BOLLINGEN SERIES LXXXV

Selected Works of Miguel de Unamuno

Volume 1

Selected Works of Miguel de Unamuno

Edited and Annotated by

Anthony Kerrigan, Allen Lacy, and Martin Nozick

1. *Peace in War*
2. *The Private World*
3. *Our Lord Don Quixote*
4. *The Tragic Sense of Life*
5. *The Agony of Christianity*
6. *Novela/Nivola*
7. *Ficciones: Four Stories and a Play*

Miguel de Unamuno

Peace in War
A Novel

Translated by
Allen Lacy and Martin Nozick
with Anthony Kerrigan

Annotated by Allen Lacy and Martin Nozick,
with an introduction by Allen Lacy

Bollingen Series LXXXV · 1
Princeton University Press

THIS IS VOLUME ONE OF THE
SELECTED WORKS OF MIGUEL DE UNAMUNO
CONSTITUTING NUMBER LXXXV IN
BOLLINGEN SERIES
SPONSORED BY BOLLINGEN FOUNDATION.
IT IS THE SIXTH VOLUME OF THE
SELECTED WORKS TO APPEAR

Printed in the United States of America by
Princeton University Press
Princeton, N.J.

Table of Contents

Peace in War

Introduction

Language, Slogans, and Existence

IN 1897, THE YEAR in which Miguel de Unamuno y Jugo, then thirty-three years old, published
his first novel, *Peace in War*, Pablo Picasso, aged fifteen, won honorable mention in a national exhibition
in Madrid for a large painting entitled *Science and
Charity*. The parallels between these two works—and
between the subsequent careers of their creators, who
with José Ortega y Gasset, Pablo Casals, and Federico
García Lorca constitute the greater part of Spain's
legacy to the twentieth century—are immediate and
striking.

Remarkable for its technical proficiency, *Science and
Charity* shows an impressive mastery of the Academic
style of late nineteenth-century painting, blending realistic and romantic elements, didactic and inspira-
tional intent, and the mawkish sentimentality that was
already painfully evident in Picasso's large canvas of
1896, *First Communion*. A genre painting, *Science and
Charity* depicts a deathbed scene in which a young
woman lies exhausted by a wasting disease, most likely
tuberculosis, under thick bedcovers in a shuttered room
with stained walls of ancient plaster. On the left a
stylishly dressed doctor (modelled on Picasso's father,
also an artist) sits and takes the patient's pulse. At the
right a nun offers the sick woman a cup, while holding
a child who stares towards the bed in uncomprehend-

ing fright. Utterly conventional, Picasso's painting makes no intellectual, moral, or aesthetic demands whatsoever on the viewer, even though it does depict what the German existentialist philosopher Karl Jaspers called a "boundary situation," a moment when the ordinary horizons of everyday life are radically altered by a question impossible to ignore.

We are in the presence of death, and a question must be asked—though not necessarily the one Picasso poses: in the presence of death is it science or charity, medicine or religion, the cure of the body or the care of the soul, that should concern us? Certainly the answer Picasso gives offers little satisfaction (though painterly mastery is almost enough to ask of a fifteen-year-old: profundity can wait its time). The painting's message is that we need both science and charity, but that in the supreme moment of death it is religion that gives meaning to the life of a dying human being, a soothing drink to her lips, and hope to those who, for a time, survive. Thus *Science and Charity* remains a cliché, merely one more deathbed scene painted near the end of a century uncommonly fond of deathbed scenes in both painting and literature.

The most remarkable thing about *Science and Charity* is what is *not* there: the artist's power to make us feel pity and terror, to grab us by the hair, shake us free of our comfortable and conventional assumptions, and force us to look around us with fresh and astonished eyes. This painting provides a window through which we peer to see . . . precisely what we expect to see. It has no hint of the Picasso to come, the visionary painter who would finish the work of the Impressionists in shattering the notion of painting as a window on reality, who would radically alter spatial and temporal relationships in art, who would explore the hidden erotic currents of human existence, and who would in 1937 bring forth *Guernica*, his agonized cry against the cold and methodical aerial bombing of civilians in the ancient Basque town of northern Spain. In its flat representation, its collage-like figures, its gray newsprint palette, its women screaming silently over their dead children, its brutal bull and its tormented horse, *Guernica* stands a pole away from *Science and Charity*. It offers us terror, not sweetness, the world as it is at its cruelest, not the world as we would like it to be in our more sentimental moments.

Peace in War bears a striking resemblance to Picasso's early painting. Like it, this novel looks backwards into the nineteenth century for its substance and technique, borrowing freely from both literary realism and literary romanticism. It looks at society with a realistic—and sometimes ironic—eye, and it depicts nature with such broadly romantic strokes that modern readers will be tempted to skip whole paragraphs about scenery, about mountain vistas and roaring oceans and peaceful forest glens concealing the fierce struggle for survival taking place underneath the solitude. There are some hints in *Peace in War* of the Unamuno to come, the Unamuno who was to write odd and disturbing novels dominated by personalities located in no identifiable time or space, but for the most part this is a fairly conventional historical novel. Besides detailed descriptions of misty crags and crashing waves, it is filled with battles and military gore, set pieces in which the author addresses the reader directly, and, yes, deathbed scenes, several of them, stock deathbed scenes the young Picasso might well have illustrated. One of the major characters, young Ignacio Iturriondo, dies suddenly and violently of gunshot wounds in the battle of Somorrostro during the second Carlist War, but he is killed with a cliché as well as a bullet: as he falls to the ground, all the events of his life pass before him in a split second. The three other characters who die in the course of *Peace in War*—Doña Micaela Arana, the mother of the girl Ignacio secretly loves; Don Miguel Arana, Doña Micaela's brother-in-law; and Ignacio's mother, Josefa Ignacia—all die in bed, attended by priests and family, amid tearful farewells and lamentations. (And they seem to die, respectively, from fear, timidity, and grief, rather than from specific medical causes.)

Like *Science and Charity*, *Peace in War* has a didactic intent, lessons taught about the course of history, about time and eternity, about death-in-life and life-in-death, about the famous and their follies and about ordinary people, who have their patient and noble courage as well as their follies. Above all, *Peace in War* has lessons to teach about the vexing problems of the Spanish past and the Spanish future. As Martin Nozick has pointed out in *Miguel de Unamuno: The Agony of Belief* (New York, 1971; Princeton, 1982), the most comprehensive critical study of Unamuno in English, this novel has its origins both in a short story, "Solitaña" (1888), and in *En torno al casticismo* (1895), a series of five articles published in the journal *La España moderna*, which in the course of a penetrating analysis of some of the maladies of nineteenth-century Spanish society, raised fundamental questions about Spain's relation to its own traditions and about its intellectual dealings with the rest of Europe. (These essays were not published as a book until 1902, but when such writers as "Clarín" [Leopoldo Alas] called attention to them in 1898, when Spain was in shock over losing the Cuban War with the United States, they served to make Unamuno the acknowledged spokesman for the literary generation which took its name from the national disaster, the Generation of '98.) And *Peace in War* has a far closer connection with Unamuno's numerous philosophical and cultural essays, both early and late, than it has with his later fiction, the novels and short stories which followed.

Over eighty years after its first publication, *Peace in War* undeniably presents the late twentieth-century reader with an initial difficulty—its unfamiliar setting in the Basque country during the second Carlist War (1874-1876). This conflict was an immediate part of Unamuno's experience. He was ten when the Carlist army put his native Bilbao under prolonged siege. The first shell in the city's bombardment—an ordeal described at length in the most touching section of *Peace in War*, where the effects of the siege on the citizens are explored with detail and compassion—fell outside the Unamuno house on February 21, 1874. In a superb memoir of his childhood, *Recuerdos de niñez y de mocedad* (1908), Unamuno writes that before that date, "I keep only fragmentary memories; after it comes the thread of my history." The siege of Bilbao marked the end of his rather dreamy childhood and the beginning of his awareness of the larger history in which he was situated. The siege was burned into his memory; much of the dialogue in *Peace and War* comes from conversations he overheard, and many of the incidents—such as people eating bean-bread and then cats and rats as the supply of food ran out—were familiar to him. The child of a Carlist family who later came to despise Carlism for its narrow vision, its dogmatism, and its impossible political program of returning to a past that never truly existed, he pays close attention in this novel to the issues at stake in the second Carlist War, both the real ones and the ostensible ones.

But no matter how vivid the events of the second Carlist War may have been to those who lived through it, no matter how crucial the issues it involved, no matter how important the political and military leaders who took part in it, all these things are now obscured by the passage of time. Pachico Zabalbide, a character modelled on Unamuno himself but a decade older, muses to himself fairly late in the novel:

> *Of the entire war, what would remain?* A few dry reports, a few lines at best in future history books, some passing mention of one of the numberless civil wars whose meaning the actors in the drama would carry to their graves.

Pachico is squarely on the mark. Few modern readers of *Peace in War*, except for those with a special interest in Spanish history, have even heard of the Carlist Wars. In fact, many standard histories of nineteenth-century Europe fail to mention either the Carlist War of 1833-1840 (the Seven Year War) or the second Carlist War.

Although there are deeper social and religious issues, in one sense the Carlist Wars arose out of a family squabble over an inheritance—the inheritance of the Spanish throne. When Ferdinand VII died in September 1833, he left two daughters by his fourth wife, María Cristina of Naples, whom he had married in 1829. The elder, who was just three years old, became queen as Isabella II, with her mother as regent. But the succession was disputed because of the ancient Salic Law limiting the throne to males born in Spain. The law had been secretly revoked in 1789 by Charles IV, and at María Cristina's urging Ferdinand VII officially promulgated its revocation soon after Isabella's birth. After her father's death Isabella's claim to the throne was promptly challenged by the first Carlist Pretender, her father's brother, Don Carlos María Isidro de Borbón, who had strong support from conservative political and religious elements hostile to Liberal philosophies and policies at work in Madrid, to the Masonic lodges which helped shape these policies, and to those who wanted a constitutional monarchy or even no monarchy at all. In 1833, particularly in the Basque provinces, Carlist sympathizers rose in guerilla warfare to support Don Carlos' claim to the throne as Carlos V. The Carlists fought under the leadership of such fierce mountain chieftains as Don Tomás Zumalacárregui and Don Ramón Cabrera until their cause was finally defeated. The war ended in the north of Spain in August 1839, when the Carlist leader Rafael Maroto, after prolonged secret negotiations with General Baldomero Espartero, signed the Treaty of Vergara, which recognized Isabella II and renounced Carlos V, in exchange for protecting the financial and legal interests of officers in the Carlist army. Espartero defeated Cabrera in the Catalonian theatre in 1840.

The military war was over, but by no means the underlying conflict of ideas about the Spanish past and future, the war between Jesuits and Freemasons, between Traditionalists and Liberals, between those who wanted Spain to make the Pyrenees a barrier insulating her from the ideas of the French Revolution and those who wanted her to open her doors to the freer intellectual winds of modern European thought and culture.

Carlism was defeated, but it was not dead. Don Carlos resigned as Pretender in favor of his son, Carlos Luis, conde de Montemolín, whom the Carlists knew as Carlos VI and who was captured by the central government after a Carlist insurrection at San Carlos de la Rápita in 1860.

The downfall of Isabella II in 1868 led to a second

chance for the Carlist cause. Toppled from her throne by military uprisings in the September Revolution of that year, she fled into exile. There were those who wanted to proclaim a republic, but they were blocked by military men such as Francisco Serrano and Juan Prim. In 1869 a constituent Cortes reaffirmed the monarchy, but there was no monarch. Serrano served as regent until a king could be found. Several members of European royal families declined the Spanish throne, but in 1870 Prince Amadeo, the second son of Victor Emmanuel II of Italy, agreed to accept it. On December 27, 1870, the day Amadeo arrived in Spain, Juan Prim, his principal supporter, was assassinated by unknown parties. The new king's short and uneasy rule began, ending with his abdication in February 1873. Soon after, another Cortes proclaimed a republic—which had three presidents in one year's time. But late in 1874 the monarchy returned when a military uprising led by General Martínez Campos brought in Isabella's son, Alfonso XII, then a student at the Royal Military College in Sandhurst, England, as king.

Against the background of this turbulent and confused political history, Carlism began the resurgence of its old hopes. During the first days of Amadeo, Carlist forces again began to gather in the mountains. The Pretender Carlos V, before his death in 1861, had surrendered his claim to the throne to his brother Don Juan de Borbón, who in turn passed it on to his son Carlos María de los Dolores Borbón y Austria—the Carlos VII of Unamuno's novel and of the second Carlist War. Don Carlos entered Spain in late May 1872 but was quickly driven back to France by General Moriones. Meanwhile, the Carlist army held Navarre, the three Basque provinces, and much of Catalonia. In July 1873, Don Carlos returned to Spain and set up a government of sorts at Durango, in Vizcaya. In the following year his forces besieged Bilbao—a commercial city where Carlism had never been strong, despite the strong sympathies toward the cause in the surrounding countryside—for three bitter months. Under Alfonso XII, the Liberal army made deeper and deeper inroads into Carlist territory, finally forcing Don Carlos' surrender and retreat to France in March 1876.

But these historical facts, the deeds of figures in public life, the current events that the newspapers record, and the past events stored up in history books, interested Unamuno very little in themselves. Although battles and kings and generals and proclamations appear in *Peace in War*, Unamuno's real concern lies elsewhere, so much so that the novel gives only a very cloudy and obscure picture of the war which is its backdrop. What excites him is not the history populated by kings and generals but what he calls *intrahistoria*, infrahistory, the quiet and unrecorded lives of ordinary people who are born, who work, who breed, and who die leaving scarcely a trace of their existence behind. They vanish like smoke, though they were flesh, these ordinary people who may suffer and die in war in the service of causes they do not understand, ideas which in no way touch the substance of their personal being. In *En torno al casticismo* Unamuno writes:

> All that the daily papers report, all history "of the present moment," is but the surface of the sea, a surface which is frozen and crystallized in books and registers. . . . The newspapers say nothing of the silent lives of millions and millions of men without a "history" who at all times of the day and in all countries upon the globe rise at the order of the sun and go to their fields to follow their eternal and

quotidian labor. . . . That infrahistoric life, as silent and continual as the very bottom of the sea, is the substance of
progress and the true tradition . . .

"Progress" and "Tradition": in the political arena these
were opposing slogans, but Unamuno saw them as
peacefully united in the lives of ordinary people. *Peace
in War*, then, is not so much a historical novel as it is
an "infrahistoric" one, a kind of snapshot album freezing isolated intimate moments in the life of a people
and presenting them as a collective portrait, told in
small fragments of a kind that nineteenth-century his-
torians never put in books of history.

Like his fictional alter ego Pachico Zabalbide, Unamuno frequently challenged his critics: "No one will
ever classify me!" "This mania for classifying everything . . . is absurd," he wrote in "La enseñanza de la
gramática" in 1905. "I recall that once a certain individual, after speaking to me at length, asked me,
'And you—what are you?' I answered him, 'Put me
under *miscellaneous*.' " And indeed, like Søren Kierkegaard and Friedrich Nietzsche, he does defy clas-
sification, for he was social critic, novelist and play-
wright and short-story writer, essayist, philologist,
professor of Greek at the University of Salamanca,
university rector, literary critic, outspoken opponent
of those in high places, controversialist, indefatigable
writer of prefaces to the books of others, translator,
poet, journalist, and all of these at once. He was a
public figure as well as a private man, but he was never
a man of party. "I, who am not a man of any party,
have not come to bring a program, have not come to
bring you something specific. I do not like these things
people call concrete solutions," he said at a conference
in Madrid in 1906.

But Unamuno is best known as a philosopher, albeit

a very odd sort of philosopher who wrote novels and short stories, who said once that he wanted to write philosophy in the kind of language people used in buying chocolates, and who knew that Spain presented him with some extraordinary problems if he wished to make himself heard.

Unamuno is often described as an existentialist—or perhaps a forerunner of existentialism, a proto-existentialist, and with good reason. He has strong affinities with Kierkegaard (whom he read, in Danish, long before the Germans discovered him), Nietzsche, Heidegger, Jaspers, Sartre, Camus, and Marcel, to the extent that all these thinkers can be placed under one heading despite their differences. Like them he emphasized the personal and the individual over the collective. Martin Heidegger did not exceed him in his suspicion of *Das Man*, the every-man and no-man, the creature who speaks of himself as "one" rather than "I"—the human being who lives abstractly, doing all that "one" must do, refraining from all that "one" must not do. Like all the existentialists, Unamuno understood that human beings must die, we know we must die, and then we try to conceal our knowledge by strategies of diversion amounting to bad faith, inauthenticity, or what he simply called "the lie." ("Here in Spain," he said at another conference, in Barcelona in 1906, "we breathe the lie, . . . we eat the lie, we are all massaged with the lie. People do not tolerate that someone says openly what he says in private.") Unamuno knew the limits of reason and logic and understood that we often must make fateful choices in the absence of any good reason to choose one thing over another—sound existential insight, all of this.

But it has been insufficiently noticed that Unamuno is also a linguistic philosopher, that if he is a Spanish

Kierkegaard or Heidegger, he is also a Spanish Wittgenstein. Much of his thinking on particular issues grows out of his conviction that human beings are better defined as animals who speak than as animals who reason. Scattered throughout his writing there is a coherent philosophy of language—which among other things helps explain why he wrote novels as well as philosophical essays. I wish now to explore this philosophy of language and then to show how it bears on his concerns in *Peace in War*.

One widely held and commonsensical view—a view unalterably opposed by Unamuno throughout his career—holds that language is merely a vehicle, a container, a medium. According to this view, language expresses something which precedes it. We have a thought, and then we try to find the words to formulate it to ourselves and to convey it to others. We perceive something—a dark flashing of wings in a green tree and a tiny squeak of terror—and then we name our perception: "an owl killing a baby squirrel in a hollow swamp maple." We experience an emotion, and then we name it "love," "envy," or "joy." According to this view, at some time in very early childhood we begin to experience the world and to think about our experience, until at last one day we acquire the vocabulary to name the thoughts and experiences we have already had. Language is a vehicle for communicating what is already known. It reports experience; it does not constitute experience or make it possible. Language is always about something else, something logically prior to it: sense data, percepts, concepts, emotions, experiences, jiggling molecules and colliding atoms, the necessary truths that reason or experiment can discover. In opposing this view (as he consistently did from the early 1890s until his death in 1936),

Unamuno called it by many different names—dogmatism, delegation, ideocracy, diversion, abstract speech, intellectualism, the lie, the vanity of vanities—but here we'll call it "logical realism."

There is a subspecies of logical realism which recognizes that ordinary language is often imprecise but goes on to claim for some special type of discourse not only precision but also fixed and static truth, genuine knowledge rather than opinion. This privileged universe of discourse may be a philosophical system, a system of theology or divinely revealed truths, or a system of scientific knowledge. Thus for Plato most human beings wallow in ignorance compounded by their ignorance that they are ignorant. The best that can be hoped of these sorry creatures is that they will somehow stumble on—or be indoctrinated with—correct opinions they can never really understand. The ignorant use words like "justice" and "piety," but since they cannot define them—"give an account" of them—the words are empty in their mouths. They are left only with the words for humbler things—"jug," "tree," "path." Fortunately a small class of men does have the ability to rise up from the world of appearance and mere opinion into true knowledge of reality. These are the philosophers, those who are privileged to know every thing as it truly is and who are therefore fit to rule.

But there is a stubborn problem with philosophers from Thales to our own time: they often disagree. They disagree about what questions are to be asked, and they disagree about what answers are suitable. And so another variety of logical realism holds that while human reason is incapable of attaining any final and immutable truth, divine revelation does offer absolute certainty about the nature of the universe where we have our habitation, about human destiny, about what we must do, say, feel, hope, obey, and believe. The literal-minded shall find comfort, for the system of divine truth contained in creed and catechism is available not only to the intellectual few but also to the unthinking many. It is only necessary to take holy water and recite the creed, for our Holy Mother the Church has doctors to answer even the questions we cannot clearly state to ourselves. Thus some religious people are often smugly certain about some very odd things, such as the exact date and hour of the world's creation, the best person to occupy the Spanish throne or the Oval Office, and the sharp distinction between human beings and mere animals (a distinction which makes it moral to eat a chicken but immoral to abort a human fetus—or for that matter the other way round). But there is a problem with rigidly dogmatic systems of religious certainty which are believed by their passionate adherents to constitute the sum of all truth: many such systems exist and they disagree on fundamental points—especially about what is fundamental. Protestant Christian fundamentalists come in a great many varieties. Some of them are not on speaking terms with one another, and it perplexes the spirit to imagine any of them holding converse with an Islamic fundamentalist. A further problem with systems of religious certainty—and with the political sentiments they often carry as extra baggage—is that they have been known to bring men to kill or torture one another in their name. (We often resort to violence to preserve what we take to be certain, seldom, if ever, to preserve our uncertainties.)

Finally, there are the scientific systems of certainty—although the scientific community is much more modest in its claims than was its nineteenth-century counterpart, which Unamuno, after a passing flirtation with positivism in the 1880s, thoroughly criticized for mis-understanding its own endeavor. According to the ear-lier view at least, an understanding of science that originated with Galileo and Descartes, the scientist has Reality trapped in his laboratory: observing it, weigh-ing it, classifying it, arranging it in ever tidier boxes and compartments, putting it on display in glass cases in museums, as he formulates hypotheses, objectively turns them into theories as he accumulates more facts, and then awaits their final emergence as Proven Truths of Science. Those who speak of "vinegar" and "water" are ignorant children; the final word belongs to those who have learned to speak of "CH_3COOH" and "H_2O."

Unamuno utterly rejects both the commonsensical view that language is merely an expressive medium for something that precedes it and the more specialized varieties of logical realism which would give privileged status to dogmatically held systems of philosophy, the-ology, or science. Any certainty which rests on the failure to attend to the implications of the fact that human beings are, before anything else, *language-users*, men of flesh and bone, yes, but also men who speak and in their speaking bring themselves and their world into being—any such certainty is almost surely false and illusory, for it is bought far too cheaply. Like Wilhelm von Humboldt and Alexander Bryan John-son before him and like Benjamin Lee Whorf, Edward Sapir, and Ludwig Wittgenstein, Unamuno held firmly to the conviction expressed most succinctly in one sen-tence from Martin Heidegger's *An Introduction to Met-aphysics* (New Haven, 1959): "It is in words and lan-guage that things come into being and are."

It is in words and language that things come into being and are. A human being is not primarily the featherless biped or the animal who reasons; he is *homo hablante*, the animal who speaks, from whose speech grows into being the public world common to all and the private world peculiar to each person—and a host of intermediate "worlds," communities built on our acts of speech. Thinking grows out of language, not the other way round. In the essay "*Dostoyeusqui sobre la lengua*" (1933), Unamuno took sharp exception to the Russian novelist's reference to language as the "form" or "wrapping" of thought: "Language is not the form, body, or wrapping of thought, but thought itself. One does not think *with* words, . . . one *thinks words*." "One feels with words," he writes in *Tragic Sense of Life*. Love, he says, "does not discover that it is love until it speaks, until it says, 'I love you!' " Likewise perception depends on the word, for how can we perceive a color without a name to separate it from every other hue in the spectrum of visible light? (Painters, whose tubes of oil paint teach them names like rose madder, alizarin crimson, Prussian blue, and cadmium yellow, know, unlike most of us, that shadows are colored.) The concept is also given in language—or, formed by poetical and metaphorical processes, comes to be incorporated in a given language.

As regards the special claims of systems of philosophy or theology that they provide certainty, Unamuno is adamant: their certainty is illusory. Against the Cartesian model of the philosopher as someone who seeks certitude through methodical caution, he offers himself as a man dedicated to sowing uncertitude everywhere on every matter of vital interest. Every philosophical system, he argues in *Tragic Sense* and elsewhere, is personal and autobiographical, no matter what claim it may make to being public, objective, and universal. He admits that there may be great human

value in religious faith, but faith has to do with the
way we live amidst doubt, ambiguity, and uncertainty,
not with the doctrines we trumpet forth as being absolute truth—and may be willing to protect by burning
a few heretics by way of an edifying warning to others.
And science, in its deepest roots, turns out for Unamuno to be poetry, its truths the truths of poetry. In
the essay "*Sobre el cultivo de la demótica*," (1896) he
wrote: "Science is built with language, and language
is in its essence metaphorical. 'Matter,' 'force,' 'light,'
'memory,' 'spirit'—all metaphors!"

Unamuno knew Kant's thought well, but where
Kant posited a set of universal categories, built into
the human mind, which give experience its structure
and make it impossible for us to compare things-in-
themselves with our experience of them, Unamuno
posited an enormous, growing, and potentially infinite
number of sets, some overlapping one another, some
incommensurate with one another, all given in, with,
and through human language—both the languages of
the world (Spanish, German, English, and others in
the Indo-European group; Arabic and Hebrew; Basque;
Tagalog; Hopi; Chinese . . . and so on) and the specialized languages associated with particular human
activities (chemistry and physics; aesthetics and ethics;
gardening and golf; bridge and canasta). Each of us
lives, it would seem, a polyglot existence.

Unamuno defines language as "a system of metaphors with a mythic and anthropomorphic base."
Throughout his writings he clearly thinks about language somewhat as Ludwig Wittgenstein did, as being
"games"—of which there are many, some related to
others, some not. Each such game is made up of a
limited set of mutually coherent concepts and the tacit
and explicit rules for their use.

The upshot is that Unamuno is an extremely pluralistic thinker who was pained to find himself living in a society of absolutists of a variety of stamps, all warring with one another in a quite tragic and wholly unnecessary way. If language precedes thought and perception and feeling, it is clear that the Spaniard and the German and the Englishman will all inhabit slightly different worlds—will think, perceive, and feel in accord with the differences in their native tongues. (Kant, Unamuno points out, thought in German, and despite the universality of his intentions, his own philosophy is shaped at certain points by linguistic accidents, such as the rhymes and rhythms of German speech. Recent investigations by psychologists studying early infancy suggest that within the first few weeks of life human beings pick up the rhythms of their native tongues, rhythms that remain with them even unto the grave as an unconscious part of their personalities: as the cradle rocks, so does the bough break.) It is equally clear that there will be family resemblances among the Spaniard, the German, and the Englishman, since all speak and think in an Indo-European language and thus, unlike the Hopi or the Cherokee, organize their experience and their understanding of reality within a framework of *subjects*, *verbs*, and *objects*, thus making the world a place where some things do things to other things, and that's the end of the matter.

The specialized languages of philosophy, theology, and science must be interpreted in a new way, once they are understood *to be languages*. If a philosophical system is an autobiographical statement rather than an assessment of what must be self-evident to anyone who is not deliberately perverse, then philosophical disagreements appear in a new light—and thus Unamuno had more taste for philosophers like Kierkegaard and

William James, who admitted that truth is personal and subjective, necessarily and inevitably incarnate in a particular human life, than for those like Plato and Hegel, who proclaimed the need to transcend subjectivity. If religion is a language game that serves to color the world of those who play it, then there is no justification for people to kill each other—or even to be rude to one another—over religious differences: those who play the Basque game of *pelota* have no just cause to massacre those who prefer cricket or croquet. Furthermore, the conflict between science and religion which so troubled the nineteenth century and which still remains with us to a lesser degree utterly vanishes. Science, which Unamuno called "Cataloguing the Universe," employs such concepts as 'causality,' 'force,' 'matter,' and 'energy,' and uses them in accordance with rules calling for economy of explanation. Although he believed that in its deepest roots as a human activity science draws on something closely kin to religious trust and faith, Unamuno did not believe that 'faith' was itself a scientific concept. 'Faith' belongs to another language game altogether—to religion, where it is employed with such other concepts as 'God,' 'soul,' and 'immortality.' We may thus have Newton and Darwin, and the Book of Genesis as well. (And Unamuno is vindicated in his odd practice—odd, that is, to the literal-minded of various persuasions—of addressing scientific groups, preaching to them from the text "Remember, O man, that thou art dust," while speaking to the pious about the glories of human evolution.)

Properly we are all polyglots. There is no rule restricting us to one language, though we can speak only one at a time, and it is important to note that some language games are incommensurable with each other. It is vanity and nonsense to prove anything about God or the soul, for 'proof' is part of the language of logic and mathematics and, Descartes notwithstanding, it does not operate conceptually in religious thought. There may be right and wrong ways of using languages, but there are no wrong languages and no correct ones. Languages are not right or wrong, but they may be rich or scanty, expansive or restrictive, imaginative or pedestrian, free or inhibited. Those who live the richest lives are those who speak and think and live in the most languages, who dwell in "many mansions"; who speak Spanish and French and German; who can read Dante and Shakespeare, Darwin and Kierkegaard, Marx and de Maistre and J. S. Mill; who are capable of standing transfixed before a Rilke sonnet, a Bach passacaglia and fugue or a Mahler symphony, a nude by Rubens or Renoir, or a mathematical equation stated with elegance as well as economy.

We must, however, keep our languages straight, take care to attend to the incommensurability of some with others. In *Tragic Sense* Unamuno points out that although we may speak about the roots of an ash tree it is purely foolish to ask a mathematical question about its cube root. Likewise, there is a language pertaining to *things* which appraises them according to their utility, but this language is inappropriate if applied to *persons*. I may say that a streetcar is useful in taking me to my lover, but if I appraise my lover entirely according to her utility something essential is surely lost. (I am entitled to specify exactly why I "love" my automobile, but there is quicksand at my feet the moment I begin to catalogue the reasons I love my wife.) Again, the words "good" and "bad," which function well enough within the language game of giving a moral assessment of human action, are for Unamuno— though not for many of his Spanish contemporaries—

wholly out of place if used to assess ideas. In one of his classic essays, *"La ideocracia"* (1900), he asks:

> Good and bad ideas, you say? To speak of good ideas is like speaking of blue sounds, of round odors, of bitter triangles, or, even better, it is like speaking of wise or foolish money, or of heroic or criminal bullets.

Unamuno clearly understood the problem of what Anglo-American linguistic philosophers were later to identify as "category mistakes," the confusion arising when concepts appropriate to one field of discourse are applied to another, where they are not appropriate. Perhaps his most interesting novel, his *Candide*, is *Amor y pedagogía* (1902), which explores the tragicomical existence of one Don Avito Carrascal, a man who is so committed to science that he even sets out to marry and to raise a son scientifically. (One thinks here automatically of James Mill's attempt to raise his son John Stuart Mill according to the principles of Jeremy Bentham or of B. F. Skinner's determination to introduce the principles of behaviorism into his own home.) The child is to be a genius, and thus when it is born Don Avito immediately plunges it into a basin of water to determine "the specific gravity of genius." His educational scheme is finally disastrous for his son and his own hopes, for he has mistakenly assumed that anything human beings can do is better done "scientifically." Some things—making love, caring for a garden, and raising children towards a reasonably sane maturity—stubbornly resist this assumption.

Unamuno wrote no book entitled *The Philosophy of Language*. His linguistic philosophy is diffused throughout his writings, often on matters that would seem to be far off the topic. But it is summed up in his "Ultima lección académica," his last formal address

*xxvii**

to the students and faculty of the University of Salamanca on September 29th, 1934, and in two poems from his poetic diary, the *Cancionero*. Addressing the solemn assembly at Salamanca, he said:

> There is no chasm between the word and the fact. . . . Man leaves behind some bones in the earth and a name in the air, a name in history, which is woven of names. . . . The substantial man is his name, the person. What is it to define something but to give it a name? "My name is—" means "I want to be—.". . . Each man must form for himself and re-form for himself his own idiom—*idiom* means *ownership*—within the common idiom, enriching himself from it and enriching it by enriching himself in it. And thus it is, students of Salamanca, that I have tried during these years, in a Socratic way, to teach you to learn the very language you speak, that you would come to the light and that I might also learn it from you, all of us together. . . . Every language carries implicit—no, *incarnate* is the better word—within itself a feeling—one feels with words—a cofeeling, a philosophy, and a religion. So does ours also. Bringing that philosophy to light is a work of philology and of the history of language. So-called "universal philosophy," what is it but the history of universal human thought incarnate in the word? . . . Man is the animal which speaks.

One untitled poetic fragment in the *Cancionero* asks:

> Would you get to the bottom
> Of things? Then go to the depths
> Of words, for names
> Are the viscera of being.
> We have built the dream of the world,
> Creation, in proverbs.
> Your task: repair what is built.
> And, if by chance you give God
> His right name, you will make Him
> Truly God, and by creating Him
> You will create yourself.
> . . .

A second poem from the *Cancionero* develops still further the connections between speech and creation. Addressing God directly, Unamuno writes:

> Father, when I call you *Thou*
> With visceral intimacy
> I become godlike in Thee,
> I create myself.
> My afternoon turns to morning.
> In Thee, Father, *I* see *myself*;
> *You* see *yourself* in me, my Father.
> Calling you *Thou* becomes calling myself *I*
> And we are one in blood.
> *You* create *me*, *I* create *You*
> In this dialogue which burns
> And the words become gigantic.
> Men understand themselves by speaking
> And the name becomes the thing;
> Forged by the conflagration of suns—
> Cold word!—the diamond.

The name becomes the thing: language always creates a world. But it does not necessarily create a pleasant world or a humane one. In the Book of Genesis, God brings heaven and earth into being through the word and shortly thereafter sets Adam at the task of naming what He has created. But the serpent also speaks and in very short order teaches both Adam and Eve the art of deceitful speech.

Unamuno's ideal is an ever-growing and ever-changing system of human language that is faithful to its own nature, that recognizes that the uncertainty underlying every act of speech is also an invitation to enrich the world by poetic creation, and that realizes that all truths are partial—that anyone who claims to know the truth utterly and for all time is necessarily a liar.

Liars also create a world, a demonic one. Unfortu-

nately the world they have created was Unamuno's—
and is our own. No human being since the Garden of
Eden, since the slow ascent of life out of the primordial
slime and muck by means of chance and natural selection, has ever tortured or killed another to preserve
his own uncertainty, to hold fast to the everlasting
ambiguity at the heart of all that is. But millions upon
millions have died that others might be certain that
they had the truth, tanked up in the ready-made slogans and catchwords that move them into battle against
their opponents. The dogmatist is more than dogmatic; he is also dangerous. The serpent still speaks
in people like Celestino, the young Carlist lawyer in
Peace in War who memorizes phrases from political
propagandists like Aparisi Aguado in order to impress
other people by reciting them in his club. Celestino is
a fraud. He is that most despicable figure among those
who live by words, the plagiarist—the man who steals
the words of others and then seeks to benefit by offering them as his own. He talks, but he does not *speak*.
He uses superficial slogans unthinkingly rather than
speaking honestly out of his own depths; he remains,
then, a man without depths, a cardboard figure, a self-
parody. Celestino would be comic if he were not also
dangerous. It is better to remain silent, for meaningless
catchwords have an unfortunate way of moving us to
acts of cruelty and violence. Our own century offers
ample evidence of the terrible efficacy of short and
mindless phrases to stain the earth red with blood and
to lead to the extermination of millions: it is not very
far, we have seen, from "Strength through Joy" to
"The Thousand-Year Reich" to "Tomorrow the World"
. . . to "The Final Solution of the Jewish Problem."

It would be surprising if *Peace in War* did not reflect
the philosophy of language which Unamuno had worked

out as early as 1895 in the essays later published as *En torno al casticismo*. And indeed, I should like to argue here, this novel is not really about the second Carlist War at all, nor even about its characters and what happens to them. They are all shadowy and poorly fleshed: Pedro Antonio, the owner of a chocolate shop in Bilbao, who lives from his memories of a soldier's life in the first Carlist War; his sweet wife Josefa Ignacia, who tends her good man but prays for a child; Ignacio, their son, who escapes from the drudgery of office work into brothels and long nature walks into the hills around Bilbao and who finally dies in a war he doesn't understand; Don Juan Arana, a prosperous Liberal merchant who reads the French economist Bastiat for inspiration and worries over his fearful wife Doña Micaela and his timid brother Don Miguel; Don Miguel himself, who seems almost a classic case for Freudian analysis, considering his neurotic fear of the open countryside, his determination to live by routine and habit, his secret collection of obscene pictures, and his unconscious, basically incestuous love for his pretty and sensible niece Rafaela.

What *Peace in War* finally comes down to, I strongly suspect (and what rescues it from being merely one more historical novel from the nineteenth century about events that somehow hardly seem to matter any longer), is that it is a novel about *jabber*, in which it is abundantly rich: idle political discussions among friends in the nightly *tertulias* or intimate conversational gatherings; children taunting one another in the streets; soldiers shouting friendly obscenities at one another in the trenches dividing enemy armies, during a lull in combat; pompous, meaningless sermons in village churches, and open-air Masses said by armies who repeat the liturgy mechanically and know that God approves their cause—all these things combining to form a chorus of demonic jabber. There is no clearly defined hero in this novel—Ignacio is a tedious dullard, and Pachico Zabalbide is an intrusively autobiographical spokesman for Unamuno himself—but there is a villain: the slogan.

Listen to some of the voices in this novel for a moment—

"Down with our chains, slaughter the monks!"

"Let's get the Moor!"

"Listen, you, I'll get my brother and he'll hit you in the snout!"

"God wills it, and the King commands."

"The mission of the armed revolution is to destroy!"

"Down with things as they exist!"

"Spain with honor!"

"Constitution or death!"

"God, Fatherland, King!"

"Take faith away from man and he'll live like a pig!"

"Liberalism is foreign and revolutionary, but liberty is Catholic and Spanish."

"Long live Don Carlos!"

"Long live Spain! Long live God!"

"Even though we're beaten, we're the victors."

Even though we're beaten, we're the victors. Someone who can say such a thing is capable of turning a blind eye to almost any atrocity. These words come from a priest, but they are demonic jabber, an echo of the words of the serpent in a garden long ago when men first learned to lie.

*   *   *

Peace in War has its solid virtues. It also has some notable flaws that will not escape the reader's attention. The diction is often self-consciously "poetic," especially when the topic is nature. I could multiply examples easily but will restrict myself here to commenting on the end of the book—one of the most overblown pieces of metaphorical nonsense in late nineteenth-century European literature. My own critical hunch is that the true ending of the novel comes with our last sight of Pedro Antonio—widowed, bereft of the son in whom he had placed his hopes for a comfortable old age, but still a man who has learned acceptance and who lives without complaint or resentment. *Peace in War* falls to pieces once Unamuno turns his attention from Pedro Antonio to Pachico Zabalbide, who climbs a mountain overlooking Bilbao to contemplate the city, to gaze at the sea and the clouds and the sierras, to consider the bloody history of Vizcaya, and to Ponder the Deeper Meaning of It All. The entire final passage is a compendium of wonderfully atrocious examples of the pathetic fallacy; furthermore, it displays a poor grasp of elementary botany when it speaks of parasitic mosses sucking the sap of the noble race of beech trees to which they cling. But Pachico does offer us the interesting notion of salvation by irony, and underneath the silly language and the colliding metaphors in this account of a young man fleeing the follies of history for a raw encounter with the world of nature, there is a point, a point made recently and much more eloquently by John Fowles in his splendid book *The Tree*:

> There is something in the nature of nature, in its presentness, its seeming transience, its creative ferment and hidden potential, that corresponds very closely with the wild, or green man, in our psyches; and it is a something that disappears as soon as it is relegated to an automatic pastness, a status of merely classifiable *thing*, image taken *then*. Thing and then attract each other. If it is thing, it

was then; if it was then, it is thing. We lack trust in the present, this moment, this actual seeing, because our culture tells us to trust only the reported back, the publicly framed, the edited, the thing set in the clearly artistic or the clearly scientific angle of perspective. One of the deepest lessons we have to learn is that nature, of its nature, resists this. It waits to be seen otherwise, in its individual presentness and from our individual presentness.

Unamuno would have said, "Yes, precisely. Nature lies, but only to liars. But it has some lessons for those who mean to speak the truth."

ALLEN LACY

Stockton State College
Pomona, N.J.
November, 1981

The Chief Fictional Characters

LIKE MOST historical novels, *Peace in War* mingles fictional characters with "real" or historical ones. But unlike the writers of most other historical novels, Unamuno made little effort to flesh out the generals and politicians in his narrative, for one of his constant refrains was the notion that fictional characters in a novel or a play have a more enduring and solid existence than the world-historical beings who briefly strut across the battlefields and parliaments of this earth to command, for a time, the attention of people who read newspapers. Unamuno seems to have been correct in this matter. Who today, except for the occasional specialist in nineteenth-century Spanish history, will know the name of Juan Prim or King Amadeo, much less the names of Basque generals like Don Castor Andéchaga? In any event, the historical persons and events are explained in the notes and indexed at the end of the volume.

For the benefit of readers, here is a cast of the chief characters in *Peace in War*.

Carlists

Pedro Antonio Iturriondo ("Perú Antón"), owner of a chocolate shop in Bilbao

Josefa Ignacia ("Pepiñasi"), his pious wife

Ignacio ("Iniciochu"), their only son

Don Emeterio, Pedro Antonio's brother, a country priest

Don Pascual, Pedro Antonio's cousin, also a priest

Gambelu, Don Eustaquio, Don Braulio, Don José María: all friends of Pedro Antonio, who gather for the nightly *tertulia* in his shop

Juan José, a friend of Ignacio

Rafael, another friend of Ignacio

Celestino, a lawyer of Ignacio's age, whose dedication to the Carlist cause tends toward boring fanaticism

Anti-Carlists or Liberals

Don Juan Arana, a merchant of Bilbao

Doña Micaela, his wife

Juanito, their elder son, a childhood friend of Ignacio Iturriondo

Rafaela, their daughter

Marcelino, their younger son

Don Miguel Arana, Don Juan's brother, a timid bachelor

Non-Partisans

Pachico Zabalbide, a young skeptic (and a character Unamuno modelled on himself)

Don Joaquín, Pachico's uncle

Chronology

Derived partly from Raymond Carr, *Spain 1808-1939* (1966) and Martin Nozick, *Miguel de Unamuno: The Agony of Belief* (1971, 1982).

	1833
September	Death of Ferdinand VII, followed by accession to the throne of Isabel II (1830-1904)
October	Carlist rebellion against Isabel II begins in north
	1834
July	Don Carlos appoints Zumalacárregui as commander-in-chief of Carlist forces in north
	1835
June	First siege of Bilbao and death of Zumalacárregui
	1839
February	Maroto shoots his enemies at Estella; Carlism disintegrates
April	Espartero and Maroto begin negotiations
August	Treaty of Vergara; end of war in the north
	1840
May-July	Espartero defeats Cabrera; end of Eastern Carlism

Chronology

1841
October   Basque *fueros* suppressed

*   *   *

1859
November   O'Donnell lands at Ceuta: Moroccan war

1860
April   Ortega's Carlist pronunciamiento at San Carlos de la Rápita

1864
September 29   *Miguel de Unamuno born in Bilbao*

1868
September   Admiral Topete pronounces at Cadiz; joined by Prim and Serrano. Isabel II leaves Spain for France

1869
June   Constitution of 1869; Serrano as Regent, Prim as Prime Minister

1870
November   Amadeo of Savoy elected King of Spain: a constitutional monarchy

1872
May   Don Carlos crosses frontier but fails to start Carlist war

1873
February   Abdication of Amadeo; establishment of Republic

June   Revival of Carlism and military successes in north; General Concha killed at Abarzuza

July   Cantonalist risings in Alcoy, Cartagena, and Andalusia

Chronology

(1873)

December | Beginning of Carlist siege of Bilbao: 125 days

1874

March 27 | Battle of Somorrostro

May 2 | General Concha enters Bilbao, bringing the Carlist siege to an end

December | Alfonso XII proclaimed King of Spain

1876

June | Promulgation of the Constitution of 1876

* * *

1880-1884

Unamuno at the University of Madrid; bachillerato 1883, doctorado 1884

1885

November | Death of Alfonso XII, followed by regency of María Cristina for Alfonso XIII (1886-1941)

1890

July | *Unamuno at work on "Paz en la guerra" while teaching in Bilbao*

1891

January | *Unamuno married to Concepción Lizárraga*

July | *His appointment to chair of Greek at the University of Salamanca*

1895

Essays composing "En torno al casticismo" published in periodicals

Chronology

1897

Spring

His religious crisis
Publication of "Paz en la guerra"

1902

Publication of "En torno al casti-
cismo" in book form

*   *   *

1936

December 31   *Unamuno dies in Salamanca*

Peace in War

Author's Warnings for the First Edition

IN THIS PRINTING there are errata, not a few of them of some importance, which can be attributed to the fact that the very special circumstances under which this work was brought out prevented my correcting it with the care which all such publications should have. The fault is mine, because many of these errata come from mistakes in the original manuscript. Although the reader will know enough to correct them mentally for himself, I think it is my duty to place at the very beginning of this work, and not, as customarily, at the end, a list of the principal errata—especially those that alter the sense of the context.

[. . .]

Besides, there are some words—very few—which are used only in the region where the tale is supposed to unfold, but these either are explained in the text itself or can be understood from context.

As for spelling, I have frequently tried to reflect colloquial pronunciation.

Of course, there are probably many true cases of sloppiness of language, since it is not external grammatical exactness that concerns me to any extent. I am always drawn away by my obsession with content and internal form; such an obsession prevents me from seeing clearly, at each step, the merely external form of what I write. I do not believe, furthermore, that respect for established *literary*—and, we might say, *official*—language should be unlimited; therefore, I deliberately allowed many so-called mistakes. And since I now see that I am defending myself, I shall go no further.

And as I beg a thousand pardons of the benevolent and well-intentioned reader, who, after purchasing this book, finds that the defects I have just pointed out make its perusal difficult. Let everything else follow its course.

Author's Prologue to the Second Edition

THE FIRST EDITION of this work, published twenty-six years ago, in 1897, has been out of print for some time; that is why I have decided to publish this second edition. And on this occasion I did not care to retouch it, nor to polish its style in accordance with my subsequent style of writing, nor to change it in any way, except for correcting typographical and other errors. Now that I am a year and a half short of sixty years of age, I do not think I have the right to correct, and certainly not to reshape, the person I was when I was thirty-two, in life and in dreams.

Here, in this book—the book of who I was—I invested more than twelve years of work. Here I gathered in the flowers and the fruits of my experience of childhood and adolescence. It contains the echo and perhaps the perfume of the most profound memories of my life and of the life of the town where I was born and raised. It contains the revelation of what history—and art—meant for me.

This work is as much a historical novel as it is a fictionalized history. There is scarcely a detail which I invented. I could document its most insignificant episodes.

I think that apart from any literary and artistic (or rather, poetic) value it might have, today, in 1923, it is as pertinent as it was when it was first published. What we thought, felt, dreamt, suffered, and experienced in 1874 when the explosion of the Carlist bombs jolted my childish dreams could serve as lessons for many young people of today—and many not so young.

This novel contains sketches of landscape, outline, and color of a given time and place. Later I abandoned this procedure and forged novels outside of any given place and time, skeletal novels, like intimate dramas, and I left the depiction of landscapes, skyscapes, and seascapes for other works. Thus in my novels *Amor y pedagogía*, *Niebla*, *Abel Sánchez*, *La tía Tula*, *Tres novelas ejemplares*, and other lesser writings, I did not want to distract the reader of the tale from the unfolding of human actions and passions. I brought together my artistic studies of landscape and skyscape in works like *Paisajes*, *Por tierras de Portugal y de España*, and *Andanzas y visiones españolas*. I do not know whether I have been successful or not in this differentiation.

As I again hand over to the public, or, better yet, to the nation, this book of my youth, which appeared one year before the epoch-making year of 1898—to which generation I am said to belong—this tale about the greatest and most meaningful national episode, I do so with the profound conviction that if I am leaving anything to the literature of my country, this novel will not be the least of all. If Walt Whitman said, in a collection of his poems, "This is not a book, it is a man," allow me, my fellow Spaniards, to say of this book which I am again publishing, "This is not a novel, this is an entire people."

MIGUEL DE UNAMUNO

Salamanca,
April, 1923

I

SOMETIME in the 1840s, in one of the so-called Seven Streets of Bilbao at the nucleus from which the city had grown, there used to be a small old store, of the type which occupied half the length of the entranceway and which was entered through a hatch-door hung from the ceiling and affixed to the roof once it was drawn up. This was a chocolate shop, full of flies, in which a variety of goods was sold. According to the neighbors, it was a little mine which was making its owner rich. It was a current saying that in the basements of those old houses in the Seven Streets—under the bricks, no doubt—there lay sacks of gold coins, hoarded coin by coin from the first days of that mercantile city out of an unquenchable will for savings.

At the hour when the street grew lively, about midday, the chocolate vendor could be seen, in his shirtsleeves, his elbows on the counter, his shaven, florid, self-satisfied face made vivid by his stance and his linen.

Pedro Antonio Iturriondo had been born with the Constitution, in 1812. His first years he lived in a village, slow and lifeless hours spent in the shade of chestnut and walnut trees or minding the cow. When he was taken to Bilbao at a very early age to learn the use of the chocolate-grinding pestle under the supervision of a maternal uncle, he proved a serious and timid worker. Because he learned his profession during that patriarchal decade that was brought about by the Hundred Thousand Sons of St. Louis, Absolutism symbolized for him a tranquil period of youth, work-days spent in the darkness of the shop and holidays at dances on the plain of Albia. From hearing his uncle's talk of Royalists and Constitutionalists, of Apostolicals and Masons, of the regency of Urgel and the *ominous* three-year period between 1820 and 1823 (which, according to his uncle, forced the people, tired of liberty, to demand chains and an Inquisition), Pedro Antonio gained what little knowledge he had of the nation where chance had placed him and where he lived out his life.

During his first years of work he often went to visit his parents, a custom he abandoned after he met a fine girl named Josefa Ignacia at one of the Sunday dances. She was the epitome of serene calm and sweet, diffuse joy. Following the advice of his uncle, he decided, after thinking it over awhile, to make her his wife. The matter was about to be arranged when Ferdinand VII died and the Carlist insurrection broke out. Pedro Antonio, twenty-one years old and respectful of his uncle's wish that he make a man of himself, joined the Royalist volunteers which Zabala raised in Bilbao, thus setting aside the chocolate pestle in order to defend with the flintlock musket his faith, so threatened by the Constitutionalists—the legitimate heirs of the Frenchified sympathizers of Napoleon, as his uncle said. Uncle added that the people, who had driven off the Imperial Eagles, would know how to sweep out the Masonic residue which they left in our house. As he took leave of his betrothed, Pedro Antonio felt like a man who is called on to drive a cart just as he was getting ready for bed. But Josefa Ignacia, swallowing her tears and putting her trust in a God who both grants time and takes it away, was the first to encourage him to carry out his uncle's wishes and God's, as revealed by the priests. She assured him that she would wait, use the time to gather some little savings, and pray for him so that as soon as the good should triumph they might get married in peace and in the grace of God.

How the seven glorious years glowed in the memory of Pedro Antonio! It was worth hearing him tell the story, his voice breaking toward the end, of the death of Don Tomás, as he always called Zumalacárregui, the chief who was crowned by death. On other occasions he would relate the story of the siege of Bilbao ("this same Bilbao in which we live"), or the Night of Luchana, or the victory of Oriamendi. Best of all was his account of the Pact of Vergara, when Maroto and Espartero embraced each other in the middle of the sown fields, between the two veteran armies who cried out for sweet peace after so much long, hard warfare. How much dust they had swallowed!

After the Pact was signed, Pedro Antonio returned home to Bilbao, putting aside the blackened rifle to take up the pestle. The Seven Year War vivified his life, nourishing it with a warm ideal made flesh in a world of memories of glory and fatigue. Thus, in the year 1840, twenty-eight years old and back at his job, he married Josefa Ignacia, who handed over her stocking filled with savings. From the first day they fitted into the same mold, and the comforting warmth of his wife—that epitome of serene calm and sweet joy—tempered his memory of the heroic years.

"Thanks be to God!" he would say again and again. "Those years are past now. How we suffered for the Cause! What sacrifices! Nothing but grief! . . . A fine reward we got for war! It's only good to talk about afterward . . . peace, peace. Let whoever wants to govern do so. God will call him to account in the end."

As he repeated this, he savored the honey of his

memories. Josefa Ignacia, though she knew it all by heart, always found the episodes of the Seven Year War to be entirely new. She was never quite surfeited with the idea that her good man had been a soldier of the faith. And she never quite saw, beneath his hymns to peace, the embers of his love of war.

Following the deaths of his parents and of his uncle, who left him the chocolate shop, Pedro Antonio was weaned away from his village. Nevertheless, he did not stop dreaming of it from time to time, immured in the tiny shop as he was. His gaze would wander after the cows as they passed along his street. Often, as he dozed beside the brazier on winter nights, he could hear the crackling of the chestnuts roasting and see the black iron chain for the pots hanging in the smoke-blackened kitchen. He found a special delight in speaking to his wife in Basque when, after closing the shop, they were alone to count and lock up the day's money.

Pedro Antonio enjoyed the novelty of every minute in his monotonous life, the delight of doing the same things day after day, the fullness of his limitations. He would lose himself in the shadows, passing unnoticed. Inside his skin, like a fish in water, he enjoyed the intimate intensity of a dark and silent life of work, taking pleasure in his own reality rather than in the appearance of others. His existence flowed along like the current of a gentle river, with a soundless noise which would go unnoticed until it met an obstacle.

Every morning he went down to open up the shop, happily greeting all his old neighbors, who were busy at the same task. He would stand about for a while, watching the village girls going to market with their bit of produce, exchanging a few words with those he knew. After taking a look up and down the street, always a busy marketplace, he would await the usual events. At nine, on Thursdays, the Aguirre family's maid would come for her three pounds of chocolate; at ten, some other maid. By way of novelty, there were always the unexpected chance customers, whom he often regarded almost as intruders. He had his own congregation of customers, a true congregation inherited for the most part from his uncle. He took care of these parishioners, keeping abreast of the course of their illnesses, taking an interest in their ups and downs. He treated the maids with familiarity, especially those who had served the same families for a long time, giving them advice and, whenever they had colds, candy to soothe their throats.

He took his meals at the back of the shop, from where he watched over the counter. In winter, he looked forward to the hour of the *tertulia*, the customary gathering of friends for conversation, and when it was over he went to bed eagerly, to sleep the sleep of children and of the pure of heart. During the week he provided himself with a supply of small coins, and on Saturdays he put them on the counter to hand out one by one to the poor as they came by to beg. If the beggar was a child, he would add a piece of candy.

He dearly loved his little shop, and he enjoyed the reputation of being a model and doting husband—a *chocholo*—among his neighbors, who left their wives in charge of their shops while they went off to taverns to chew the rag. For years his gaze had calmly wandered about that small space, leaving in every corner the imperceptible aura of peace and work. In every corner slept the vaguest echo of moments of his life, forgotten since they were all the same and all silent. He loved the gray days with soft rain because they drew him closer to the intimate shelter of his shop.

Hot, bright days struck him as ostentatious and somehow indiscreet. And how sad it was for him on summer Sunday afternoons when the neighbors closed their shops! Standing in his own place, open because it was classed as a confectionery, he would gaze at the sharp outlines of the shadows of houses in the silent but wakeful street. What enchantment, on the other hand, when he watched the fine insistent rain falling on gray days, in slender threads, falling gently, and he just out of it, covered and cozy!

Josefa Ignacia helped him in the shop, chatted with the customers, and enjoyed her peaceful life secure in the knowledge that her husband lacked for nothing. Every morning at dawn she went to Mass at her parish church. When in her old prayer book—with its grimy edges and large type, the book which spoke to her in Basque and was thus the only one she understood—when in this book she arrived at the blank space in the prayers where one was to ask God for some special benefaction, she asked, every day, year after year, mentally, not daring to move her lips because of shyness, for the gift of a child. She liked to pet and fondle children, a practice that irritated her husband.

Pedro Antonio liked the winter, for as soon as the long nights were joined to the gray days, and the endless persistent rains had come, the *tertulia* would begin in the shop. He would light the brazier, place the chairs around it, regulate the fire to keep it going, and wait for his friends to appear.

They came, wrapped in gusts of wet and cold. First on the spot, blowing on his hands, was Don Braulio, called an *Indiano* because he had been to America. Don Braulio was one of those men, born to live life, who live it with all their souls. He was in the habit of taking long walks in order to test what he called his "hinges and bellows." He called America "over there." Throughout the year, he commented on the lengthening or the shortening of every day, according to the season. Next appeared, in order: Gambelu, a former comrade-in-arms of Pedro Antonio, rubbing his hands and wiping his clouded glasses; Don Eustaquio, a former Carlist officer protected by the Pact of Vergara, under whose terms he lived; the grave Don José María, who was not a regular visitor; and finally, Don Pascual, a priest, Pedro Antonio's cousin, who stirred up the air in the room when he undid his cloak. Pedro Antonio savored it all: Don Braulio's blowing on his hands, Gambelu's rubbing his; Don Eustaquio's wiping his glasses; the unexpected appearance of Don José María; his cousin removing his cloak. He was happy simply watching the small rivulet of water which ran along the floor, formed from the great dripping umbrellas the visitors one after the other left in the corner. Meanwhile, he stirred the fire in the brazier with his brass fire-spoon.

"Not so much, not so much," Don Eustaquio would call out. But Pedro Antonio liked to see, as he separated the ashes from the embers, the coals glowing red and seeming to palpitate. They reminded him of the undulating flames of the open kitchen fire in the farmhouse where he was born; crackling flames whose many tongues licked the smoky walls; flames he had fallen asleep watching on many nights; flames which made him think of living beings—chained but longing for liberty, harmless in their place, but terrible when set free.

The *tertulia* had been organized shortly after the end of the war, and that conflict was discussed there in minute detail, as was the trouble stirred up later in

Catalonia by the Montemolinists. They commented on the articles in which Balmes, writing in *El Pensamiento de la Nación*, called for the union of the two dynastic branches, or they listened to Gambelu quarreling with Don Eustaquio over what the former called the treason and the latter the Pact of Vergara. Don Eustaquio, a supporter of the Pact, waxed indignant at the government's issuing terrible circulars by way of reply to Montemolín's proffer of an olive branch in his Bourges Manifesto and at their allowing the statue of the Pretender—whom Gambelu and the priest accused of being a liberal and a Mason—to be decapitated in Madrid, while he inveighed furiously against the line of Orleans, a family of monsters. Don José María, in the meantime, assured the company that England was "with them," and he insisted that "the autocrat" (his name for the Czar) would never have recognized Isabel II. When Gambelu replied by chanting

> And the Rushians who appeared
> Were all made of coal,
> Folderol, folderol!

the grave gentleman would only smile, as if asking himself, "Can there really be men so childish?"

The Montemolín insurrection broke out in Catalonia. The supporters of the Pact of Vergara did not spare their sarcasm, heaping it on those Catalonian officers who benefitted from no Pact at all, and the *tertulia* grew lively with daily battles between him and Gambelu, who idolized Cabrera and blamed the rich for all wrongs. Cabrera's entrance into Catalonia, his victory at Aviño, his strange humanity, the union of Carlists and Republicans, and the end of the war, all furnished fodder for the *tertulia*. So did the news of the Italian revolution unleashed against the Pope, the feats of Garibaldi, and the gossip that flew about concerning the garment and sores of Sor Patrocinio. Everything, in Don José María's eye, seemed unhinged; everything, according to Don Eustaquio, was going well; and everything made Pedro Antonio exclaim, "Now it's time to go to work and begin to live. Enough adventures. It's time to take reckoning."

All the while, Josefa Ignacia knitted, counting the stitches and sometimes dropping one, overhearing many things which became part of her without her being aware of them at all. When something held her wandering attention, she put down her work and gazed at the speaker with a smile.

It was not always a public event which furnished conversational material for the *tertulia*. Sometimes they turned their attention to past happenings. This was a special predilection on the part of Don Eustaquio, an old-fashioned *bilbaíno*, a partisan of Maroto, and a man nostalgic for his own former prosperity, which he identified with the salad days of the city.

"What times they were, Don Eustaquio!" the priest would exclaim, drawing him out.

With a gesture signifying "Don't force me to speak," Don Eustaquio was off. What times they were! There were no factories then, nor any bridge but the good old drawbridge we had, only the old Catalonian forges in the province, and the clean cabin, "clean as a little silver cup," was a hearth where everyone lived together. What traditions! The children used to undress on board any one of the little boats in the harbor and swim in front of the port houses, right in the middle of town! And business? In that town, where the famous Consulate of the Sea ordinances were first promulgated, the merchants used to play cards using bales of cotton for stakes. Everyone knows the song that goes

> A great traveler
> and Lord of England
> saw many lands
> and came to Bilbao:
> our commerce
> our wealth
> our grandeur
> left him amazed.

Utopia, it was Utopia in those years between 1823 and '33 when they, the Royalists, were in command, and the new Plaza, the city council's cemetery, and the hospital were all built by relays of men working for nothing.

"Then came '29, the year of the freeze," observed Don Braulio.

And with an air of saying "Now that one's butted in!" Don Eustaquio went on, speaking of Constitutionalists and Progressives, of the year '40, of tariffs. And when Pedro Antonio, poking the fire in the brazier, would attribute the establishment of tariffs to the urging of the big merchants, who had been hurt by the contraband carried on by the small merchants, the supporter of the Pact of Vergara would exclaim, "Be quiet, man, be quiet. It's hard to believe that you ever served the Cause. Do you dare to defend that Progressivist outrage? Do you dare defend Espartero? Would you go as far as to defend the barbarism of Barea?"

"For God's sake, Eustaquio! . . ."

"I tell you, and I'll always say so, that that was the end. . . . I have to laugh at the Progressives of today! . . . At that time—take note, Don Pascual—at that time, right here in this town, in these very streets, in

Bilbao itself, they sang, 'Down with our chains, and slaughter the monks!' I heard it, I heard it myself. And they tore down the churches . . . they even tore down the tower of San Francisco. . . . Since the year of the Revolution, since '33, everything has gone wrong . . ."

"What about the Pact of Vergara?"

"The devil of a pact, or a stew! The Liberals of today . . . those? They're not worth a thing. . . . Don't say any more, Pedro, not another word . . ."

"We'll not see again another slaughter of monks," Gambelu added. "The Liberals today haven't got the guts they used to have. . . . They're nothing . . ."

"It's worse all the time . . ."

"What are we to do about it! As long as there is peace, let God's will be done," Pedro Antonio concluded, by way of a moral.

Don Braulio would thereupon take out his watch, and the company would begin to break up when he exclaimed, "Gentlemen, it's ten-thirty!" Sometimes, when it rained, they would stay a bit longer, waiting for the weather to clear, and the conversation would go on, as sleep threatened to fell Pedro Antonio.

The great revolutionary storm of '48 burst upon them. The priest worried over "the Italian question," and would argue about it, irritated that there was no one to oppose him. Terrible events followed on each other's heels: the Pope fled Rome, and the Republic was proclaimed; and France lived through bloody days. Josefa Ignacia kept opening her eyes wide and dropping her knitting, as she heard tell of men who did not even believe in God, but then she would begin to doze over her work again, muttering something or other between her teeth. Pedro Antonio was secretly delighted with the terrible news of social upheaval. He felt the hidden pleasure of someone sitting next to a fire, watching from a window the wild wind blowing and from his refuge feeling pity for the poor foot traveler. Whenever he could put together a bit of savings, he would take it to the bank, thinking as he did so what it would be like if he had a son to whom he could leave it.

On one of those nights, in '49, after the *tertulia* broke up, man and wife were left alone to add up and put away the day's earnings. Poor Pepiñasi, all blushes and stammers, said something to her husband Peru Antón, whereupon his heart gave a leap, and he embraced his wife, exclaiming, with tears in his eyes, "Blessed be the Lord!" In June of the following year they had a son, whom they called Ignacio, and from thenceforward Don Pascual became Uncle Pascual.

During the first months, Pedro Antonio felt disoriented in the presence of that poor child, born to them so late, who seemed on the point of being carried off by a cold draft, an attack of indigestion, or some invisible nothing coming out of nowhere. As he retired for the night, he would bend over the little boy's face to listen to his breathing. Often he would take him up in his arms, gaze at him, and exclaim, "What a good soldier you might have made! . . . But thank heaven we live at peace. . . . Good boy!" But it never occurred to him to kiss the little fellow.

He proposed to bring up his son in simple Catholic strictness, and in the ancient Spanish manner, with the help of his cousin the priest, all of which amounted to the boy's kissing his parents' hands when he went off to sleep and when he got up and to his avoiding the familiar form in addressing them (a nefarious custom, sprung from the Revolution, according to Uncle,

who took it upon himself to inculcate the holy fear of
the Lord in his little nephew).

And the child would be in great need of this in-
doctrination, for the times were getting impossible, as
Pedro Antonio began to contemplate the future of the
world. Uncle Pascual's commentaries about the assault
of the priest Merino against the Queen made a deep
impression on the chocolate-maker, who seemed to see
Lucifer, disguised as a priest, silently creeping out of
the Invisible Valley to corrupt the world.

These first years of his life molded Ignacio's virgin
spirit, and the impressions left on him at that time
became later the soul of his soul. Inasmuch as his parents spent the entire day in the shop, he was scarcely
ever at home, where he rarely went except to sleep.

His real home was the street which ran into the
market, encircled by the horizon of the looming mountains. The houses in the street were ancient, many of
them bowed, with wooden balconies and asymmetrical
openings; houses where the cares of families seemed
to have left their mark; houses built with wide lengthy
eaves which made the long street narrow and dark.
Not far away stood the enormous portico of St. James,
with its cemetery, where the children used to gather
on rainy days, their fresh voices resounding in the
vault. The street—parched, cut across by narrow an-
gles of shade, resembling a tunnel covered by a piece
of sky, usually gray sky—seemed to grow gay when
it sensed the children running its length and calling
out. Nor was it somber there, for its shop exteriors
boasted a great kaleidoscope of lively-colored berets,
belts, suspenders as well as yokes, shoes—everything
hung out to allow the villagers to touch and handle
them. It was perpetual market day in the street, and
on Sundays coveys of country folk walked down the

middle, coming and going, stopping to examine the goods, bargaining, making as if to move on, only to return and pay for the item they then carried off. Among them all, often mimicking and mocking the people, Ignacio was raised.

The boys had their own special calendar of diversions, according to the season of the year and to the weather; from the water mills set up in the rainy current in the middle of the street when there were heavy showers to the imposing spectacle of Corpus Christi week, when they saw and heard the city trumpeters in red coats sounding their long solemn notes from the balconies of the Town Hall in the darkening twilight air.

Ignacio's best and closest boyhood friend was Juanito Arana, son of Don Juan Arana of the House of Arana Brothers, a Liberal and a man of substance.

The founder of the House of Arana, Don José María de Arana, had been a poor diligent tailor, no fool, who had invested the few meager savings earned from the sweat of his brow in merchandise from the colonies, placing orders for small consignments which came along with general cargo or with the large cargoes consigned to the big commercial houses of the city. He had set up shop behind his tailoring establishment, and he would leave off his cutting, blow on his fingertips, and go and sell codfish to a customer. The story was told of him that on one occasion in placing an order he had made an error in his figures, adding some unintended zeroes, supposedly to his undoing, since he found himself with an entire shipload consigned only to him, without means of paying for it. But he found creditors. The merchandise in question was in short supply, the price was up, and so he sold everything. This unexpected profit greatly enlarged his resources and awakened his latent sense of commercial initiative, inspiring him to undertake even greater ventures to lay the basis for his children's fortunes. This was the way, in short, that the lazy and the envious explained his wealth. Some slanderers even asserted that the good gentleman had finally come to claim that his mistake had been deliberate and calculated. In any case, at his death he left his offspring a fine store of capital and an excellent line of credit. On his deathbed he urged them not to split up but to continue the business as a joint stock company.

There were two sons: Don Juan, the elder, who directed the affairs of the commercial house, and Don Miguel. Don Juan was a slave to his office. He was there when it opened and he stayed there until it closed, except for visits to the docks to watch the arrival of ships consigned to him and to oversee the unloading of their cargo. As he walked among the goods in his warehouse, he was prone to be carried away by mercantile sentimentalism at the thought of the vast extent of the world and the infinite variety of lands that nourished commerce.

"Commerce will do away with war and barbarism," he would exclaim.

How happy he was the first time he read about "the commerce of ideas"! That even ideas should be subject to the law of supply and demand! He was a lukewarm Progressivist with a conservative cast to his character.

His father, Don José María, had not been able to provide his children with a brilliant education, but he did well enough by them, for they had learned enough about business and, among other attainments, some French, begun in the courses at the Consulate.

Don Juan traveled on business, and his voyages

endowed him with an even greater love of his *bochito*, which was his name for Bilbao. In the course of his travels he discovered Political Economy, to which he grew passionately devoted. He subscribed to a French economics review and bought the works of Adam Smith, J. B. Say, and others, especially Bastiat, who was then very much in vogue. He savored Bastiat as if he were a poet. After reading a few pages of his *Harmonies*, he would sink under the weight of his vague meditations into a sweet torpor similar to that which follows a hearty meal, finally falling asleep with Bastiat in his hands. Whenever anyone would remind him of the legend of his father's extra zeroes, he would reply haughtily that such a large credit would not have been forthcoming if his father had not always paid his smaller debts formally and religiously—for him, religion and formality were the same thing—and would add that it was his father's good credit that had made the mistake a fruitful one.

"It is very easy to talk of luck," he would say, "but difficult not to let it slip between one's fingers."

His wife, Doña Micaela, was the daughter of an émigré, one of the Seven Year War émigrés, who had died in the siege of 1836. Her family had suffered considerably in that war, and she had been raised amid shocks and flights. Any little thing was enough to set her off, and so she avoided contacts with people. All forms of pain became obsessions with her. She suffered from nightmares, and loud sounds set her teeth on edge. Her life had been a torment affording no rest nor respite. The unexpected bewildered her, and whenever she read the newspapers she kept repeating, "Good God, how much suffering there is!" When she reached the proper age, she married Don Juan, hoping to find repose at his side. And the union was fruitful.

Each time his wife bore him another child, Don Juan would meditate on the Malthusian law and then apply himself with even greater ardor to his business, so as to assure his family a future wherein they could live on the work of others; grateful to Providence for conceding him the luxury of being able to afford numerous children, he would oblige by resigning himself to life. Over and over he repeated that the breaking down of the least wheel in a great machine, the simple breakdown of one of the minor cogwheels, was enough to throw the whole movement out of kilter; he thought of himself as he said it, and of his importance within the machinery of human society.

Don Miguel, the younger of the Arana brothers, was a real bachelor, with a reputation as a rare bird, and he lived alone with his maid, a fact which furnished the idle with no small theme for talk. As a child he had been weak and emaciated, an object of mockery to his playmates, in consequence of which he developed a sickly sense of the ridiculous, so that he was preternaturally sensitive to the sound or sight of anyone saying or committing absurdities. He was a believer in the power of suggestion, in forebodings, and in sudden impulses. In the street he amused himself by counting his footsteps. He was an expert at solitaire, of which he knew forty-four kinds. This game was his delight, rivaled only by the pleasure of sitting alone by the fire, conversing with himself. He also liked to go on pilgrimages and to sing to himself while watching others dance at festivals. At the office he worked hard, demonstrating a respectful affection for his elder brother.

The firm of Arana Brothers was liberal by tradition and Catholic in the ancient manner, its name figuring among the first in every pious fund-raising drive. They pursued business with a passion, never neglecting the grand business of salvation.

Don Juan Arana's son Juanito was Ignacio's great friend, his schoolmate since the earliest times. The hours spent on school benches grew longer and longer in Ignacio's mind. Ill-equipped to endure such torture, he would amuse himself by hitting his neighbor. One of those boys given to pleading bodily needs every other moment as a means of escaping his enforced, boresome immobility, he consequently learned filthy habits in a dark, malodorous cubicle. As soon as the boys felt the air in the street, the air that was the *aperitif* of life, they leapt and raced about, imbibing as much of it as possible. How linked are games and freedom!

There in the street, with the boys from the city school, the *free* school, they went through their first sexual swaggering, as they ran after girls, dashing through town after them, scaring them with mice and making them cry, the poor timid things!

"Listen you, I'll get my brother . . . !"

"Go call him, I don't care! I'll bust him in the snout with a ball . . ."

The brother would appear, and the belt in the snout would follow. Battle would be joined to the accompaniment of a chorus: "Go on, get him by the ear!" "Knock him down!" "You're afraid of him . . . !" "He can beat you!" One of the boys would say a prayer that his friend and protector might win. They would grab hold of each other, and, amid the cries—"Hit him!" "Trip him up!" "Get him on the ground!" "Look at him biting, like a girl . . . !"—they would beat each other up, until one of them fell underneath, and the one on top, all sweaty and sniffing up his snot, would demand, brandishing his fist on high and holding his opponent by the collar: "Give up?" When the beaten boy answered "No!" the victor would smash him one on the mouth and ask again: "Give up?" The cry of "*Agua! Agua!*" warned of the approach of the *alguacil*, the constable, and this news would break up the fight, the boys dispersing, the two combatants sometimes going off together, without obvious rancor, but with one of them surely bearing a grudge and the other feeling proud. And it was in one of these fights that Ignacio got the better of Enrique, the street's bantam cock, a bully, a boy none of the others had been able to beat and nobody could stand up against ever since he got the better of Juan José, his only rival for street boss. They hated him, just hated him . . . !

What stone-throwing fights they had! Fights between gangs organized in the streets into offensive and defensive alliances! Ignacio never forgot the day they got hold of a brazier from the Marian sanctuary at Begoña, near Bilbao, filled it with dry grass, and set it on fire just to watch the spectacle of the smoke.

The older people complained because the rock-fights interfered with their promenade; newspapers drew the attention of the authorities to these young ruffians; all of which increased their fighting zeal, as they saw themselves objects of attention to their elders, who were their public. Whenever a gentleman brandished his walking-stick at them and threatened to call the constable, they fought the more furiously, so that he might admire their courage and skill and the newspapers print them up as "youths."

The African war broke out. All Spain thrilled to the traditional cry of "Let's get the Moor!" and the campaign was on every tongue. As the infantry regiments marched off, the boys went wild with excitement. Stories from the front sharpened the valor of the street gangs, among whom the name of Prim was universally known.

Around that time the boys also used to go watch, with mysterious fear, the trees at Miraflores shedding tears, where they had been hit by bullets from the firing squad that cut down the unfortunates captured at Basurto and implicated in the plot behind the uprising of San Carlos de la Rápita.

When he was eleven and on the eve of making his First Communion, Ignacio was a suntanned, blond youth who walked with a firm step. His somewhat deep-set eyes gazed calmly out from beneath a wide forehead. He made his First Communion before he was twelve, and it was the first of a series of regularly observed Communions, received with a simple punctuality on the appointed days.

During his preparatory phase, he would repair to the parish sacristy to study doctrine in the company of the other boys and girls getting ready for the Sacrament, the boys on one side, the girls on the other, all seated on the floor. Ignacio, without knowing why, gazed long on Rafaela, Juanito's sister, who kept tugging at her skirt, to cover her shins. The noise of the street reached the quiet dimness of the sacristy like a fresh and happy echo of the world.

The solemn day arrived, around Easter time, the festival of spring, and that day they were all young heroes, in their resplendent new First Communion clothes. An occasional girl wore white, showy and swell. Almost all the others wore black, for any other color was not nice, "proper only to *those* people," in Uncle Pascual's words. They were all heroes of the day, little angels. The older people came to admire them; it was the day of their entrance into the world of society, the solemn declaration of their religious coming of age. When Ignacio returned home, his parents kissed his hand, a reversal of roles, and while his mother wept, Uncle Pascual told him, "Now you're a man."

Uncle Pascual concentrated all his affection on Ignacio, who was his constant concern. At the family gathering at nightfall, before the *tertulia*, he would have the boy read aloud, usually from *The Lives of the Saints*. From this book Ignacio learned about the courage of the martyrs; about St. Lawrence, who asked that he be turned on the fire so that he might be roasted on both sides; about tender virgins who praised the Lord from within bonfires. Uncle also brought with him a collection of semihistorical legends from the Crusades. On the nights after Ignacio read from this book, he dreamed of godly knights, of warring monks, of Saladin and Godfrey of Bouillon. When he dreamed he heard the Crusaders cry out, "God wills it and the King commands!" he saw them just as they were pictured in one of the illustrations, raising their crossbows to the heavens and singing to Almighty God at the sight of Jerusalem.

Uncle Pascual often stayed for supper, but no matter how much his cousins urged him to come and live with them, he always declined, for he was put off by the idea of becoming a part of the private life of a family for whom he cared so deeply.

The priest, absorbed in Ignacio's care, tried to keep his nephew's soul unspotted and to protect his sacred store of redeeming beliefs, so there was no lack of little moral and apologetical sermons, for which Ignacio served as audience.

Often his father's tales of the Seven Year War came on the heels of Uncle's sermons. These stories brought to life in Ignacio's mind those figures in a coloring book he had so often colored as a child, figures of men in great helmets standing against men in great wide berets. In his mind's eye he saw them make their way over the craggy terrain, in ferns and gorse up to their knees, carrying supplies through a gorge or descending through chestnut groves with their bayonets at rest. Sometimes the boy could hear their shouts. Dominating all else in his imagination was the great figure of Zumalacárregui-of-the-dark-gaze, the warrior-chief of the engraving, showing him in a wide-brimmed beret and a furry sheepskin jacket, with a mustache running into his side whiskers, that dominated the seldom-used parlor. Taking him out of the engraving, Ignacio imagined the chief looking down on Bilbao from the height of Begoña or staring into the valleys obscured by the smoke of combat.

"Poor Don Tomás!" Pedro Antonio would exclaim. "They killed him, killed him between the two of them, a monk and a medical man and both of them in the pay of the Masons."

In the mind of the old soldier of Don Carlos, the Masons were the hidden power behind every dark machination, the explanation for the failure of the Holy Cause. Since there was no visible power that to him seemed capable of such a triumph, he fell back on the unknown and the mysterious, creating a diabolical divinity against which man could do nothing.

Overcome with tiredness, Ignacio would rub his eyes and watch with a dull gaze as his father thought about the Masons.

"Ah, Iniciochu!" his mother would say. "You can't last much longer. Your little eyes are begging for sleep. Come, son, go to bed and sleep, you're tired out . . ."

"But I'm not at all tired, Mother," Ignacio would say, struggling to keep his eyes open.

"Go on to bed," Pedro Antonio would say. "I'll tell you more about it some other day."

After kissing his parents' hands, Ignacio would go off to bed, a thousand confused images swimming around in his head. Often, the childish bogeyman that slept at the bottom of his soul would wake up in his dreams, dressed in Masonic garb.

His father's stories aroused in Ignacio abstract images of men and places, figures etched in copper, and he would hear again and again the clamor of ancient battles. Within him, the world, his world, began to take shape, the true world, one very different from the world that filtered into him through the senses, the false world.

The years preceding the September Revolution furnished the *tertulia* an abundance of subject matter on European, Spanish, and local events. The failure of the construction company building the railroad between Tudela and Bilbao had affected nearly every part of the town. The panic was general. There were many who wept over their lost savings, savings made on the basis of some small sale or sacrifice. Stocks quoted at 100 had gone down to 5, and soon, it was said, the certificates would serve only to wrap candy.

Those who complained the loudest were the ones who had lost the least, or who had lost a small portion of inherited capital, money they had never had to earn for themselves; those who had been deprived of the fruits of their own work went on working and wept in silence. Among the most vociferous complainers was Don José María. Overexcited, he saw everything in the worst light. The spoliation of the Pope and Garibaldi's entry into Rome seemed to him storm clouds charged with hailstones. He spoke of *the Corsican*—as he called Napoleon III—and of *the Austrian*, *the Russian*, and *the Englishman*, and went on endlessly about Magenta and Solferino, about Savoy and Lombardy. He talked vaguely about the momentous mysteries of international politics, and he thereby aroused Don Eustaquio's contempt and Gambelu's playful humor. Gambelu kept repeating that Narváez had gotten his wings clipped; he was awaiting the fracas with childish anticipation.

The year 1866 ran its course, providing them with much to argue about, for it was a year of pronunciamientos and blood, of firing squads and terror.

Uncle Pascual was much upset by the recognition of the Kingdom of Italy, a development which threw all of Carlist Spain into a commotion and which began to alarm Don Eustaquio, who thought he detected a violation of what had been tacitly agreed to by the embrace on the field at Vergara. Don Eustaquio then was moved to pity the poor Queen.

The priest gave vent to a certain quantity of vague rancor, product of the profound irritation which most things caused him. Believing man to be naturally bad, he called for "a big stick," called for it at every turn, and would not let up until he was submerged in the myths of Aparisi, where he could bathe his embryos and abortions of ideas in the stream of thought which holds that Carlism is "the Affirmation."

Pedro Antonio would listen delightedly as accounts of the Italian campaign were read aloud, carried away with enthusiasm for the Zouaves, for the Christian warrior, whose dignity and rank—in Uncle Pascual's opinion—was the highest after that of the clergy itself.

When Don Juan of Bourbon renounced his claim

to the Crown in favor of his son Carlos, the priest
called the father a Liberal and a heretic, Don Eustaquio
maintained that the rights in question were unre-
nounceable, and Gambelu exclaimed, "It's really better
that he renounce his claims, because, after all, could
we have called ourselves 'Juanists'? Carlos was our
man, and Carlists are what we are, that's our name
. . . but, 'Juanists'? Ugh!"

Were they to lose the name that bore with it all the
hopes and memories of some and the hatred of others?
Carlos! That was a name redolent with history, evoc-
ative of the green years! Vulgar John! John Fleece!
John Soldier! Poor John . . . ! The sonorous name
roused them, though they never saw the man beneath
the name, so that the frequent letters from Trieste
published by *La Esperanza* were received coldly by
the *tertulia*, just as they coldly received a grimy letter
badly worn and tattered from much handling which
Don José María took out of his wallet one night, a
letter stating that the young Carlos was one of the best
horsemen in Europe, lauding his pure love of Spain,
and describing his wedding.

Meanwhile, to the sound of the Riego Hymn, the
Revolution drew near, on its own, like a cyclone following its fated course; concurrently, the European
gust blew upon Spain. Conspiracies flowered. Progressives, democrats, republicans, Carlists worked in
the shadows. Palace abominations were retailed, and
it was said that a nun with the stigmata was in control
of the court.

"Perico," the priest would say to his cousin Pedro
Antonio, "you who have children, tremble for what is
to come!"

As the *tertulia* broke up, its members thought vaguely
of the future, of the struggle which was to ensue be-

tween the national will, bound to the whole being of the people and held together by tradition, and revolutionary reason, goaded by new and brazen impulses.

Often, after the *tertulia*, Pedro Antonio would have to wake up his son, who had fallen asleep over a penny-dreadful, and see that he got to bed.

For some time now, Ignacio had taken to buying religiously, from the blind man who sold them in the marketplace, *pliegos* or penny-dreadfuls—loose sheets bound by reed strips to a cord, and offered for sale to the curious, usually by blind men. They were all the craze among the local boys, who bought and traded them.

Those *pliegos* contained the flower of popular fantasy and history. Some of them were stories from the Bible, others were Oriental tales, some were medieval epics of the Carolingian cycle, or novels of knight-errantry, or the most famous stories from European literature, the cream of patriotic legends, the feats of bandits, and narratives of the Seven Year War. They were the poetic sediment of the centuries. After having nourished the songs and stories which have consoled the lives of many generations of men, going from mouth to ear and ear to mouth, told and retold beside comforting fires, they now lived on through the good offices of blind street peddlers, in the evergreen fantasy of the populace.

Ignacio read them falling asleep and scarcely understood them. Those written in verse quickly tired him, and all of them contained words which were beyond him. Sometimes, on his way to sleep, he would gaze slackly on the rough and ready engravings. Very few of those legendary figures clearly impressed themselves on his mind: at most, Judith holding up the head of

Holofernes; Samson tied up at the feet of Delilah; Sinbad in the cave of the giant; Aladdin with his magic lamp exploring the cavern; Charlemagne and his twelve peers "hacking through turbans and coats of mail" on a battlefield where blood ran like rainwater; the gigantic Fierabras of Alexandria, "who was a tower of bones" and feared no one, bending his head over the baptismal font; Oliveros of Castile dressed now in black, now in white, now in red, his arm bloody to the elbow, looking up from the tournament field towards the daughter of the King of England; Arthur of the Algarve battling against the monster with the arms of a lizard, the wings of a bat, and a tongue made of coal; Pierre of Provence, fleeing with the beautiful Magalona on the rump of his horse; Floris the Moor leading Blanchefleur the Christian woman by the hand toward the beach, gazing at her all the while, although her own eyes are downcast; Genevieve of Brabant, half-naked and huddling in the cave with her small son, beside the hind; the corpse of the Cid Ruy Díaz del Vivar the Castilian stabbing the Jew who had dared touch his beard; José María the highwayman holding up a stagecoach among the crags of the Sierra Morena; the cranes carrying off Bertoldo through the air; and, more than any other, Cabrera, Cabrera on horseback, with his white cape flowing behind him.

These lively visions, fragments of what he had read in the *pliegos* and seen in their engravings, appeared in his mind with uncertain contours, and in his mind's ear he heard the echo of exotic names like Valdovinos, Roland, Floripes, Ogier, Brutamonte, Ferragús. That world of violent light and dark, filled with ceaselessly shifting shadows—the more vague they were, the more vivid—would descend, silently and hazily, like a cloud, to lie upon his spirit's repose, and there take on the flesh of dreams, gradually and unconsciously becoming part of his soul. And from the depths of the past a world would loom up in his dreams while he huddled cozily in his father's quiet confectionery shop, withdrawn and half asleep, amid the noise of the *tertulia*. It was a world both rough and sensitive, in which knights both killed and wept, had adventures between prayers and jousts, and owned hearts of iron for battle, hearts of wax for love; a world of beautiful princesses who rescue from prison adventurers they have barely glimpsed and yet love; of giants who get baptized; of generous bandits who, commending themselves to the Virgin, rob the rich to get alms for the poor; a world in which Samson, Sinbad, Roland, the Cid, and the highwayman José María rub shoulders. And, as last link in that chain of heroes, there stood Cabrera, giving the seal of reality to that world and its way of life: Cabrera exclaiming, as he burst forth from a turbulent youth, that he would "make a noise in the world"; Cabrera, whirling round and round like a hyena, roaring like a lion, tearing out his hair and vowing blood vengeance as he called out General Nogueras to single combat for having had his poor mother—seventy years old!—shot down; Cabrera, going from victory to dizzy victory until he fell exhausted. And that man still lived. Gambelu and Pedro Antonio had seen him with their own eyes, a man of flesh and blood and a hero from another world at the same time, a living Cid who would come back some good day on horseback and bring with him the enchanted world of the heroes, where fiction is bathed in reality and shadows take on life.

Ignacio would fall asleep, and his world would sleep with him. The next day, as he emerged into the cool of the street, into the light of day, all those fictions, though faded, colored his soul and sang to him in silence.

One night, as he was leaving the *tertulia*, Uncle Pascual caught sight of boy's *pliegos*. Turning to Pedro Anotonio, he said, "Take those things away from him. There's all kind of stuff in them."

One morning in the year 1866, returning home after Mass, Josefa Ignacia called her son to carry him off to the sacristy, where he saw a petition, covered with signatures, protesting against the recognition of the Kingdom of Italy.

"Sign, Ignacio, to make them give back to the Pope everything they have stolen from him," his mother said.

Ignacio signed, thinking to himself as he did so, *What a lot of signatures! They'll have enough trouble just reading them all.* He felt a bit humiliated that his mother had fetched him and brought him along, instead of letting him come alone.

The sacristy was full of priests talking about the disputed recognition, which had caused a terrible outcry. They spoke about the religious ceremonies being held by way of amends and about the petitions of protest appearing everywhere with the signatures of thousands of people, old and young, men and women, ancients and infants at breast.

"This will bring down the throne of Doña Isabel!" exclaimed one priest, as he went off to say Mass.

For some time now Pedro Antonio and his wife had been thinking seriously of what they were to do with their son, already fairly grown up. They used to whisper interminably about the matter in bed. They were of a mind to place him behind a desk in a counting house before he took up his expected duties in the shop. Later he might find this mercantile apprenticeship useful, once he was in command of the family business, expanding its sphere of operations while his parents rested in his shade.

These meditations, repeated thousands of time, helped Pedro Antonio dream of his rosy future, his peaceful old age. Every day he would go sit in the sun at Begoña with his wife. He would be amused by his grandchildren. He would wait on customers for the fun of it, and the business would sail along before the favorable wind provided by his tradition of credit, the soul of all commerce. He thought that there was none better to ask about a position in a counting house than Arana, their neighbor, whose son was such a friend of Ignacio. But Pedro Antonio did not want to decide the matter definitively without first seeing Uncle Pascual.

Consulting him one day, the couple explained their plan.

As he took a pinch of snuff, Uncle Pascual told them, "I think it is well, very well for you to be thinking of making a man of him. I've been thinking about the same thing for some time. I think a counting house is right for him. Arana's is a good one, but I would prefer another. It's not that Arana is bad, no! He's a good person as far as that goes, a serious man of commerce, but . . . you know that he's a Liberal, one of the biggest. And his son, that snot-nose, is a bit more than a Liberal, with some unsavory ideas in his head, I understand. Just imagine: he doesn't go to Mass on Sundays . . . !"

"Jesus, Mary, and Joseph!" exclaimed Josefa Ignacia. "That can't be, it must be just talk. . . . Why, we know them all, him and his family. Why, we saw him born, as they say . . ."

"Well, that's the way it is," Uncle Pascual went on, helping himself to another pinch of snuff. Then he added, in a slightly preaching tone, "We must be careful of Ignacio, keep him away from bad company. Watch out now, with the ideas currently in vogue. He's at a critical age, and we have to handle him very carefully. You can't be too vigilant, and he has—thanks be to God—a good foundation, a noble one. Those ideas, those ideas will turn that silly Arana boy upside down if his father doesn't keep him in close check. . . . But then of course his father . . ."

He fell silent, his thoughts busy with Ignacio, who was at an age when blood overcomes reason. He pondered his nephew's character. As his cousin was talking to him, he was thinking that the lusts of the flesh cool off with age but that spiritual pride stays with us to the grave. He was, at that time, working on a sermon.

"Keep a sharp eye," he continued, "a sharp eye on rationalist arrogance. . . . Other evils are preferable."

He went on to adduce further cases, all of them abstract, since his mind had moved beyond Ignacio, beyond the house of Arana. As he rose to go, he said, "So now you know. You asked me for advice, and I've given it, but it's my opinion that Arana will not say anything if you don't think of him as regards Ignacio's education in business. Some other counting house, Aguirre's, for example. . . ."

He waited a bit, his cousins kept silent, and then he left. The parents decided to place the boy in Aguirre's counting house.

"Well, I think Arana is a good man," said the mother.

"Good, yes, good . . . as far as being good is concerned, he's a good man. But you know what Uncle Pascual said."

They placed Ignacio in the counting house. At first things went well for him, because of the newness of the experience. But very soon the boy began to hate that rack—in the form of a three-legged stool—upon which he was stretched, calculating the amount of other people's money. His hatred of his desk gradually became hatred of Bilbao, of cities in general. He would have liked to be a member of the furthest-removed parish, live in the remotest corner, in a place where no city person had ever set foot. In a city like Bilbao, it was the grandsons of countrymen who made mock of new immigrants from the villages. It annoyed him to see the way city people treated the *batos*, the people they called hicks, and he began to conceal the fact that he was from Bilbao at all. For want of a knowledge of Basque, he began deliberately and ostentatiously to mutilate Castilian Spanish, which he had learned in the cradle from parents who in *their* cradles had lisped in Basque.

In the same measure that he hated the city streets he loved the countryside. He waited for Sunday with real impatience, so that he could escape with Juan José. The streets of the city stifled him, the nightly stroll inspired revulsion. But what a lovely thing was the woodland! The woods! The woods where there were no dandies or ladies, where they could let out a yell in the clear air if they wanted and let their shirttails fly!

They would set out on a Sunday after the noon meal, sometimes in oppressive heat, at the hour of burning dead calm, when the wind dozed and the motionless trees gave no coolness. They would climb the mountains, avoiding the well-marked paths and propelling themselves by holding on to the undergrowth, making their way through the gorse, breathing in its warm aroma and the scent of heather and fern. They would force themselves to climb long and far, scarcely stopping for breath. When they reached the top—disappointed that there was not yet another climb ahead of them—they would sprawl on the ground to gaze at the sky and feel the grass at their backs and let their sweat evaporate in the open air, the highland air, the breeze of heaven which sometimes carried shreds of clouds along with it. Sweating was a pleasure, and with it they felt the evil humors of the city streets quitting their bodies, leaving them like new men. An immense panorama spread out before their eyes: the giants of Vizcaya, and, at the foot of the great peaks, sometimes fog filling the valley like a fantastic sea on whose limitless surface the tops of smaller mountains floated like islands and in whose ethereal and vaporous depths Bilbao from time to time glimmered like a submerged city.

The friends would climb down filled with pride at having conquered the height. They would stop to drink a bowl of milk or a glass of the light, bitterish *chacolí* wine of the region in some farmhouse with a begrimed religious print affixed to the courtyard door. Juan José, bent on exhibiting sympathy and interest, would ask endless questions as they engaged the householder in conversation.

At that time Ignacio was much bothered by visits and company. He would avoid encounters on the street with girls he knew. He blushed red greeting Rafaela, now a fine young woman, with whom he had so often played as a boy. He refused to go for a stroll in the Campo del Volantín—"like the dandies," as he put it. He became a devotee of *pelota*, which he played well and frequently, in the afternoons before repairing to the counting house, and he put all his soul into the

game. He challenged all comers, bragging as he displayed the calluses on his hand and asked people to
feel them.

But since he could not play games or climb mountains every day, and he had to wait for Sundays, and
they were sometimes rainy. On wet afternoons, under
a leaden sky across which black clouds scuttled, there
was nothing to do but retreat to a *chacolí* tavern to
play the favorite local card game of *mus*, to have a bite
to eat, and to chat.

Present on these occasions, besides himself, were
Juan José, Juanito Arana, and several others, among
them a certain Rafael, a chap Ignacio could not abide
because after a few glasses of wine, he would string
together verses and more verses, whether or not any-
body wanted to hear them. The verses were from romantic poets like Espronceda, Zorrilla, the Duke of
Rivas, Nicomedes Pastor Díaz—verses with drumbeat
cadences which Rafael recited with a heavy-handed
insistence. It was all a late echo of the literary revolution which had broken out in Madrid, where Clas-
sicists and Romantics battled each other in the theaters,
much as the partisans of María Cristina and the Carlists
fought it out in the Basque country.

In the tavern the boys talked of everything. Rafael
would fill his bell-shaped glass to the halfway point,
hold it up to the sun to judge its color and clarity,
would down it in one swallow, and then hang his head
low, like a man in meditation. After they all had a bite
of something to eat, Juan José would light up a cigarette and call for a deck of cards. Ignacio would horse
about with the maid, whom Juanito pawed, and Rafael
would declaim:

Peace in War

Give me wine: to drown
My memories. Let life
Fly by, and strife.
The tomb will bring me peace.

"I hope they burn down the counting house!" Ignacio shouted, as if it were a maxim for any fine afternoon.

It was a Sunday in spring. A violent norther sent black clouds scudding desperately across the city sky, and heavy rain showers alternated with thin squalls.

Ignacio and his friends took refuge in a tavern where they ordered a big spread and began to yell, argue, and sing until they were hoarse. Ignacio did not take his eyes off the girl serving them. He was restless and irritated with himself, and he ended by quarreling with Juanito over politics. When they left the tavern, there was still part of the afternoon left, and they debated where to go next. Ignacio kept quiet, a prey to inner agitation, while Rafael, dissenting from the general decision, went off reciting:

In a sea of boiling lava
My head is blazing . . .

That afternoon Ignacio had been listening to these verses of the Romantic poet with unprecedented interest: their sing-song had even succeeded in entrancing him, as he kept ogling the little waitress. His mind was in a whirl, he seemed to feel the wine circulating in his head, and he wished he could throw it up, and his blood along with it. And thus it was that he followed his companions to a suffocating hole in the wall, where for the first time he knew the sin of the flesh. When he came out and felt the cool of the air and saw

*41**

the people passing he felt shame. He gazed at Juanito, suddenly remembered Rafaela, and, flushing red, asked himself, "What have I done?"

Once the dam was broken, his blood spilled over, and he was unable now to forget the new way of life, so that a period of carnal indulgence began for him. The tavern feasts became regular events, and sometimes vomiting them up afterwards in unclean retreats. But it was not always the same: oftentimes he would go home, have the lightest of suppers, and then go to bed, where he tossed and turned in great restlessness, regretting not having finished up the afternoon in the brothel, prey to a desire that could have sent him running back and, at the same time, filled with the self-loathing he always felt on returning from such places.

When, some time after he had entered upon this path, it grew time for him to go to confession, he did so with true contrition and shame, stammering and in confusion, and confessed his sin. Afterwards, he was surprised at the naturalness with which his confessor listened and how unimportant it seemed to him. This fact calmed him, so that once more he gave way to his passion, surrendering after a very short struggle with himself, a tussle of an almost purely theatrical nature; in the end he grew accustomed to confessing and repenting the same old sin again and again.

Just as he had never felt his own heartbeat when he was in sound health, so he had never felt the palpitations of his conscience while sound of spirit until now, when both his heart and his conscience had painfully awakened. He had lived without sensing life, in the air and under the light of heaven, but now he never fell asleep as soon as he lay down, and at times the very sheets seemed to scald him.

The manner in which Juanito and his other friends

treated *those* women also offended him. The first of them he had sinned with had aroused pity in him. He thought her a victim, and now he was glad to listen to Rafael's tearful poetic recitals, many of which were filled with laments for fallen women.

One night Pedro Antonio summoned his son. He questioned him and obliged him to make a clean breast of it. Abashed, the father found no strength to reprimand the son.

To himself Pedro Antonio murmured, "It's because of his age! Good God, what times we live in! . . . I'll watch over him. . . . But it doesn't surprise me in someone of his temperament. Until such time as he gets married. . . . Just as long as he doesn't lose his soul! . . ."

When his poor mother got an inkling of what was going on, she wept in silence, and, when Ignacio saw her eyes all red-rimmed, he shut himself up in his own room to weep. Josefa Ignacia's mind was awhirl with the image of the she-devil of a rouged woman in low shoes, wearing red stockings and standing at the door of one of those houses, a woman she had seen one day when she was visiting a friend in that direction. The woman's dismal, glassy-eyed look was still strongly fixed in her memory.

One day, when the couple were spending an evening with Uncle Pascual, they told him about their son's latest activities. The priest fell silent at first and then delivered a homemade homily, advising them to calk the seams in the boy's head so as to keep out fatally impious currents, and also to separate him from Juanito Arana. He added that all this would pass, since it was merely a sign of hot blood, and that the worst danger was spiritual pride. Finally, he undertook to

take charge of his nephew, to direct and admonish
him.

Pedro Antonio went to bed with an easier mind,
somewhat recovered from his stupefaction and murmuring, "May God's will be done!" His wife was more
in the dark than ever about the business of spiritual
pride, but on the other hand she half-glimpsed the
mystery of iniquity that lay in the concupiscence of the
flesh, and she trembled with worry at the thought of
the strange diseases which come without warning and
kill in shame, turning the body into a loathsome living
cadaver. Since the poor woman had the gift of tears,
she cried at every step, asking God to save from pride
and concupiscence the son of her flesh and spirit, to
keep him safe from that dismal, glassy-eyed look. She
redoubled the care she lavished on her son. When he
was asleep, she would go see if he had gotten uncov-
ered, saying, "Take care of yourself, bundle up close,
and don't get up yet if you don't feel well. I'll send a
message to Aguirre." At meals, she urged him to take
second helpings. All the tenderness of her first years
of motherhood flowered again. And all these attentions
and niceties were the shame and bane of Ignacio.

It was then that Uncle Pascual took his nephew under
his wing, and had him come walking from time to time
the better to instruct him. He loved the boy as much
as he could, but he was especially engaged in shaping
his ideas, viewing him as primarily material for education. Ideas, a social bond, were everything in his
eyes. It never occurred to him to look at a man in a
deeper way, or to see in him anything but a member
of the Church or an outsider. When he admonished
his nephew about the sins of the flesh he argued from
reasons of prudence, meanwhile striving to confirm

him in the faith of his fathers. A man of fixed ideas, the priest repeated to Ignacio everything he had read in Aparisi Guijarro, who pleased him by a certain hazy quality of emphasis. The boy listened to him in wonder. He thought about Cabrera as his uncle told him that Carlism is affirmation; that just as the infernal serpent promised our first parents that they would be like gods, so Liberalism promises us that it would make us like kings—so that God will turn us into beasts, as He did with Nebuchadnezzar. Uncle Pascual was most intent to inspire in Ignacio a contempt for Liberals, a belief that they were pig-headed, ignorant, and cowardly. He stirred him up to such an extent and preached so spiritedly against human "rights" that Ignacio launched upon a period of intense religious show.

Ignacio carried a torch in almost all the religious processions. He liked challenging the idea of human "rights" and was ready to come to blows with anyone who mocked religion. He greeted all priests, kissing the hands of those he knew. He doffed his hat when he passed churches. At the sight of the Viaticum processional, he would kneel on the ground, on both knees, with greater fervor the larger the crowd. He kept repeating, in season and out, that he was an Apostolic Roman Catholic, and a Carlist to the death, on his sternest honor.

But in his blood he had not forgotten the path of sin. Sometimes, after having walked in the streets in the morning with a torch in his hand, challenging the "rights" claimed by this cowardly society, he would go that same night to glut his flesh. Once, when he saw a harlot cross herself at the sound of a thunderclap, he felt a lump in his throat. Then, when he further caught sight of her scapulary and at the same moment remembered Rafael's verses, he felt a holy pride for the blessed land where a healthy sap runs, as it runs in oak trees, beneath the mistletoe. Poor woman! She was a Basque! And no doubt the victim of some Liberal!

When Juanito Arana would bring up his weakness and throw it in his face, Ignacio would reply, "I may be a libertine, even a lost soul, but I'm Catholic still. I'm only flesh and blood, but the Faith . . ."

There was still time for him to repent truly, because God abandons only the proud, who do not believe in Him. This was his line of thought as he recalled the examples of those hardened sinners who always retained the habit, acquired in childhood, of saying a short prayer to Holy Mary on retiring, even though they did it mechanically and half asleep, and who were finally saved and assisted by the Virgin in their last moments. "If I did not believe in Hell, what would become of me?" he thought, and the thought filled him with pride. To him a believing libertine was a cavalier figure, a man prodigal with spiritual treasure, someone whom our greedy, superficial, and cowardly society does not know how to appreciate. Thus did he freely translate his uncle's sermons.

Numbed by sin, Ignacio's flesh did not plague his spirit, letting him sleep virginally in his faith. Hard upon a session in the confessional, he would vow not to give in; a little later he would tell himself that it was only a matter of necessary hygiene, a way to avoid worse evils and uglier vices; and once he had fallen, he had his faith to console him.

When his parents suspected that he had not reformed, they hastened in alarm to Uncle Pascual. Ignacio's mother wept. His father mused vaguely. The priest told them, "I'll find some solution. I think something has already been accomplished. . . . He'll settle down once he gets married, and then, disillusioned, he'll put in at a sure port, to work for the Faith, which is what's needed nowadays. Not everyone can be a St. Aloysius Gonzaga. . . . It's a bad affair, but we'll try to find the solution, and it would be worse if he took up some other vice, like that Arana brat. . . . We must take the times into consideration, Perico. . . . We have to be careful, but you can't make him stay home for prayers; there is some evil that is almost inevitable. . . . It's a matter of patience and of feeling out the cure. . . . But don't think that for all that I'm going to glorify vice, like those French writers lacking shame or faith. . . . Frenchmen, after all . . ."

Later, he spoke alone to his nephew, and when he saw him bow his head in shame said, "Ask God for help. . . . You've still got a lot there to draw on!"

He delivered a little sermon, urged him to persevere in his Faith, and, as a distraction, led him into the Carlist club.

Ignacio's faith grew stronger. He understood nothing of philosophy nor other complications, but he never took up such deep things. He had been handed the Book of the Seven Seals still sealed, and he believed in it without needing to open it. He once told Juanito and Rafael in an argument that for his part he favored raving atheists, fanatical demagogues, and that if he were not a Carlist Catholic, he would be an atheist and an incendiary, because the worst people of all were the meek, the moderates. . . . Consumptive souls! He did not believe in the virtue of the unbeliever, pure hypocrisy or satanic pride at most, nor did he believe that there existed either atheists or young men who at seventeen had not committed abominations.

"Take Pachico, who is an unbeliever, and passes himself off as the most proper of chaps . . ."

"He's just a half-wit, and the Masons have made him worse. Even though he says the opposite, he really believes. You can see him every day on his way to Mass . . ."

"If he heard you now I know what he'd say: that the blood cools with the years while the head hardens . . ."

Ignacio had never been so curt with strangers as he was in this time of his life, and he had never been so overcome with embarrassment on meeting Rafaela in the street and having to greet her.

The absence from the city of the one whore who had exerted her fascination over Ignacio coincided with the effects of weariness and of Uncle Pascual's work upon him, so that he returned, with the good weather, to his jaunts into the country, a habit which brought him peace. He became enveloped in the tranquillity of the countryside: a balsam rose from out of the warm green earth and cured him of the fumes of the city streets, the fumes of human breaths on which were borne low desires and lewd sighings.

Ignacio and his old friends met and set out for distant *chacolí* taverns and *romerías*, saint's day pilgrimages. Some Sundays they had country dinner in the village, a practice which pleased Pedro Antonio and his wife, who thought it a good distraction for the boy. After a large meal, the friends would lie in the grass, contemplating the countryside and talking. At dusk they would set out for home.

At sunset, the light would fade off into shadow, and the blue mountains in the background would stand out against the white sky. It was the hour of evening air, that time when all the senses are sharpened, when the sweet fading colors of twilight give rest to the eye, when the fresh odors which arise from the earth before nightfall revive the nose, when the ear catches the occasional sound of a dog barking or a child crying— sounds arising against the noisy din of locusts like voices of the valley itself. Ignacio and his friends usually came home by the mountain roads. Without conscious awareness, Ignacio let the voices of the valley penetrate deep within him, as it gradually grew darker. He lost himself in his surroundings, with his soul open to the fugitive flow of impressions, watching the unmoving procession of haystacks and of trees, listening to the cries of children, sharp and clear in the valley air. A villager, leaning on his crook, watched Ignacio and his companions from the side of the road. Another greeted them awkwardly. The blue smoke from a farmhouse hung in the distance ahead of them, and cows placidly browsed on the grass without raising their heads, the last thing the friends saw against the quiet background of darkening night. The whole party walked along in silence, absorbed in their trek, until they suddenly heard far-off bells and saw a villager take off his hat to pray. Rafael then might shout out the famous verses of Zorilla—

> The noise that cuts the wind
> Is the funereal sound of a bell . . .

And the vibrant voice of Juan José would rise up to sing—

> *Au . . . au . . . aupá!* The bell ringer
> Is about to ring, *ay*, for prayer.
> *Ay, ené*, I'll die.
> *Maitía, maitía*, come here . . .

At which they would all burst into song together—

> Though the bells call to prayer
> I'm not stirring from here
> The girl with the red kerchief
> Put my mind on mischief . . .

Rafael would wail tremulously, his face turned up to the sky and his hand over his heart.

When one of them on the heights would catch the first sight of the starburst of the streetlamps in the darkness of Bilbao, he would signal to his companions, without stopping in his song. The solemn notes and cadences of the *zorcico*, which seemed to dance a solemn dance of their own, now began to displace the sounds of the country. As they came into the city streets, they lowered their voices, while the real sons of the people bawled their wild songs in the middle of the same streets to attract the attention of strollers and to draw to themselves the curiosity of the public. Once home, Ignacio went to bed muttering, "Tomorrow, the counting house, the damned counting house!"

These excursions gave peace to his turbulent spirit and quieted him down for the entire week, since his soul had expressed itself in those songs. He liked singing more than music; he enjoyed giving his voice to the wind as an outburst of energy which relieved his soul.

Juanito Arana's bold mode of thought and expression came to the attention of his father, who felt it necessary to call the boy aside and take him to task, more to soothe Doña Micaela than for any other reason. The old man considered religion, without being clearly aware that he did so, as a kind of divine political economy, a matter of resolving the great business of our salvation

economically, securing the greatest possible eternal fe-
licity at the expenditure of the least possible temporal
mortification. To comply with the forms was enough:
punctuality was the guarantee of credit.

Face to face with his son, the father told him that
he had been aware of his follies but had kept his peace
out of prudence. Now, however, seeing that matters
were getting out of hand, he found himself obliged to
insist that the boy toe the line, since many people were
going around condemning him for the way he was
bringing up his son, even going so far as to lay the
blame for all those wild doctrines on the father.

"You're still young," Don Juan said, "and you don't
know the people among whom you live. When you're
my age, you'll think differently. You've got to know
how to get along, and all those ideas can only get you
into trouble around here. Besides, what do you know
about all those things? I'm not asking you to become
a canting altar boy, a saint, or a fanatic like the confectioner's son, but a little religion is no obstacle. And
most of all, enough of these mad declarations! You
don't even believe them yourself. Most of them are
pure verbiage. In matters like this, it's best to follow
the teachings of our fathers; otherwise you'll just lose
your head without gaining anything useful. Just look
at the English, a practical people if there ever was one.
In their country, each man practices his own religion
and has the good taste to refrain from arguing about
it. It's not like here, in this poor Spain of ours. Of
course, a country like ours, where the majority doesn't
even know how to read. . . . Well, let's thank God for
having allowed us to be born in the true religion, and
leave it to the priests to worry about meanings. And
would to heaven that they actually tended to their
business! But you tend to your business, and don't

butt into other people's. To one degree or another we've all gone through this stage of yours. . . . So don't give us any more cause for complaint . . ."

After this speech, Don Juan went off to watch over the fortunes of his house of business, satisfied with his good sense. The son remained behind to mutter, "Some theories! What a pack of foolishness!" But very low, very low indeed, so as to avoid shaming him, a voice within said, "Come now! If he weren't that way, he probably would never have made the small fortune he's going to leave you when he's dead."

Gambelu amused himself with the revolutionary proclamations which Prim, Baldrich, and Topete issued beginning in the summer of 1867. Speaking of clerical despotism, the pronouncements promised the abolition of the tax on food and the military draft, the reduction of property taxes, the maintenance of rank, the promotion of field officers who supported the Cause, and demobilization of all soldiers following victory. They all concluded with a call to arms. Gambelu was particularly amused by the statements to the effect that there was nothing worse than mutiny and nothing more sacred than revolution; by Baldrich's motto, "Down with the existing order!"; and most especially by the claim that they had only one goal—the struggle itself.

"That's the way the Liberals are," Don Pascual would say, "destruction for its own sake."

"Look, Perico," Gambelu would say to Pedro Antonio, "this business of theirs about 'The mission of the armed revolution is to destroy amid the storm' is divine, especially the part about the storm. . . . Don José María says slyly that Prim doesn't understand how to destroy silently . . ."

Toward the end of 1867, there had been comment in the *tertulia* on the news of the proposed offer by the revolutionaries to give the crown of Spain to the young Carlos: he would be a constitutional king with revolutionary sanction, his legitimacy attested by universal suffrage. Among the members of the circle this report provoked bitter discussion, during which Pedro Antonio poked the fire with an air of apparent indifference toward that contentious and merely diverting theme. Gambelu was elated that the Progressives should call upon Cabrera. Even the priest did not look askance at this development, for he reserved his hatred for the Moderates. On some nights, Don José María would put in a brief appearance, arching his eyebrows and wagging his head until at length he would get up brusquely and exclaim, "Well, now, I've got things to do!" and go off to sleep.

"Godspeed!" Don Eustaquio would say to him, but when he was gone he would exclaim, "Idiot!"

The year 1868 found them all impatient, the priest in a state of irritation because the oft-trumpeted "fracas" was so long in coming. From time to time there was word of a raiding party putting in an appearance. With the restriction of the press, a clandestine press took the place of the legal one. Abominations and atrocities were told about the Queen and her court; these tales caused Don Eustaquio to exclaim "Poor woman!" He felt a protective pity for her, since he considered himself one of those to whom she owed her place on the throne. Don Braulio, proprietor of a small property in Castile, worried over the crop failure that year, when not a single grain of wheat was to be found; but the priest took pleasure in this scanty harvest, without really wanting to. They talked about the deficit and took the death of Narváez as a bad omen. When

Don José María announced to them a great Carlist meeting, scheduled to be held in London under the aegis of Don Carlos in honor of Cabrera (who was sick and unable to travel to the young Pretender's residence in Graz), a meeting which was to be a kind of Council of clergy, nobility, and the entire Spanish people, Pedro Antonio exclaimed, "Glory be to God! If only Don Tomás were alive . . ."

"We still have Cabrera," Gambelu answered.

Don José María added, "It's a question of saving the country from a Spanish '93!"

"What's that?" Gambelu answered.

And when they had explained it to him, he was left desirous of a " '93," for he wanted to see how things would change, things that were already very old and very familiar. He recalled the days in which he heard the cry "Death to the monks!" resounding in the streets, days full of vigor.

Don Pascual grew impatient to learn the results of the London gathering and to know more about the exile of the generals to the Canary Islands, and he would urgently tell Pedro Antonio that in Austria they were harassing religion, that the Pope was the victim of the revolutionary fury, and that Russia persecuted the Catholics. He privately diverted himself by sniffing the winds of stormy change, in a time of struggle and of sharp definition of contending sides.

At length it became known that the London meeting had taken place, that Cabrera had been unable to attend because his wounds from 1848 had opened up, and that Don Carlos had been received with the cry of "Long live the king." It was said that the old leader was going to put himself at the head of the party, and that the throne, the aristocracy, industry, and commerce were about to atone for their sins.

"All of them, every one, has contributed to the general disorder," the priest assured them.

"We'll go to the polls," Don José María added. "We'll get involved in parliamentary riots and seditions, and then . . ."

Ignacio had become uneasy, listening to the constant talk of the coming revolution. He imagined skirmishes in the streets, barricades, and raiding parties. Up until then, everything had been a matter of proclamations: one on the 17th of September signed by Topete, and one on the 18th signed by both Topete and Prim, who had joined forces to call the citizens to arms.

Gambelu fled the side of the old and identified himself with the young, moved by the announcements of the coming revolution, something he awaited along with the youngest. He told Ignacio, "That's my man, Prim. Once again he calls on us 'to get rid of obstacles amid the storm.' He's a man who likes a fight!"

The next day, the 19th, it was learned that the railroad line to Seville had been cut to prevent the arrival of the regiment from Balien. All the newspapers were wrought up. On the 20th, having joined the mutinous Serrano and other deportees of the Canary Islands, they issued a collective manifesto depicting official public immorality. The revolt of San Fernando was re-enacted, the cry of "Spain with Honor" reverberated, and the fight was said to be a matter of life or death.

"And a matter of the budget," added the priest, pleased.

"That poor lady, the Queen, in Lequeitio . . . !" exclaimed Don Eustaquio.

The rebellion offered freedom of the press, education, and religion; universal suffrage; and the abolition of the death penalty and the draft. The Navy rose in rebellion and was joined by the city government of Seville, followed by Córdoba, Granada, Málaga, and the entire province of Andalucía. When he learned of these events, Gambelu explained, "Hurrah for confusion and the salt of the earth in the land of the Most Blessed Virgin! Up with uproar!" Every day was filled with dramatic events. Like Gambelu and Ignacio, everyone else waited anxiously for night, for the hours of sleep which would bring the great news closer by cutting down the time spent waiting. The cities of Andalucía were shortly joined by El Ferrol, La Coruña, Santander, Alicante, and Alcoy.

"Everything's burning like a house afire, Don Pascual! The yoke of immorality, the dawn of triumph, the holy revolution, the fortress of tyranny, prostitution, and scandal. . . . There's a fine storm brewing!"

The poor queen, seeking refuge among those who had brought her to the throne by fighting against her, trembled before those who formerly courted her.

Word finally arrived of the battle of Alcolea, seven miles from Córdoba, on the banks of the Guadalquivir. Novaliches was vanquished by the insurrectionaries, and when Madrid heard the news, that city also rebelled. The government resigned, to be succeeded by a revolutionary Junta. To the cry of "Down with the Bourbons!" the coats of arms of that dynasty were destroyed, the Ministry of the Interior was assaulted, and, "amid the storm," the "existing order" remained.

When Pedro Antonio learned on the 29th that the Queen had fled to France from San Sebastián, he recalled the bloody Seven Years, when Doña Isabel was an adored child and, exclaiming "Poor lady!", he felt that the Pact of Vergara had been broken.

Ignacio went into the streets to see what was happening.

A lieutenant of the border guards and a couple of soldiers in the second row of seats at El Arenal were yelling "Long live liberty!" and "Down with the Bourbons!" People were coming and going at the Café Suizo and groups formed to discuss the news at length. Ignacio felt someone giving him a quick hug and heard Juanito happily exclaiming "Now we can breathe!" The air was exactly the same as always.

The band was ordered out, and it marched through the streets of the city playing the Riego Hymn, with a swarm of children leading the way. The music recalled a whole world to some of the older people, and it made the children gambol.

When the band went down the street in which Pedro Antonio lived, the sound of the Riego Hymn brought tears to the eyes of Doña Micaela, Arana's wife.

"What's the matter, Mama?" Rafaela asked, her own heart enlivened by the music.

"That music can only bring trouble. . . . Getting rid of the Queen means war. You don't know what war is like . . . ," her mother replied. The memory of her childhood anguish oppressed her, and the notes of the march drilled into her, giving her a headache.

Pedro Antonio and Gambelu stood in the doorway of the shop, as the band broke into the Espartero Hymn.

"This must be the 'storm' that Prim was talking about," said Gambelu. "It gladdens my soul, you know."

A mere slip of a boy went by singing—

> He died with a sword in his hand
> Defending the Constitution!

"Does your father teach you such nonsense, boy? So, Riego died with a sword in his hand, did he? It was on the scaffold he died, and in tears. He had to be dragged there in a basket . . ."

"Listen, in a basket . . . says he!" the boy exclaimed, and after taking a few steps he turned around and yelled at them, "Carlists!" Then he broke into a run. A bit further along he turned around again to yell, "Carlists! Worse than Carlists!" Then he disappeared, following the music of the band.

"It's begun!" murmured Pedro Antonio as he entered his shop.

And Gambelu hummed—

> Constitution or death
> Will be our cry.
> If any traitor does defy
> Death will be his due.

In the Basque country there was widespread satisfaction that the revolution brought back what Espartero had taken away: the *fueros*, the special legal rights and statutes of the region, were restored, and the last legal possessors of the pike were to hand it over to those elected by the people. It was recalled that the vanquished Queen had never sworn to uphold the Basque laws, though she had three times visited the *Señorío*. The priest, nevertheless, predicted evil results from the fall of the *corregidor*, the *alcalde de fuero*, and the *ordinarios de hermandad*, and he filled the air with invective against the Pact of Vergara whenever Don Eustaquio was present, forcing this worthy to exclaim, "Well, now the priests can lead us into a new war, so we can lose the little that's left to us."

All of them, though, and especially Ignacio, Gambelu, and the priest, were exasperated with the promoters of the revolutionary movement, who had betrayed their expectations of something more profound and more tragic. They made mock of the Glorious Revolution, for it had all added up to no more than a lot of noise, the burning of Bourbon coats of arms and portraits of the Queen, the issuing of endless proclamations, the parading of banners, the firing of rounds of ammunition into the air, and nothing more serious than the one episode at Santander. "That was a real storm," Gambelu reiterated, "a genuine storm, and no make-believe. . . . Long live liberty! Long live the Queen! And straight shooting from the cannon's mouth. That's it, and not that horseplay about the pretty general's entry into Madrid, so he could step out on a balcony to talk, and everybody hugging each other in public. Shameless goings-on! And then that Italian comedian that was said to have spoken from a carriage about the fraternity between Spain and Italy. . . . The expulsion of the Jesuits, the suppression of the monasteries, all those things they announce are no more than reflexes, hoaxes. . . . They don't dare. I'll bet they don't dare. Ah, Perico, we'll never see those days again, when we heard the cry of 'Death to the monks' resounding in the streets. The present generation doesn't amount to anything." And, saying this, Gambelu turned toward Ignacio, who was present.

For the priest, the matter of supreme interest was the reorganization of the Carlist party, an endeavor to which Don José María devoted himself with zeal. He appeared at the *tertulia* one day like a child with a new pair of shoes to announce the abdication of the Pretender Don Juan in favor of his son Carlos, and to read the note from Don Carlos addressed to the sovereigns of Europe, wherein he declared that he foresaw the need to reconcile the loyal and useful institutions of our epoch with the indispensable institutions of the past, leaving it to the Parliament, freely elected, to write a definitive Constitution for Spain. After reading the note, Don José María looked over his audience with the air of a man waiting for a response which never came.

In one manifesto the revolutionaries proclaimed a family monarchy, born out of popular rights and consecrated by universal suffrage, a popular monarchy abolishing the so-called divine right of kings. Other elements, meanwhile, demanded a republic. To all of this, toward the end of '68, the Carlists prepared themselves for the elections to the Constitutent Assembly, in an attempt to triumph by means of "ratiocinative reason."

Ignacio was deeply disquieted. A throne had been riotously brought down, but now he feared Don Carlos would be silently elected, with no opposition and without paying the price for triumph—in short, inauthentically. And that would mean no chance for another Glorious Seven Years.

As direct consequence of the revolution, he became totally absorbed in the life of the Carlist club. He passed all his free time there, in company with Juan José, his other outing-comrades forgotten.

At the beginning of 1869, Ignacio, commissioned to distribute ballots, was beside himself as he watched the villagers come down to vote in platoons led by priests. He was delighted: they seemed to him like victors. When the voting closed down for the night, he went to the club, from whose suffocating atmosphere he emerged half-intoxicated. There was much crying out on all sides, and revolutionary excesses were narrated in detail. A child had been baptized in the name of Satan; novenas, rosaries, religious offerings, all were of no use; it was necessary to do what had been done in Burgos, where the Governor had been dragged at the end of a rope after he had tried to take away the sacred vessels.

"The revolution will devour itself. We must leave it to its fate," said one.

"And then it will devour us all. . . . A stick is what's needed, a big stick."

The two tendencies dividing the Carlist party were clearly visible in the club: one advocating force, and one living on hopes. The first cited the apocalyptic phrases of Aparisi; the second sighed for the return of Cabrera. In that bubbling caldron Ignacio felt like a fish boiling in water. All the instincts of his blood, the impulses which had led him into sin, gained in vigor and found immediate release in the form of a longing for war. Hopes and expectations? Let mere circumstances put Don Carlos and his ideals on the throne? A peaceful triumph? That would be a lie, a usurpation, a larceny! Without resistance and war, his triumph was irrational.

At the club he met, among others, a certain Celestino, a young Carlist lawyer recently taken out of the university oven and certified as "done," who burned with the oratorical fever with which the revolution had infected Spain. He was one of those men whom the newspapers call "our contributor, the illustrious young man," a machine for producing phrases and quotations, a man who saw in every matter a thesis complete with objections and rebuttals, a man who pigeonholed everyone, and stored away every opinion properly ticketed. His narrow-minded education had confirmed the congenitally one-sided and pedestrian tendency of his spirit. Kant or Krause was always on his lips, and he was capable of arguing with himself.

He went strolling with Ignacio, whom he sought out in the club, for he needed an "O thou beloved

Theotimos" relationship in order to launch into his monologues and display the full measure of his knowledge.

His talk was a devilish hodgepodge about divine right and national sovereignty, filled with dizzying quotations from Balmes, Donoso, Aparisi, De Maistre, St. Thomas, Rousseau, and the Encyclopedists. He knew his quota of Latin sentences and, in discoursing grandly on the Salic Law and the dynastic question, would add "Eris sub potestate viri": he expatiated on the failure of the fusion between the two royal branches, on centralization and the law of Basque rights, on Carlos III—putrified by Liberals and opponents of the Vatican's power to make ecclesiastical appointments— and on the grand days of the great Fernando and the great Felipe. He prophesized the collapse of Spanish society unless it were saved by the man of Providence, and he pondered the virtues of old-fashioned and true Spanish democracy and of liberty prudently understood. He despised the epoch in which he lived since it did not yield to his thesis and its corollaries and since he could not label it according to the formulas of his imagination, as he did the past patched together from bone-dry books. The flesh of facts, warm and living, was something alien to him, as alien as their skeleton was tractable. The past was submissive to syllogisms. The past belonged to his much-admired compilers of printed intelligence. And so, though he disdained pure philosophy, albeit with reservations and qualifications, he exalted history, the teacher of life. "These are facts" he would exclaim as he cited reports of events, printed words, bare narratives of mere occurrences. Considering himself capable of constructing, out of his own imagination, historically and in typeface letters, a political machine in the antique Spanish style, he deprecated those who built a Constitution philosophically according to the modern French style, and branded them Jacobins. All his historical discourses revolved around Lepanto, Oran, Otumba, Bailén, Columbus, the Cross and the Throne. He was a Castilian, a Castilian to the marrow of his bones, he said, and knew only Castilian. He spoke "in Christian," calling bread *bread*, and wine *wine*.

He called the Liberals perverse idiots who didn't know the Mass halfway through, nor have a crumb of serious history, fake savants and faddish philosophers, philosophasters, charlatan Encyclopedists, inventors of conflicts between religion and science, people who called priests ignorant—*priests*, who had saved the world from barbarism! He knew all about the Liberals' flashy sophistries, none of which had moved him. Vain Knowledge, which swells the head and gives no comfort at all!

Ignacio, overcome with stupor, like a boy drowsy from an hour of reading, would say to himself, "What a lot he's read!" And he came to develop toward his mentor the loyalty of a dog for his master. And the little lawyer loved him in the way a haughty man loves the good fellow who admires him, with a spark of protective compassion. "What a noble chap! He's all right!" he said to himself. "Such men are needed if great things are to be done. They are the lever of Archimedes." And in a lower tone, almost inaudibly, a voice whispered to him from beneath the bookish debris accumulated in his soul, "And you, you yourself are the fulcrum."

Ignacio came to depend on Celestino to put his feelings into shape for meditation. Out of the great mass of garble which spouted from that living phonograph, Ignacio absorbed the bulk and quintessence: the Liberalesque world is abominable, while that other world, that world of dreams and truth, is paradise. He admired Celestino's virtue and knowledge: not one vice, not a single one! Always at his books, at his books alone!

The strong but blurred pictures in Ignacio's imagination were enlarged, and the lively figures of the heroes of the Seven Years were joined by vague, grave heroes of Old Spain. Cabrera re-emerged larger than ever.

All that intellectual travail, all that world of ideas, reflected in his mind, formed a compact mass above which floated like a pennant the words "God, Fatherland, King," a phrase full of potent mystery. Reducing the motto to the bare formula G.F.K. Ignacio engraved it upon a thousand objects. It was a formula—the vortex of a pyramid of the throbbings of the flesh and the longings of the blood—that leads nations toward heroism and men toward death, like the S.P.Q.R. of the Romans or the modern "Liberté, Égalité, Fraternité" of the French. God, Fatherland, King! In Ignacio's imagination, God was an immensity of power infusing everything, the Fatherland a blazing field ringing with the noises of wars, and the King the arm of God and the stave of the Fatherland. The King! For some time now the young Carlos had been called the hope of the Fatherland, and Ignacio frequently saw his photograph. There was one, circulating from hand to hand, which pictured him with his family, seated, with one of his children on his knee, an open book in his hand—a feature which charmed Celestino—but a book at which he is not looking; his wife stood beside him, the smallest child in her arms; another child stood farther off, and his brother, Alfonso, dressed as a Pontifical Zouave, leaned against the French mantel. It was altogether a family scene, in a modest room. Looking at it, Ignacio involuntarily thought of Rafaela, of the loose woman in his life, and of his father's Seven Years.

Don José María furnished them with a thousand intimate details of the Pretender's life, to which Don Eustaquio added, "Let's see what Carlos the Terse has to offer!"

Absorbed in the life of the club at this time, Ignacio scarcely ever saw his old comrades. He divided his free time between Celestino and Juan José, and the growing political agitation stirred his spirit more and more. He could see that things were going from bad to worse, that there were growing hunger, rascality, suffering, and crime. Why? Because of the cowardice of the Catholics, who let a handful of rascals without religion lord it over the land. "It's pretty thick," said Celestino, "when an entire nation of Catholics is in thrall to the sons of the Frenchified, to Liberals baptized by Napoleon with the blood of the people and confirmed by Mendizábal with the gold of the monks. Is this the nation of the Second of May?"

On Sundays they would leave the club in bands and head for the country dances or the *romerías*, the pilgrimages to local shrines. In the Plaza de Albia, any time after the call to prayer, one thing could be counted on: a brawl! The musicians, wearing white berets, were all Carlists. Provocation came from one side or the other, but it always came.

Ignacio, Juan José, and some others wearing the white beret would meet, armed with truncheons, ready for the fray, and prepared for a Christ-the-King row. They usually returned in great good spirits, covered with sweat, yelling with joy and singing "*Ay, ay, mu-tillac!*"

At an excursion on one of those afternoons, Ignacio met up with Juanito, Rafael, and a certain Pachico Zabalbide, whom he knew very indirectly, though they had gone to school together for a time, and who fascinated him because of his fame as a rare bird. Ignacio stayed to chat with Juanito. The look that Pachico gave him then, as he gazed at Ignacio's truncheon and beret, penetrated to the marrow of his bones, shaming and unnerving him. Suddenly there was the sound of yelling, the cursing of men and the shrieking of women, numbers of whom began to run as the crowd eddied about. They edged closer to see what was happening—except for Pachico, who remained seated while the lances of the authorities separated the combatants.

That night, Ignacio could not forget that mocking, deadly look. The recollection of Pachico calmly seated in the middle of the turmoil caused him great disquiet.

Francisco (Pachico) Zabalbide scarcely retained more than a shadowy memory of his parents. Both were dead by the time he was seven, and the orphan boy was adopted by a maternal uncle, Don Joaquín, a rich bachelor, who, taken up with his devotions and business affairs, barely paid any attention to his nephew, unless it was to address him a kindly sermon or have his company at Rosary.

Pachicho grew up a delicate boy. At school he was noted for his timidity and his keenness, and also because he was one of those who was first to get tears in his eyes when moving passages were read aloud. He took delight in singing plaintive songs, like the one about the martyrdom of Saint Catherine on "a wheel of knives and razors, Ah! yes! on a wheel of knives and razors."

To his fearful spirit, influenced by these stories and legends, the dark was frightening, and he fled past dark places in trembling haste.

At night his uncle made him say the rosary, along with the maid, and often had him read aloud from *The Lives of the Saints*, after which Don Joaquín would always add some word of comment. His uncle affected a sober faith, free of witchery and superstition. He believed only in those miracles the Church had certified as true and commanded him to believe. He disdained "those people," as he called those who had not been instructed in doctrine and who did not know what the official faith included and what it did not.

Pachico, at puberty, was weak and sickly, prey to a consuming inner turmoil and to a certain timidity which turned him in on himself and gave him the burning desire to know everthing. He listened to his uncle intently and learned also to disdain "those people," soaking himself in the high purpose of the official faith. He came to manhood after passing through a youthful stage of mysticism and intellectual voracity. He wanted badly to be a saint, mortified his flesh by staying on his knees when they most pained him, and lost himself in vague dreams in the darkness of a church filled with organ music.

He enjoyed most the days of Holy Week, when he followed the liturgy in his prayer book in Latin and Castilian, saying solemly the same prayers the priest said, and not the prayers made up for "those people." The black altar cloths, the statues of Christ wrapped in purple percale, the wooden clappers on the bells, all the liturgical changes of the season captured his interest.

Sometimes, without knowing why, he trembled like a leaf. He would never be able to forget the deep impression church retreats left on him, especially when the voice of the Jesuit, occasionally interrupted by dry, isolated coughs from the congregation in a candlelit church so dark they could hardly see one another, told how the devil hand once appeared before a sinner, the devil with his goat's hooves going *click*, *clack*. Pachico grew frightened and afraid to look behind him. Sometimes, when he was alone in his room, he felt as if some invisible being was silently approaching from behind. The night he heard about the devil's footsteps was a bad night for him. He had nightmares and cried out in his sleep. The next morning his uncle said dryly, "Don't go back to the retreat. It's not good for you."

He gave himself up to fervid reading, devouring the few books in his uncle's library. Many nights, with an open book before him, he would end by contemplating the soft light of the candle. Its flame seemed like a living being, a timid creature which contracted and expanded unceasingly, drawing back at the slightest movement or breath of air. Although often prey to sudden convulsions, it gave a calm and tranquil light. When he went to bed and snuffed it out, he could still see its wick glowing like a many-colored jewel. Poor soft timid light!

He dreamed about the books in that meager library, dreamed a thousand vagaries. He was carried away and exalted in imagination when he read Chateaubriand and other purveyors of Romantic Catholicism. He tried to make his faith rational. He listened to sermons. He became an apologist for dogma and, like his uncle, a disdainer of "those people," those who repeat, "I believe what the Holy Mother Church be-

lieves and teaches," all the while remaining ignorant
of what the Church teaches and believes.

His years of preparatory school had filled his mind
with dead formulas, beneath which he half-glimpsed
another world, a world that gave him a thirst for
knowledge, but he was also filled with the dry luke-
warmness of his uncle's house. When he was eighteen
years of age, in 1866, his uncle sent him to study in
Madrid. It was a time in which the winds of rationalism
and of Krausism were blowing. Pachico almost cried
as he hummed Iparraguirre's "Adiyo," leaving the peak
of Orduña behind him, leaving his Basque countryside
for the tumult of new ideas in the capital city.

During the first year of school he went to Mass every
day and to Communion once a month. His Basque
land was much in his thoughts—not the one that belonged to reality but the fancied one he had gleaned
from his reading, one full of dreamy melancholy.

He continued at the same time working on his faith,
bothered more than anything else by the dogma of
hell, the dogma that finite beings should suffer infinite
punishment. The labor of rationalizing his faith gnawed
away at it, despoiling it of its form and reducing it to
a shapeless pulp. Thus it is that leaving Mass one
Sunday morning—for a long time he had gone only
on feast days—he asked himself what such a ritual
could mean for him, and he stopped going from that
day on. He suffered no soul-wrenchings for the moment, for it seemed the most natural thing in the world.

Concurrent with this act in which his faith was
stripped from his mind, a sudden flood of numberless
vague but resounding ideas filled his head: fragments
of Hegel and of positivism, recently arrived in Madrid,
which proved most meaningful for him. And like a
child with a new toy, he gave himself up to playing

with his reason, inventing new philosophical theories, childish and symmetrical arrangements of concepts, like solutions to chess problems.

At the same time, he explored the world of fantasy and read the great poets whose fame drew him to them. The titanic world of Shakespeare, a world of gigantic passions embodied in suffering mortal bodies, filled his dreams and peopled his mind with the ghosts of Hamlet, Macbeth, King Lear. . . . The heroes of Ossian, wrapped in crepuscular clouds, also wandered through the scene, joining their voices to those of the torrents cascading from the mountains. When he grew tired of reading or studying, he worked on a monotonous psalmody, weaving segments of musical reminiscence in a kind of langorous humming, as continuous as an endless chain, by means of which he projected out of himself the ever-shifting longing of his soul.

When his uncle learned of the change that had taken place in Pachico's mind, he took him aside and spoke to him of his poor mother in such a way that he left the boy deeply moved and in tears. The old faith struggled to be reborn, so that Pachico went through a crisis of retrogression. Don Joaquín returned to the charge, urging him to confess and to consult with the local priest about his doubts, to which the boy said, "But they aren't *doubts* . . . !" His uncle, with tears in his eyes, begged him then to do as he asked, and left him alone in the little room where he had so often pored over the pages of the Church apologists.

After a night of insomnia and mental torment, he went, half-dazed, with his uncle on the following morning, the anniversary of his mother's death, to make his confession. Without going into detail, he limited himself to telling his confessor that he harbored certain doubts, and did not mention what they were. The priest gave him advice regarding human prudence and spoke against reading in general, recommending diversion and outdoor life, as well as the *Confessions* of St. Augustine, adding, "Not the *Soliloquies*! Those are too strong yet."

When Pachico left the confessor, in disillusion with the effort he had made, he said himself, "The poor man probably thinks I haven't read the *Soliloquies*, or that I'm still suckling at the breast . . ."

Pachico, once the crisis passed, returned to pursue the course of his own ideas, avoiding all conversation with his uncle.

He lived an inner life, huddled up in his spirit, hatching his dreams. His spiritual state was that of those who, on the basis of their former faith—sound asleep but not dead—have received another, and who long for an unconscious faith that would be a synthesis of the two. He grew impatient with himself because sometimes his ideas flowed too fast while at other times they came so slowly they seemed static; because he had days of intellectual drought, days without a single idea to be seized from out of the tumult of his agitated spirit; and because he could not retain everything he had learned. He was prey to depression. "Why study? Better to live the fleeting moment! Since knowledge is as nothing alongside the immense sea of ignorance, what good is it to study? What good is a sip from the inexhaustible sea, which leaves behind only greater thirst? Better to contemplate from afar."

He would take several books to bed with him, and then go from one to the other, reading none of them. Should he read the work of the genius consecrated by previous generations or the latest product of scientific experiment? Disenchanted with the latest novelty, bored with the similarity of one novelty to another, he went

back to the ancient and eternal. He would put the light
out to give himself over to meditation, and, if he was
not overcome at once by sleep, he was tormented by
the terrible mystery of time. Once something was learned
or done, what was left of it? Was he any greater than
the day before? To have to pass from yesterday to
tomorrow without being able to live the entire series
of time simultaneously! Such reflection led him, in the
solitary darkness of the night, to a sense of death, a
vivid emotion which made him tremble at the idea of
the moment when sleep would bear him away, terrified
at the thought that one day he would sleep never to
wake again. It was a wild terror of nothingness, of
finding himself alone in empty time, a mad terror that,
deprived of breath, smothering, he was falling forever
through eternal emptiness in a terrible fall. Hell itself
terrified him less than nothingness, for hell was for
him a cold and dead image, but an image of life, after
all.

He was easy enough in his dealings with other people, though he had the reputation for being a serious
eccentric. He talked a great deal, and his conversation
annoyed many people; it was pedantic and tiresome.
He always tried to dominate discussions, and if he were
cut off he would stubbornly return to his point. People
also felt that he converted his audience into an abstrac-
tion, and that, since he himself was wrapped up in his
own opinion, any conversation was a pretext for a monologue, while the other participants were reduced to
geometrical figures, examples of humanity whom he
dealt with *sub specie aeternitatis*. For his part, he was
much concerned with what other people thought of
him, felt wounded when he was judged harshly, and
strove to be liked and understood by everyone.

Such was the person who at this time went about in the company of Ignacio.

The first time in many years—since childhood—that Pachico and Ignacio spoke to each other was in Juanito's company, and Pachico took delight in making himself out as odd for the benefit of the confectioner's son, in confusing him and upsetting him by uttering the greatest paradoxes and the most sweeping exaggerations.

They walked out into the country. Pachico grew tired climbing the slopes and forced the party to stop from time to time so he might catch his breath. He breathed heavily during these halts, straining his lungs and full of apprehension. Ignacio, watching him, told himself, "Poor chap! He won't live long! He's tubercular!" On the summit they lay down for a good while, almost without speaking, while Pachico reveled in the joyful sight of the trees, the clouds, the whole countryside bathed in light, a sight so different from the sad one of domestic objects, the creation and slaves of men. The panorama was like a mosaic, made up of fragments of fields and farms running the gamut of greens, from the faded yellowish color of harvested wheat to the soiled blackish hue of a copse, altogether a grand vista. The marks of human labor scaled the slopes, reaching nearly to the heights. Patches of moving shadow, of cloud-shadow, ran along the fields, and high above, with its wide wings spread and seemingly immobile, floated a hawk, the symbol of power. A serene calm flowed from everything, and the silence made them all silent.

When they descended, they repaired to a *chacolí* where, after he had something to eat and drink, Pachico's tongue was loosened. He spoke in half-meanings, explaining himself obscurely and by insinuation, leaping from one point to another, apparently without caring whether or not he was understood. He said that everyone was right and that no one was right. As far as he was concerned, Carlists and their opponents were all the same, all of them moving in their designated spaces like chess pieces moved by invisible players on a board. He said that he was not a Carlist nor a Liberal nor a Monarchist nor a Republican—and that he was all of them at once. "Me? Wear a label, like some dried-up, hollow insect pinned down in a specimen case, ticketed as belonging to *this* genus, *that* species? A political party is nonsense!"

"But our party is a communion!" exclaimed Ignacio, recalling one of Celestino's phrases. But he felt a flush of shame as he uttered the words and wished he could have taken them back.

"It's all the same. A 'communion' is nonsense, too!"

"What are you, then?"

"Me? I'm Francisco Zabalbide. Don't get offended, but only idiots can think alike and subscribe to the same program . . ."

Ignacio was wounded to the quick by Zabalbide's insolence in calling people idiots and seeing them as imbeciles, rather than as rogues. He much preferred Juanito, who considered him an obscurantist, an ultramontanist, a factious fanatic, but at least not an imbecile. Zabalbide was too elastic: he denied nothing, he seemed to concede everything, but it was all only a way of coming back to his original thesis bit by bit, of turning everything he had seemed to accept into its opposite. He said very seriously that the Carlist party might or might not make Spain happy, but that it made no sense as long as it didn't have power, and then he concluded, "Things are as they are, they can't be any other way, and there's only one way of getting what you want, and that's to want everything that happens. What's left over is the right to stamp your feet in protest." Ignacio didn't know whether to feel sorry for someone who said such things or to get mad at him, so he just exclaimed, "What an outrageous thing to say!"

The next day, also a holiday, they met again, knowing that the same questions would come up once again. Juanito, as a result of some remarks he had heard his mother and his sister make after they heard a sermon, launched into an attack against priests, monks, and nuns, calling them all lazy loafers and adding that it was necessary to take Purgatory away from them.

"Take Faith away from man, and he'll live like a pig!" exclaimed Ignacio.

"And besides," said Juanito, looking at Pachico, "even if I wanted to believe, I couldn't. What I can't comprehend I simply can't comprehend."

"Come on now, you really do believe, of course you believe! You're just playing a role, trying to make yourself seem more interesting. You only say these things because of Zabalbide here," Ignacio said.

Then Juanito brought up Ignacio's affair with the loose woman. Ignacio flew into a rage, and some bitter words were exchanged, while Zabalbide smiled and kept quiet. After the argument died down, he began to speak calmly but forcefully, saying that religious dogmas had once been true, true in the sense that men had produced them, but that today they were no longer either true or false, having lost all sense and substance. He spoke at length, in an unceasing monologue, until his two listeners went off with their heads hot and their feet chilled, a tumult of obscure ideas running through their minds from their collision with thought so strange to them.

One afternoon in April, Don José María went to Pedro Antonio's shop, and the two friends talked of the Constituent Assembly, which had been convened on the 11th of February, and of the feats of the Carlist minority as concerned the religious question, which was the main bone of contention.

"We must talk in private," said Don José María, with a mysterious air.

Pedro Antonio led him to the workshop, and his guest continued, "As you know already, the triumph of our cause is near at hand. We've won the Army over, and the country is alarmed by the blasphemies and atrocities heard in Assembly . . ."

"What's he driving at?" Pedro Antonio wondered to himself, since he wasn't at all alarmed by such blasphemies.

"But for all this, money is needed. Yes, money is needed. You're a good man, and besides, I'm not talking about a charitable donation. No, it's a matter of your assuming some of the obligation . . ."

"What obligation?" asked Pedro Antonio mechanically, suddenly alarmed as he recollected the bankruptcy which overtook the Tudela railroad line.

"An obligation of two hundred francs . . ."

The word "francs" astonished Pedro Antonio, who was used to counting in reales, ducados, or duros.

"An obligation of two hundred francs," repeated Don José María, "to be credited to His Catholic Majesty the King, Don Carlos VII, as authorized by him. The money will be exchanged for a regular government bond, at three percent interest, to be paid starting the moment the King ascends the throne. Between

now and that time, the interest will be five percent.
The bonds are being issued through Amsterdam . . ."

"I'll see about it," said Pedro Antonio, interrupting
his visitor to avoid further bother, and also because he
heard Uncle Pascual calling him.

"Talk it over with Father Pascual and then decide,"
said the conspirator as he left.

A few days later Pedro Antonio handed over part
of his savings, which he had to withdraw from the
bank. From that moment on, he began to take an
interest in the political developments in the nation and
in the moves made by young Don Carlos.

The Constituent Assembly furnished the *tertulia* with
much to talk about. They discussed the chatterings of
those parrots in Madrid who were such experts at
wasting time, and they celebrated the trouncing Manterola was said to have given a golden-tongued politician whom Uncle Pascual made fun of. But the priest's
soul went out to Suñer, who had declared war on God
and tuberculosis. For him he felt a secret affection
because he thought that at heart he really was a believer.

Gambelu held that it was necessary to gag the or-
ators, for argument was a waste of time. Everyone
ought to know what he must believe, what he must
seek, what he must do, and what he must hope. Neither rhetoric nor philosophy is of any use, if contrary
to the people's will. Every person knows what's good
for him, and only God knows what's good for everyone. "In this country," he exclaimed, "the one who
knows the most exploits the one who knows the least.
The city exploits the country, and the rich exploit the
poor. We give careful study to the best ways of ruining

our neighbor. Lawyers make lawsuits, and doctors make sick people . . ."

"Don't talk such nonsense," the priest interrupted.

"And the priests are the ones who make the sins," Gambelu added jokingly. "In this country of ours, a handful of former rich men will be sticking it into the poor people tomorrow, turning everything upside down and deceiving the people. If Don Carlos were to summon me . . ."

"Now it's come out!" Don Eustaquio exclaimed.

"Glory be to God!" Pedro Antonio added.

". . . If Don Carlos were to summon me, I would advise him to take all the offices and public buildings out of the city and scatter them around the country. I'd suggest that he force the rich to support the poor and to educate all the orphans. And he should double the taxes of the rich, so that the more they have the more they would have to pay . . ."

"We know all that already!"

"As I was saying, what good is it to argue with the godless? Either believe or don't believe. And as far as believing is concerned, it's all a matter of wanting to believe, of humbling yourself. Then faith is granted as a kind of prize . . ."

Then the priest spoke up. "Thank God you've managed to say something worth saying."

"Anyone who accepts our principles is a Carlist, and there's nothing more to discuss."

"The Liberals devour each other," added the priest. "They're like the Protestants, whose freedom of conscience in religious matters turns everything to dust. Discussion divides people, but faith unites them . . ."
He took a pinch of snuff as he watched the effect of his words.

"Things are going badly," Don Braulio ventured to suggest. "Everything costs more."

"I know the solution!" Gambelu answered.

"You may know the solution," Don Braulio said, "but things are going badly. Village girls are wearing low shoes and linen blouses. . . . These railroads and these damnable factories!"

He fell silent. For a moment they all thought back to the good old days when their blood was still hot, and then farther back still to the times of which the history books spoke. They had known only adults and old people in the generation before their own, and in the generation that followed theirs they knew only young people. Thus they saw antiquity in the past, in the time of their childhood. The oldest among them had lived only two-thirds of a century, and what was that compared with the men of a century ago, of three centuries ago, of a thousand years ago? A thousand years! In comparison to a thousand years, their own age amounted to nothing at all.

"I've lost count of the Constitutions I've known," Don Eustachio said.

"They're imported from France," the priest observed. "*Liberalism* is foreign and revolutionary, but *Liberty* is Catholic and Spanish . . ."

"The best thing is to resign ourselves," suggested Don Braulio.

"What a world it would be if we all did that," Gambelu put in, "if good people gave in to the bad. God helps those who help themselves. Look here, Don Braulio, we're like the dog, and God's like the master . . ."

The priest smiled. Pedro Antonio wondered, "Where did he read *that*?"

They both looked at Gambelu as he continued, "The

dog licks the hand of the master who punishes it, but it doesn't lick the whip. We must break the whip and yet lick the hand of God . . ."

"We must fight for God's justice to placate his wrath," added the priest, who had at last found his phrase.

"It wouldn't be right for us all to be saints," Gambelu insisted.

"Don't say crazy things," the priest interrupted.

"We don't need saints. What we need are absolutists—yes, absolutists, intransigent men. Those of us who, thanks to God, know the truth shouldn't compromise with lies. Just as I said before, nowadays the government is run for the rich at the expense of the poor, when it should be run for the poor at the expense of the rich . . ."

When it grew late and eveyone was tired of Gambelu's incoherent talk, heard so may times before, the *tertulia* broke up.

Celestino, the Carlist lawyer, was in despair.

Ever since July, when the letter had appeared from young Don Carlos to his brother Alfonso, and through him to all Spaniards, he had spent all his time talking about it in the club to a group which had received the letter coolly. A thousand and one times he pointed out the new and larger vision on the part of a claimant to the throne who, wanting to be the king of all Spaniards and not just of a single party, respected the agreements which sanctioned established practices, strove to make all the provinces of Spain equal to the Basque provinces, and would grant the country liberty—*liberty*, the daughter of the Gospel, not *Liberalism*, which is the son of Protest. Don Carlos understood that the King belongs to the people and should be the most honorable of all men, the father of the poor and the

guardian of the weak. Above all, he would save the
treasury by living like Henry the Sufferer and dressing,
as a good Protectionist should, in the cloth of his country. All of this was received in the club as in a void,
and the idea of exporting the regime prevailing in the
Basque provinces to the rest of Spain was met with
suspicion and admonitions. Special statutes for everyone is the same as special statutes for no one: that was
the hidden thought. To make a privilege universal is
to destroy it. The talk at the club was all about Basque
rights and religion, not about restoration of the monarchy. Let Don Carlos swear to uphold the Basque
privileges, leave them in peace—and the Castilians could
go hang.

Celestino suffered. He suffered from the murmur of
conversation in Basque, which was unintelligible to
him. He suffered because of the general hostility which
pervaded the atmosphere. He realized that as soon as
his back was turned he was treated as a hick, a book-
worm, and a pedant, and he feared the moment when
those who still respected him would turn upon him
too. And sure enough he was accused, in various cliques,
of meddling and practicing the eloquence which he
hoped might one day win him a rich wife.

Sometimes, irritated by the tone taken in certain
discussions, he would get up and leave, hoping that
Ignacio would follow him. And then, finding himself
alone, without his "lever of Archimedes," he would
mutter to himself, "Idiots! Fools! Dolts!"

Ignacio meanwhile kept quiet as his idol was slowly
torn from him. He felt as if a weight were being lifted
from his soul, that he was being freed from a tyrannical
relationship. How could he have been so blind? Remembering Pachico, he said to himself, "A great pair!
How would they be able to understand each other?"

Still, even as he freed himself from Celestino's influence, his former affection, never extinct, exerted an intermittent influence. The Carlist lawyer scarcely appeared any more around the club, and Ignacio had to think up some excuse for visiting him. He finally recalled having lent him a copy of *The Life of Cabrera.*

He arrived at Celestino's house in some confusion, like a man doing something wrong. The Carlist lawyer, who was reading, stood up and greeted him with the casual gesture of a man waiting for someone else. His look seemed to ask: What are you after? What right have you got to come here? Why don't you go see your own people?

Celestino began to talk about the club, examining the motives of his detractors, calling them "fanatics," and assigning himself the role of victim. "You'll see whether or not these people can bring back Don Carlos if we Castilians don't put ourselves to it." And without any transition he added, "I was just reading one of Aparisi's pamphlets. Here it is . . ."

"Do you have many of his works?"

"Almost everything that's published."

"Would you like to lend me some?" Ignacio breathed easier, feeling he finally had a reason for his visit.

After a while, the lawyer said, "Very well." He seemed to entertain the unspoken question: What do you want them for? What will you get out of them?

Lending books always pained him, making him feel that he was being robbed of his wisdom. It especially pained him that other people would find in them the phrases which he repeated so much.

Ignacio left with a number of pamphlets. At night he read them in bed until the candle was used up and sleep overtook him.

How lovely everything would be when Don Carlos

would triumph! And there was no other salvation now: it was either Don Carlos or the incendiaries, tradition or anarchy. And that prince was no inconsequential figure: educated in adversity, descendant of a hundred kings, related to the most important rulers of Europe, maintaining social relations with the Napoleons. . . . It was necessary to resist the barbarian invasion, for the hour of expiation was approaching for industry, for business, for all those who had helped undermine the fatherland. The people, virtuous and well-off, would prosper and be happy under the traditionalist monarchy.

Ignacio fell asleep to dream of Pelayo and his cross on the heights of Idubeda, of the Cid, of Ferdinand the Saint, of Alfonso of the Navas, and all of them soon became confused with Roland, Valdovinas, Ogier, and others of that stamp. At the magical cry of "God and Country!" the King would bring new birth to Spain. Hospitals would appear, as would asylums and monasteries, and writers and artists would spring up.

Some of the current pamphleteers wished to go back to a time before Philip II, nullifier of the rights of Aragon, even further back than Charles I, hangman of the Castilian *Comuneros* uprisings. They argued that after the September Revolution of 1868 in Spain only one throne and one people were left, and that the people would place Don Carlos on the throne. Municipal excise duties would disappear. The public payroll would be reduced to one-third its present level. There would be political rights, but not military drafts. Finally, Don Carlos would do away with the death penalty—by eliminating crime. By 1880, Madrid would be something to see, filled with the palaces of princes. The Manzanares River would no longer be a dirty, ridiculous little stream as in former times. The people

would be madly happy at seeing every man given justice, the King summoning the poor to his table, handing out prizes to the Institute children, and presiding
at the dedication of artesian wells. In short, they would
adore him, seeing in him a king who was brother to
his subjects.

This was the Utopia pictured by the pamphlets.
Besides the latter, there were a number of humorous
Carlist newspapers: *El Papelito*, *Rigoleto*, *Las Llagas*,
El Fraile, *La Boina Blanca*. Then there were earrings
and brooches in the form of a daisy bearing the initials
of Don Carlos, printed handkerchiefs, tobacco pouches,
and chromo-lithographed matchboxes . . .

It was 1870, a historically decisive year. Six or seven
candidates contended for the unhappy throne of St.
Ferdinand, among them one Italian, one Frenchman,
and one German. The struggle between the last two
of these was the pretext Prussia would use to establish
itself upon the ruins of the Sacred Germanic Empire
and set loose its allies on corrupt Napoleonic France—
to the great delight of Uncle Pascual. And then—to
the great indignation of the same man—when the Roman Pontificate was deprived of the support of France,
of the ancient protectorate of Avignon, this Pope was
despoiled of the temporal power (given him by Charlemagne) by the Italians invading the Eternal City,
and the Papal States were annexed by the King of the
Lombards—the new Alaric!—on the 2nd of October.
The battle of Sadowa and the assault on the Porta Pía
summed up a critical moment in the long history of
the stuggle between the sword of the Apostle Peter
and that of the Apostle John. Once the people of the
Latin Revolution were defeated by the army of the old
Germanic Reformation, the ties which bound the Pon-

tiff to his terrestrial domains were broken. And as the
last act of this age-old war between the Papacy and
the Empire unfolded, as the French howled in the sway
of their revolutionary ardor and of the Germans inebriated at Versailles, and the Ghibellines sang Garibaldi's hymn to a single and redeemed Italy, there took
place, in a small corner of the Lake of Geneva, at
Vevey, an event of incalculable importance, according
to Don José María, an event perhaps destined to re-
solve the very complicated issues of the day: Don Carlos took upon himself the leadership of his great community, rent by the internecine struggle between the
old elements and the new. He would lead them in
battle against the Revolution in Spain and ascend the
throne of his ancestors. Later, he would deal with the
Revolution in Europe, so that other nations and dy-
nasties might be held in check and order established
between the Emperor and the Pope, while he inaugurated, in the shadow of the Latin Cross, a new era
in the universal history of the old races.

The earth of Europe was aflame, and the Spanish
earth with it. On the 10th of June, under the pretext
that it was the saint's day of Doña Margarita, the Carlists issued official announcements and celebrated the
feast day and subsequent days, as a way of mustering
their forces. A short time later persecution against them
intensified. In July, they were aroused by an assault
on the Carlist club in Madrid. The club's members
fled through the streets, hearing the *Trágala* sung at
them and shouts of "Get them!" as they were blud-
geoned. The club was closed down, and the Carlist
press ceased publication in the capital. It was all in-
supportable.

"Well, at least here no one will lay a finger on us!"
Juan José exclaimed when he heard the news.

That summer some of the Carlists took to the hills. In the province of Vizcaya they were led by a priest. The rising at Escoda was a failure. All these hasty moves were condemned in the *tertulia* at the chocolate shop. When Don José María was sought out, they found he had disappeared.

Uncle Pascual, especially, felt his spirits rise. Bit by bit, each new event shook his soul. In April, the Pope had launched against the winds of revolution his encyclical *Syllabus errorum*, a bold challenge by the Papal Church to the spirit of the age. Later that year the infallibility of the Pope was voted, thereby closing Gregory VII's iron ring. Meanwhile Paris, the holy city of the revolution, was lit by the red glow of the Commune. All these things were reflected in Uncle Pascual's consciousness like the unfolding of a mysterious and terrible act in the drama of humanity. The Paris Commune and papal infallibility seemed closely bound together, like the devil's work and God's joining together to meet a common purpose. The priest took pleasure in both, trusting the Commune would force people into the arms of the infallible Pope. He believed in the devil as he did in God, often without distinguishing between the work of one and the work of the other. Although he wasn't aware of it, it could be said that for him, in an unconscious Manichaeism, God and the devil were the two terrible Persons of the same august Divinity. He felt a brotherly tenderness towards the destroyers, the pious Satanists, for they were his brothers in faith in that Divinity, but he truly hated the Liberals, those weak Mephistopheleans who were the real unbelievers. His military spirit saw the world as divided into two armies, one beneath the Catholic banner of Christ and the other flying the Masonic flag of Lucifer. He despised informers, amateur theoreticians, the indifferent, and the indecisive. Blasphemy seemed to him, after all, to be only a kind of prayer turned upside-down. His silent irritation with Don Juan Arana and his like only increased when he saw they kept calling themselves Catholics and kept being considered Catholics, even while they totally ignored the new dogma of papal infallibility. It angered him deeply that infallibility had turned out to be a failure, since there was no way of telling the difference between those who took it seriously and those who paid it no attention whatsoever.

When he learned that there was a move to enforce the law of civil marriage, which was to take effect in September, he gleefully said, "That's it, that's the way!"

For Pedro Antonio it was a day of awakened memories and feelings when a monument was unveiled in the municipal cemetery to commemorate those who had died defending Bilbao against the soldiers of Charles V in the Seven Year War. The sermon in the open air to the silent crowd called to his mind the night at Luchana, that nighttime battle during a furious storm in whirling snow, at the precise hour when "Glory to God in the highest, and on earth, peace, good will towards men" was being intoned in the temples of the Catholic world. The chocolate vendor gazed at the distant mountains, those witnesses to that old struggle, standing beyond that stone statue of a woman holding a crown high in each hand, one for the victors and the other for the vanquished. Both sides came together that day in the prayer of the preacher, who ended with the invocation: "Glory to God, peace to the dead; and among the living, unity and charity!"

"For God's sake!" Pedro Antonio cried out when

Gambelu told him that the priest who had stirred up the lees of his soul was a Liberal and a Mason.

Meanwhile, the preacher, who had concentrated all his mind at the beginning of the sermon on the thought that he was attending a religious event having nothing to do with differences of worship or belief or church, left to words of congratulations, thinking about the time once, in Switzerland, when he had heard one and the same bell bringing Catholics and Protestants together in the name of God under the arches of the same temple.

The next day, still under the impression of that open-air sermon, Pedro Antonio saw Don José María, whom everyone had believed to have left the city, silently entering his shop. The conspirator called him aside to induce him to subscribe to the voluntary and repayable fund issued that year. Pedro Antonio refused. Hadn't he already contributed?

"But this is at twenty-five percent annual interest, to be repaid in the first two years that the Duke occupies the throne of Spain."

No matter how much he kept talking about the twenty-five percent interest he could not persuade Pedro Antonio. But in a few days Pedro Antonio again took out another part of his savings to buy Carlist securities.

The streets of Guernica, where the General Autonomous Councils were assembled during July, rang with the cry of "Viva Don Carlos!" and resounded with the old Carlist songs. The fight grew stronger between the Council and Bilbao, whose spokesman was received in triumph when he withdrew to his town by way of protest. Bilbao had the same number of votes as the tiniest parish in the province, though it contributed forty percent of the levies! Scandalous! For their part, the Carlists considered the jailing of the local deputies a provocation on the part of the spiteful mercantile city.

All Spain was burning with a premonitory fever, just like Vizcaya. There were uprisings that summer.

The final limit, according to Uncle Pascual, came— the limit after the law of concubinage. It came with the imposition as king of the son of Victor Emmanuel—Victor Emmanuel, excommunicated, the Pope's jailer. In 1871 the new King, Amadeo, entered Madrid on January 2nd, a cold morning. Across the snow, before anything else, he went to the still-fresh corpse of Prim, who had been assassinated on his account.

Don Juan Arana, who had become a supporter of Amadeo, thundered against the Paris Commune, which was going unrestrained in France, and against the Pretender Don Carlos, who was touring the French border, fraternizing with Republicans. And when the good man was surprised to find his son with some lithographs depicting the new King in an unpleasant and vulgar caricature he cried out in indignation, "This is an outrage! With stuff like this, we'll have no need of Absolutists and Communists! Don't have any more to do with Ignacio, nor with that Pachico . . ."

"But, Father, they're the ones that . . ."

"No more, no more! They're fanatics!"

One morning in the spring of '71, Pedro Antonio told his son that one of his nephews was getting married in the village. Since he could not go himself, he wanted Ignacio to go.

Don Emeterio, Pedro Antonio's brother and a parish priest, awaited his nephew to take him to his house, where Aunt Ramona came to the door with two pairs of sandals. Her eyes were glued on Ignacio's footwear, wet from rain. Both the boy and his uncle the priest had to change their shoes to keep from tracking in mud on the waxed floor. He was hardly across the threshhold after this act of purification than Aunt Ramona brought blushes to his face by giving him two noisy kisses, one on each cheek. And he a grown man already! Her house, filled with furnishings whose only use was to be constantly cleaned, was like a little silver cup which was polished every day with a chamois. In the parlor there were mirrored globes, some enormous seashells, a piece of chinoiserie cabinetwork brought from the Philippines by Aunt Ramona's late and short-time husband, a man who had been a ship's mate. On the walls there hung a painting of his ship, *The Maiden Adela*, as well as other paintings of saints and virgins and a faded piece of framed embroidery. The whole place exuded an air of cozy tastelessness and excessive symmetry. Aunt Ramona—"the widowed old maid," as her brother the priest called her in moments of good humor—gratified her instinct for cleaning upon that house. Although she had no other duties except taking care of her brother and also had the help of a maid, she hardly found free time to go to Mass on Sundays. Since taking care of the house left her no time to take care of herself, she went around looking like a raga-muffin.

The priest let her be, and for his part he took care of his orchard and little garden, slept his siesta, read his copy of *La Esperanza* from cover to cover, and walked every afternoon with his assistant to the spot where his parish ended and the next one began, and there they would meet with some other priests in a little house. They would discuss the news in their newpapers, and return to their respective villages at dusk. On winter nights, the priest would get together with the doctor, the schoolmaster, and a local man who had been in America, to play cards. They would talk a great deal about each hand and the way it had been played, and then they would return home to begin the whole business again the next day. Don Emeterio's chief diversion lay in the huge feasts the priests in the villages of the area put on from time to time—banquets which usually led to endless rounds of *banca*, a card game on which some of the players staked their entire savings.

Don Emeterio's philosophy was that of the Book of Ecclesiastes—Solomon-like—and he spent most of his life sleeping and eating, almost the only pleasures of his existence.

Ignacio's first visit was to the family of the bridegroom, Toribio, whose parents insisted that he eat something. This was the only form of hospitality they knew, and the only kind that was within their means.

He went to bed completely worn out. When he woke up the next day, his aunt told him that the wedding had already taken place in the bride's village and that the wedding party would be arriving any moment.

The marriage had been arranged by the parents and the matchmakers with all the careful negotiation such matters require. The bridegroom contributed a house worth six thousand ducats, a sum which the bride's father had to give her future parents-in-law as a dowry. The bridegroom also contracted to pay for a second-class funeral for his parents when they should die. Thus the wife bought an inheritance and a man to work it for her. How much negotiation had been necessary to arrive at this arrangement, and how many times the couple had come close to breaking off before it was all settled!

As the sun came up Ignacio and the other guests

waiting at the bridegroom's house heard the creaking of the carts bringing the bridal furniture. The cart-wheels had been rubbed with resin and they fairly *sang* along the road. They could hear the shouts and cries of the wedding party resounding joyfully across the green of the countryside, and occasional yells of greeting, which they answered. Finally they could make out, through the trees, bathed in the first rays of the sun, the moving white promontory of the wedding cart, so loaded down that it was a blessing to behold. On top of the bed lay the distaff, like a crown—the distaff, the symbol of household tasks and holy family equality. Other carts came behind carrying more furniture and swelling the procession, and alongside them there were women bearing baskets full of presents. In the lead, a friend of the bridegroom was firing salvoes of blanks.

"How lovely!" exclaimed all the old women, wiping eyes grown moist at the recollection of their own old distaffs, with which they had spun the thread for their children's swaddling clothes and for their own awaiting shrouds. Presently the rest of the party appeared, all in their Sunday best, the bridegroom silent and wearing the look of a little boy who has just gotten away with something, the bride serene, blushing, and happier than a lark. She was a fine girl, sound, wide in hip and shoulder, a strong and willing field hand, whose wholesomeness proclaimed that she would be a robust mother and a splendid breast-feeder.

A space was cleared and the trousseau was spread out piece by piece before the wedding party. The whiteness reflected all the lively rays of the early morning sun. One woman called out a description of each item and gave its price as everything was laid out in sight of everyone. At the end of this exhibition she added a few words to the effect that the bride, for her part, was bringing with her something else with which to give her husband pleasure. It was a customary quip, at which everyone smiled.

Then came the long and leisurely feast, at which the bride's brother, a seminary student, did most of the talking. Everyone laughed at his witticisms. Ignacio, despairing of being able to follow the fluent Basque, his glass constantly being refilled before him, gazed at the fair face and the cowlike eyes of a blonde sitting across the table. Meanwhile, the student, his eyes flashing, joked with the girl, sending her into peals of laughter.

When Ignacio finally got up from the table and went to lean over the old wooden balcony, his spirit was clouded. He felt his blood pounding in his veins, and everything looked hazy to him, while there awoke within him the impulses he had felt the first time he fell into the sins of the flesh. The steamy smell of the country-side aroused him. When the dancing began, he danced with frenzy, to sweat away his feelings of desire. He watched the village girl with the fair face and the cow-like eyes leaping in front of him, against the deep green background of the countryside. The seminary student danced too, spinning like a top and yelling loudly.

They had hardly rested after eating before they were forced to eat again. Ignacio felt nauseated. When night fell, he went off with the seminary student to take some girls home to their farms, hardly knowing what was taking place. The wine, the heavy meal, the excitement of the dance—all these things dulled his senses. The student, completely tipsy, joked with the blonde girl, making her laugh with her whole being, as he poked at her and filled the air with his noise. The wild laughter, seeming to come out of the very earth, rang distantly in Ignacio's head, which felt like it was plugged up with burlap. He felt an impulse to grab the girl who was with him, rub hard against her, roll on the ground with her, to fuse his being with hers—but he restricted himself to caressing her face while she laughed at his poor stammering Basque. He was inhibited and timid. Without knowing why, he thought of Pachico and how he would have looked at him mockingly if he had been there.

The next day, tired and exhausted, after a night filled with lustful dreams, Ignacio was awakened by his uncle calling out, "How are you now? Have you slept it off?" He passed the day in low spirits, almost sorrowful, in the company of those guests who were still there. The student had recovered his usual timidity and seemed to be ashamed in Ignacio's presence.

On the following day, early in the morning, the newlyweds left the warm comfort of their bed to return to battle with that eternal earth in which they would one day be buried. For Ignacio the hours passed as slowly as oxen, and he chafed at being idle in a village where everyone was working.

On the fourth day of his visit, the nuptials having been concluded officially, he was awakened very early by Aunt Ramona's comings and goings, and he leaped out of bed for an early walk in the country. The sun was beginning to shake the mountains from their sleep. The mist began to rise and disperse, a few patches remaining in the trees to be blown away by the wind. As the sun turned the peaks golden, they began to cast their shadows before them. Like the voices of the mountainside, there came occasional sounds of bleating flocks, answered from the valley below with a plaintive, drawn-out lowing of cattle. Ignacio, having forgotten all the political disputes of the city, let himself fall under the spell of the countryside.

It was a holiday, a holy day of obligation, and he was to discover what that meant in a village where everyone worked. From the earliest hours, the road was filled with women in shawls. Aunt Ramona was among them, hastening to pray for the husband who had died so young. Ignacio made his way from the mountain to the parish church, the heart of the village and the source of its unity. Everyone who had been baptized there gathered on Sundays and feast days, coming from their scattered valley and mountain farms, to honor their forefathers, who slept under the floor of the church.

When the bells had stopped ringing, the people waiting in the portico began to go in to Mass. In the first row, in the most important pews, sat those who wore the long black capes of a year of mourning, even if they were mourning children who had died a few moments after birth. Ignacio had heard few Masses with as much satisfaction as he heard this village Mass, in mystic and silent communion with his parents' kinsmen, as the chorus of villagers raggedly answered the priest in the ancient liturgical language they did not understand, in sonorous Latin. And then, while the priest rapidly said the responsory for the dead before the tombs over which wax tapers burned on the wooden crosses, Ignacio remained in the atrium, at the door of the church, which was the original site for the people's assembly. As Ignacio stayed in the shade of the temple, among the landowners, many of these men came up to greet the son of Peru Antón of Elezpeiti, and most of them did so as his kinsmen. It was something to behold, the way they spoke in short phrases, the local men in their sparse Castilian, Ignacio in his very poor Basque.

Among themselves they talked about life's cares, and they asked Ignacio, as an outsider from Bilbao, about political developments, although these hardly seemed to interest them very much. The day of the Glorious Uprising had been for them like any other day. As on all other days, they had sweated over the living earth which engenders and devours men and civilizations. They were the silent ones, the salt of the earth, men who raise no outcry in history. Unlike city people, they did not complain about the Government nor blame it for their troubles. Neither drought nor hail, neither disease nor pestilence, was caused by man, but by heaven. Living daily in close touch with nature, they understood nothing of revolutions. They were endowed with resignation by their experience of nature, which bears no malice and treats all men alike. Nature worked upon them without regard for their social standing, and it made them religious. They did not view God through other men. And for them the primitive and direct connection between production and consumption had not been broken. They entrusted their seeds to the earth and to heaven, and they learned to wait. They kneaded the dough for their bread, and they blamed no man when the crop of corn was scanty. They depended on their bit of earth and on the strength of their arms. Nothing stood between them and their lands but the head landlord, whose right of ownership they accepted quite simply as one more mystery, as natural as everything else that happened to them in their daily lives. They submitted to him as oxen submit to the yoke. Just as each of them individually had forgotten his first crying breaths of life, so the memory of the beginnings of human history, when slavery and property were born together as twins, had been blotted out from their collective consciousness. They lived face to face with life, taking it seriously but simply, spontaneously, openly, and unreflectingly, and they awaited the next life without thinking about it. In their countryside, they were rocked in a silent song, a lullaby for death. They tilled their lives, and without conscious reflection they allowed the heavens to bring forth the fruit. Submerged in resignation, they lived with no concern for matters of progress. Their lives unfolded as slowly as a tree grows, casting its motionless reflection in the water. Although their lives were never the same for a single moment, they nevertheless appeared to be unchanging, as if seen in stilled mirrors.

After Mass, most of the men went to the tavern. It was their collective secular home, their stock market, and the center for their contacts and contracts. Inevitably, they ended up by having a hearty meal. In the tavern they immersed themselves in their chief concern—money. And there they permitted themselves almost the only diversion in their lives—a little drink after doing business.

The villagers all thought alike, thought the things they heard from the mouths of their priests. And the priests were beginning to feed the flames.

An educated villager, the second son of small property holders, a man who had gone from the spade to the book, the village priest receives in his head the weight of dogma. When he returns to his town from the seminary he is greeted with respect by his former playmates. He is their brother, but he is also the minister of their God. He is the son of the town, but he is also father to their souls. He had left them, had gone away from that small property holding in the valley or

97

on the mountainside, but now he brings them eternal truth. He is the trunk of the village tree, where its sap is concentrated. He is the organ of the common conscience. He does not impose his ideas; instead, he awakens the ideas that are asleep in everyone. When he speaks from the pulpit to his parishioners who are huddled together, he sends down the Divine Word like a heavy shower. In his age-old language he recites to them the age-old dogma. And this exhortation directed at the silence of his parishioners has a powerful effect, for it resounds inside them like a living echo.

O enlightened century! So much steam, so much electricity! But what of God, who is the true steam, the true electricity? And railroads? Railroads have brought corruption to even the remotest valleys. Families hardly gather any more to say the Holy Rosary. And in the very moment when the good countryman leans at twilight on his spade to remove his beret and prays, prays on the land he has watered with his sweat, the business man is sitting in his office in Bilbao, plotting deceit and worshipping the Golden Calf. How the good old customs have been dying! That is why God, in the strictness of His wrath, visited mankind with droughts, floods, and plagues of cattle. He punished everyone, punished everyone so that good people would rise in His defense.

The priest's voice was the voice of disturbed calm, of weakened resignation, the voice of someone worried by the lack of contentment among his neighbors.

Instead of reproaching them for their vices, he reproached them for the vices of others. *It was a sign of the times. Little by little the spirit of the farmer was waking up against the spirit of the merchant, the man with the spade against the man with the ledger. The poor villager, with time only for working his land, had stored up his ancient dogmas. Then he was robbed of them by*

*unscrupulous peddlers, who had offered in exchange a
lot of theories imported from nations of unbelievers, just
as they had already robbed him, little by little, of his good
gold coins in exchange for the paper money the Liberals
had invented. And these Liberals were merchants and
seamen, newcomers, people from families no one had ever
heard of. People from Bilbao were entering the smaller
towns as if they were conquerors, trampling on the farmer's land and insulting his women.*

In the portico after Mass, the priest would again go
over the most important points in his sermons, stating
clearly some things that his respect for God's temple
had kept him from presenting as the Divine Word.

Ignacio made friends with one of his uncle's tenants,
a countryman named Domingo, taking such a strong
liking to him that he was with him almost constantly
during his stay in the village. A sudden spell of sentimentality about country life had overtaken him, the
return of feelings left over from his early mountain-
climbing days.

He would set out almost at dawn and stay away
through dinner, until nightfall. He would accompany
Domingo to the farm, eager to lend a helping hand.
He busied himself shucking corn or shelling beans
with the other boys in that kitchen with its blackened
ceiling. He would spend almost the entire day there,
fascinated by the morning prayers, the saying of grace
at meals, and the angelus, when the only public voice
of the village filled the solemn air with its soft metallic
music. In one corner of the house, behind the large
kettle hanging from the center beam, Domingo's
grandmother, an old lady whose mind had grown dim
along with her sight, spent endless hours telling her
rosary, praying for the blessed souls in purgatory. Ig-

nacio felt sorry to see her cast away there like old and useless furniture, getting leftover scraps from the table as alms. The old woman's dead eyes wept at the touch of a warm and youthful hand resting a moment on her wizened hands. It was the hand of an angel, no doubt! "What a good gentleman, may God bless him!"

At nightfall, when Domingo stopped work, he and Ignacio would sit in the lee of the wind, next to the luxuriant corn fields. Taking his tobacco pouch from his beret, the villager would fill his clay pipe and watch the red cow against the background of the green field. Ignacio, seated next to him, kept silent.

"This is a sad thing for a Bilbaíno," Domingo would begin, launching into his favorite theme about *gentlemen* who worked with their heads, a kind of work he thought much harder than the work of the fields. He was intrigued by the subject, for though it was difficult for him to think things through, he took everything as a lesson to be learned. But he kept to himself his private opinions, which he had not quite formulated.

The two friends would fall silent. While Ignacio drank in the countryside's peace like sweet milk, Domingo would suck away at his pipe and gaze fondly at his cow. Because she gave him calves, milk, fertilizer, and work, she was his mainstay and his pride. He had started life with the loan of a cow, then had bought another and sold the calves at the Basurto fair. They had yielded forty gold duros, the beginning of his savings, still put securely away at the bottom of his private chest. It might be said that his race, by virtue of its long association with the ox, had taken from it the resignation and the quiet strength, the laboriousness, and the slow pace with which they followed this beast behind the harrow and the plow, step by step along the fruitful furrow. It could also be said that his race, taken out of its native pastures, was like the bull furiously charging to show off its wild feats far from home.

Ignacio began to enter into Domingo's quiet and withdrawn life. His wooden farmhouse was one of the oldest in Vizcaya. It was a beautiful witness to the life of the shepherd who has become sedentary and settled, a living testimony to a period of transition from tending pastures to caring for fields. The granary and especially the stable occupied Domingo's attention almost entirely, so that the result was a stable with living quarters added on for human beings. About the whole place there was something vegetative, as if it had sprouted from the very earth as a spontaneous flowering—or as some geological caprice. A grapevine covered the front of the house, and ivy covered its sides in an embrace through whose green web the windows peered out. The house somehow suggested the outlines of a human face on which the silent sorrows and the dark joys of unknown lives had been impressed. The old rustic house seemed born there, sad and dignified, shaped by rain and storms of snow and wind, condensing within itself both the harshness of its rural surroundings and human efforts to surmount them.

The ground floor was half kitchen, half stable, with a thin partition between, through which cows could put their heads to take their feed. The livestock and their owners thus ate together as a family. There was no chimney, and therefore, Domingo said, the smoke strengthened the beams of the house and kept the sleeping quarters dry. The smoke sought its exit through the windows or the roof, like steam from the sweat of the farmhouse or like the incense smoke from an altar. Since Domingo's cows ate next to him, he could scratch their necks as he ate his own cornbread and milk or his potatoes, listening to them breathing heavily and chewing their cud. And for their part, when the table blessing was said, the cows looked at him with their sweet damp eyes filled with resignation, as if they wanted to take part in the ceremony. When they lowed, their mellow voices resounded through the smoke-blackened kitchen. In winter they warmed the household with their body heat and with their fermenting dung, while the family slept with every opening sealed off, breathing the thick exhausted air.

Every night Ignacio went to bed with a delight he hadn't felt in a long time, but after a short time the warmth of the bed would bring lewd images to his mind, against which he tried to defend himself. He tried to pray. Sometimes he would get out of bed to cool himself off. It was like returning to those days when he had most struggled with sin.

At dawn he would rush to the old farmhouse in the countryside, passing on the way the house where lived the girl with the cowlike eyes he had danced with at the wedding—though her house wasn't on the shortest and most direct route. Whenever she saw him, the girl would smile and stop doing her chores for a moment. She didn't speak Castilian, and he didn't speak Basque, so they played the game of exchanging between them the few phrases each knew in the other's language:

"Good morning!"

"*Egun on!*"

"Crazy man from Bilbao makes fun of village people."

"*Nescacha polita, ederra . . .*"

She would laugh with all her heart, from the depths of her being, while Ignacio devoured her with his eyes. Once, when he found her sitting on a haystack, the

smell of the hay overcame him so much that his blood
rose to his throat and he felt his heart beat with thoughts
of violence even as she gave him a smiling look. Her
loveliness was the picture of health. She was the daughter
of air, water, and sunshine. She had the same calm joy
as did the countryside. Her face had the freshness of
the earth. She stood on the earth's surface like an oak,
although she was also as agile as a she-goat. She was
as elegant as an ashtree, as solid as an oak, and as full
of plenty as a chestnut. And the peace of the mountains
was reflected in her eyes, those large, cowlike eyes.
She was like a product of the village, a condensation
of mountain air. She had been nourished on a sturdy
cow's milk and corn from the sunny fields. For Ignacio
she embodied everything in the life of the village, and
everything he felt during those days was summed up
in her image.

Nevertheless, there were times when he was overcome by the deep sadness of the village, the subtle
melancholy which welled up out of that silence whose
voice seemed to be the unceasing noise of a stream,
and times when he felt oppressed by the country's
monotonous gamut of green, from the pale yellow-
green of the wheat to the black-green of the distant
woodlands.

On his way back to Bilbao a few days later, Ignacio
was thinking about Rafaela, but the village girl was
still on his mind, and he realized that the two looked
a bit alike. He hardly had set foot on his dark street
filled with the kaleidoscopic spectacle of goods on public display before he felt deep affection for Bilbao, which
repelled him when he was too close and which called
out to him when he went away. The shadows in the
street seemed to embrace him and to call up the memories of his vanished childhood. And there in their

darkness he again saw the image of the village girl as she had appeared to him one morning at a turn on a country path, her skirt gathered up, her feet in sandals, a sickle in her hand, her head half-covered under a bundle of hay, her fresh mouth smiling out of a face tanned by the sun of the fields.

The visit to the village gave Ignacio new vigor, and when he talked later on with Pachico, he no longer found his paradoxes quite so absurd.

After the great public demonstrations of July 18th, the twenty-fifth anniversary of the elevation of Pius XI to the papal throne, when there had been bunting and lights everywhere and everyone had shouted "Long live the Papal King!" in the very face of Amadeo, the usurper King and son of the Pope's jailer, Uncle Pascual spoke of war, making Pedro Antonio sigh as he thought of the savings he had pledged to the Cause.

Gambelu, outraged at the appointment of a usurping Liberal provincial government, called for an understanding between Don Carlos and Cabrera.

"All these new laws, a new Constitution, new regulations!" he exclaimed. "Here we've lived for centuries with our usages and customs. . . . For decent men, the commandments of God's law are sufficient. The law and its tricks are for the others . . ." His opinion was shared by everyone else who found thinking hard work.

"Our own democracy! When the King comes, from him on down—we're all equal." And he would go on to develop his program of "Fight the city and make it hard for the rich."

On all sides there was talk of the coming war, and the sparks flew everywhere. The young, who had been nurtured by their parents' memories of the Seven Years, did not want to be less than their elders. Ignacio feared that the crisis might be resolved without a war. Pedro Antonio recounted the feats of the great epic of his life more warmly than ever and longed harder than ever for the return of Don Tomás, whose mere presence would have called up victory.

The people, the clergy, and the militia all conspired. The nobility openly defied King Amadeo and helped arm the "Conspiracy of the Mantillas." The only class which resisted the popular current was the one Mendizábal created when he tried to stop Spain from being a monastery-barracks.

Agitators from the other side of the Ebro River infiltrated the Basque country in an attempt to shake the people out of their timidity. There was not so much agitation in Castile, where people had enough to do to earn their daily bread.

At the club, there was talk of the coming uprising. Everything was said to be ready, waiting only for a signal. Open warfare was preferable to a mockery of peace. The Carlists thought they had been abused a thousand times over, and they preferred dying in battle to the last man to suffering insults from foul-mouthed newspaper writers. That swarm of petty rancors was disgusting, and it would be far nobler now to take firm hold of things, to give the enemy a splendid drubbing, to break each other's heads if it came to that, and then, black and blue from the blows exchanged and out of breath from fatigue, for the victor and the vanquished to embrace, sweat on sweat and breath to breath. It would not be war but triumph. They would rise as a mass and the Liberals would have to give way; the mercenaries of the Revolution would give way to the Sons of Faith. They were going to war because they wanted peace, true peace, peace built on victory.

There would be no campaign, merely a military parade. This prospect annoyed Ignacio, as did the role assigned the army. It was also rumored that Cathelineau, the hero of La Vendée, was expected to put in an appearance.

Aroused by the moral atmosphere of war, Ignacio would sometimes leave the club and wind up at the little hutch of a brothel he had known before. When he got home late his mother's cough would say clearly, "Why at such an hour? What have you done, my son?" He would go to bed with his head on fire as he thought about his promise to take to the hills.

Towards the end of '71, it was said that Don Carlos, renouncing war, had put himself in the hands of Nocedal. Despite this, there were rumors and mysterious hints spread around by military men dressed in civilian clothes and the constant repetition of "Soon it will be!" It would all end up, Don Eustaquio was assured, in medals, titles, benefits, María Luisa sashes, and promotions, all of which the government would eventually come to recognize.

"We'll get nowhere with speeches!" Uncle Pascual exclaimed.

"Cabrera, Cabrera," Gambelu would repeat.

"How much better it would be to submit the question to the Pope's adjudication!" Don Eustaquio would add.

"What simple-minded innocence!" the priest exclaimed. "Keep the Pope out of it! He has his business, and we have ours. Our own kings, who were the most pious of men, knew how to keep the Pope in line in temporal matters . . ."

"Infallibility . . ."

"Don't talk rot! Infallibility has to do with matters

106*

of faith and morals, and whenever he speaks *ex ca-thedra*, which has nothing to do with the present case
. . ."

"Yes. 'The law and its tricks.' . . . Some priests!"

"Some ignoramuses!"

"The priests are told to preach peace, and they preach war!"

"Christ came to bring war . . ."

"And you people to draw your living from the State."

"And you, you," said the priest in a slow, deliberate voice, "you're a loafer who lives off the Budget! . . . And you will be lucky if the Covenant doesn't affect you . . ."

They parted, one mumbling "Aggressive brute!" and the other, "What an old codger!" But the next day each would feel a need for the other, and the one who arrived first at the *tertulia* would impatiently await the other's arrival. They mutually needed one another and used the *tertulia* to annoy one another with a stream of veiled allusions. On days in which one would seem to get the better of the other, the one who had lost would go away in smoldering silence, but the truth was that they cared for each other, in an affection that took the form of rancor, a sign of the solidarity between belligerents who complement one another. Each needed the other in order to get rid of his annoyance over the state of affairs, and each poured out his annoyance on the other's head.

Uncle Pascual would come in and start at once, "Well, Don Eustaquio, congratulations!"

"What for?"

"Espartero, the Duke of Victory, has been named Prince. . . . And it takes some crust to call the Covenant a victory, too!"

In some such way would their skirmishes begin,

sometimes over Carlist matters, sometimes on the rhetorical storms in the Cortes or Parliament, and sometimes on the uprising being planned. Gambelu would interrupt to bring up Cabrera, in whom he put all his hopes for salvation.

Ignacio did nothing but think about the campaign. There was no question of resignation now. Only people with consumptive souls could resign themselves and quibble over trivia under the yoke of tyranny, becoming head-wagging, word-mongering revolutionaries. And, when they finally grew tired of so much indignity and wanted to lift their voices in protest, they would find themselves spitless from so much idle talk. Weak-willed men, they were capable only of some kind of convulsive attack. War! War at any price!

The uprising would be mere child's play, a cinch, a mere question of posing a threat. There had been enough novenas, Te Deums, and expiatory services. Those Liberals who had something to lose would be intimidated and end up helping their enemy. There would be no bloodletting. They would take over Bilbao without firing a shot, and Don Carlos' horses would drink the waters of the Ebro River four days after their entry into Spain, and after thus refreshing themselves they would continue on their triumphal march on Madrid.

The elections would be the pretext.

But the Liberals had also armed themselves. Don Juan enlisted in the militia, fearing the agitated Volunteers for Liberty more than the Carlists themselves.

When the elections took place, they were as scandalous as the Carlists had warned. Men sank back to their lowest instincts. As in a tribe of savages, moral law applied only to members of one's own party. It was not wrong to kill the enemy. Troops of men, each incapable of stealing on his own, stole election lists. The semi-criminal elements of society floated upward, and in all things the depth of criminality appeared. The people, in exercising its sovereignty, broke every law and showed itself nakedly to be both tyrant and slave.

In the *tertulia* they discussed the way in which the entire opposition had hurled itself against the government: radicals, moderates, federalists, Carlists, pro-dynastic groups and anti-dynastic ones. The legislature might be called "the legislature of Lazaruses," since many people who were dead when the election took place had been resurrected when the votes were counted. Some voting tables had been presided over by garrison colonels, and at others the voting lists were "protected" by cannons.

"The die is cast! *Alea jacta est!*" exclaimed the priest and stood up. "Don Carlos has already spoken: 'Carlists! First to the ballot boxes, then, wherever God takes us!' "

"Better the evil we know than the unknown good to come," murmured Don Eustaquio, taking cover in this refrain which sums up the conservative skeptical spirit and its egocentric fears.

II

Dear Rada:

The solemn moment has arrived. Good Spaniards are calling for their legitimate King, and the King cannot ignore his country's call.

I order and command that on the 21st of this month the uprising take place in all Spain, to the cry of "Down with the Foreigner! Long live Spain! Long live Carlos VII!"

I will be among the foremost in the most dangerous and exposed post. Those who do their duty will merit well from the King and the country. Those who do not will earn the direst severity of my justice.

May God keep you.

Carlos

This emphatic order called up a fleeting spring uprising. On Sunday, April 21st, those who were committed to the Cause gathered in the club, after hearing Mass in order to rid themselves of care. From there they made their way into the countryside, in groups made up mostly of villagers living in the town. Some of the men danced and leaped to the sound of the fife, as if they were taking part in a festive religious holiday. There were even some who put off their spring marriages until the demonstration had been carried through.

From the market square, Don Miguel Arana watched the march of the Volunteers, basking in the reflection of their joy and taking pleasure in their carefree youthful impulsiveness. What wouldn't one give to be able to set out like that? Who wouldn't delight in dancing freely through the streets, turning war into a festival? The world was theirs!

Torn between respect for his parents and his longing to take to the hills, Ignacio went to Mass with Juan José and then followed along a good distance of the route. He sensed dimly that without his parents' support he would never be a true Volunteer.

Anxious days followed for him, in which he would climb alone to the heights surrounding the town, and gaze at every fold in the terrain, trying to find the men on his side. He hoped that they would enter Bilbao, now that it was without garrison.

The following Sunday morning Don Juan Arana, who had only the most superficial relations with Pedro Antonio, came into his shop on the pretext of buying a sweet.

"Did you see those bumpkins last Sunday?" he suddenly asked the confectioner. "They vote with their guns, and then have the nerve to call our side illegitimate."

"It's all in God's hands."

"I don't know what it is you people want . . ."

"What *we* want?"

"Well, now, yes, your friends. These people who let priests run around loose are to blame—these priests who abuse the confession box in such a way . . ."

"Don't say such things, Don Juan!" Josefa Ignacia said.

"I stand by what I said," he continued, hotly determined not to see himself contradicted. "No fewer than forty priests have taken to the hills. . . . What do you think of that?"

"I don't believe it."

"And why shouldn't you believe it, woman? And in the face of all this, the bishop hasn't issued so much as a pastoral letter. . . . They ought to shut down that cathedral, it's a center of conspiracy." *I must have a strange effect on them*, Don Juan thought to himself. *They're surely saying to themselves "He's mad!"* Just then Gambelu and Don Eustaquio came in, so he continued, "Nothing will come out right until they crush these country bumpkins. . . . These people must be wiped out. They're the kind who ask for more water the more it rains. . . ."

"Halt! Stop right there!" Gambelu exclaimed.

"Just you try wiping them out," Pedro Antonio said calmly.

"General Serrano will come. . . ."

"Was it to say these things that you came here, Don Juan?" asked Josefa Ignacia. Her question was like a pitcher of cold water poured on Don Juan. For a moment he saw himself as he must seem to them, and he understood the looks they were giving him. Out of a sudden inner irritation, he composed himself, picked up his purchase, and went out saying, "This is a center of conspiracy!" Once in the open he breathed freely and thought to himself, *I really gave them a good piece of my mind.*

"Not altogether wrong," said Don Eusebio, then added, "It's here!" He took out the communiqué Don Carlos had made on the 2nd of May. It contained the obligatory points: the sacred fire of Independence, kept alight through forty generations, and so on. After hearing it read, Pedro Antonio asked calmly, "And where are our people now?"

It was the first time he had called the men of the uprising "our people."

When Don Juan reached home and met the serene glance of his daughter, he realized how foolishly he had behaved at the confectionary shop.

What panic there was in Bilbao on Ascension Day, all because of four shots heard above the market square! The village women ran around in a fright, some of them dropping their purchases, while the shops shut down as quickly as they could. They feared at any moment the appearance of the enemy, which the day before, only a couple of miles away, had cornered a column which had gone out from the city. Don Juan crossed the street running to arm himself, while the confectioner smiled, his elbows on the counter. Bugle calls sounded down the empty streets. From time to time a head peered out of a window to see what was going on. Ignacio, who was on his way to meet his people, heard crying from one house. From another he heard someone call out, "Landlady, look and see where they're coming from," which was answered with "Some soldier you are!"

"What will happen when they see the real thing?" Pedro Antonio asked when he learned that the whole business had been a joke played on the town by four "enemy" children.

Days of anxiety followed. Don Juan was furious at the resistance the bumpkins were putting up at Mañaria and Oñate, after the news of the net drawn around Oroquieta and the rumors that Don Carlos, their King, had fled, or been killed or imprisoned. He wanted to see Serrano crush them within the triangle planned to entrap them. And then, all of a sudden, there was talk of a pact. A covenant! Bilbao shrieked to the skies.

Without having had a chance to raise a finger, the people of the loyal town would be the scapegoats.

With Juan José, who was already back from the brief "campaign," Ignacio went to the reception Bilbao gave to Serrano, the pact-maker, whom Ignacio hissed.

"It's because of milksops like this fellow that it's easy for your father and his friends to raise a rebellion. . . ."

When Ignacio discovered that the man who had spoken to him was Rafaela's father, he asked him, "Who has said anything offensive to you?"

"Enough of your impudence!" Don Juan exclaimed. Then he turned to a little boy next to him who was enjoying himself by trying out his prowess at whistling and said, "Louder, louder!"

The uprising passed by like a summer cloud, but it left behind the germs of endless disputes. A pronunciamento by peasants, born out of an order on a piece of paper, it ended in a pact. No more than a mutiny, it had fallen of its own weight. Time, which allows resistance to build up, had nipped it in the bud. Furthermore, the rebels had presented themselves to the enemy in a block like a metal ingot instead of in a fluid mass like quicksilver which spreads out but later comes back together. And it was all because of the order.

Don Juan, infuriated by the pact, paced around his desk, muttering, "Hit them in the pocket, where it hurts! Bear down on the country people! Confiscate, according to the old law, the goods of those who took to the hills and those who encouraged them. . . . Enlarge the militia, and let the province pay for it—except Bilbao, of course. Take the right to say Mass away from these mountain-loving priests. . . . The pocket, where it hurts! Off with these religious confraternities and congregations, they're against the law! Serrano, you milksop! You call us Liberals to such and such a percent, abandon us to those rebels, and then come out with the statement that you cannot be influenced by local sentiments but only by the example of the warriors of antiquity. . . . Milksop! Figurehead! . . . Juanito!"

"Papa?"

"Another thing: I don't want to see you in the company of that confectioner's son again!"

One afternoon in a *chacolí* Juan José retraced the brief campaign for Ignacio.

Over three thousand men had mustered, formed into seven battalions. Many young men were sent home for lack of weapons. In fact, military drill had started with some men bearing rifles and others sticks. What hurrahs there had been for the battalion which had disarmed twenty-five Civil Guards, after a brief exchange of fire! It was a pleasant stroll they were taking, especially at first. Farmers would come out to offer them water, bread, milk, eggs, and cheese. As the "sisters" of the Volunteers, carrying changes of clothing, streamed along the footpaths, they made the green hills resound with their high spirits, as if they were on a religious procession, a local *romería*. The population of the villages came to see them pass. Surrounded by cheering country people, they breathed in the spring air which swept across the meadows and they arrived in Guernica, where four thousand men had assembled amid cries of enthusiasm as if they were ready to play pelota, the ball game of the Basques. They shouted "*Viva!*" to religion, to the Basque laws and privileges, and to Spain, with an occasional shout of "Down with the Foreigner!" and cheers for Carlos

VII and whatever he ordered or commanded. Right
there and then they elected and proclaimed their Dep-
utation by armed suffrage, in the face of the intruder.
Then came the skirmishes, the sad death of their chief,
who had been wounded in front of his men, and a
night march under an intermittent moon, a march which
took them twenty-one hours across hills and fields of
brambles. Some of the troops slept on their feet. And
then the final weakness, the abandonment, the pact.

When Juan José finished his narrative, the two friends
stood looking out over the panorama before them: the
mountains disappearing up into the mist, a dream landscape, and Bilbao lying quiet below them.

That night Ignacio dreamed that bands of villagers
descended on the city, and that Rafaela ran around in
terror, while her father moaned in despair as his shop
was sacked.

The summer flowed along peacefully while the war
continued in Catalonia.

King Amadeo visited Bilbao, and Pedro Antonio
could not repress a sigh of compassion when he caught
sight of him on foot, walking down the main street of
Begoña with a remarkably small retinue in a pouring
rain which caught them fully exposed.

Don José María visited the confectioner regularly,
bringing him the latest gossip and minutiae from the
Carlist Olympus, tales of the dissidence surrounding
Don Carlos, whom he considered a type of Caesar, of
fallings-out among the Junta over his secretary and
court favorite. The good man had become an enthusiastic partisan of Cabrera, and he could not abide
Uncle Pascual's quibbling over the fact that the Carlist
chief had married a Protestant. In the priest's eyes the
model was General Lizárraga, whom Don José María

titled "El Santón," the devout chief who, in the belief
that God gives each nation the King it deserves, crossed
his hands over his breast, consulted his conscience,
and, accepting the King he had been given to serve,
bowed his head and asked only that if his King were
a scourge, he be shown mercy and the King converted.

"It's generals like that we need!"

"What we need is a program," retorted Don José
María,"a definite program. . . . Fewer warriors, fewer
heroes, and more thinkers!"

And the good gentleman, persuaded that ideas rule
the world, as astronomy guides the stars, projected
official visits on his part of this one and the other one,
and would go about in silent converse, arching his
brows and gesturing, altogether unaware of the spectacle he was creating.

Ignacio and Juan José meanwhile were avidly reading the reports of the Catalan campaign. They raised
their spirits reading about that guerrilla war based on
stealth and surprise attacks on cities in broad daylight,
with bullets flying through the streets. It was exciting
to read about "a second Cabrera," about the "devil of
the Crosses," in the Liberal nomenclature, and about
the former Papal Zouave, Savalls, a kind of mountain
cat, whom the King asked to reach into his heart, take
out some of the sacred fire burning there, and scatter
it over his troops.

Autumn came and went quietly. At the beginning of
winter, guerrilla bands and proclamations multiplied.
The feats of the priest Santa Cruz made a large impression, and there was much talk of Ollo's deeds.

Finally, Christmas Eve came around, the longest of
the winter celebrations, a night on which, drawn up
around the hearth, protected from the threats of the

dark night, the fruitful family, in union against the
dark forces of Nature, commemorated the religious
mystery of the descent of the redeeming word to the
wandering Holy Family in a poor hovel, which was a
brief stopping place in their outlaw way on a long cold
night, where the angels sang "Glory be to God in the
highest and peace on earth." It was a celebration of
Christ's descent to shine his light on those who lie
down in darkness and to set our feet upon the path of
peace. It was the eve of Christmas, the Basque *gabón*,
a feast peculiar to the Basque race, on a night shared
with all other Christian nations, with a particular and
private physiognomy which makes of it a feast proper
to each race, with the traditions pertaining to each
people.

Pedro Antonio celebrated it in the confectionery shop.
It was the sweetest familial feast in his life of limited
plenitude; he seemed to dance in the very atmosphere,
basking in the summation of his life carried on in all
the small corners of the tiny shop where the imperceptible haloes of his thoughts of peace and work reposed. It was the feast of the gray days, of the heavy
rains, of the hours of rest and rumination around the
fire.

When the confectioner let himself go with a little
wine, he could feel the heavy burden on his spirit
lighten, which was weighed down with the dank darkness of the workhouse where he labored over his mortar and pestle. The generous wine whispered to him:
"Arise, Lazarus!" And, once the ice was broken, the
youthful Pedro Antonio arose. He would play the gallant to his wife and call her beautiful; he would make
as if to embrace her and she would shyly shoo him
away. Uncle Pascual, who always joined them, would
laugh as he smoked his cigar. In such moments Ignacio

felt uneasy, unable to drive away his improper memories.

Pedro Antonio would sing the chorus of the most common of all Christmas songs, repeating it over and over, since he did not know the rest:

> *Esta noche es Nochebuena*
> *y mañana Navidad . . .*

Then he would summon up Basque songs out of the past, all slow monotonous chants, heard in meditative silence by his wife, his son, and the priest.

He would insist his son dance with his mother. When the priest left, Pedro Antonio felt easier and, withdrawing into the world of his memories, he would recall that this night of peace around the hearth in the spirit of the family was also, in his interior world, a night of war.

"Christmas Eve. *Nochebuena*! Thirty-six years ago tonight Espartero came here . . . *Nochebuena! Nochebuena!* What a terrible night it was! The young had gone off to celebrate *gabón* with their families. . . . It was snowing . . ."

Once again he told the story of the night of Luchana, concluding, "If Don Tomás were still alive . . . ! Even at my age he'd still be able to shoulder a musket . . ."

"Don't say that, Peru Antón . . ."

"Don't you say anything, love. What do you know of these things? Here's Ignacio here, and he will not be less than I was. . . . We brought him up to serve some purpose, and he's the son of his father . . ."

His father's innermost voice had a profound effect on the son. It shook him. He heard it that night in bed, where he lay sleepless, overtaxed by the glut of events. His mind spun in that interior world of his own. His flesh, gorged with food, was lashed with thoughts of the brothel. His blood, feverish with wine, called up scenes of battle for him, and there, at that final point, he saw the hazy image of the mountains.

A few days later, when Don José María called him aside, Pedro Antonio thought to himself, *Here comes a new levy, a demand for money.* "I'll give my son, but as for money, no more," he said.

The conspirator went away, denouncing the confectioner in his mind. *He wants his son to make good on his investment in the Cause*, he thought.

The new year came around. King Amadeo worn out with his troubles, abdicated. The Republic was proclaimed. And now the Carlists could exchange their cry of "Down with the Foreigner!" to the simpler "Long live the King!" which was no longer ambiguous.

Ignacio and Juan José tramped the mountains around Bilbao, eager to see some sign of the Carlist forces, waiting for Ollo and his men from Navarre to appear any moment at the gates of the city. They carried all the proclamations which were issued on all sides these days, and they read them with gusto: up there on the heights, conventional rhetoric moved their simple hearts.

These proclamations heaped abuse on the foreign intruder's dynasty: it had *confounded in the dust of oblivion and disdain* the reign of the son of the excommunicated jailer of the immortal Pius IX. The proclamations redoubled amid the din of *the scandalous noise of the revolutionary bacchanal*, but there was the assurance that *what God does is permanent and floats above all earthly tumult*. They announced that the hour had come: *Why wait when society had come apart, chaos threatened, and the waters of the deluge were newly rising? When the religion of their ancestors was being oppressed, the fatherland abused, the legitimate monarchy reviled, and property menaced? When the priest had to go begging for his sustenance, when the Lord's mother moaned, and the slaveholders of blacks in Puerto Rico were being menaced? Victory or Death! The Lord of Hosts does not abandon His own, if they rally with faith around the holy flag which waved over Covadonga and at Bailén, and if not caring or counting the number of their enemies, they truly willed to be free even though now enslaved.*

The Catalans were reminded of their past glories, when they imposed their laws upon the Orient; the Aragonese, of the Virgin of the Pilar, who had expelled the French revolutionary army and would fight alongside them; the Asturians, of the shadow of Pelayo and the Virgin of Covadonga. For their share, the Castilians were roused and incited against *that gang of cynical and infamous speculators, brazen-faced dealers, local chieftains, and shady police who, like toads, were growing bloated in the polluted swamp artificially forming from the confiscated property of the Church.* The population was further aroused against *those very same ones who lent money at thirty percent interest, who expropriated the forests, the pastures, the ovens and even the forges, those who got rich buying up the lands of the commonwealth for a handful of silver, using a thousand tricks, and did so shouting "Order!" sometimes or "Anarchy!" other times.* Furthermore: *All that muck and all those dregs will be swept away. The day of reckoning is at hand.*

They were being called to arms! They were about to oust the tinsel-patriots, those who made treason out of the ruins of Voltairean "moderation," those who used the blood of the loyal to concoct the black treason of Vergara. The apathetic and the duped were about to bite the bitter dust of remorse!

They summoned to their side all the soldiers of the nation, the soldiers of Isabel, those of Amadeo next, then of the Republic, all those, in short, who had never served Spain. Enough of civil warfare. They would all be victors. The King opened wide his arms to all Spaniards. He would respect all accustomed and acquired rights. He would throw a veil over the Concordat; he would take to his bosom "even those toads who had grown bloated in the polluted swamp of amortization." War! The spirits of his ancestors would be with him! To arms! War on the heretics and freebooters! War on the thieves and murderers! Down with the existing order of things! *Santiago, y cierra a España!* St. James and close Spain, especially against *them*, who were worse than Moors! Long live the Basque and Aragonese and Catalan statutes, the *fueros*! Long live the franchises of Castile! Long live Liberty correctly interpreted! Long live the King! Long live Spain! Long live God!

The hills and woods remained calm and serene, as immutable and silent as ever, providing grazing space on their slopes, furnishing water to the arroyos which murmured on down between their stones.

All this rhetorical clamor in the unceasing proclamations worked on the imaginations of Ignacio and Juan José, who, after reading it all, would gaze up to the silent heights, waiting to see them crowned with the crusaders.

Don José María, meanwhile, diligently pursued the definitive program.

For his part Pedro Antonio frequented all the council and chapter meetings in company with his cousin the priest. Ignacio once noticed his mother wiping away her tears. Ignacio had been absent from his desk for some time now and had very little to show in the way of work. His father talked at length about war and the slow pace of recruitment. More and more he called up his own past military glories. By means of frequent veiled hints and insinuations, he sought to have the initiative come from Ignacio—who meanwhile waited hopefully for some sign from his father. And thus arrived the day on which a natural meeting of minds came about spontaneously within the family, a tacit understanding and accord.

Pedro Antonio was looking for a time when he and his son would be alone, but at the same time he was avoiding such a meeting. Once they were alone, but he told himself that it was really still too soon for a frank talk. But finally one morning when Gambelu was in the shop Ignacio walked in, and Gambelu said to him, "What's this? Do you expect to keep hanging around like this? You should show yourself as your father's son. . . . To the field! Off to the hills!"

Father and son both started talking at once, the son saying "As far as I'm concerned . . ." and the father saying "I won't be the one to stop him . . ."

The ice broken, more talk followed, and Uncle Pascual appeared on the scene to confirm the joint agreement of father and son and to prepare his nephew for his duty. A campaign such as he would take part in would be a solemn, grave, and serious matter.

When Josefa Ignacia learned of the decision, she accepted it with the same resignation she had shown forty years before, when Pedro Antonio made a similar decision. She reached into her bosom and took out an embroidered patch she had secretly made and gave it to her son. On it were stitched the words "Stop, bullet!"

"You'll be leaving right after Holy Week and Easter," Pedro Antonio told his son. Ignacio hardly slept that night. Now, now, he was a true volunteer in the crusade. It was the crowning moment of his life. A world opened before him. He dreamed of strange happenings in which an odd mixture of persons descended through the gaps in the thick mountain underbrush: Charlemagne, Oliveros de Castilla, Arthur of the Algarve, El Cid, Zumalácarregui—and Cabrera.

Ignacio and Juan José spent Holy Week walking in the mountains; on Passion Monday they watched, from the top of Santa Marina, the bulk of the Carlist forces some five miles outside Bilbao. They saw the troops moving about as on an anthill, and they itched to climb down and join them.

Who would have guessed it? That mass of men, that troop which hid from time to time amidst the forest cover, that handful of volunteers, was the hope of God, King, and Country. They were the men of the fields, the volunteers of the Cause.

They avidly took in the view. The mountain ranges were like rows of backdrops: cordilleras like petrified waves of an enormous sea, their colors fading away into a distance where they were lost.

Behind the somber barrier of the mountains and under a darkling sky, there were occasional glimpses of some little green valley, a mosaic of sunlight, a paradisiacal corner, a green lake of reposeful light. And the entire scene, with its great waves of mountains in intermittent shadow and light and rays filtering through from the darkened clouds, produced a sense of overwhelming serenity.

Around Easter they went to a dance for farm girls and danced their fill. They met Juanito and Pachico and bade them a formal farewell.

"Who knows, some day I may be of use to you!" Ignacio told them.

"Enjoy yourself!" exclaimed Pachico.

On one of those days, when Lagunero appeared in town in his sheepskin, Ignacio heard someone call out "There goes our new Zurbano!" His heart swelled with fellow feeling as he watched him, smiling.

At times Pedro Antonio felt himself transported back to his own years of glory. The comings and goings of the troops, the bugle calls: everything excited his memories. When he caught sight of Lagunero's sheepskin, he, too, conjured up the vision of Zurbano, of the terrifying Barea, and he recalled for his wife that October of '41 when, just married, they lived through that "Peace" made up of hatreds between the moderates and the progressives, and when on the feast day of Santa Ursula, Zumalacárregui, the Tiger in the Sheepskin, entered Bilbao. What a day! The confectioner closed down his shop and set about consoling his wife, telling her stories of the war, while the rest of town was running to the Sendeja, leaving the streets vacant behind them. And what days followed! They were days when a strict edict forbade even the wearing of a beret or a mustache, days when people went in terror to view the cold, inert corpses of the prisoners taken the night before.

"Get on with you, Ignacio, go out and put an end to them . . ."

On April 22nd, Josefa Ignacia placed the scapulary around Ignacio's neck, added the embroidered talisman against any bullet, and kissed him goodbye. Ignacio then listened to a homily by Uncle Pascual, who, when he had finished, embraced him and went out with Pedro Antonio to look for Juan José. The boy was bidding his mother farewell when they arrived. From the doorway, she called, "Don't leave a *guiri* alive, even as a token! War on the enemies of God!

Don't come home until Don Carlos is King. And if they kill you, pray for me in heaven."

Pedro Antonio accompanied them to the Puente Nuevo, where a Carlist advance party was stationed. He called out to the chief of the party, spoke with him, and then turned to his son and said, "We'll see each other from time to time." Then he returned to the town, his soul burning with a tumult of memories of his seven epic years, and especially with the memory of the day in '33 when he joined the uprising in Bilbao with Zabala. He saw Don Juan at the door of his warehouse, and he greeted him without the slightest rancor.

When Ignacio and Juan José presented themselves at headquarters in Villaro, the commander received them coldly. "What have you got?" he asked. He quickly examined their letters of recommendation, told them that they would be enlisted the next day, and turned aside to resume an interrupted conversation.

"What have you got?" Why, they had a will to fight! Was that any way to greet volunteers? The whole scene smacked of an office, mere routine, without any apparent enthusiasm.

They spent that night on the floor of a large hall, unable to sleep a wink, full of vague anxiety and longing. The next morning they received orders to join the Bilbao battalion. Ignacio made a gesture of disgust. They were putting him in with the very men he was trying to avoid, youths from his home town, former cronies from the street and the club, all his rowdy friends, when what he wanted was to be among villagers, among men of the open fields.

The battalion strength at that point was about a hundred men, many of them armed only with poles.

"We meet again!" cried Celestino to Ignacio when he saw him eying his non-commissioned officer's stripes.

Yes, they met again: another encounter with the former idol whose spell he had broken, but only seemingly, it appeared. Ignacio met the spirit of divisiveness, not of war, and now armed and sporting stripes. Celestino's sword appeared to him like a sharpened tongue, serpent-like. And then it struck him—he understood, even if only dimly in the depths of his spirit, all the emptiness of classified ideas, the hollowness behind the verbiage in all programs.

Since it was the season of Easter duty, all the volunteers routinely received Holy Communion, a Communion hurriedly administered. They received the mystical bread of the strong in spirit as if it were a disciplinary service. Among them were some who had not received Communion in years.

Ignacio felt downcast among that band of tired and poorly-armed men, who made tours of the villages demanding donations and rations, each man helping himself as best he could, and risking a possible contact with the enemy. The entire affair was as hopeless as trying to draw water from an empty well.

"Quite different from what we did in April," exclaimed Juan José.

And Celestino commented, "It's all the same. Everything will get done. The road to Rome is long and slow, not a matter of quick leaps."

A new routine now began for Ignacio. It was a time of marches and counter-marches, of enforced hikes, made difficult by the irregularity of the terrain: a task to break down the strongest men among them—and all of it merely to raise some rations and go on living. Spring snow still covered the woods; a cutting wind struck them in the face. They walked now along dark ravines in whose depths a river murmured among the underbrush, steeped in humidity. Crossing a gorge, they were liable to come out onto a fertile plain or upon a vista of a distant mountain range near the sea. At times the dark panorama covered over with black clouds would give way to a green oasis bathed in light which fell from a rent in the clouds. Often they walked under a fine drizzle of rain, as slow in falling as it was enervating, and it sank into their bones and spirits; it turned the landscape into a kind of smoke which then liquified. They walked for the most part in silence. When they saw the farm workers busy at their small plots in the peace of the fields or the smoke coming from the chimneys of the country houses, they forgot they were on their way to war. War in the silence of the fields? War in the peace of the groves of trees? The trees offered them rest in the shadow of peacefulness, and the men sometimes took the opportunity to lie down under them, among the tree-trunks, which seemed like the columns of some rustic temple, holding up the vaults of foliage penetrated by the sweet light of the sun.

Ignacio took a new view of the volunteers, for he now saw them through other eyes: finding himself among like-thinking comrades, he felt he was one of them. When armed men bound for battle come together they see themselves as a separate caste and look upon the peaceful men of the fields almost as inferior servitors. Whenever they came to a cluster of houses and called a halt to rest, or for the night, they would cry out in authoritative and resolute voices for the "*Ama!*", the mother and household head. And they would all gather in the great kitchen, as if it were occupied territory, to dry off in front of the family hearth. The entire household would soon join them, the children hiding silently in corners in order the better to scrutinize the exotic visitors. Some of the soldiers would call the children over to them, ask them their names, and let them handle their weapons. They treated children habitually with a tenderness they had never felt for any children before. Ignacio would often sit one of them on his own knees, asking the few questions he could manage in the Basque vernacular. He could see himself in these children, who looked at him with innocent calm one moment, with timid bashfulness the next.

Both Ignacio and Juan José had been vastly annoyed at the outset because they had not been issued real rifles, but once they had been equipped with them, they found them a heavy burden. What a weight! They shifted them constantly from one shoulder to the other, never comfortable; meanwhile Celestino sported his sword.

Ignacio had to wash his own clothes and, while he wrung out his shirts in the freezing water, he was ever aware that Celestino's stripes entitled him to have his shirts washed by an orderly.

"The Republic has just been proclaimed and now is the time to gather strength instead of going to pieces," announced the little lawyer-at-arms.

Ignacio could not stand the sight of the other's stripes, or of his naked sword, which was like an idle tongue. Compared to a rifle reeking of powder, compared to a firearm which detonates amid fire and sound and can kill at a distance, was that little sword any more than a toy? Was it anything but the symbol of braggadocio? In disgust at the company of his old friends the street rowdies, he determined to ask for transfer to another battalion, specifically the one which was drawn from the men of his father's village. Permission was granted, and he went off with another man, the two of them walking alone and freely through the woods. At Urquiola they came upon Durango's battalion: one hundred men effectively armed with Remington rifles.

His spirits began to rise. There was talk of a victory gained at Eraul, a town in Navarre, of a decisive cavalry charge, of a cannon captured from the enemy. The church bells rang out to mark these gains. Ignacio, enrolled in Durango's battalion until he could find the one he had been assigned to, straggled in exhaustion from town to town.

All the formal discipline and the mass drill, of which he was just a small part, following along in the footsteps of everyone else, struck Ignacio as ridiculous. If it were a regular organized army, made up according to a strict mathematical pattern, with its regular square formations, if it were an army which had to be drawn up for grand parades and maneuvers, in front of the honorable fathers of families holding their children by the hand to come to see the spectacle, well and good! But out here in the woods, up in the free mountains, what difference did all this make? Without realizing it clearly, Ignacio was beginning to discern that what is ordinarily called discipline is not the quality which makes an armed force what it should be. He began to perceive that they should never form themselves into an army at all; that as soon as they became regular soldiers they would cease possessing the special force which lent them effectiveness and which made any sense. In effect, to try to form a regular army organized in the systematic manner and in accord with a modern tactical pattern was much like the search by Don José María for a definitive program. Was it not the very Liberalism they were fighting against which had created the idea of such an army?

At last, thanks be to God! At Mañaria, the scene of last year's rising and glorious battle, they encountered two-hundred *guiris*: a mixed group composed of regular soldiers and nationals from Durango. Ignacio's heart beat faster when he was stationed on the left side of the road, at a point where he could see nothing at all. He was burning with curiosity to get out into the middle of the road to see what he could see, to see what it was all about; just then he heard a whine over his head; he felt cold all over, and leaned against a tree. "The same thing happened to Cabrera," he thought, and he could feel his face was flushed. He could hear the shooting, but could see nothing. When he found the men around him beginning to run, in obedience to some voice of authority, he ran with them. Later he learned that they had pursued the enemy to the very gates of Durango.

So this is the way it was! This was war? He had left home for this? They went on from town to town, from hill to hill, without rest; sometimes they followed along dusty, sleepy roads, sometimes along ancient rocky causeways, sometimes along old riverbeds which, drained dry by irrigation ditches, served as roads through the canebrakes. They received contradictory reports, and they grumbled that the whole campaign was a wasted opportunity to bring down the Republic, which was in a sad state, and give it the coup de grâce. The Republicans were busy with an election campaign. One of their agents crossed paths with the Carlists as he was on his way to Bilbao from Durango. He stopped and had a meal with them; they offered a toast to Don Carlos, while he toasted the Republic. Ignacio was altogether distraught: he recalled the scene at Mañaria; he was sick to death of the endless canebrakes and hedges and of the hills and forests which all resembled one another.

"This is headquarters for the priest Santa Cruz," he heard someone say on one of those days, as they were entering Elorrio. He felt like a little boy who is told he is being taken to see a white bear. For the entire countryside resounded with the name of the priest from Hernialde, already a legendary guerrilla-fighter, whose extraordinary feats were discussed by everyone, some in awed admiration and others in denigration. His passage signified terror. When they felt his presence, anyone of any distinction in the village would begin to tremble, while the town itself would turn out to hail him in a frenzy. The life and deeds of this wildcat made the rounds everywhere by word of mouth. Everyone knew how in '70, when they had planned to seize him as soon as Mass was over, he made his escape dressed as a villager. He was again imprisoned as a result of the Amorebieta Pact, and fled again, after he let himself down from a balcony and hid for twelve hours in a thicket alongside the river. And everyone knew how on the 2nd of December he had recrossed the border with a force of fifty men, who grew like the proverbial snowball, sowing terror in all directions, battling their way through valleys and over mountains, fording rivers at flood, leaving in their trail the victims of Santa Cruz's firing squad. Mocking the enemy who put a price on his head, he made guerrilla war in his own style, rebellious and intransigent to all discipline, inciting hatreds between opposing bands, the Whites and the Blacks, and all the while reviled by the hypocrite, the master saint, Lizárraga, who called him Hyena Heart and Sacristy Rebel.

Cries of "Long live religion!" and "Long live Santa

Cruz!" could be heard on all sides, while the populace ran in crowds to hail his passage. The priest's partisans came to about eight hundred men, grouped in four companies. They were an effective-looking lot, with the appearance and air of smugglers about them. Over their heads several flags waved: one was a black flag with the words, in white over a white skull, "War Without Quarter," and another flag, red, proclaiming "Death before Surrender." And still others.

Under the spell of this scene, which mesmerized him, Ignacio's spirit took over from his conscious mind, so that he recollected José María in the Sierra Morena, and a series of confused images, all in a tangle, a misty cloud of evocations, of Charlemagne with his twelve peers cleaving their way through turbanned coats of mail; the giant Fierabrás, a tower of bones; Oliveros of Castile and Arthur of the Algarve, the Cid Ruy Díaz, Ogier, Brutamonte, Ferragús, and Cabrera with his wildly flapping white cape. All the images crowded upon each other in confusion, without his being clearly aware of it all, and his soul filled with a silent sound which evoked a world in which he had lived before he was born, and to this was linked in some mysterious way the warmth of his father's chocolate shop. And without knowing how, by some odd connection, he recalled Pachico watching the partisans of Santa Cruz.

This state of mind was something genuinely ancient, something authentically characteristic, something which, reflecting the hills and forests, lent life to the vague ideal of the people's Carlism. They constituted a band, not the embryo of an impossible army. These forces seemed to grow out of the turbulent times of factional warfare, of war between armed bands.

Long live Santa Cruz! Long live the priest Santa Cruz! Long live religion!

133

"Is he the one on horseback?" Ignacio asked.

"No, that's the secretary. Santa Cruz is the one beside him, the one with the staff."

Santa Cruz was a man of narrow forehead, brown hair, fair beard, and a taciturn countenance. He seemed not to hear the acclamations of the populace, whom he gazed upon with indifference. He was zealously intent on shepherding his flock, leaning on a long staff, and with no weapon but a revolver under his ash-colored jacket. His tucked-up blue breeches revealed the legs of an indefatigable hiker, and he was wearing only rope-soled sandals.

Amidst the cries of "Long live Santa Cruz! Long live religion! Long live the *fueros*!" there was heard a shameless "Down with Lizárraga!" The priest, meanwhile, paid no attention and watched over his own men.

That afternoon they were privileged to hear about the priest's feats from the mouths of his own volunteers. There was no one braver than he, nor more clever, nor as good, nor more considerate, nor more serious than Santa Cruz. He was a man of few words, who walked by himself for hours. When he gave an order, there was not a lad who would dare match those eyes in that full-bearded face under a beret, for he was a man who could order someone shot with the greatest calm in the world. No, war simply could not be waged in the manner of the saintly Lizárraga, with poultices and novenas. One's own blood must be saved, and never mind the enemy's blood. Be forewarned, and be wary! If they did not put their enemies in front of a firing squad, they would find *themselves* up against a firing squad. The priest always gave the necessary orders for the best of reasons, and he always allowed the condemned man half an hour to put himself right with God. It was his custom to explain to his young soldiers the reason for the punishment. This one was shot because he lost those men; another, because his treason resulted in the loss of several others; and that woman, because four men were captured on her account. When he asked the boys if they were satisfied with the verdict, they would call out, "Yes, sir!" And the discipline was done simply. Poor carabineros! It did no good for them to shout weeping "Long live Carlos VII!" It was too late.

"Do you all remember," said one of the lads, "when we took that second lieutenant prisoner, and he was recognized? Santa Cruz asked him, 'Are you the one who spat in my face when I was caught with Arrézola?' The lieutenant answered, 'Yes, I was the one.' And the priest said to us, 'Take him to the crossroads and . . . four shots.' We let him get drunk and when we got to the crossroads and he was most relaxed we put three shots into his head."

And that man who sowed terror would preach to them in a way that brought tears to their eyes when he spoke of warfare.

"He must speak to you of religion . . ."

"Santa Cruz doesn't go in for religion, he goes in for war," someone said.

They went in for war, and they were doing well at it. They went their several ways, came together again, ate and drank well. The villagers brought out bread and wine and meat, and sometimes Santa Cruz ordered that his men be given coffee, cigars, liquor, and ten reales a day as long as the contributors were able. He was the one and only in command: below him, everyone was equal, bore the same arms, and carried out the same tasks. A common soldier displayed the same courage as an officer, and if the officer went too far in his authority, woe betide him! Many a time in the high woods, as they were seated in a circle, Santa Cruz would force liquor on them, and then invite them to drink again, another round! True enough, he was a hard man, he was hard on those who deserved it, hard on the enemy, but with his own, he was severe but good. He had put a thief before a firing squad, and— better leave women alone! He was inflexible on the matter of going too far with women. He was never known to have shown any weakness himself as regards them, nor did women soften him in any way; he had gone so far as to have a pregnant woman put before a firing squad. There was never a question of being surprised serving under such a man, either, for he was ever on the alert. He slept out in the open, spending the night on the balcony of whatever priest's house he was staying in, and kept everyone on their feet. One of the lads recalled a night when, on sentry duty and nodding off, he was awakened as from a nightmare, with trembling heart, by a voice which called out, "Eusebio!" He shook even more in front of the priest, who said only, "Watch out for the next time!" Sleep was no longer tempting.

No one was privy to the headman's plans. He would receive his many confidants, and would then issue orders for a march no man knew where. They would follow him over hill and dale and through canebrakes and into canyons, with the snow sometimes up to their knees, cursing, damning, even threatening the elements, and he always up in front with his stout staff: "On, on! Forward!" He was so sure of himself that he knew that if he threw himself over a precipice all the men behind would follow him, still cursing. What would they do without him? And thus he wore down the

enemy and the four columns of Miqueletes who were
sent to track him down, his head having a price on it.

After all was said and done, it was an amusing life
they led. The burning down of that railroad station
had been lovely—and even lovelier to see the locomotive reduced to rubble! The train was of the greatest
help to the other side. Trains, an invention of Lucifer,
impeded the development of the war. They were the
enemy, a potent means of Liberalization. What a pleasure to destroy those objects, to see them made into
rubble! Let them make new ones! And when they
heard the King was about to make a pact with the
railroad company, one of the lads spoke out: "The
King and an agreement. The King is just another
temporizer. . . . Just that! He's appointed Commandant General of Guipúzcoa that churchling who is not
even from Guipúzcoa. . . . We all know what the King
wants. . . . The only man among us is Don Manuel
de Santa Cruz. Who are the *guiris* afraid of? What a
small price they've put on the King's head! The chiefs
don't want us because they want to compromise and
dilly-dally. Battles . . . campaigns . . . a great big stew!
They sit and laugh. . . . The thing to do is to wear
them out, arouse them, make life hard for them, and
when they come down on us, we'll simply disappear
like quicksilver, scatter and join up our forces later,
and make life harder for them still. We'll wear them
out. Lizárraga would like to take the lads away from
Santa Cruz, and hand us over. . . . He wants our cannon. . . . They've got plenty to keep them amused with
the one they captured at Eraul!"

"But that's not how to make war . . ."

"It's the way Cabrera began, before he had enough
men to show his face."

Shortly after this exchange, they caught sight of the

priest. A mother was pointing him out to her son, and an old woman crossed herself at his sight. The entire town followed him with eyes full of tenderness and love. They loved this man who was the vessel of their frustrations, this son of the fields who, overfed and living an idle life in a village and denied any relationships of the flesh, had let his excess of life force escape in acts of ice-cold cruelty.

He was a man of an earlier time, leading a medieval horde. Ignacio was stirred to his roots, to the history he bore at the depth of his soul where the spirit of his forefathers slept.

They spent a week running from town to town, entire days in the canebrakes and brambles, and all this running hither and yon was beginning to wear on Ignacio. He seemed to have seen every new landscape a hundred times before, so that even change became monotonous. Always the same hillsides, the eternal oaks and chestnuts, the unending ferns, the unvarying heather, and the ever-present flowering gorse, whose flower was like golden frost. This was the hard fact of the mountain woods, not Ignacio's dream of it. But, then, whenever they reached the heights and they halted to rest, with the sight of the valleys at their feet, their spirits would soar and their breasts would fill with a new kind of fresh air.

Finally, he found the battalion to which he was assigned and reported to the head man, who had him put into uniform and promoted him to sergeant upon learning that he was the nephew of Don Emeterio, the priest.

They composed a band of some one hundred and thirty men, poorly armed with English flintlock rifles. Among the members of the new outfit, he found old friends including the student who had been at the wedding and some youths from his father's village. He was now uniformed in a gray coat, red trousers, and a white beret.

There was talk of the new forward thrust which was due, of the Cantonalism which tied the hands of the central government at Madrid, of the lack of discipline of the government army, of the disorders in Bilbao, and again, of the Carlist victory at Eraul, of the surprise of Mataró in Catalonia, and finally of the fact that they were going to join forces with the main part of the army, the King's army, the embryo of the definitive army, that very afternoon.

They were advancing along the main highway, between high mountains covered with forest, when they heard a far-off sound of troops and then, around a sudden turn in the road, the sight of them: "There they are!" Some four thousand men were coming towards them; Ignacio's small band of troops joined them in their flight.

The raggle-taggle mass they had joined was like a giant undulating serpent. Hauling the cannon captured at Eraul, it was now in full flight from the enemy. The men all wore the talisman saying "Stop, bullet! The Sacred Heart of Jesus is with me!" Their flying feet scarcely made a sound, since they were all wearing rope-soled sandals.

Over that living mass two standards waved: the flags of the First and the now-famous Second battalions of Navarre. On the first was proclaimed the Immaculate Conception of Mary, with the national colors and the words "God, Country, King." Its reverse showed St. Joseph against a green background. On the dusty white silk of the second flag another "Immaculate" shone in the sun, its reverse side bearing the red cross of St. James, the patron saint of Spain, and his motto: "St. James and have at them!" Watching the sweet Virgin and her most gentle husband dominating that horde of warriors, Ignacio remembered the skull on Santa Cruz's flag and couldn't help thinking that his flag was more genuine, more fitting, and more manly. He recalled what Pachico had once told him about the Papal Guards who marched in martial arrogance through the leafy promenades of Rome to the applause of the cardinals. Pachico had said that some sentimental priest should write a book about their exploits; illustrated with fancy steel engravings, it would bring tears on winter evenings to its soft-hearted and childish readers. "What a difference between these little gentlemen and mercenaries dressed in opera costumes and those manly Chouans in royalist Brittany or those counter-revolutionary Vendée farmers who stood up to the great French Revolution!"

The multitudes which came out to receive them told them that they were close to Lequeitio. The outcry was great, and the hurrahs drowned one another. The people wanted to see, touch, and kiss the cannon captured at Eraul.

Lizárraga approached his men of Guipúzcoa. At his order, beneath the waving banners of the Virgin Immaculate, the mighty voice of the crowd swelled up in the hymn to St. Ignatius of Loyola, the knightly saint, Christ's knight. The music seemed to want to scale the heavens in order to fall in a fuller and more solemn cascade back to the earth and then lose itself in the unceasing noise of the sea and the eternal silence of the mountains. The people cheered the troops who were advancing to the beat of the hymn to the captain of the Jesuits. Ignacio felt his soul expanding in his chest, and as the wind off the immense sea played across his body he dreamed that they were marching like this into his town, his Bilbao, and that Rafaela was waving a white kerchief at him from her balcony.

They scattered to look around the town for billets, and then they went to look at the sea, to watch the waves break against the shore. Ignacio stared out over the vast liquid plain, dreaming idly of lands beyond the clean line of the horizon. He would have liked to ship out, if he could, to find adventure, to see new worlds, to get to know new people with exotic customs and tastes, to live a full and rich life. Facing the immense and monotonous sea which concealed such a wealth of marvels that it drove him to a frenzy of fantasy, he thought of Sinbad the sailor and his stupendous adventures.

The call to prayer sounded. Surrounded by the multitudes, the troops from Guipúzcoa drew into formation in the plaza, presided over by their devout chief. They all said the rosary together. The weak voice of the chaplain was heard from time to time, and then came the massive inarticulate swell of the crowd like a sea. The litany was called out, to be answered by the long-drawn-out hissing of the *Ora pro nobis*, which carried over into the first part of the *Agnus Dei*. When the litany was over, the crowd took another breath, seemed to swell up, and once again hurled at the heavens the hymn which went on to dissolve in the monotonous and eternal litany of the immense sea.

Watching Lizárraga, Ignacio recalled the saying about Santa Cruz: "He doesn't go in for religion, he goes in for war." What secret motive caused the rancor between the warrior-priest and the devout general, between the terrorist priest and the military man who believed in rosary beads?

How many different sorts of people served under the white flag! Pious crusaders with pure souls, former members of the Congregation of St. Luis Gonzaga; hereditary Carlists, the sons of the verterans of 1833; boys attracted by an adventurous life of which they knew nothing, all of them anxious to be heroes; aristocratic libertines; sons of noble families who had run away from home, some of them having fled their parents' reaction to the disasters of June; deserters; adventurers from everywhere who swarmed around like drones around a hive; people bent on vengefulness against others; some who were paid for the blood they spilled; some who wanted revenge for a sister who had been seduced by someone on the other side; quite a few who were attracted by nostalgia for combat—but most were there without knowing why they were there. Some were there merely because others went. Some were there out of despair, some out of sheer brutality, and a goodly number so that they could live without regular work. The sons of ancient nobility—the Mugica family, the Avendaño clan, the house of Butrón, vultures who centuries before had laid waste to the entire countryside, challenging the towns who, like octopuses, were sucking away some of the benefits of the lands the aristocrats preyed on—now directed their armed peasant followers once again to harry the townsfolk, the sons of commerce. The stilled voice of dead centuries of ancient feuds was here brought back to life.

That whole popular movement surging out of the depths of the people, out of the formless and protoplasmic mass from which nations are made, all that movement rising up out of the people—would it be possible to mold that mass into a military pattern, into the cadres of a nationalist militia, to systematize those

armies which had grown out of the forging of nationalities? Would it be possible to subject that mass to
the disciplinary hierarchy, to a subordination from grade
to grade, without a single gap in the order? To turn
those bands into an army, to make a well-defined program out of their inarticulate aspirations?

Did they know where they were going, where they
came from, and by what spirit they were impelled?

The insurrection had already grown to formidable
proportions, and it was gaining ground, especially in
the old kingdoms of Aragon, León, and Navarre. Daring men raised armed followers and made themselves
their natural chiefs, restricting their fighting to their
own home territory. And thus, little by little and from
below upward, like vegetation taking over the ground,
the Carlist insurrection was formed, while federal Cantonalism strove to resist from the industrial cities of
the Spanish Levant.

The makeshift unity of Spain was torn to shreds
once again: the sons of the Pyrenees and of the Ebro
River turned against the spirit of the Castilian table-
land.

That night Ignacio and his comrades heard the story
of Eraul, that victory gained by the boys who had
rushed into combat against the opinion of their chief.
It had been a victory of enthusiasm and lack of discipline. It filled them with ardor to hear tell of those
bayonet charges, while Lizárraga cried out "Long live
God! War on hell and its satellites!" and the young
men ran into battle yelling, "Long live God! Let us
at them!" What enthusiasm the men from Navarre had
for Radica, their chief! They loved the leaders who
came up out of the people, not those imposed by the
King, those leaders who had to prove themselves the

bravest to justify their posts and save their prestige. On the other hand, they grumbled about Dorregaray, the commander in chief, that phantasm who put on airs with his great beard and his arm in a sling.

Everyone was now contented and hopeful. With their enthusiasm they had captured the cannon from the enemy, thanks to an unforeseen charge. The unforeseen! Is not the unforeseen the decisive factor in war as it ought to be?

In their huddles the boys spoke about the motives which had made them take to the hills.

"I was about to go to America," one said. "When you marched by, my father called me and said to me, 'Farming is no good, times are hard. You know that the family is large and our land small. The passage to America costs money. . . . Get along now! Go off to war and learn how to live!' What more could I want?"

"Well, my people didn't want me to go at first, but as everyone was going, every day someone else, I couldn't be left to be the last man there. . . . I wanted to go where others dared. . . . My grandfather told me, 'If you only knew what this means . . . !' When I'm a grandfather—provided we get through this—I'll say the same."

"In my case, they looked on me as a tramp because I wanted to go."

"Well, I'll tell you the truth, I prefer this kind of life, even if it is rough, to working regularly for a living. As it is, we don't even know where we'll sleep tomorrow, nor where we'll be, nor what will become of us. . . . And then, we get to see a bit of the world."

They were all impelled by the primitive instincts of the wandering predatory life, instincts which welled up in them from the immutable source of inner being where dwells the soul of the souls of the remotest ancestors.

Ignacio was soon up to his ears in the monotony of the nomadic life of the battalion. Everything was regulated. That wasn't war, it was the office job all over again. And there was constant griping. One man grumbled about everything; another made up to his chief; one of the volunteers never tired of repeating to one of those who had been pressed into service that it made him ineligible to change to some other battalion. Half a dozen Castilians, renegades from the regular army, ate by themselves apart, disdaining the rest of the company. The worst of it all was that no one had any experience of warfare, any exploit, to talk about.

Ignacio, while he dealt with everyone, had made no special friends; he could not truly call even one man friend. Though they were all joined together in a fighting force, something nevertheless separated them. Come together in a united cause, each man lived within himself and for himself. Concurring in a common action, they remained each in his own little world, his spirit impenetrable. Something made them children again and reawakened in them all the small envies and jealousies and petty wrangles of childhood. At the same time, what a breath of fresh childhood in games and innocent diversions! What a pleasure it was when, formed into a chorus of four or five, they would intone the popular old songs, singing with a wavy rhythm, in cadences as monotonous as the very mountains: always the same in their incessant variety!

From his father's letters Ignacio learned that Gambelu proposed to join the Carlist camp in search of civil employment; that Don Eustaquio went walking with an ex-seminarian, who feared lest the Carlists

might put him back in the very same monastery; that
Don José María was frequenting the French frontier,
and that he and Josefa Ignacia would soon be leaving
Bilbao.

During the month of June, ever since parting from
the victors of Eraul, they spent their time in marches
and counter-marches. Once Ignacio passed through his
father's village, where a *romería* was taking place.

His aunt Ramona was at the door to greet him, and
seeing him in military outfit, did not dare suggest he
change. His uncle embraced him and, taking him aside,
he made clear that it would be "inconvenient" to put
him up in the same house as the battalion commander.
Ignacio went off to his cousin Toribio's house; it was
the same Toribio whose wedding he had attended.
The newly married couple already had a child, who
was bawling in his crib, while his parents sweated
away working the land. They were totally in the dark
about any such thing as a war and absolutely innocent
about the course of history. For their part, there could
be war just as there might be a thundershower, or a
year of drought, or an epidemic among the livestock.
The Blacks were to blame for everything! The worst
aspect of warfare was the levies made on their stocks
in order to provide rations, the slow sacking of the
peaceful farmers' granaries. They failed to understand
a whit about the blackness of the Blacks, or the whiteness of the Whites.

What a world! What a world of mysteries out there
beyond the horizon, beyond the peaceful green fields
which were subject to the uneven mercy of the open
air under the eternally silent mountains! What a world
of cities, where men thought only of undoing whatever
was already done and of changing the eternal round
of things!

At the *romerías*, to which all the young people from the surrounding areas came, it was they, the irregulars, who were the heroes of the fiesta. Girls came from the adjoining village and hamlets dressed in their Sunday best, and they lined up with smiling aplomb waiting to be asked to dance. The blonde country girl with the cowlike eyes saw Ignacio in a different light, now that he was a soldier. In one of the dances, he saw to it that she was invited to join. There she was, solemn and serious, between two escorts, in a scene capturing all the serenity of the open fields. He played up to her with agile and flashy pirouettes, while she did not take her huge eyes off her dancing feet. What leaps! What energy! Let them see if there was a like pair of legs present, or such a chest, such a soul! The ceremonious weaving of the traditional dance turned into a dance of caprice. And Ignacio danced without pause, beside himself as he realized that of all the dancers he was the center of attention, as well as her real partner. At the dance's end, his comrades applauded him and he took the girl's hand. He pulled her towards him roughly so they could bump against each other amid cries and genial laughter. Then they danced a Basque ring-dance, everyone joining in its ceaseless whirl.

The shrill sound of the pipes rose over the monotonous beat of the drum, as those men had risen over the monotony of their hours. The music Ignacio could hear was merely the accompaniment to the dance, but the dance itself was the body's music. Ignacio's limbs lost their numbness. He grew drunk on the air. His vision of the countryside was blotted out, and he took full pleasure in his energy and in the health of his body. The pure joy of his own movements drove him to cry out, while the girl, serene and solemn, smiling at his contortions, danced rhythmically and ritually, with liturgical gravity, like a tree shaken by the wind's rigid cadence.

There in the open air on the green field among the serene mountains, dance attained all its deep meaning as a hymn to the movements of the body, a primal striving for rhythm, and a living fountain of grace. That dance, there in the village, was the purification of work, a burnt offering of human energy. Except in the freedom of the dance, how could bodies bent over the hard earth, and arms and legs aching from toil, find their refreshment? And how could the guerrillas express better their protest against the marches and counter-marches down stony roads and paths where they dared not take their eyes off the ground? What refreshment is found in the dance!

Ignacio invited the girl to a drink and then, as the day darkened, he was determined to take her home to her farmhouse. They walked the country roads enjoying the calm air of that time of day. From time to time they encountered another couple, a boy walking along with his arm around a girl's waist, and sometimes two girls walking with a boy between them. In a dance of the voice, the young people filled the air with shouts of joy which echoed across the foothills. As they came to a branch in the footpath Ignacio quickened his step to be alone with his companion, somewhat apart from others. In a sudden impulse he grabbed her and planted a kiss on her apple-red cheek.

"Stop it, stop it now!" she cried out, and ran back to the company of her girl friends. There she gave out a long and vibrant yell which cut through the serene twilight air and echoed in Ignacio's head like a shout of both victory and mockery, a strident sound out of life's plenitude.

When she was close to her place, the blonde turned

back to Ignacio and shouted out *"Eskerrik asko,"* Basque for "Many thanks." She ran for home, and Ignacio heard a yell: *"Bilbotarra, choriburu, moskorra dau-kazu?"* "Bilbao man, hare-brained, are you drunk?" And then, a little later: *"Agur, anebia!"* "Goodbye, brother!"

Ignacio did, in fact, return to camp inebriated from the countryside and the dance. He felt the blood puls-ing in his head, and he breathed in the breath of the earth like an aphrodisiac. The bugle—late, this special night—sounded retreat, and Ignacio returned to mo-notonous reality. So this was being at war? This was war? And battle? when did that take place?

Everything came down to marches and counter-marches, running around the hamlets surrounding the district capital on muddy paths in persistent rain, evad-ing the enemy. It was a game of hide-and-seek.

The rain drenched Ignacio's spirit with sadness, and as it swept in across the fields in wavering indecision it seemed to suffer in silence. Ignacio passed through his father's village again and caught sight of the blonde, who waved at him with a handkerchief from her farm-house. He thought then of Rafaela in Bilbao, imagining his entry into the city.

One afternoon he helped an old man who had slipped and fallen. The poor old fellow, half-paralyzed, turned to him with his eyes brimming with tears and thanked him in halting Castilian. He said that if a bullet were to hit Ignacio he hoped it would not seriously wound him; either that, or that it would kill him rather than causing him to lose an arm or a leg, rendering him useless for work.

"I'd rather stay alive and crippled than die."

The old man shook his head. "Short a leg, no. Short

an arm, no. All in one piece, all in one piece . . . and if not all in one piece, dead. Man can't work, no good. . . . In the way, just in the way!"

And he went off limping, while Ignacio watched. The crippled man seemed bent permanently in the posture of someone spading the earth.

He repeated the old man's words to himself, "If not all in one piece, dead." Was it possible he himself might be left crippled, broken, useless—he, Ignacio, a strong, sound youth? His sense of his own healthiness kept such imaginings from his conscious thinking, but they descended into the deepest layer of his spirit, where the sorrows of war were building up, where everlasting disillusionment was being nourished.

The war's monotony was interrupted when Ignacio was sent off with some other soldiers to recruit men between the ages of eighteen and forty in the small hamlets of the region. They found one man hiding in a silo, and it proved hopeless to pry him out, even with the exhortations of the chaplain in the party. Some fathers refused at first to hand over their sons, but the chaplain lectured and threatened them until they finally yielded. Others handed over a son as the adornment of their house. They would have to emigrate to America otherwise anyway, since these families were too large; let them go off and learn to live. There were still plenty of women, old men, and oxen. In any case, Bilbao must be taken.

In a few of the farmhouses, there were tears and lamentations and long kisses by the mother; but at most places the men and boys would come forth with a certain gravity as if merely doing their duty. At one place the mother herself went to fetch her son, and she took leave of him saying, "Go for the sake of religion, even if it means dying."

They mostly came out without a murmur, serious of mien, like sons dutifully coming forth to be married to the girl their parents had picked. The principal consideration in most places was the loss of a farm hand before the seasonal work was done, before the threshing was accomplished. Sometimes the fathers had to go in place of the sons.

On the way back to camp, Ignacio had a strange experience while leading the levy. One of the conscripts bolted and ran into the planted fields; a volunteer aimed his rifle at him, but Ignacio stopped him from firing, "Let him go. He'll be back on his own." And the runaway did just that: he came back by himself, filled with shame and fear.

The towns swarmed with recruits, who ambled around in groups, striving to appear joyous, or even indifferent, devil-may-care.

All over Vizcaya the levy was exacted among the men of silence and toil.

Then came the marches and counter-marches, in escaping from an enemy column. Some of the men got lost along the paths in the dark. Weary with walking, they regained their morale along the heights of Bizcargui at the sight of the green valleys slumbering in the sunlight, contemplating the petrified waves of the mountains under a radiant sky. There, down there below the range of mountains, lay Bilbao, and in Bilbao the little nest where Ignacio had been born, a place of shade and rest.

The enemy column had gone, its pitiful troops unable to put down the rustics, while the irregulars had the entire countryside to feed on.

Ignacio received a new pair of shoes and a little money with a letter from home. Pedro Antonio was of a mind to leave Bilbao, where the volunteers of the Republic were beginning to arm, but at the same time he was convinced that the insurgents were a mere handful who would be undone with a wave of a wand.

On the other hand, a general picture was painted calculated to raise the Carlist spirit: the country was said to be going to pieces, and the Republican army was pillaging, assassinating, and raping at San Quirse de Basora. They were already beaten anyway, an army which taunted its officers, while they, the Carlists, the Crusaders of God, Fatherland, and King, were merely waiting for the King to cross the frontier. The Carlist troops, levied by force, demanded arms instead of the wooden guns they were issued; wherever they were convinced that real rifles would not arrive, they threatened to go home.

Stubborn and resistant as clods of earth, they were like the earth, too, in that once they had been plowed, they were passive, resigned to having their roots torn up, and understanding only blind resistance or meaningless aggression.

Volunteers! These men who had been forcefully torn from their woods and mountains turned out to be truer volunteers—in the sense that they gave their wills to their task—than the violent men of the city. Their will was the will of active resignation, something of more substance than the will of turbulent imagination.

It was raining hard when they arrived at the inlet of the bay where the smuggled arms had been put ashore and hidden. There, at the foot of an enormous dark rock which seemed about to fall into the sea, they were issued their arms amid great excitement. They took the covers which were wrapped around the guns and used them as shelter from the storm. Persistent and stubborn, the rain went on lashing the sea.

Two thousand five hundred rifles were distributed among three battalions.

They instantly became other men. They marched back to the village with their rifles pressed to their chests, giving thanks to God for the luck of the smuggled arms.

"The marching back and forth is over now," Ignacio said to himself. "The war has begun."

The newly armed men were received with festivities. The Republic was going from bad to worse, and the Cause was on the up. The forts of the Basque region fell into their hands while the enemy regrouped. There was word of a surprise ambush of an enemy column in Catalonia, of the imminent arrival of the King in the country, and of the battalions from Vizcaya in Bilbao.

In a solemn religious service the new weapons were presented to the God of the Armies. When the rifles were offered up in the pious act, the chaplain elevated the Host in bloodless sacrifice to the Archangel St. Michael, "the supreme prince of the principalities of heaven, captain of the archangelic militia, and defender of Christian armies," who was asked to defend Carlos VII as he had defended Hezekiah against the power of the Assyrians when he slaughtered one hundred and eighty five thousand of the enemy in a single night. They asked that the Archangel vouchsafe them the same zeal as was vouchsafed King Josiah; that he endow them with the confidence of King Josiah, the wisdom of Solomon, the courage of David, and the piety of Hezekiah; further, that he send, in their favor and aid, the celestial squadrons he had sent in aid of

Elisha and Jacob; all in the service of Jesus Christ and
His greater glorification by one and all in the universal
peace of the Church. The people and the assembled
battalion responded to this prayer by mechanically repeating, "Forgive us our trespasses as we forgive those
who have trespassed against us."

That same day, the feast day of Our Lady of Carmen
and the anniversary of the triumph of Santa Cruz at
Navas de Tolosa as well as of the beheading of friars
in '34, Don Carlos entered Spain to repair the damage
done by the disaster of Oroquieta. He entered the country at the same point his grandfather had thirty-nine
years before, by way of Zugarramurdi, the scene of
infernal witches' sabbaths in the past.

A Te Deum was sung. General Lizárraga preached,
followed by the parish priest. A rosary was said for
the friars beheaded in '34, at the time of the plague,
and the soldiers shouted out "Long live the King!" in
answer to "Long live Spain!" from the King from the
heights of Hachuela. They said three Ave Marias to
Our Lady of the Angels of Pourvorville, and then the
King strolled among the ranks of his soldiers, mingled
with them, and then and there freed seventy-five prisoners from Eraul.

Meanwhile, Ignacio was beginning to get his bear-
ings. In all the marching back and forth, he had forgotten all about his ideas. Carrying out his duty, he
simply waited for war. Ideas? Where were they now?
Where he was now, no one spoke of ideas or of principles. Once in action, everything had been turned into
movement, and ideas all boiled down to a personal
matter for him alone. Transformed into action, they
converged all around him in pure action which en-
gendered new ideas of its own. "Principles" had merely
been the bait to lure him and others into a war to fulfill

a mission still hidden in the mystery of the future. Ignacio one night remembered how Pachico had said that both sides were right and that neither was right, that victory alone decided who was right. But when they all set off at dawn, he felt himself to be a part of the whole, part of the mass: reality took over, living reality. The enemy: there was the final meaning. The enemy? And who was the enemy? Why, the Enemy! The Other!

Three days after the King's entry into the country, three battalions, one of them Castilian, were emplaced along with Ignacio's on the heights of Lamíndano, above the hamlet of Villaro, in the rough overgrown valley of Arratia, ready to take on an enemy column which was based in the village, between the road and a hill.

They were finally to enter combat. Ignacio thought of everything but of dying. Die? He felt strong, and he felt a need to win and go on living. Death was still an abstract idea. The fullness of his health made him unfit to comprehend death.

Two companies were detailed to attack a bridge, and Ignacio remained with the rest. A Castilian outfit was deployed to the enemy's right and center. They all felt they had to shine in front of the Castilians, not to be inferior to them in any way.

Around three in the afternoon firing broke out, and the enemy advanced under the protection of an artillery barrage. When Ignacio heard the whistling sound of ammunition over his head, his heart suddenly felt chill. He felt around for the medallion his mother had sewn for hours and hours out of the materials of her soul, with its prayer to stop a bullet. At the first sound of a shower of bullets, the landscape liquified in his sight and his body grew weak. He was paralyzed with a chilling fear by the subtle whistling sounds, like invisible snakes in the air. In the stone-throwing battles of his youth, he could see the enemy, the boy who threw the stone, and he could watch its trajectory. But here? The enemy was far off, scarcely more than a confused movement in the bush, nothing to hate in some concrete way. This warfare was something cold, mechanical, and businesslike, something which proceeded by formula. It was a lie: a true lie.

Compared to the high-spirited spontaneity of a childish stone-throwing contest, what a farce this was! What an empty illusion that turned to dust at the slightest touch! The very size of the field of combat made it seem meaningless.

The whistling sounds of the bullets continued, commonplace things that seemed to do no damage at all.

At the cry of "Fire!" they charged the enemy's right wing. Thrown into disarray and having lost its position in the woods, the enemy retreated to a hermitage. Meanwhile the men who had been sent to take the bridge returned, without having taken it.

When Ignacio heard the order to attack, he went forward with the men around him. The heather and fern were obstacles which caught him up constantly. Once near the hermitage's portico, Ignacio found himself surrounded by Castilians led by an officer from the other battalion.

They fell back, held for a spell, and then went forward again. But why had they fallen back? Why the holding action? Why the new advance? Ignacio looked around and could see the enemy close by. Seeing some enemy troops fleeing even as they fired back, he ran after them. This was now the third charge they had made. Ignacio soon found himself on the hermitage grounds but was stopped by a fallen soldier crying out for water. The Castilians pressed on, bayonets fixed, and the enemy force disappeared into the village. And that was all there was to it!

Could that really be called combat? When Ignacio saw the wounded, he began to believe that it had been combat. Around him the men were talking about the action. Vying with the others, the Castilians claimed they had taken the hermitage. Each of them told some detail of the action, some exploit, and Ignacio began to feel a clear sense that he had actually witnessed it all. Little by little he reconstructed the events of the advance, incorporating into his vague impressions of the things he had overheard his own experiences—the shouts he had heard, the way some of those in battle had looked as they fell.

By nightfall he had made his own the legend built up by them all. But once he was alone, everything seemed to blur into an empty dream.

The only things he could remember personally, as lived experience, were the trek through the heather, the wild vegetation holding him back, and the group of soldiers he had seen firing as they retreated.

And they returned to the marches and counter-marches, to crossing through woods and gorges which seemed to be the same ones but might not have been, to the vexed and fatiguing life of campaign. Meanwhile, it was said that the insurrection was taking shape.

At the beginning of August they were en route to Zornoza to join the King, who was making his way toward Guernica.

The noisy tide of people grew by the moment: children, a scattering of women who ran to the head of the crowd, and the cry of "Viva!" rose in a repeated and compact sound.

The figure of the King appeared: a tall, well-built man magnificently astride a beautiful white stallion, his uniform covered with the dust of the campaign, on his head a grand large white beret with a gold pompon; he was surrounded by generals.

As he passed Ignacio's battalion he halted and asked if they were the Lamíndano outfit.

A woman whispered to another, "What a handsome man! But he looks so worn with weariness!"

How beautifully he rode! He was the image of a King, and the people flocked round his throne, wild with excitement. The King! The invisible halo that mysterious word always calls forth surrounded him. The King! Children saw in him the hero of a thousand tales. For their elders he was the focal point of a thousand memories. Intoxicated by the shouts, the cries of "Viva!" and the milling of the crowd, they all gazed up at the great man high above them on his horse.

The battalion escorted him as far as Guernica. All along the way, on the heights, in the dark gorges, on the broad plain, the inhabitants of the scattered houses came down to see the spectacle. Children lined the road, veterans of the Seven Year War came to see the grandson of Charles the Fifth, and women carried their infants in their arms.

Stretching out before them was the peaceful plain of Guernica, a broad lake of mosaic green where the corn waved like whitecaps on the sea, the town nestled against the foothills of Cosnoaga alongside a wall of trees, and the raked and upright coastal peaks pointed to the sky. To their right they could see the noble bald mountain of Oíz, its giant spine bathed in light. Nature received the King indifferently, with neither gesture nor salute.

The entire town turned out for his entry. Some old women wept, some mothers raised their infants high so they might see him, other mothers, with babes in arms, forced their way through the multitude, while their babies squalled. People struggled to kiss his hand, his foot, whatever they could reach, and one woman, who could reach no other part, kissed the tail of the horse which served the King as pedestal. An old woman crossed herself with the two fingers which had just touched the King; another touched him with a long bread loaf which she immediately packed away with avaricious care. The smallest children squirmed in between the legs of their elders or climbed the trees. All the while a prolonged "Viva!" swept through all the people, their eyes fixed on the King, their hearts beating faster.

"What is a king?" asked a child.

And he was answered, "The one who commands above all others."

One voice cried out, "Long live the savior of humanity!"

As Ignacio ran his eyes over the crowd, his eyes lighted by chance on the blonde village girl with the cowlike eyes, who, once she had acknowledged Ignacio, saucily threw back her head, shook out her long hair, and turned her gaze once more upon the King. Ignacio saw Domingo, the farmer, who had left his labors to come for the spectacle, which he watched with a distant look.

"He's so handsome, so handsome!" said the women, both old and young.

One young woman was beside herself, shouting in a loud voice, crying "Viva!" in such a desperate manner, waving her arms about, her eyes sparkling and her cheeks glowing feverishly, that she soon infected some of her companions with her ardor.

"If he were not robust and handsome and not called Carlos but Hipólito instead and was ugly to look at, then 'Goodbye, Legitimacy! Goodbye to the Cause!' " Ignacio heard a familiar voice say nearby. The voice shook him. It was surely Pachico's. Ignacio turned around quickly, but could not see him.

"There's a King for you! Right there! How well the crown would suit him! And the royal mantle!"

"Long live the Lord of Vizcaya!" a stentorian voice shouted above the noise of the crowd's "Vivas!"

Ignacio drew near the church where Basque kings took the oath, by the Tree of Guernica.

"He's going to swear fealty to the Basque statutes, the *fueros*," the people were saying.

"No, not yet," explained one man, "he's going to promise to take the oath as soon as he's seated on the throne."

Don Carlos approached the tree and, in front of the shrine in the shadow of the church, he knelt and prayed. Then he stood up and a general hush prevailed. In the silence, Ignacio could make out only unconnected phrases: ". . . my heart . . . God . . . lack of piety and despotism . . . my beloved Spain . . . noble and honorable people of Vizcaya . . . heroic and loyal earth . . . venerating the Tree, symbol of Christian liberty . . . I promise you . . . my august ancestors . . ." This was followed by resounding cries of "Viva!"

When he had already retired for the night, Ignacio received a visit from Gambelu and Josefa Ignacia. His mother hugged him to her breast and kissed him, and, running her hands over him, asked, "You're not hurt, are you? You don't need anything, do you? Have they done anything to you?"

They spoke of the King. His mother brought Ignacio the sweet remembrance of Bilbao. She seemed to have brought with her the dark and humid atmosphere of his father's chocolate shop.

"Your father wants to close the shop and come here, to be closer to you. He says it's impossible to stand Bilbao any longer. Sweet Jesus, how much longer can this go on? Those Blacks have rocks for souls. They know they cannot hold out, but they go on merely to torment us."

She had decided to come out to the country with Gambelu to see him—after such a long time away! And besides, she would see the King . . . The King! What a powerful figure! That was a King for you! Zeal to see the King had merged with the force drawing her to see her son.

The following day was one of complete joy, for they met Juan José and his mother and they all ate together. Juan José's mother urged them to kill as many of the Black party as possible, while Josefa Ignacia smiled as she gazed at her son, and Gambelu, rubbing his hands, predicted that there would soon be a triumphal entry into Madrid.

Juan José, full of hopes, saw everything in rosy colors, expecting great things from the faith of the Volunteers. He daydreamed about what Spain would be like once Don Carlos was seated on his throne. He spoke wildly of combinations of strategies, developing a complete campaign plan for taking Bilbao within twenty days. He made comparisons with the Prussian siege of Paris and what he called Moltke's tactics. He went on interminably in his critique of the war operations and the organization of the forces.

"Take care of yourself," Ignacio's mother said to him in parting.

Enthusiasm began to soar again, spirits to be lifted. The Liberals were concentrating. Lizárraga had captured several hamlets and was getting ready to take Eibar, the arms industry center, and Vergara, where the Covenant had been signed. Don Carlos had joined forces with Ollo, and everywhere one heard, "On to Bilbao, to Bilbao."

From the heights of Archanda, the scene of his childhood pranks, escapades, and stone-throwing battles, he gazed down on his city one August day. Night had fallen, and he could follow the procession of lamplighters. He thought of the little neighborhood of the Seven Streets, of his father, of his friends, of Rafaela, asking himself, "What are they doing at this moment? The last thing they might be thinking of is me. Just imagine if we were to enter the city tonight." And then: "It was right over there we had a stone-fight, and it was in this very house that we hid for refuge . . ." The house had been burned, and presently a farmer came out of the remains and walked towards them.

"Those *guiris!*" he shouted, shaking his fist at the city below.

"What happened?"

"I've sent for my son, who works our trade in Bilbao, so that he can go off to kill *guiris* . . ."

"Well done!"

"They've burned down all the houses around here," said the farmer, pointing at the ruin of his own house. "There was nothing to be seen but fires all around. The people down there in Bilbao were probably having a good laugh at our expense. . . . They ran up a flag on Morro, the headland. . . . They've built fortifications to fire from. . . . They've burned my house, and we've had to go live at a brother's house in Za-mudio . . ."

He let up for a moment and then shouted, "Bilbao must be burned down!"

Ignacio gazed at the man standing in the night among the ashes of his home and ready to take on Bilbao.

"Bilbao must be burned down! If you could have seen! They made us come out, take out our things and, right here, beside the cart stacked with our furniture, we watched the flames. . . . The poor cows mooed in fright, the calf hid under its mother in fear, the wife and kids cried. The troops paid no attention. 'That'll teach you,' they said. Bilbao must be burned down!"

It was time to settle the long quarrel between the town and the country, between the city and the plain, which made up the sometimes bloody history of Viz-caya. The landed peasantry would once and for all choke the octopus of the city, the distillery which si-phoned off their earnings in taxes. The headquarters of deceit must be burned out.

Down there at their feet, behind a fold in the moun-tain, dominating the city, rose the ancient walls of the castle tower of the Zurbarán clan, testimony to a time of armed brigands, of those rough ancestral chiefs of the plain who resisted with their own bands the for-mation of the towns. That ancient manor house was and remains a monument to the turbulent period when Vizcaya passed from the clan organization of a pastoral society to the civil rule of merchants and towns; from a society governed by custom and tradition to one governed by written laws and the ordinances of com-merce; from the patriarchal household open to every wind to the dark city streets where men are closely packed; from the mountain to the sea.

The long dispute between the rustic and the man of the town, between the man of the mountain and his savings and the man of the sea and his greed, was about to be settled.

And then again began the marches and counter-marches from hamlet to hamlet. Ignacio was fed up with it all.

At the end of the month, a breath of hope animated the ranks. One afternoon, as they entered a small town after a hard day's march, they heard the bells of the church ringing out joyously. A disheveled woman, her eyes red from crying, seized hold of her husband's arm—she had obviously been quarreling with him—and, forgetting her quarrel, cried out: "They've captured Estella. Estella has fallen to us!" She was overcome by the idea and invited everyone to dance: the bystanders were amused by her sudden change from quarreling to wild enthusiasm over victory in a greater quarrel. Women appeared in the doorways of their houses. Estella, the holy city of the Carlists, had been taken.

Estella had fallen, and the Jesuits had been reestablished in Loyola, the birthplace of the Society's founder.

And then when in a few days the battalion was received in triumph in a small coastal town, Ignacio felt that his troop was getting its deserved reward, for it had been the Carlist spirit which had fought and won at Estella; the spirit of all the Volunteers had supported the victors at Allo and Dicastillo. They were all equally members of the victorious army.

At Durango they rested from the marches and counter-marches and used the time to receive instruction and schooling. Pedro Antonio, who was more intent than ever on leaving Bilbao, came for a visit with his son. They were joined by Gambelu, recently named a customs man, and by Don Emeterio, the village priest, who was Pedro Antonio's brother.

Gambelu was delighted with the appearance in the field of Don Castor Andéchaga, now seventy years old, and with his proclamation to the men of Vizcaya: "May the fighters who humbled the power of Rome in these mountains be reborn in their sons, under that sparkling sky where cowardice never made its nest, among the murmurs of those woods where the weak never found refuge and where our hearts beat with courage at the signal of battle from the churchbells in our valleys. Keeping in mind the glories of our ancestors and the ignominious present, may we perish honorably in battle rather than suffer in dishonor violation by a handful of brigands. Our forest can still supply us with iron and wood to arm ourselves with lance and shield. We have right and justice on our side. History is in our favor. Faith makes us live. Hope inspires us, religion protects us, and our fathers will give our sons their blessing." The reading of the proclamation brought forth the ritual chorus of "Viva!"

"This is all very well," exclaimed the priest when he heard the proclamation, "but haven't we done enough preaching war, and putting new life into the weak, without their coming now to take our money with the excuse of a forced levy? All for the Revolution and a *pax Christi*. . . . I don't plan to hand over my funds: that would be an attack on ecclesiastical immunity. . . . We are beginning to be more liberal . . . all we need now is a Mendizábal!"

"He's a priest after all," said Gambelu. "So hang on to your funds, so that the war effort may die of consumption. The Liberals will take care of you and your Masses. . . ."

"Of consumption? May God send you a good case

of consumption! . . . Communion at Loyola, and the consecration of the King, canary seeds! . . . Silly little generals, one gaga from old age, another from pure piety, another a big phantom, and in Loyola a lot of hypocritical protocol: everyone talking about their new posts, whether he'll get to go here, there or somewhere else. . . . What we need is Santa Cruz . . ."

"This is the way it went on last time! . . . May everything work out in God's own way!" murmured Pedro Antonio.

In point of fact, the insurrection was beginning to ferment. It was rumored that two generals refused to shake each other's hand; that another general, under the spell of his mistress, invented fictitious feats in order to climb in rank.

Like many of the men of Vizcaya, Ignacio looked to the knight-errant, the seventy-year-old Don Castor, armed with the iron of his mountains and the wood from his forests, with his gaze fixed on Bilbao. As he thought of him, he also entertained visions from his nebulous world of Oliveros, with his forearm bloody to his elbow; of Arthur of the Algarve, locked in combat with the monstrous dragon with arms like lizards, the wings of a bat, and a tongue of fire; of Charlemagne and his twelve peers laying about them with naked steel upon the enemy's turbans and coats of mail; of the Cid Ruy Díaz; of Cabrera, riding his horse with white cape flying behind; of all the magical figures roughly carved in wood.

"I'm doing my duty," he would tell himself in periods of depression. "Let the others settle with their own consciences. The enemy may well be stronger. It doesn't matter! I must fight on—and never mind winning. Let them win if it be God's will that they win."

And he would dream that everything depended on himself, that his effort was the one that counted, and that there had often been unknown heroes who had fought for lost causes. "If I were only a general now!" And he wove fantasies of how he would conduct matters if he were: he drew up plans, actions, and battles, but then it would all end in vain and insignificant dialogues with the King, or in domestic scenes with Rafaela.

Was all this really war? Marches, counter-marches, then again new marches and counter-marches, the day of the great battle nowhere in sight. Waiting for the grand climax, he would anxiously await nightfall and the quick sleep which would bring the supreme day closer.

Meanwhile, the simple-minded Pedro Antonio thought and thought about what would become of his money. He recalled sacrificing part of his savings in the enterprise of raising Carlist capital, which made him feel justified but not satisfied. The poor man was at his wits' end. He could not penetrate to the heart of the mystery, to the terrifying and occult power which served the Carlist uprising to grasp its prey and maintain its own life. He attributed everything that went wrong to the Masons and their Invisible Valley, the symbol of everything infernal and mysterious.

Who but the Masons had brought the Seven Year War to an end? Who but the Masons, through their hidden manipulations, had brought about the desire for sweet peace after so much hard warfare, after their treachery had rendered vain the best efforts of the Carlists? It was clear that no human power, no open and clear force, could have beat them; there existed, then, some occult and mysterious power, against which all courage and bravery came to nought.

167

The battalion escorted the King in a tour of his domains. Finally they arrived at Estella, the holy city of Carlism, and the city received them in joyous turmoil. It was around Estella that the Carlists were continually being forced to carry on the war and establish their hold. For days the two armies marched and counter-marched, making the round in a continuous dance and contradance: they would inflict some slight wounds and then come together as whole units again; they struck like fighting cocks with their beaks and then backed away to stand upright.

They spent about a month around Estella, in drill and military maneuvers, and Ignacio regained some of his calm after the grueling field excercises. He met up with Celestino and, when he hailed him with a "Hello!" the other retorted with a "Stand at attention!" The blood rose in Ignacio's head and he said in Celestino's ear, "Go to hell!"

Celestino, red with shame and guilt, went off without a word. Ignacio was left with a sense of heavy disquiet, filled with vague fears. That night he listened without much understanding to Gambelu, now installed at Estella, complain at the course events were taking, which augured a bad result. His ears were also battered from hearing the customs agent's song:

> What do I care whether
> there's peace or war;
> a land-pirate is what I am.
> . . .
> I count out the pieces of eight—
> "Long live religion!"

"Is it possible that the incompetents running war think that you can fight without money, or that pesetas are to be sown like seed corn? Land-pirates indeed!

As if a war was waged only by those who dodged bullets? 'To the right, march! Battalion stand firm! Fire!' and then out with the money, and whoever gathers the funds is a land-pirate, and has to have his palm greased. . . ."

In the town, now become home for the Carlist forces, everyone's reaction to the campaign became more defined as each man exchanged his impressions with others. Legends were buttressed, complaints against the command were widespread, and above all, everyone gambled.

There Ignacio began to get some idea of the diverse personalities of his comrades and to find some for friends. One afternoon when all was quiet, he learned that the war had given freedom of choice to one comrade who had been a seminarian when he took the field. His parents had obliged him to study for the priesthood, but it was only his mother who felt a sense of true vocation—the vocation of being a priest's housekeeper. "To have a priest for a son, to keep his belongings in order, to take care of his money, and then to play the part of his mother when he preached the Sunday sermon—these were all surpassingly sweet! To have him always at home, and to have no chores other than those of an old mother, to have a priest for a son—here is the comforting rod and staff for old age. And besides, the other children would have in him an uncle for their children, someone to dry their tears. And especially, could there be a truly well-off family without one member to give it status and importance by being a priest? Priestly celibacy is perfect for the mother's vocation." The boy was not interested and went into the seminary against his inclinations; but he gave in to his parents because, after all, what difference did it really make to him? But now, once out in the field of action, a free man, his true character came out in all its nakedness.

"Come now, Diegochu," the men would taunt him, "didn't you have a woman last night?"

And then, rubbing his hands, he would recount the usual gallant adventure, with a maid, or the daughter of a household—almost all of it pure invention. A soldier is a bird of passage in time of war: women liked the brave lads because, quickly forgetting their conquests, they would not be bandying their names about the marketplace, and they would display discretion towards a feminine conquest.

"Too many lads will die in this damned war," Diegochu would say, ending his narrative of adventures with a moral. "We must show our hand. Take the case of Domingo here: he was going to get married in a few days and he came to camp thinking it was all a matter of batting his eyes open and shut. . . . His girl is waiting for him."

"Bah, this will all be over in quick order and, as soon as we lick them, I'll stick my head in the noose. In the meantime, it's a matter of killing *Blacks* . . ."

"And then turning people into Whites. And you, mama's boy," he called out to a youngster who was trying to hide himself, "come on now, as if we didn't know what happened between you and the maid when you were out making hay together . . ."

"Let him be," said Ignacio.

Amusement increased, when Diegochu's father, a veteran of the Seven Year War, appeared in Estella to visit his son, having walked all the way. The old man wallowed in invidious comparisons: the present war reached his weakened senses only dimly while the green impressions of his youth remained strong. "That was a war, now! Those men were really volunteers! You're a sad lot compared to them! This civil war is over-civilized!"

He would relate the stories of the battle of Oria-mendi, the night of Luchana, the expedition to Madrid. The old man's tales stirred Ignacio's own childhood memories of winter evenings when he listened to his own father's accounts with open-mouthed wonder.

Above all, he remembered a night in which he and Juan José heard Gambelu's account of the expedition carried out by the Carlist chief Gómez in that first war. The boys did not even know the places he named: Santiago, Léon, Albacete, Córdoba, Cáceres, Algeci-ras. But it was clear enough to them what Gómez had done, with a handful of brave men whom he picked up—and sometimes lost—along the way. They had made forced marches, bivouacked, and then repeated the cycle. They made their way with carts across arid plains and intricate sierras, avoiding entrapment by two or three enemy armies close on their heels, sometimes one side winning and then the other. But they entered large cities without meeting resistance and made a tour of half of Spain, coming back at midyear to their point of departure. The first Sunday after they heard of these wonders, the boys organized an escapade to the woods to search out boys from other towns and engage them in combat. And now, was the war they were waging anything more than an escapade by grown-up children?

Brought back to the reality around him, Ignacio felt a total absence of ideas. He felt that the loud struggle of ideas all came to an end with the war to which they had led. He stubbornly recalled Pachico phlegmatically explaining in the *chacolí* the paradoxes of skepticism.

The Republican rooster, shaking its crest, its neck-feathers stiffening, showed its spurs and cackled as it surrounded the King's troops.

While Estella celebrated the birthday of Don Carlos and the arrival of his brother at the camp, the battalion was ordered into the field on November 4th. Under a torrential downpour, they made their way through harsh uneven ground. They traversed the slopes of somber Montejurra, to defend the city and gorge of Villamayor, between Montejurra itself and the heights of Monjardín, advance sentinels to the city.

Robust, ancient Navarre, invigorated by the breath of the nearby Pyrenees, offers a most varied landscape. On the north and east, intricate mountain ranges covered by twisted growth hold the snow, give rise to storms, and separate and guard Navarre from France. In these mountains Roland's last trumpet blast sounded, accompanying the barking of Altobiscar's dog. The mountains turn into placid valleys and unfurl at length into the placid banks of the Ebro River. The sharp menacing vertebrae of Montejurra form, together with the rugged Monjardín, a defile which in turn opens out on to La Solana, here traversed by the highway from Arcos to Estella: on one side Villamayor in the foothills of Monjardín, with Urbiola along the way, and on the other side the spurs of Montejurra, Luquín, Barbarín, and Arroniz.

The Republicans, wise in the ways of the terrain, advanced along the highway with the aims of enveloping the two wings of the Carlist forces, occupying the heights and falling upon Estella. The King's troops spread out among the five villages under cover of the wooded heights. Ignacio's battalion occupied Luquín, at the center of the line. At last, battle was about to be joined, formal and serious, with troops locked in combat. Here was, in the center and base of operations, the now famous battalion from Navarre, which had been victorious at Eraul; on their right, the troops of Ollo the organizer. It was vitally important not to let down those brave lads from Navarre; if possible, they must outdo them.

On the 7th, at about ten in the morning, they saw the enemy make their way through the defile at Cogullo; they spread out over Solana like a tide inundating a cove surrounded by mountains. They opened fire. The noise made by the reports from the mortar on their left, stationed in front of the church of Villamayor, and the sound of the howitzer hidden among the planted fields of Luquín on their right, reassured them, and they felt safe under the covering fire which came from the two artillery pieces from time to time. After each salvo, the report was followed by cheers, a general outcry, and red berets flung into the air.

Now, *now*, the enemy would see what they could do with that kind of support. They felt safe under cover of the artillery. Their bayonets were fixed and ready.

The enemy climbed slowly, while the Carlists shouted "Long live the King!"

Ignacio and his comrades received the order to regroup a bit higher up, while the invading wave advanced and tried to cut off the Carlist right wing as they themselves occupied abandoned positions in the Carlist center. Ignacio fired calmly, without emotion, in complete relaxation. Some bullets whistled overhead. Shouted commands were heard: "Higher up! Move back and up." Ignacio kept climbing.

Ignacio saw enemy shakos emerge from among the planted fields. He went back through the hamlet with his own troops, and on emerging on the other side and climbing the foothills of the somber and formidable

Montejurra they saw that the enemy was everywhere. Meanwhile the Carlists were taking to the higher woods. On the highway, the inhabitants of the abandoned hamlet were loading their already packed carts with food and furniture, taking everything from their houses with them, their children piled on top of the furniture. Other inhabitants of the area, most of them women, were crying out to the troops, encouraging them by shouts not to leave a single Black alive. From Barbarín, the Carlists were removing their cannon by hand, since there was no time to load it on a wagon. As they retreated from one end of the village, the enemy occupied the other end.

The Carlists had been forced to abandon Urbiola, and as the enemy advanced there was the danger that they would be cornered. The men from Navarre began to retreat in a wave, falling back onto Ignacio's battalion and sweeping them along with them towards the left wing. They feared that the enemy, after taking the highway pass, would fall upon Estella. They crossed the highway. Like a torrent in a sudden storm, when the waters fall from a height into the sea, which receives the fresh water while roaring against it, the Carlist mass now swept toward the pass between Villamayor and Urbiola to keep the enemy out, to block them, by battering against them. "The King looks to us, lads!" the officers shouted, and voices could be heard here and there crying out "Viva!" for the King.

Ignacio was running with the other ranks when he was met by a sudden wave of men coming back in great heat. What was happening? "That was a clever move!" Ignacio heard a man say. What move? thought Ignacio. New ranks fell back toward the stalled possession. "The King is watching us, lads. Stand up to them!"

Now they were running again. At last he caught sight of the enemy shakos, but only for a moment, and from a considerable distance.

When night fell, the soldiers of the Republic, weary and without food, slept wherever they chanced to be in the abandoned hamlets. Ignacio's battalion bivouacked in the thick undergrowth of somber Montejurra, waiting for the battle to come. They learned that the cannon on the Carlist right had fired blanks in order to raise the boys' morale and give them the faith that brings courage.

Ignacio was greatly disturbed. What was that action, that "clever move," which had stopped their advance? What was the reason for their abandoning the hamlets and beating their way backwards before they had so much as seen an enemy really close up? There had been no hand-to-hand meeting, no real clash of forces at all. The successor to his childhood rock-fights had turned into a travesty of a charge, with noise being all that counted. Men had come to mortal grips only as individuals moved by mutual hatred, not as human masses. This wasn't the action he had dreamed of. They weren't making war at all, merely following orders from the chiefs who played with them like pieces in a chess game. That was why they so urgently desired bayonet charges, close combat, a collective duel. They would never completely become an army but would forever remain a guerrilla band. They had received no training in hierarchical discipline and traditional tactics. They were merely a mass of men who had volunteered for the Cause. They had not been schooled in intricate moves on the open plains, but had formed themselves by marches and counter-marches across unoccupied mountins, irregular terrain made for ambush and surprise.

Still the great day was bound to come on which they would wage real war, hand-to-hand combat, and learn, at last, what the enemy was like. They would learn how to mete out their force like veterans do. His spirit tense, Ignacio imagined tumultuous scenes in which he slashed away at turbaned troops in coats of mail. He pictured shakos battling military jackets on a battlefield red with blood flowing like rainwater. He still dreamed of the giant Fierabras of Alexandria, a tower of bones which he, a modern David, would fell with a single stone. Awake, he dreamed ceaselessly.

The 8th dawned, bitter with rain, and as the light came, so did the bullets. The firing grew heavier. For two hours they endured the rain, the cold, the fog, and the bullets. They were a sad lot: wet to the bone, waterlogged in body and spirit. They were powerless to do anything about the elements. All they could do was resign themselves and endure. A heavy spiritual pall oppressed their very souls. They were like a flock of sheep surprised in the open country by a storm. All the pent-up disillusion of the campaign oppressed Ignacio. And then the firing stopped.

The clouds broke up about noon, and a fathomless blue sky appeared; the King rode among the troops to the echo of "Viva!" From time to time the shrapnel and grenades of the enemy shattered the calm. When Don Carlos rode by, Ignacio heard a "Viva!" escape from his own chest.

For Ignacio it was a day of dreary expectation. The morning rain made his very soul soggy. Weary from lack of sleep, he lay down still fantasizing about the great battle, all confusion and muck, still to come. Another day lost! Another day of miserable rain in his soul! For, in all truth, an obstinate, constantly dripping cold rain had been falling in his soul since the start of the campaign, so that it sank deeper and deeper until the landscape of his spirit was covered by a great fog and diffuse with a monotonous rain. Yes, it was raining in his soul: hour after hour of monotony.

"Don't you hear that?" asked a voice, rousing him from his sleep in the pitch dark. "They're firing again, moving around, probably planning their action."

Action! A military blow! It was exactly what he was looking forward to: hoping that the action would do away with the sad soaking of those monotonous days, shake out his soul, carry him along in a whirlpool of movement.

They emerged into the open. The troops were assembled on the field, where the officers, their chief at the center, were preparing for a night attack. The dark hours could be counted only by the rhythmic fire of the enemy.

Dawn broke and a voice rang out: "They're retreating!" Ignacio felt his heart sink into the morass of rain which had accumulated there. The Carlist troops were deployed both left and right, entire battalions inspired by the enemy's retreat.

During one halt, Elío, watching the ebb of the enemy tide, murmured, "Good. Very good." The torrent of volunteers flowing down from the heights occupied the fields the enemy left to them, without a skirmish, without battle.

When Ignacio entered the deserted village of Urbiola, he heard wails, curses, supplications. The fact was that the King's cavalry had set about slashing the enemy wounded as they lay in the street, as well as any and all stragglers. Some soldiers were running like chased hares cornered by dogs and looking for a burrow.

The villagers, some of whom still stood by their

loaded carts, were watching the chase, the hunt. The women shook their fists and shrieked, "Go after them! Go get them! *Guiris*, assassins, thieves!" The children, their eyes wide at the sight, looked at their parents and at the town, the smallest caught up in the skirts of their mothers, who had turned into veritable furies.

The battalion went through the town after the Republicans, but the latter had set up guerrilla positions to impede an advance while the bulk of their troops were abandoning the town and had passed Cogullo.

"If we had artillery, we'd drive them back to Madrid!" someone said.

It was the day of the Patronage of Our Lady.

The Carlists started back towards Estella, carrying with them for burial in a small hamlet along the way the tattered corpse of a man they claimed was Moriones, the commander of the Republican forces. While the liberated town set its bells ringing to proclaim victory, elsewhere Liberal Spain celebrated the triumph of the Republican general by running bulls in the streets and setting their own bells ringing. The idle on both sides debated which side had won. Victory was still hidden in the mysterious future, where all weighty questions are decided.

Ignacio, again dispirited and crestfallen, asked himself if there had even been a proper battle, let alone a victory. How different those heated rock-fights of his childhood had been!

When his battalion entered their home town, the cheers of the immense crowd which greeted them almost drowned out the bells. Ignacio fell into his mother's arms and tasted the poor woman's bitter tears.

"What a sight you are, my son! Are you ill?"

He went from her arms into those of Pedro Antonio, whose beating heart pressed against his own.

The troops assembled in the plaza, where their commandant addressed them.

On those days he spent near his parents, Ignacio breathed more comfortably, hoping to recover his strength. His mother watched him and watched him, saying over and over, "What a sight you are! What ails you, my son?"

"Nothing, Mother, nothing."

"Yes, there's something. . . . Have you been wounded?" The poor woman thought he was hiding something from her.

After a few days he left the house to go look down on Bilbao from the heights where he had ventured so boldly in his childhood. Bilbao lay there below, surrounded by the protecting mountains, which seemed to jostle one another to get a better view of the city nestling among them. The city was like a landslide which had tumbled down the foothills until it came to a rest in the valley. There was the city, now, beside the river which was its lifeline. Down there was that red sea of tile-roofed houses, pressed together densely and compactly, with paths running through them like ravines. Down there in those houses were his friends, in one of them Rafaela. There, in that dark slit was the street of his childhood, a street where it was always market day, a kaleidoscope of shoes, sashes, leather yokes, pottery, cloth, all manner of odds and ends. When the echo of some music from the town reached the ears of Ignacio and the comrades who had gone with him to the heights, one of the battalion's clowns answered it with a cowbell.

"We've got to enter the city," one soldier said. "I've

already made a list of all the skirts I'm going to take out dancing."

"I'm going to beat up Ricardo . . ."

"I'm going to set fire to the office where I worked!"

Ignacio thought of Celestino and his imperious "Stand at attention!"

"And we'll levy a heavy tax on the rich!"

Juan José, more hopeful than ever, described in minute detail their entrance into the city. "You'll see, you'll see, when we take the city, the looks on the faces of Juanito and Rafael, that fool with his little verses. And Enrique: especially him. He's sure to remember the day you thrashed him on the street and he had to run off sucking up his snot along with his blood . . ."

Ignacio ached all over, and that filled his soul with sad premonitions which were only enhanced by reading the pastoral letter from the Bishop of Urgel, who wrote: "Woe to you if you allow sin to penetrate your ranks, and you come to be like these Republican hordes who sow desolation and mourning wherever they go." The Bishop went on to add that God would abandon them for their sins and abominations, as He had cast them aside in 1840 when He used the traitor Maroto as the instrument of His justice. Ignacio, on reading that victory is not attained by the power of an army unless God is on its side, called up the blurry, chill images of what he had seen at Lamíndano and Montejurra. He remembered running when others ran. He remembered the sight of villagers crowding around their carts and women wailing over the wounded while children cried and did not dare hang on their mothers.

The rain and the sun seemed to have settled into his body as rheumatism, and his soul to ache from the slow stubborn rain of the monotonous days.

Ignacio's bad state was growing worse. The hardships of the campaign, all the marching back and forth from one place to another, all the climbing up and down, caused him to break out all over with boils and blisters. He was swollen, and his bones seemed to grind against each other. The doctor ordered him to rest, so he went with his parents to Pedro Antonio's village, where they were staying.

He stayed in bed, falling into a kind of sweet stagnation in which he felt himself getting better as the warmth of the bed counteracted the slow and persistent rain that had soaked him and penetrated him to the bone. War seemed as distant as a story, and the world a dream. His mother watched over him and cared for him. Rafaela appeared in dreams in which she took his pulse, rested her hand on his forehead, waved away the bothersome flies of autumn which were as stubborn as rain, brought him water to drink, and straightened his blankets. And, when he closed his eyes and fell into a deep sleep, she would kiss his forehead.

At other times, at dawn when he was just waking up, a warm ray from the rising sun would take shape in an ethereal body like the village girl with the cowlike eyes. The trilling of the birds at dawn would sound to him like her vibrant and open laughter. Then the village girl would be transformed into Rafaela, until his mother came into his room and his vague dreams would vanish as he woke up fully. He would wake up feeling better slept than he had slept since he was a child. So he went to sleep each night quite eagerly.

One morning his mother felt his forehead and asked with ironical sweetness, "What did you dream last night?" He felt himself blush.

The regime of the campaign had strengthened him,

invigorating his body and purifying his soul by contact with the hardness of the earth. At times he felt the brutish and fleeting desire of his carnal flesh, but he had cleansed the dirty and persistent lust of his spiritual flesh. The woodland air had hardened him, cleansed him of the pestilent vapors of the street, taken away the disgusting scabs infecting his soul. He had become pure and strong, like the newborn child of parents who loved one another in the Lord.

His spirits rose one morning when Domingo, the landholder, visited, seeming to bring with him a breath of fresh air from the days when they had shucked corn together in the old farmhouse's smoky kitchen, that cosy human nook of work and peace.

Another day, Juan José came calling, red-cheeked from the mountain air. "We're going to Bilbao!" he said.

"Soon I'll go with you!"

Juan José unfolded for him a plan for the city's siege and then went on to talk about the consequences of its capture. It was as good as done. How were those peace-loving merchants going to hold out, when they were interested only in trade? It was all clear sailing. Within four months, Don Carlos would be on his throne, and everyone who now belittled him the most would hurry to pay him court. Once Bilbao was captured, what else could it do but declare itself a Carlist city?

Ignacio stayed two months longer with his parents. He felt born again and took pleasure in all the small things of daily life. On sunny winter afternoons he contemplated the barren trees in the still-green fields. In the distance the jagged spine of Oíz showed white under its blanket of snow. He spent Christmas Eve with his parents and uncles. It was an intimate Christmas Eve, warm and peaceful. Pedro Antonio told his old tales no longer, for he sighed for his little shop. Everyone went to bed at ten o'clock.

Like someone listening to the rain, Ignacio listened to his uncle Don Emeterio comment endlessly on the progress of the war. He spoke of the coming fall of Bilbao, the longed-for victory, the villagers in whom old passions lived on, and the anxiety of other villagers who were afraid that the urban colossus would crush them.

Don Emeterio's commentaries were especially lively and picturesque on the more and more frequent days when his friends celebrated some piece of good news with a huge meal and abundant drink. Now, how were they to celebrate victories except by eating? Was there any other festival in the village or any other diversion to take its place? Wine loosens the tongue and expands the imagination. Warm food, easy intimacy with friends, a glass in front of one—that was how the news of the campaign could take on life, enter into legend, and become the stuff of prophecy. What joy, the joy that arises from a warm stomach! Then they felt especially fond of the out-of-the-way village, with its odor of the countryside, its free air which cools the overtaxed mind. The green fields, open to every breeze, were a great appetizer and a great digestive. Often the commentaries about the war campaign would end in rustic philosophical dialogues in the spirit of Solomon and Ecclesiastes. Bread alone would have only lessened the brilliant duels.

On the 22nd of January of '74, Ignacio heard the bells tolling a victory. Portugalete had been taken. Towards the middle of February, when no one talked of anything but the siege of Bilbao and the coming bombardment, he rejoined his battalion. When his father put his hand on his shoulder in farewell, the boy felt a lump in his throat, tried to speak, swallowed hard, and then murmured in a smothered voice, "We'll meet in Bilbao."

Glad that she could hold back her tears, Josefa Ignacia hugged her son to her breast.

III

F ROM ABOUT THE MIDDLE of 1873, Don Juan lived in constant indignation at the government's apathy. Was it for this that he and his son had taken up arms? It was intolerable to see soldiers wandering around drunk at nightfall, while others wasted time in card games by the light of tiny candles on tables placed in the open air of the marketplace. It was a shame to see them wrapped in their blankets, lying on the ground next to their rifles on the cobblestones of the Plaza Nueva.

Lack of discipline undermined the army, eating away its strength. It was all natural enough: the authorities had insisted on carrying democracy into the ranks, filling the soldiers with egalitarian preachments. After the cries of "Down with the draft!" Had come "Down with the gold braid!" And then the demoralizing "Let them dance!"

The circle, meanwhile, drew ever tighter: even ships had a hard time getting in. News was hard to come by, and so rumors for fear to feed on filled the void, during those days on which a changing sky brought them heat alternating with a dank humidity.

"They're practically on top of us!" Grumbled Don Juan when, after word of the retreat from Montejurra had gotten through—news which fell like a lightning bolt—the conscripts were fired upon: they went through their military maneuvers at the very entrance to the city. At the same time, the hamlets and villages set their bells to ringing at the liberation of Estella.

By November, Don Juan took to wandering around the wharf, now turned into a marketplace. He was saddened at the sight of the piled fruit, the crowded cattle. It was a wartime market with the look about it of a dumping ground for booty, and possessed none of the rhythm of natural commercial circulation: it was no ordinary warehouse, but resembled, rather, a military encampment where imprisoned sheep bleated while hogs wandered about. It was not the same wharf on which the city used to receive cargoes of cacao for transshipment to all of Europe. The war reduced commerce itself to a barbaric process, the open market of a nomad people. He would walk home sadly, and his very soul would shrink as he took a turn around his own lonely dark warehouse, whence all life had departed.

"We have hake at thirty cuartos a pound . . . cheap at such a time," his brother told him one day.

"Lucky man!" Don Juan replied gravely.

Don Miguel amused himself with the accumulation of events, and grumbled only silently and to himself about the inconveniences the soldiers caused, about the enforced billeting and the scarcity of goods in the market.

He kept following his niece Rafaela about, furtively, at some distance, down streets and walkways, whenever she went out with friends or with Enrique, her brother's neighbor. "Well now, there he is, that bumpkin," he'd say to himself, "He's capable of carrying her off! She's fallen into the hands of a fool, and he'll confuse her and make her dizzy! He doesn't deserve her, no, he doesn't deserve her." And he would follow her from afar, like a sneak thief. He visited his sister-in-law on the slightest pretext, to tell her, for example, that hake from Laredo was available at the market at so much a pound. Such visits gave him the chance to see his niece. He felt stung by a sense of his own ridiculousness, but kept giving her furtive glances.

Rafaela's little brother would tease her by saying, "Don't you think we see you two? As if we didn't know what you're up to!"

"Shut up, nitwit!" she would scold, turning scarlet.

"Hah, hah, just so she can tell everyone she has a boyfriend!"

"Marcelino! You're being rude. Keep quiet now!" Uncle Miguel would exclaim, growing pale while his niece turned red.

And once at home, after trying in vain to keep his mind on a game of solitaire after supper, he would carry on a silent conversation with a sweet shadowy figure of his imagining.

The day he most enjoyed in those times was San Miguel's Day, when the people of Bilbao could not go on the usual mounted procession, the *romería*, to Basauri, and moved the festival to the Arenal. It was a mild September day, and many of the fearful who had left town at the first alarms and difficulties had returned.

Don Miguel was vastly amused by the sign hanging in front of the cemetery: "Entry Forbidden." In a good mood, he repeated the phrase to himself and said, "They don't even grant us the inalienable and unwritten right to die."

On that peaceful day, when the mountains lay in the quiet of autumn and the sun, caught in the cobwebs of a cloud, rained down like a slow shower of gathered light on the countryside, the old bachelor Don Miguel could enjoy the same pleasures as other men.

187*

He took to the street while it was still early, at the hour when the man in the scarlet cape and blue pants who played reveille on a tambour and tin whistle was waking up those sleeping in their beds. That song of the dawn sounded, in that town encircled by mountains and inhabited by the descendants of country people, like the trilling song of a caged bird remembering the wood where it was born. The sound of the tin whistle, as sharp as the green of the mountains, rising above the steady monotony of the tambour, spoke to Don Miguel of the freshness of the countryside, where birds trilled away above the steady murmurs of the streams.

The streets were filled with groups of youths wearing red berets and white drill pants and jumping about and shouting. Some had dogs and guns for hunting figpeckers, with all the necessary gear—leather bags, cartridge belts, dusty green cloaks, game bags, puttees, and pilgrim's stew of fried hake and bread. The little dogs were brown and fleecy and fine-snouted. How often had Don Miguel himself set out, filled with the freshness of youth, when the joyous robin was already singing away to salute the sun of a new day!

All those groups of strolling pilgrims on a *romería* felt as fresh and joyous as youngsters about to play a prank on someone. They could shout and do childish things in public, letting out all their souls into the free air.

Don Miguel arrived at the site of the improvised *romería*. It was just what he wanted—the countryside brought to the city streets, a *romería* near at hand, nestled in the town. Where the streets opened onto the Arenal, every one leading to the festival, flags and pennants were hung. What a beautiful sight! An image of the open countryside had been brought into the little gardens of the town, now filled with punch bowls and glasses and pitchers. There were tents and leafy huts. There were games of chance, employing knives and rings and hoops and dice. Beyond the yellowing foliage of the autumnal landscape there was the autumnal sea-scape of the fishing gear and nets of the ships in their Sunday best. Nearby, four steps away, were the city streets, concealed in shadow, awaiting the pilgrims, along with the rows of houses whose hearths would give them warmth.

Don Miguel laughed like a child as he watched the make-believe hunting dogs point at trees empty of birds and as he watched children laughing at the comical sight. The sizzling of the cooking oil and the odor of hake frying made him feel like a new man. He almost took part in a game of ninepins made out of planks from the "Battery of Death." For a while he followed behind the giant figures of papier-mâché, running along with the children as in his childhood, when he drew back as his playmates ran in front of the figures. He was carried back to the days of his youth, and he was completely a part of his surroundings, as if in some spiritual womb. He took delight in each new thing, growing young again as the pilgrimage progressed in its round. A cart appeared from out of the town, dec-orated all over, the horses drawing it bedecked with bells, carrying young people adorned with dahlias who made the road resound with their cries and shouts. That was how Don Miguel liked the country: reduced to human scale and brought to nestle close up against the silent streets.

Won over by the freedom around him, he stayed on to eat in the open air at Las Acacias, at a noisy table where the talk was of war and peace and of the damned Cantonalists, who disrupted the army. Past *romerías* of San Miguel were recalled, those that had been held in the cool valley of Basauri, with smoke from the portable stoves rising up over the trees amid the sounds of guitars being strummed and of food being fried. Don Miguel ate silently, thinking to himself that no other *romería* had ever been so intense, so intimate, so much like a large family gathering. He was enchanted with the table talk and the shouts of the vendors. "Cigars!" "Cold water!" "Fritters!" He felt warmer and warmer as he heard the innumerable shouts unite in one overwhelming resonance in the air. When he heard that a company was going to dance the *aurresku*, he hurried to the scene with his napkin still tucked under his chin, his feet ready to break into a gambol. He wanted to put an end to his everlasting inhibitions for once and for all, to shout out the secrets that he told himself in his hours of intimate conversation with himself.

It was almost an audacious act of defiance for him to run about with his napkin left tucked under his chin: he was willing to risk ridicule.

He wandered from group to group for a while, like a child. For a time he followed a small boy mounted on a donkey, with a red beret and a tassel of esparto grass, a blue percale band across his chest and a wooden sword in his hand, who was accompanied by a drummer and a swarm of children armed with sticks. The mounted child wore a sign reading "The Entrance of King Chapa into Guernica."

All the stores in town closed for the afternoon, and the population flooded to the Arenal.

So: the enemy would not let them go out into the countryside? Well, then, they would bring the countryside home, and that was that! How could they welcome autumn without a field outing, without filling their lungs with good country air, without a tumble in the fresh green field?

This, this was a true *romería* now, in the Arenal of everyday, in the little garden of the city. Don Miguel preferred it to a *romería* in the open countryside, just as he preferred the tiny garden on his balcony with its flower pots to the forest, where he would feel left alone and abandoned by everyone.

As he got closer to the *aurresku*, his heart gave a leap: Enrique was dancing the Basque dance in front of Rafaela, who looked at the ground being trodden by the dancer's feet. Don Miguel's eyes followed his niece, in and out of the tangle of the dance, face to face with her suitor, the two of them there close together. When her eyes met her uncle's during one of her turns, she felt faint, while Don Miguel felt his blood ready to burst in his head and his soul about to leap from his body. He hurried off to another group of dancers and began to dance like someone bedeviled, a desperate man courting ridicule, it seemed to him.

"Bravo, Miguel, for once I see you act the real man!" one of his friends called out. Don Miguel, smiling, danced all the harder.

"Come on, Miguel, step lively! Life is nothing but a dance, and whoever doesn't dance it is a fool."

They applauded him in his awkward clumsiness, and he felt his life renewed as he gave himself over to the intoxication of the dance. His inhibitions melted away, and he felt like a child again, new and fresh.

Later, after a break for food, he found his niece again just as the trumpet call sounded above the noise of the celebrants. The noise died down, the trumpets blared, and Enrique told the girls, "They're calling us!" He started off and then came back to say goodbye to Rafaela. After he left, Don Miguel went up to Rafaela and made some vulgar remarks. He had drunk enough to be brave, and he was excited by the dancing.

"Well, now, you surely had yourself a good time," he told her in a low voice. "There's nothing like having a boyfriend."

"That's all just talk by that little brother of mine, Marcelino," she answered, turning red.

"No, it's what life is all about! What a marvel to be young. . . . Ah, if I were only fifteen years younger! That was the time when I'd sit you on my knee and make you dance and you'd run your hands over my face and say, 'Pretty uncle, pretty uncle . . .' "

"You're still young," Rafaela said, but when she said it she felt anguish and shame.

"I'm still a rare bird, and that's worse than being old . . ."

A little later, as he was on his way home, as exhausted as if he'd had a day of hard work, he overheard someone say, "Even Miguel Arana danced this afternoon."

After dark, when the last echoes of the festival were to be heard faintly down the street, the poor uncle sat by himself after supper, trying to distract himself with solitaire. He began mumbling to himself, "Good God, what did I say? What have I done? What a ridiculous spectacle! I was drunk . . ." And he went to bed, to be in the dark, alone, where no one could see him, to lose consciousness in sleep.

What a day it had been when the besieged city had brought the famous Basauri *romería* to his Arenal! It was a prologue to the days of martyrdom, as he prepared himself for the trying times ahead by taking part in that *romería*, that family festival! What a day it had been, when he had been able to enjoy the make-believe freedom of the countryside, right where he often walked, between the shaded streets and the river!

Doña Micaela's days were filled with dark foreboding. Not even the care that Rafaela gave her helped distract her. She brooded about the Seven Year War, which had troubled her sickly childhood. She worried over the prices in the market, and predicted castastrophe as the cost of meat soared. She worried over the fact that village girls began the wine-pressing ahead of time. She worried about some nuns who had abandoned a certain convent and about some families from a distant quarter of town who had invaded the inner part of the city to take over some abandoned houses.

She was saddened by the review of the auxiliaries carried out by the mayor, when she saw her husband and eldest son wearing their Scottish caps, muskets over their shoulders, lost among that multitude of men of all ages and conditions, armed shopkeepers.

The peaceful families watched their men marching past in review, armed and assigned to military units; they all knew each other and could scarcely grasp the meaning of that aggressive formation.

Like the rank and file, the officers carried their rifles over their shoulders; the signs of their rank were sewn into their caps, the only item of uniform they wore. Their status could be made out only by their civilian clothes, so that a deep sense of equality held all these men of such disparate condition together. The predominance of somber dark colors struck a more serious note than the colorful uniforms of a regular army.

Doña Micaela found some outlet for her feverish state by putting used clothing in some sort of order, clothes which the neighborhood brought forth for the tattered Volunteers, who, uprooted from their lands and labors, were now to be battered by the chill autumnal wind of the equinox, which they called the *cordonazo de San Francisco* and which made their teeth chatter.

She went through wardrobes, disinterred some old coats belonging to Don Juan, and dreamed over them. When their wedding clothes came back to view, she thought back to their quiet honeymoon, which seemed like a dream of long ago. She cleverly remade her husband's useless formal coat by cutting off the tails, feeling a strange delight in repairing those clothes, the relics from the quiet years spent at their peaceful hearth, the remnants of their sweetly monotonous years.

But these simple pleasures were always being spoiled. Marcelino, the youngest son, was a devil of a boy. He ganged up with some other snotty brats, and they made mock warfare parallel to the real fighting. The coming and going of the troops, the marching columns, the arrival of boats with armored helms, the shooting, the fleeing townspeople, and especially the continual blare of the bugle in the city streets, had been too much excitement for their children's minds, making them all eyes, ears, and legs. Their lives were out of control.

Doña Micaela suffered constantly, wondering where the boy was. She lost her breath one day when she found some bullets in the boy's pocket. Surely he would be delivered dead to her one day. One night, when it was already getting late, she lit a lamp to St. Joseph even as she sent someone out to look for the boy. When he finally appeared, all red and sweaty, and she learned that he had followed the troops to see a fire, she began to run her hands over him and murmured, "You'll be the death of me!"

"Women," thought the boy, "they shriek at the sound of a mouse!"

Pedro Antonio had decided to close his shop and go to the country, where he had his son and his savings invested. The city imposed a tax of sixteen million reales on all citizens not in arms. He could not stay where he was, for there was a silent antipathy in the air and a secret hostility in the glances of Liberal neighbors. He was cut to the quick to hear someone shout aloud as he passed "Carlist!"

"When will we be able to come back?" sighed Josefa Ignacia in a tearful voice, as her husband gave the last turn to the key in the door.

"Soon, and in triumph! We can't stay on here!" exclaimed Pedro Antonio loudly, to give himself strength at the thought of leaving his shop, his nest, in each corner of which he had built up, over the years, imperceptible auras of peaceful thoughts and work. He had a presentiment that he would not be coming back to it; his heart held a sad silence.

Uncle Pascual came to say goodbye and to wish them well, lamenting the fact that he could not go with them. A little later, just as the coach was about to set off, Don Eustaquio arrived, deploring the stupidity of the war. "Why has he bothered to come and annoy us?" wondered Pedro Antonio. Josefa Ignacia was occupied in dreaming of Bilbao itself, her nest of innocent love, the cradle of her son.

The travelers spoke of the war and the danger threatening the city. As they reached the advance lines of the Carlists, the coach drew to a halt. By the side of the road, in a hut, some Carlist villagers and soldiers were playing cards. The travelers waited patiently until, in irritation, the coachman went up to one of the cardplayers to see if he could hurry them up in carrying out their necessary duty, inasmuch as the coach was expected and awaited.

"By whom?"

"Clear us through or we'll be off!"

"I have you!" exclaimed the other.

"They've been waiting for you for a century!"

"The middle class in frock coats? Good, let them wait, I'm boss now! On with the game!"

"That race of people will have to be done away with," said one of the travelers in a low voice.

"Not if they rid themselves of your side first," answered Pedro Antonio. His wife looked at him in wonder, astounded at the audacity of the patient chocolate-vendor, who, once out of his little shop, became the Volunteer of the Seven Year War.

Some came, others left. In the middle of November, as the Arana family sat down to eat, the door opened and a loud voice, whose bold sound heartened everyone present, exclaimed, "We're here!"

"Is that you, Epifanio?"

And Don Juan got up to embrace the visitor, a lively old man, who placed his hands on Don Juan's shoulders, looked him over from head to toe with a great smile, and then hugged him to his chest.

"Well, nothing special. Only that yesterday morning some rebels came to get us out of bed, all of us Liberals, and, well! a few of us got away; as for me, you know I'll put up here. And how are you, Micaela, how are you? This is nothing: it only makes life the merrier. And you, Rafaelilla?" He held her under her chin. "I'll bet you don't care a fig for all this nonsense." Then he whispered in her ear, "I'll bet, too, you have a sweetheart—and of course, he's a Liberal, what else?"

"Always the same Epifanio."

"The same until I die. . . . I'm going to get myself properly armed. We'll shape up a good platoon among us emigrants."

The next day he went out with a small game rifle and twenty-one shot to enlist in the Auxiliary Battalion. When he was handed a Remington and some cartridges, he exclaimed, "Half a dozen would be enough, and when I'm through there wouldn't be a Carlist left standing. . . . Long live Liberty . . . Liberal Liberty!"

The Carlists attacked Portugalete to tighten the noose around Bilbao. The city would now pay for all its past sins. It stood for all that was bad. Its fall would settle the long battle between that hive of merchants which monopolized the entire estuary area and the rest of the countryside. Thus the solution for the whole history of Vizcaya was at hand.

And Bilbao would not this time have Heaven's protection, as it did in '36. It would not have the Virgin of Begoña, who had protected the city during the Seven Year War. The Carlists went to her sanctuary and, fired by holy zeal, bayoneted the Roman legionnaires in Jordán's paintings of Christ's passion. They carried the Virgin off in a triumphal night march, through defiles and paths in the mountains, on the shoulders of energetic youths. The march was lit up by the light of a burning ship in the estuary, a combustible cargo bound for the port. The Virgin's lustrous face reflected the red flames, and several of the participants took it for a sign, crying out. "A miracle! A miracle!" As they passed the cemetery one of the soldiers pointed to the statue of the matronly woman holding out two crowns and exclaimed, "There's one who stays behind. May she protect you, Bilbao!"

They carried the Virgin in stages as far as Zornoza, and another miracle was proclaimed when it was learned that the litter on which she was borne was not properly pegged.

"How happy she looks! She seems to be smiling!"

The city, meanwhile, was living through bitter and uncertain days. Its citizens were preoccupied with the maneuvers of the liberating army, which they expected to appear any day, and they prepared themselves for the critical times ahead.

It was a sad Christmas for Bilbao that year! At the Aranas, Don Epifanio recalled the heroic siege of '36, trying to rid himself of sad forebodings by talking about sad things in the past. Over and over he said, "Just so we don't run out of firewood, like last time . . ." He talked about the desperate sudden changes of fortune in that first siege, the hand-to-hand fighting in the very sewers, and the indomitable resistance of those merchants, who had learned in peacetime the courage for war.

The Christmas meal was tranquil, and when it was over Don Epifanio insisted on dancing with Rafaela. Don Miguel withdrew to his own house, where he sat by the fire and spent a goodly time carrying on conversations with an imaginary person, turning his head to look behind him at the slightest sound.

As the year came to an end, the siege worsened. On Holy Innocents' Day, the besiegers closed the estuary, the city's nerve center, and bells rang out in the neighboring villages to celebrate the event. An attempt to run the blockade proved vain.

"A new year, a new life, Micaela!" exclaimed Don Epifanio on the first of January.

"I don't think I'll get through this one."

The day after Epiphany they received a shipment

of newspapers, like gifts from the Magi. There was such a rush for them that they were auctioned off. Don Epifanio paid three duros for one. They were able then to talk about the fall of the parliamentary Republic. The Liberal element in the city council lost no time in decreeing that the batallion of Republican volunteers be disbanded. Arana spoke out against those who had forced him to swear allegiance to the Republic, against those who had allied themselves with the common enemy in elections, and he predicted that they would pass over to the enemy side, since extremes tend to meet.

Now—now that the Republic had fallen, now that a bold military leader had drowned out its pointless chatter—now operations would take on new vigor. To try to set up a Republic in the middle of full-scale warfare—who could imagine such a piece of foolishness?

By the middle of the month, Doña Micaela put cotton wadding in her ears and told her rosary beads ceaselessly whenever she heard the glass panes rattling in the office from the distant cannon fire, echoing the sounds she had heard long ago as a child.

"It's Moriones," exclaimed Don Epifanio, "come to liberate us."

"Moriones, to liberate us?" asked Don Juan, who was afraid that the Republican general might do just that.

Don Juan watched "the barometer," which is what they called the face of the general in command of the garrison, trying to find some clue in his impassive expression that would give him news about the way things were going.

News became as real as actions in the field. The

word was a powerful weapon, giving either faith or discouragement.

A working man was arrested for spreading the story of the surrender of Luchana, a wild story which was laughed at and got the man jailed as a rumormonger. When the next day the story turned out to be true, people found it hard to believe. Some minimized its importance. Some believed it, but others called it a "ridiculous and scandalous dissimulation." The communiqué published in *La Guerra*, in which those who had surrendered had promised that they would die rather than surrender, was recalled. Many people were galled by the fact that the Carlists had been received with music, and Don Epifanio exclaimed, "O bridge of Luchana! What remains of your past glory?"

The next day came the news of the fall of Cartagena, the center of Cantonalism. People breathed again. Now the Liberator would get reinforcements from the troops which had been tied up in Cartagena. They imagined in their minds how he would be received and formed martial groups in the streets. There were bets made that he would arrive before February. Betting was general: the faith which redeems was measured by the betting.

For lack of any other kind of stock market, there sprang up a game of betting on the probable events of the future.

People huddled around anyone who came from outside the city, plying him with questions. They made guesses and conjectures, betting that the Liberator was already in Briviesca, or in Miranda, heading for Bilbao. Practical jokers proposed that a gas-balloon be chartered to go to Santander to thank the refugees from Bilbao there for their advice that the city should send a commission to the court of Carlos. The Liberator was to appear twenty-four hours after the first shell was fired, and the balloon and all became a standing joke.

"Impossible!" everyone exclaimed at the news of the capture of Portugalete. Don Juan arrived home in a state of prostration. Bilbao was now left like an island cut off from the world, once the crucial line of defense, the entrance to its port, had fallen. Seeing itself left alone, the city raised its head and took a deep breath—and a majestic breath it was. Forward! Long live Liberty! The unarmed Republicans—the rabble, according to Arana—demanded arms. When it was pointed out disdainfully that Santander was haggling with the Carlists about handing over ninety thousand duros, Don Juan muttered, "But Santander has our trade!"

At the end of January, Don Carlos issued a statement from "Royal Headquarters" to the people of Bilbao telling them that if they believed that the memory of the resistance their parents had put up during the Seven Year War obliged them to do the same thing, they should consider the differences in the times. Back then, they had had an army at the entrance to the estuary, troops of foreign legionnaires, and a Queen who had been a source of hope to those not yet disillusioned. But now they had a government born of a mutiny, without so much as a flag, and with no support in Europe. He warned them that if they resisted, all the blood that would be spilled would be on their hands.

"So be it, and amen!" said Don Epifanio.

The firing fell on the ears of Doña Micaela—who was obsessed with the fact that the price of an egg had risen to one real and that of a hen to thirty—like a series of hammer blows. She could see the specter of hunger as they continued to eat up all their accumulated provisions. The poor woman suffered from the bold remarks of Don Epifanio, who asserted that the Carlists were waging war with the money of St. Peter and St. Vincent de Paul, which they had stolen from the alms boxes of the Cristo chapel.

Isolated from the world, the town dreamed of Moriones, the Liberator, already choosing the house where he would be lodged. The rare newspapers which got through said hardly a word about Bilbao, when it was precisely its troubles that should have concerned them. . . . The wretchedness of politics! The garrison grumbled because it was not paid what it was owed, and the city underwrote a loan of 24,000 duros to cover the cost. The lazy were forced to take up arms, and doors were ordered to be shut by ten at night.

Political passions burned within. Don Juan sought for an essentially conservative militia composed of "those of us with something to lose," with no rabble. He worried more than ever about political purity, and he cherished ridiculous fears of hotheaded extremists.

He did not want Bilbao to appear as the bulwark of the turbulent freedom of the triple slogan "Liberty, Equality, Fraternity." He wanted it to be the jealous guardian of its own spirit, of the quiet progress which rests on commerce, to be the guardian of liberty within order. He felt that he was a Liberal, but a Liberal without flag or slogan.

Ordinary life meanwhile went on, leaving in its slow way its infinite pattern. Isolation called forth good humor. People hoped to dance away the danger.

"Opportunists! Worse than opportunists! You've got no sense at all, and one of these days they'll bring you home with an eye or an arm missing," Doña Micaela scolded her maid, who with other maids had been going along hidden paths to dance with enemy soldiers.

The poor lady suffered more than ever over Marcelino, who now devoted himself to spying on the Carlist forces from a distance with one of the cardboard telescopes marketed by a sharp businessman, and who argued that stray bullets only hit cowards.

"Don't talk about the war in front of the boy, for God's sake!" she begged her husband and her elder son.

The day she found a rip in her boy's cap and learned it was a bullet hole, she fell into anguish. Her blood rose in her throat and she went cold all over. The boy had stuck his cap up over a wall to provoke a sentry.

"One day it will be worse!" cried Rafaela.

"Big-mouth!" exclaimed the boy. "I know who it was who told . . . Ah, she's turning red now . . . and as if I didn't know that Enrique is her boyfriend!"

"Keep quiet!" his mother shouted, and then had to go to her bed with a fever.

Rafaela wept alone in her room.

For Juanito, those were the days! They took leave of the old year with a dance, and they danced their way into the new.

New Year's Day was inaugurated with a dance at the Círculo Federal. Evil times: put on a bad face! There were dances at La Amistad, Pello, Lazúrtegui, at Variedades and the Gimnasio and the Salón, and music in the Plaza Nueva every night. From the first of the year until the 22nd day of February, the second day of the bombardment, the city's newspapers reported thirty dances and balls. There were even some in the open country, under the stars, which ended in sudden dashes to escape the whistling of enemy bullets.

In those days of great expectations, the whole city

was like a family. Courting and flirtations were easier, and people were freer in their intimacies. They worked to entertain themselves—and to make the enemy furious. *La Guerra* joked about the siege, pointing out that since spring was on the way there should be more fasting as a health measure. The fact was that people had to eat less, and they might as well try to do so uncomplainingly, with a spirit of generosity. "Accept deprivation—gaily!" exclaimed *La Guerra*.

Good humor, ordinarily missing in the daily round of petty duties, good humor, which in normal times everyone keeps to himself, now poured out of everyone as a social duty, and the result was a collective joyfulness. People with happy natures were happier than ever.

The city's Carlist partisans emigrated to Bayonne, and the Liberals went to Santander, *La Guerra* went on trying to lift everyone's spirits, raising its voice against "the hordes of despotism" who looked down on Bilbao from the heights "like greedy birds of prey." It published historical memoirs about the sieges the city suffered during the Seven Year War, calling Bilbao "the tomb of Carlism." It assured its readers that in the nineteenth century no new St. James was likely to arise, and in a "History of the Papacy" it pictured the Popes as sly masters. Meanwhile, the city sang—

> If the government wouldn't pay
> for so many crooked clergy
> they wouldn't have this rumpus,
> or this thieving by the rebels.

Don Eustaquio, the former Carlist officer, swallowed bile, because as soon as he was seen without the cap worn by the armed defenders of the city he was forced to roll heavy barrels through the streets for the fortifications, while bands of children, seeing a serious gentleman at such a task cried out, "Stay-at-home! Carlist coward!" and sang—

> Whoever wears a hat
> must be shameless
> for when the kids see him
> they call him stay-at-home!

"Bandits!" he muttered. "The Covenant . . . did me in! Pedro Antonio was right to get out of town."

Don Miguel did not go out of the house during those days, but from the glass windows of his balcony he laughed at the sight of the barrel-rollers.

The season of Carnival came in, with its dancing and music. Few masks were seen, and there was only one group dressed up like serenading students looking for a cheap restaurant. The whole town gave itself over to dancing, especially dancing in the open. The Liberator would soon be coming. . . . To the dance! In three days' time there were ten or twelve dances. Juanito was on guard duty with his company, but with some others he slipped past the sentry, who looked the other way. They invaded the Salón, where the chiefs pretended to see nothing. Out of decorum, they turned their caps backwards and flung themselves into the dance.

The heat was suffocating. Enrique waited in vain for Rafaela, who would not leave her mother alone for a moment.

Some danced, and the poor swarmed from door to door, while life in its depths wove its slow texture, an infinite pattern of small events which sank into oblivion.

"Can it be true?" asked Doña Micaela, when the bombardment was announced on the twentieth.

"No such a thing," said Don Epifanio. "They're just bullying us. Things are going badly for them in the pocketbook. They'll never be able to pay on the coupons for the loan raised by the *junta de merindades*."

"But things are going badly for us too, Epifanio: five duros for a pair of hens, eight for a hundredweight of potatoes . . ."

"Somebody's getting along. . . . The waters are troubled."

When the coming bombardment was formally announced, there was an exodus, a procession of people as if on pilgrimage, some of them feeling sorry for those who stayed behind, who in turn felt the same way about them.

They placed lookouts in the city's towers, and the firefighters and engineers got ready.

What days of intimate anguish, the days of a city under bombardment! After a freezing night, the dawn brought a pure radiant sky on the 21st of February. Doña Micaela, while her heart pounded in her head, prayed in silence. Don Epifanio had gone out very early, exclaiming "They're ringing for Mass!" But it was a call to arms. Doña Mariquita, Enrique's grandmother, came down to comfort Arana's wife, while Rafaela, deeply restless, did nothing but go out on the balcony every other moment.

The neighborhood children got together and spoke in subdued voices as they watched their elders. Their minds on the bombardment, they asked themselves what it would be like. They expected something superb and out of the ordinary.

"Chapa has just gone through Archanda," announced one man in a knot of people at the Arenal, where Don Juan had stopped.

It was one of those gatherings of the prudent people who stationed themselves under the arches of the bridge. With their walking sticks they drew tactical diagrams and curves in the sand, showing that A + B proved that it was impossible for enemy cannonballs to reach the city. They were preparing the papier-mâché giants and the music to display their bravado. From time to time they launched skyrockets into the calm of upper space.

At the last peal of the midnight bell, they heard a deafening sound. A little later, after they learned that the cannonball had fallen into the river, the bridge stood deserted.

"Isn't it obvious? You can see for yourselves that they can't reach us!" one of the tacticians said after it was learned that a second shell had fallen short.

But just as Rafaela ventured out onto the balcony to have a look down the street where the neighbors were chatting in their doorways, a crashing noise shook the glass in the windows, cleared the street of people, and hurled the girl into her mother's arms.

"Everyone into the warehouse!" yelled Don Juan as he came running in.

All the neighbors hurried to the back of the shop, where they stared at each other in suspense, awaiting what they did not know. The noise of the city's cannons answering the Carlists hammered in Doña Micaela's head. She was suffocating in the trembling air. She began to cry, and the children watched her with wide eyes. They also stared at Don Juan, who paced about giving orders, and at all the neighbors. And the little ones whispered, "Is this the bombardment? What? That noise?" And they couldn't even go out on the street to take a look!

Don Epifanio put in his appearance, assuring one

and all that it was merely a maneuver to frighten them, and then he went out again.

"They've destroyed the Sociedad's building," said someone passing by. "Faustino was killed . . ."

The fatal phrase "was killed" sank into every one's heart, and there was a general silence. The beating wings of death could be heard. Everything blurred in Doña Micaela's vision, and she let herself fall into a chair.

Enrique came in from guard duty. When he had first gone on duty at Pichón, about noon, at the first sight of smoke, he had been received with a great burst of merriment, cut short by the sound of a locomotive roaring by. The train was carrying reinforcements, some said guerrillas, to Portugalete; the city would soon be liberated.

"Tomorrow, Moriones will be here tomorrow," announced Don Epifanio, back from his wanderings. "Everyone has comments to make on what is happening, without realizing what is really going on. . . . Some think the end of the world has come. . . . Poor Faustino! He went out on to the shoulder of the highway, thinking it had been blown up, and then he got himself blown up . . ."

When night fell, Uncle Miguel entered quietly, his slow, soft step calling up again in his sister-in-law's mind the fatal words "was killed." He had spent all the afternoon behind the glass front of his balcony, watching the neighbors. The Arana family had been unable to induce him to come down and stay with them. He wouldn't leave his house, to which he was attached with the devotion of a cat.

"No, no, I'm better off there than anywhere else," he would say, looking often at Rafaela and Enrique, while mattresses were being laid down on the floor of

the shop and a quilt was being hung up to divide it
into one side for women and children and another side
for men.

That first night almost everyone went to bed fully
clothed in that dank and dark warehouse office, which
was below street level on one side. In that silence
broken by distant cannon fire, Doña Micaela trembled
in fright when she heard rats scurrying among the
sacks in the adjacent warehouse and listened to their
occasional menacing squeals. Meanwhile the children
whispered about the bombardment and what it meant.
But the little ones finally fell asleep, something none
of the adults succeeded in doing. When he saw them,
Don Juan said, "It's a happy time of life."

The next day they blocked off some of the doors and
windows with sandbags. For others they used wooden
boards and even ox hides. The shop looked like a
tannery, with the hides hung over holes. The planks
over the windows of the Arana shop shut out the light,
so that the whole place became even gloomier, as did
Doña Micaela. Restless and worn down, she was beside herself, ready to jump at anything. That night she
woke the household with a shriek of terror: she had
felt some little feet on her forehead, the light step of
some invisible creature. They had to make a special
bed for her, where she lay in a fever. Thus began
Rafaela's sad distraction in those fearful days. She spent
the entire day under artificial light, enclosed by walls
which sweated their dampness, while a continual moan
of "Jesus!" came from the bed where her mother asked
time after time about her husband and her children.

The city had a strange look. The cellars and street
floors of all the houses were blocked or blinded. Families lived in their shops or storerooms, carrying on

their daily life in what later came to be called "the catacombs." Danger brought families closer and made the whole town one crowded family facing bad times together. A person could walk around the streets as if walking around his own home. Huge stews, often cooked in a doorway, served several families, and several households shared a common hearth.

The ancient city of settled merchants took on the look of the communal dwelling of some tribe of nomads. All formal etiquette vanished into intimate familiarity.

In the uncertainty of tomorrow, they lived as if by miracle; their roots in the air, their wills free of obsession and detached from the routines of daily life, they lived with avid passion. The jolt of the siege brought out what lay behind and beneath ordinary daily life, and they could all hear the slow weaving of the infinite pattern of fate. In many of the shops the day was spent in music and dancing, the two offspring of enforced idleness. They hung out signs like "The Battery of Life," and more than one new family grew out of the physical contact of several families huddled together in dark corners.

The first day of the bombardment all of the neighbors gathered in the Arana house, but they soon scattered among other relatives, and the only ones left were Don Juan, Don Epifanio, Enrique and his younger brothers, and their grandmother Doña Mariquita. Rafaela was unnerved by the life in common that she led with her undeclared fiancé, although it was a clean and modest life they shared. Enrique himself grew restless at her sight when she was first out of bed, in loose clothes and with her hair undone, bringing broth to her mother, tending to the children, and moving with lively serenity through the traffic of the household, looking for some chore to do. Sometimes she sewed buttons on his clothes, but she would run to the head of her mother's bed whenever she met him in some dark corner of the warehouse and he spoke to her about some inconsequential matter.

The women struggled on in silent resignation, while the men took turns standing watch.

Don Miguel went every day to his desk in the office to keep up with his work, but he always refused to spend the night with his brother's family. He did spend long periods of time in the storehouse, in that household like a camp of nomads, a household which began to affect him more deeply now as he watched over the comings and goings of his niece. He began to feel more affection for Enrique, and he grew interested in the dark and tranquil relationship which was being carried on, a love affair being woven from the infinite weave of the fabric of profoundly ordinary lives. He took a deeply personal pleasure in the happiness that seemed to lie ahead for the young couple.

Every day, discovering new worth in them both, he made a point of praising his excellent qualities to her, and hers to him. He would take a walk through the streets, enjoying the sights of the camouflaged houses, collecting shell fragments, and taking note of the smallest details. Then, seated in his dining room all alone, he would play with a deck of cards, trusting that the ace of diamonds would reveal whether or not the besiegers would enter the city.

The siege opened a new world to the children, a life of lovely days without school. Enrique's brothers and Marcelino played at war, making armies out of paperfoldings. If a shell fell anywhere nearby, they would run and pick up the still-hot fragments. Using bits of rubble from the damaged house in front of them, they would bombard an abandoned shop on days when a truce prevailed, stoning the stools piled on the counter until they knocked them over; mock-besiegers, they would throw stones at the mock-besieged hiding behind that very counter.

At night, the women and children would gather around the invalid's bed and the long drown-out "ss"s of their *ora pro nobis* slowly filled the air, interrupted from time to time only by the muffled sound of a shell falling somewhere. If they heard a shell passing close, they would break off their prayer and throw themselves full-length on the floor; a long moment of anguished silence would prevail in which only the breathing of those on the floor could be heard, as well as an occasional sigh from the sick woman; then, in a stronger voice, "Hail, Mary, full of grace . . . ," they would resume the slow prayer—dream-like, mechanical, as profound as the weaving of the events making up ordinary daily life.

The people were growing accustomed to it all, and the very ones who, on Ascension Day two years before, had drawn their shutters in panic when they heard a few shots in the air now listened quietly as a shell fell, one more event in the daily round, an event incorporated into the fabric of everyday life. Masculine spirits were boosted by the vigorous courage of the peaceful women whose panic had vanished as they grew used to the bombardment. The women's courage was the true courage, courage that showed the way of peace, something very different from the bravado learned in war.

The fear of the first days of the bombardment—fear born out of surprise—had changed for many people into mute and angry irritation and then into hatred, once the bombardment was a fact of everyday life.

People came and went, absorbed in the things of their daily lives. The usual person would pass by on the street at his usual time with his usual step, as if nothing out of the ordinary were happening. People walked to work to earn their daily bread, living peaceful lives in the midst of war. As new events accumulated, they soon became part of the ongoing pattern of daily life.

Since every able-bodied man was defending the city from its attackers, a corps of veterans kept order within the city, patrolling its streets. The corps was made up mostly of those who had fought as Nationalists in the Seven Year War and who were now considered unfit to take part in standing watch or serving in the reserves. They were called *chimberos*, hunters of small birds. Among them were two or three octogenarians, armed with umbrellas on their shoulders, since rifles would have been too heavy. And these old men, calmly walking the streets on police duty, shouldering their useless weapons, were the living symbols of peace, for they awakened memories and lent a sense of calm. They were a living symbol of that peace which weaves its infinite weave beneath the superficial embroilments of war.

Like children walking alone at night in the dark, many people sang out loud to keep up their spirits, or set off skyrockets, or retold old fables. On the second day of the bombardment, Juanito went to a fancy-dress ball.

Doña Mariquita would recount her memories of the siege of 1836, while Don Epifanio played the part of a military messenger, a dispatch-carrier from one place to the next, reviving every one's spirits and then going on to add new messages of hope, like a snowball growing as it rolls. He took his turn on guard duty, as did the other grown men at the storeroom.

As the intensity of ordinary life sharpened, so did the importance of daily events. Nothing seemed trivial any longer. A story went the rounds to the effect that a youth, as he lay dying from a shell fragment, had called out: "Don Carlos never reigned, nor does he reign, nor will he ever reign!" And another about the bridge to which a verse had been written—

> In all the world
> There is no suspension bridge
> As fine as this bridge is.

And there was the tale in which an Englishman emerged as commanding officer of one of the enemy batteries; and the rumor that two ships had already been sunk; and the story of the hair-raising death of a crazy woman who had been one of the city's street-heroines, a story which particularly came home to the children, who would never again see her at the head of a military parade, directing the band with flourishes of her parasol.

Doors were never closed any more. The public clocks had stopped functioning and, at night, the only bells to ring out were the shells whistling through the air to interrupt the silence and mark the dragging course of the sad hours.

"Moriones is expected any minute. Micaela, I've seen the smoke!"

"What smoke, Don Epifanio, tell us?"

"The smoke rising from our own guns out there; we've held a meeting over by the hospital, to figure out the disposition of forces . . ."

"Do you think they will enter the city?"

"Our army? How could they not get in. . . . Our men?"

> Never into this invincible city
> Will Carlos of Bourbon set foot:
> He may walk on its ruins
> But never over its glories.

"Come, boys, don't you know the new songs?"

> Long live Carlos, without his head!
> Long live Andéchaga, without his feet!
> Long live all Carlists,
> With their hides turned inside out!

On the fifth and sixth day of the bombardment the shells increased. During one hour eighty-three shells fell, their din made worse by a strong wind out of the south. Two or more would explode at the same time, sometimes close together. The city seemed about to come down, the houses to come apart. Doña Micaela wept continuously, and her daughter, without thinking about it concretely, was awaiting her mother's final hour.

The streets were littered with broken glass and rubble. Doña Micaela ordered wood collected from the debris, so as to save on coal.

"This is irreparable, irreparable, irreparable! Do you understand, Epifanio?" Don Juan cried. "All that work lost! And if they break in on us, it will be even worse. Goodbye to our trade! Without freedom, there can be no trade."

And when he heard his daughter say one day that at least the glassmakers would have plenty of profitable work to do, the writings of Bastiat came to his mind and he made a speech about the sophistry that arises from ignorance of the unseen, leading him again to conclude that the damage was "irreparable, absolutely irreparable."

"Irreparable, you say?" asked Don Epifanio. "You'll see how all this will be repaired. And you'll see how you will be all the better for it. . . . This is a cleansing. All those derelict houses from the year one will come down, and fine modern houses will replace them. This business is like one of those illnesses that leaves you healthier than ever."

"It must mean a visit to the front by Carlos Chapa," exclaimed Don Epifanio, when on the 26th he heard church bells ringing in the surrounding villages. "If there's one thing I like about the Carlists, it's that they're always cheerful . . . and their church bells are always dancing! The bombardment begins, and the bells are set ringing. They see some smoke down here below them, and the bells start ringing! Bilbao is burning? More bells, and a young bull is set loose in the streets, while the old women dance in the square. . . . Chapa pays them a visit? The loudest possible ringing of the bells! It's all a matter of ringing the bells and setting up lemonade stands. . . . The feast is fine until the reckoning time . . ."

"You yourself are always so cheerful, Don Epifanio. . . . But tell us, just as a formality, will the Carlists break in?"

"Break in? Who? The Carlists . . . ? Where? *Here*? Keep quiet, woman, you just don't understand these rustics . . . If we put up a sign outside the city which read *Entry Forbidden*, not one of them would dare. . . . Why, they have more respect for Bilbao than for the monstrance of the Most Holy God! The ones who'll break in will be the army."

"The army with the smoke?"

"Exactly. The army with the smoke."

Later, when he was told that the Carlists' bells rang to celebrate their having pushed Moriones back, he exclaimed, "That's a lie! A lie!"

"Dorregary has written the brigadier general asking if he wants to receive the Liberal wounded in the hands of the Carlists," exclaimed Don Juan, who appeared on the scene at that moment. "He informs him of the defeat of Moriones, and advises us to surrender . . ."

"We'll die first!" exclaimed Doña Mariquita.

"Will they bring ruin if they enter?" asked the sick woman.

"Don't you worry about that, Micaela. I tell you that the news of a defeat is false. . . . They ought to throw whoever brought such a dispatch into jail."

"Sure, it's only a letter from the enemy chief . . ."

"In that case, we should answer with our guns. . . . It's a lie, a lie!"

It was not a lie, but the offer of the enemy chief, calling on the besieged to send a commission to inspect the Carlist lines, was rejected; and it was rejected after such a commission had indeed been chosen in the first moments of curiosity and anguish. Blind faith that raises the spirit is worth more than conviction that brings dismay.

Following Moriones' withdrawal, the bombardment let up for a few days, as if the Carlists were giving the city time to think, a pause in which to decide its own fate. Discouragement among the populace was general, beginning to take on shades of despair; yet they hid their feelings, overawed by the moral atmosphere created by the more militant. But now, in the lull of the cease-fire, the inhabitants were forced to consider the true state of affairs.

As long as hostilities were suspended, Dōna Micaela had the consolation of a greater number of visitors. Common apprehension brought everyone together and united them in fear, and as each one concerned himself with his own trouble, his concern joined him to the concerns of all the others. They all thought of themselves as special cases, just as a child with a bandage on his finger will exhibit it to everyone.

But there were also humorous moments:

"Shameless, they're shameless! Those people are Carlists in disguise, surely!" exclaimed Don Juan, when he heard the sound of a party next door.

"No, Juan, what they are is *young*," his wife replied.

The Carlists meanwhile were busy battering away at the tower of Begoña, where the advance forces from the city, members of the rural guard, shut themselves in for the night. The Carlists particularly detested them and singled them out for special attention.

In the city, the enemy projectiles were reforged into cannonballs, an activity which was noted with satisfaction by Don Juan, who in his role as merchant highly approved of such purposeful saving.

In order to keep up the spirits of Doña Micaela, Don Epifanio would read from *La Guerra*, which, with the passionate emphasis and the inflated phrases of hatred, hurled rhetorical apostrophes, metaphors, threats, prosopopoeias, all manner of figures of speech, in short, contained in a manual of grammar. They would lay a curse in the following manner: "A curse on you, Carlos of Bourbon, who, in order to wear on your dark head the crown of noble Spain, set her afire in a horrid war!" Nor, of course, did the editorialists forget to use hyperbole: they compared Don Carlos to Nero, and asked rhetorically if he was the one whom the priests of Rome had called King by Divine Right; they swore eternal hatred of his sinister race, and launched invectives against the Roman clergy. With theatrical hatred and overblown rancor, they hurled in the enemy's face all the tatty metaphors and worn-out phrases from the common heap.

Don Epifanio was very careful to maintain his exalted Republican role in order to keep alive the hatred on which his resistance was based.

After reading the piece "A curse on thee!" Don Epifanio recited—

> Wherever a bomb bursts
> To sow consternation
> Mothers cry out through their tears
> A curse on thee, thou Bourbon!

Everyone on guard duty felt himself to be a poet in those days.

While *La Guerra* worked to incite the anger of the besieged, who used the paper for their *autos de fe*, the Carlist paper, *El Cuartel Real*, responded in the same tone, comparing the Liberals of Bilbao with entrapped beasts, spitting at heaven with Satanic fury. Don Epifanio would find a tattered copy, one of those which have been passed from hand to hand: "We attack you defenders of Bilbao with our chests bared, with rifle and sword, with cannon and mortar . . ."

"What small-scale stuff! No comparison to the attacks by the Algerians in '36," exclaimed Doña Mariquita. "Those were men, these are . . ."

"They're rustics, hayseeds . . . ," concluded Don Juan.

"Nothing for it, but to do what *La Guerra* says. Out with the black flag, and die embracing it . . ."

"May God not wish it so!" sighed the sick woman.

"Who said anything about fear, Micaela? This rag of a newspaper blames us for not having evacuated the women and children, leaving only the men behind, for shielding ourselves behind them like barbarians. . . . See what scoundrels they are, Rafaelita! They want us to send you girls out . . ."

"What cheek! As if we didn't have a right to be here . . ."

"Your own sweethearts? That's right!"

"They say there's going to be another permission granted to leave the city," Enrique's grandmother was saying, "but I'm an old woman. I went through the siege of '36, and I'll go through the siege of '74—even if the houses fall down."

Reading *La Guerra* was Donā Mariquita's delight, but Don Juan was not at ease with what that lively paper said. The head of the house of Arana and Company, a Liberal without a flag or a slogan, a veritable muscle in the mercantile body of the city, did not like the bellicose echoes of the extinct band of Republicans; he found it hard to accept their over-strong attacks on the clergy, their retelling the infamous history of the Popes, their openly anti-Catholic campaign. "Exaggerations, dangerous exaggerations. I've always pointed out that extremes meet," he would repeat. Meanwhile, he noticed that even the women read, without reservations, articles which would in normal times have drawn their immediate protest and condemnation.

The rebelliousness which lurks in everyone was fanned now, and the sediment of Liberalism was given a good shaking. Why *moderation*, when shells were bringing down their houses and everyone lived in uncertainty about tomorrow?

Even Don Juan himself, affected by the heat of spiritual discontent, by the breath of contained fury which swept through the people, felt his own being clamor against the Carlist clergy. One day, as he recalled the past splendor of the docks, and the former traffic at his warehouse, now dead, he exclaimed—

"Even if the people of Bilbao were to turn Carlist, Bilbao would go on being Liberal, or it would cease being Bilbao. . . . Otherwise no commerce is possible, and without commerce this city has no reason to exist."

The men of the Arana warehouse took turns on patrol and guard duty. Don Epifanio liked especially the nights when he had to serve, for it was then that he was in his best spirits. The orders were that each man could have only his bed, light, water, vinegar, salt, and a seat at the fire, and there they all congregated, wage earners and rich merchants and proprietors, each of them with his little pile of victuals, canned foods and preserves and crackers to be eaten up in peaceful joy. The poor—for there were poor men among them who for a small sum served the rightful turns of other men— ate their feasts without shame. Here was a picture of true courage, the kind of courage that a man learns in the peace of work. Their gatherings were gatherings of peace in the midst of war. They became like children, and all of them fell prey to the childish humor of the soldier. Each one showed off his talents, his tricks, and even his weaknesses, enjoying the endless joy of feeling carefree. The guards stationed at the bull ring played at bullfighting, to the sound of the enemy's military band in the distance.

The jokes and jests became more frequent. Rafael, the romantic, who liked to go at night to the cemetery to recite at his father's grave the poems he had written, was frightened almost out of his wits one night when he heard a cavernous voice come from a nearby tomb in the very middle of his recital.

The explanation was simple. The militia in Bilbao—

essentially peaceful merchants playing soldier—had earlier that night listened to their sergeant, the cemetery guard, address them, suggesting that in case there was any action, they should save the wounded by putting them in tombs, leaving the truly dead somewhere else. A wounded man turned up, they put him in a tomb, and his loud outcries had later startled the romantic young man who was bent on reciting his verses to his dead father.

Life in Bilbao was pervaded by a sense of the tragicomic. Living in the midst of day-to-day siege and warfare, the children never stopped their rock-throwing mock battles.

Lively *tertulias* gathered. Writers of love ballads competed among themselves. People played Pin the Tail on the Donkey, the losers being condemned to compose ten or twenty pieces of doggerel.

> When they report to their posts
> Along with their armament,
> The men of the Eighth
> Always take along a guitar.

And what soup is there to be found like the garlic soup taken in the outposts at dawn of a placid spring? With sleepy eyes they would watch the day break, the cold wind of dawn would shake them out of their drowsiness, and they would hear the first rooster and the enemy bugle blowing reveille. Juanito would be piqued to hear the chirping of some small bird—and he powerless to shoot at it. The orders were not to fire, and they had to be content with yelling at the enemy: "Pigs! Cowards!" And the other side answered, "*Guiris*! How are you? You'll soon enough be eating rats!" And they would hold up, on the end of a pole, some good white bread.

The front lines insulted each other back and forth while the rival newspapers did the same: it was a battle of old wives, underlined by a vivid sense of familiarity in the duel, for they all felt, being from the same place, rather like brothers.

Were they not, to some degree, merely play-acting a war, dramatizing a performance for their own amusement? The war was a heightening of daily events and accidents, a game whose hidden horror oftentimes escaped their notice. For some it was a means to leave behind all domestic troubles and work.

In the eyes of the besieged there was such a thing as a *carca bueno*, a good Carlist, someone who from the advance enemy line would yell good advice to them, telling them to keep out of sight, raising their spirits in his own way.

Whenever anyone voiced any doubts about the outcome of the whole affair, Don Epifanio would take a little booklet and read aloud from it: "Article 24 says: the Volunteer 'should be altogether sure and confident in his own discipline, and, in consequence, think of victory as inevitable; he should stick to his own position in the disposition of troops, always concentrating on obeying orders, firing rapidly and accurately, and attacking the enemy with bayonet or knife whenever his superior orders it.' Now it's your turn to be confident!"

In every man war brings out the child and the savage, twins one to the other.

Whenever it was his turn to serve guard duty, Don Juan would urge that economic measures be taken to avoid an almost certain lack of food; and he had to put up with the teasing of his companions, who called him "Bastiat." On guard duty at night he would watch the trajectory of the shells and think of the slow falling away of the life of his daily companion, whose empty hours he tried to fill.

Don Epifanio, too, tried to amuse her with stories from his tour of duty, striving to throw a lifeline to the spirit which was beginning to sink in the waters of darkness.

"What about the smoke?" the sick woman would ask with a sad smile.

"Why, there are some people who are such unbelievers that they don't even see the trees which hide the view; then there are others whose faith allows them to see the wounds inflicted on the combatants. Yesterday a man back from America was lamenting the fact, over by the observatory, that he wasn't equipped with a curved spyglass so he could see over the mountains."

For the poor woman's soul, everything was depressing. Even the snow which fell on the mountain on the tenth of March gave her profound sorrow when she learned of it.

Ignacio was serving a tour of duty about a league outside Bilbao. His rest period after his illness had given him time to form a lasting impression of the campaign, which settled in his soul as painful resignation with occasional attacks of anxious hope. He deeply disliked battalion life, and he found his captain insufferable because he insisted on keeping his distance, even though the two men were old friends. Such conduct Ignacio found all the more irritating because it was justified. Justified? No more than all the rest of the military discipline against which his spirit protested. Discipline is not something which can be improvised. In a regular army it is a tradition into which every soldier enters when he joins, filling a vacancy left by someone else in a pre-existing organization. But this army? They themselves had made this army together; they were its original members. Why should he be a sergeant and his old friend a captain? What was the Carlist army but a collection of them all? Everyone knew everyone else.

Besides, that siege was turning out to be a deceitful farce. The boys who were carrying it out, almost all of them from Vizcaya, allowed provisions to be smuggled in when it was a matter of helping a relative, a former employer, or a friend. Since they had more than enough meat, they sold it at night in the house where they served advance guard duty, where it was bought the next day by the soldiers under siege, who occupied the same house during the day.

And then such weaknesses were made up for by outbursts of unyielding fury. They would suddenly be ordered to fire at anything that moved on the enemy side. Ignacio was pained when he saw some young women who wanted to leave the besieged town ordered to go back. The sheer desire to annoy people, he thought. It was, in truth, an example of the gross pleasure of exercising authority over the timid, the stupid rigidity of following rules to the letter, the kind of pleasure which fills a nobody with a sense of his own importance.

He never would have thought he could love the city of his birth as he now knew he did, seeing it suffer without glory or purpose, watching the smoke of its chimneys. And no thought of attack! One night several battalions from Navarre crossed the estuary to buttress the siege, but they were forced to come back on the orders of the marquis of Valdespina, who was fearful, some said, that the men from Vizcaya would show resentment. The Vizcayans were already muttering that it was high time to make some serious and decisive move, while up there in the heights of command they were thinking, with childish solemnity, of carrying out a methodical siege, slow and gradual, *German-style*. War had to be waged in a formal and correct way, according to the latest fashion.

The Carlist military bands played reveille, which was answered by shellfire from the city forts. Then they sang the *Pitita*, and in the front lines there was an exchange of obscene remarks and banter.

Sundays were the most pleasurable days in the camp of the besiegers. People came from the surrounding countryside villages as if on a *romería* to the mountains around Bilbao. A carriage race had been established every week from Durango to the outskirts of Bilbao. Crowds brought their lunches along to watch the event, priests and women, and villagers with empty sacks to fill if it should turn out that the city would fall, according to *La Guerra*, and there were even those who brought along empty wagons with the looting of the city in mind. Now they'd show the *chimbos* what was good for them! On Sundays, then, they would lay on the mortar fire for the amusement of the public, who would laugh in great good humor, a spectacle which infuriated *La Guerra*. The paper published thundering admonitions: "The day will come when your joy will turn to tears, your display become one of pain, and woe betide you on that day!"

"Why, this filthy rag," exclaimed a priest, biting into a slice of tongue. "They say that *their* priest is God in the Highest. . . . They must be in a bad way when their minds have gotten that twisted . . . Protestants! That's pure Protestantism . . ."

Ignacio, furious at those people and their *fiestas*, felt

like firing at them. To make the war into a game, and make a spectacle of the shelling of the city!

Sitting one afternoon on the lower slope of one of those mountains he had climbed so often on holidays when he was still an office-prisoner, he heard dimly below him the bells of his town, tolling and then dying away. The town where he was born had its own metallic language, its language of bells, and it was now telling its complaint in the voice that would perhaps give him a last farewell—the voice that greeted his birth, the voice that would hail him when he entered his home town in triumph. And when he heard the massive complaints of his town sounding forth from the sonorous bronze of its bells, what a crowd of things filled his soul! Watching the dust and smoke raised by the shells, he thought: *Isn't all of this childish? Is it anything more than a rock fight? . . . What is she doing? She must be in the storehouse, in a corner, whispering with the other one. . . . Who knows! All of them in there, in a heap, in the carelessness which grows from fear, thinking that perhaps they have only a few days left to live. . . . What nonsense! . . . Why didn't she and her mother leave the city? . . . Another shell! What barbarians for parents! . . . Does she hate us? . . . Ay! She goes along there, she must have gone out. . . . What's happened? . . . If we enter the city, ah! if we enter . . . then . . .* He tried to substitute a purer image for the brutal one that had occurred to him. *There's nothing like a conqueror, a victor. . . . I'll protect her family. No one will touch so much as a hair on their heads. Poor Don Juan! And the next time little Enrique and I come to blows, it'll be like the time I gave him a drubbing on the street.* He could already see Rafaela weeping and falling into his arms, the arms of a conqueror, while the legend of Floris and Blanchefleur stirred in the dark depths of his soul.

On March 15th, the enemy artillery having fallen silent, the city buzzed with news of the surprise capture of a troop of *carabineros* in an advance position. They had run out of ammunition after firing prematurely, like cowards, and they had surrendered in the face of a threat to burn down the house where they were hiding.

"*Carabineros*, at last!" muttered Don Juan, who had once been mixed up in the maze of contraband goods in the Basque countryside.

The poor men were warriors on the payroll, unlucky mercenaries who fought to earn their children's daily bread.

Any event at all provided material for unending discussion. In the isolated city's restricted history, everything took on added importance.

"They're buffoons, real buffoons!" Don Epifanio kept repeating, that same day, as he commented on the Carlists' unsuccessful attempt to set fire to the council house at Begoña, which was held by the city's forces. The Carlists had built a contraption of wood and wire, bottles filled with gasoline, tarred canvas, and a fuse, to be hurled by two men. The attempt to use this infernal machine failed, but it did arouse the wonder of the children who saw the fantastic device.

On that same day, the 15th of March, the suspension of hostilities made it possible for people to walk about the streets and get some fresh air. Doña Micaela begged her daughter to go out for a spell. Everyone else was up and about, working the numbness out of their limbs. The women wore housedresses only. At the Arenal girls of marriageable age jumped rope, and some of her friends made Rafaela join them. There, breathing deeply of a free air fresher than that in the storeroom, she felt her sadness begin to go away. All of them felt young again in spirit, and they laughed a great deal as they ran about. They soaked in the simple pleasure of the free movement of their limbs. Cheeks lit up, and eyes flashed once again.

Don Miguel took it all in: that vision of familial life which poured out of the houses into the street, recalling the *romería* of San Miguel which had preceded the days of anguish and worry. Now the whole town was one big family; now, even the air was more domestic and intimate. The spirit of the hearth had taken hold of the populace, which was like a nomad tribe which had settled down for a few fleeting days.

When Rafaela came home, her mother was filled with joy to see some color in her face.

"You're indulged in everything!" Don Epifanio said, "now you have your daughter to indulge you! Get up now, put on your slippers and your housedress and I'll take you by the arm, with Juan's permission, for a walk in the city. Come along now to the riverbank, to jump rope with the other venerable matrons. Up, now, one must know how to take advantage of everything. I'll bet you don't know what they've invented for fishing. They fish with falling shells! There they are on the riverbank and they hear the church bell sound a warning and the conch-shell blowing. Next, with a *whoosh . . . bam!*: a shell makes its way, head down, into the estuary. *Bang*! it explodes, and the water is covered with fish floating belly up."

> Traps and nets we need
> No more for fishing;
> We catch with dynamite
> All the bass we want.

The heightened spirits of the populace continued on through the 16th. People came out of the dreary catacombs to breathe air and sun. A thousand lies ran through the town: they told of the landing of the liberating army, of the defeat of the enemy, of a despatch calling on the city to keep up its morale. Don Juan, always provident, directed his daughter to look to the larder, and he himself put away two sacks of flour.

On the 17th, after two days of peace, firing was resumed. Still, groups of people roamed the streets, with drummers at their head, as if they were still on a holiday pilgrimage, and they tried to lift everyone's spirits.

Don Juan's hope gradually turned to resignation. His poor wife was sinking from hour to hour, and she was seized by suffocating fits of choking.

"Today's issue of *La Guerra* is very good!" exclaimed Don Epifanio on the 18th. And he read out loud an article titled "The Daughters of Bilbao," picturing these daughters as saying, in chorus: "Yes, we are completely pure daughters of the Gospel, but never ever, practitioners of a religion of blood and vengeance." They went on in such wise for a while, until the chorus stopped, and the author blessed them while the populace applauded.

"This and the article on 'A Curse on Thee' are worth an empire. . . . Come here, Marcelinín, and learn the latest:

> Carlos Chapa has a son
> He wants to make a monk—
> Which wouldn't be so hard to do
> If he used his father's hide.

"Learn it well!" Doña Mariquita urged.

"What things you teach the boy!" exclaimed Rafaela.

On St. Joseph's Eve there was intense bombing. At its height, some carpenters marched down the street in a procession honoring their patron saint. They wore red frocks and were accompanied by a cornet and a tambourine. The church bells resounded in the sick woman's head like hammer blows, confusing her so that she wanted overwhelmingly to sleep. She could barely find the breath to ask, "Will they break in?"

"How could they, Señora? Not a chance!"

The doctor exclaimed, "This is the end!" And a priest came, on the run, to hear her confession. At each stroke of the bell, she murmured, "Dear Jesus!" while she kept on saying her rosary. Her daughter and her husband tiptoed in and out of her corner of the warehouse.

A great calm, a calm filled with sadness, fell over them all. The children whispered in their corner. From time to time Marcelino went to gaze at her from the end of the bed. He had already been summoned to come and give his mother a long, soft kiss. "Always be a good boy, and don't make your father mad at you," she told him.

The sick woman slept some of the time, and then would be overcome by choking.

At dawn, an anguished peal of bells was followed by a muffled voice calling out, "Oh, the children! Dear Jesus! Marcelino!"

"He's right here, Mama!"

"All of you?"

"Yes, all of us."

An interval of supreme silence followed, and only the anguished breathing of the sick woman could be heard; her mind was filled with things to say at parting, by way of farewell, but she was so overcome by sleep that she could hold on to none of them to utter a word.

She thought to herself: *When will this end*? After a moment of anguished silence, the house shook with the detonation of a shell bursting close by. The dying woman raised her arms in terror, gave a last cry, and fell back on her pillow.

"They're firing like madmen, in a rage," yelled Don Epifanio, coming in at that moment. "Tomorrow the troops are coming in!" He went up to the bedside, looked at the woman's unmoving eyes, and grew profoundly serious. "Rest in peace!"

Her heart had given way. The world had died for her, and in her poor head the hammering had stopped, and with it had vanished all the anguish and terror, along with the phantoms which had peopled her dream of life. Now she would rest at last in the eternal reality of an unending dream.

Military sappers moved in and out of the house, the children anxiously watching it all; they longed to go out and find fragments of the last shell and to see the destruction.

Don Juan was left more stunned than grief-stricken. Doña Mariquita, wiping her eyes, got ready to lay out the body. Rafaela murmured to herself, "She's dead! . . . Dead?" Without really understanding anything, she began to give directions for the burial, for her father had decided that it should be at once. The bell which had been ringing to indicate a shelling now tolled for death. Juanito did not know what to do, as he silently wiped away the tears which the entire scene had drawn from him; but he cried as a reaction to the whole atmosphere around him, he cried from a need to cry, rather than from real pain, for he felt a great emptiness within a sense of profound calm. He wished to appear strong, but what he felt was mere coldness.

Rafaela took Marcelino by the hand and brought

him over to give his mother a last kiss on her forehead, as she said, "Mama is dead! Be a good boy always."

The boy retired to a corner of the room and broke into bitter and silent tears. Crying brought him grief, and grief brought to his mind the story of the death of Julia, the mother of Juanito, hero of his school primer. He cried from fear, but fear of what he knew not.

At noon Don Miguel arrived, and for a while he stood gazing on the dead woman. He wiped away his tears and shivered at the thought of her final hours. He sat down, took a deck of cards from his pocket, and began playing solitaire. As he played, he secretly watched his niece and thought, *How alone she will be in this world when I am dead!*

Four men came to take the corpse away, without a priest, without any accompaniment whatever. There was no sorrowing responsory for the dead, not even of the kind which is said as a kind of alms, muttered in Latin to get it over with.

When Rafaela saw the coffin, her poor mind turned to an obsessive song:

> Atop the coffin, carabí,
> atop the coffin, carabí
> a small bird rides, hurí, hurá.
> Elisá, Elisá, de Mambrú . . .

a song which floated over the dark cloud of ideas that spring from death, and which took hold of her in her shaken state:

> singing pío, pío, carabí,
> singing pío, pío, carabí,
> pío, pío, pa, carabí, hurí, hurá . . .

Without a mother! They're taking her away in a box. . . . Who will sit next to me at table from now on?

atop the coffin, carabí . . .

There's no one left for me to take care of. . . . What will I do during these days we're shut up . . .

a small bird rides, carabí, hurí, hurá . . .

If I only had a sister . . . But, both brothers . . .

singing pío, pío, carabí . . .

How many times I've sung in the atrium of San Juan, when the boys came to give us a fright. . . . A peal of the bells sounded warning of a shell. *The boys . . . they used to come . . . Ignacio, the son of the chocolate-shop owner, who's in the woods now . . . with the assassins who killed Mama . . .*

Meanwhile, the coffin with its corpse remained in the middle of the street, inasmuch as its bearers, on hearing the bell toll for a shelling, had taken refuge in a doorway.

When will this end?

She had died, carabí . . .

Yes, she's died, died! What is that? Dead . . . dead . . . dead . . .

they've taken her to bury, carabí, hurí, hurá . . .

What a bothersome song! Like a fly! What days these are!

what beautiful hair she has, carabí . . .

Whose hair will I comb now? I used to comb hers every morning . . . What will I do now at that hour?

Just then, as the recurrent song came to mind again, the infantile "pío, pío," the shell landed; the report shook her and brought her back to reality. The refrain vanished, and Rafaela broke into tears and exclaimed, "Oh, my mother!"

Don Miguel looked at her with fright, and Don Epifanio, who didn't know what to say, exclaimed, "Thank God! Cry, girl, cry!"

"Yes, yes, I know. . . . Leave me alone," she said to Enrique, who approached her to mutter the usual commonplaces such circumstances require.

That night it took Rafaela a long time to get to sleep. The pealing of the bells to warn of shells was the only echo which came from out of the darkness to remind her of reality; they echoed the slow passing of the hours over eternity, and the mystery of death over her soul. A shell crashed into the house next door; her mind and soul fused; she felt as if the report came up from the floor itself, and, finding herself still alive in her own bed she felt an obscure intuition that life is an unending miracle; when she prayed "Thy will be done," she gave God unconscious thanks for having taken her mother.

Next day, the feast of St. Joseph, the shelling was stopped. Rafaela thought: *Now she could have rested a bit!*

This is a stupid siege! thought Ignacio when he heard of the death of Rafaela's mother.

The young soldiers were anxious to go into combat and attack, and the officers did a good deal of complaining against the higher command. "Rather than surrender from hunger, those Bilbaínos will chew on wood," the old man Castor had said. One night, a patrol of three or four men approached the walls with stealth; beside one of the city's forward trenches, one of them said, "Right here. A blast of dynamite and there's your breach." Another soldier argued for occupying a neighboring house with a company of men, and, when the gates were opened in the morning to let in their scattered sentries, attacking them.

The captain grew ever more stiff with Ignacio, looking for some excuse to have him charged and locked up. Ignacio went to his commanding officer and told him his complaint, and ended by pleading to be sent into action elsewhere. The officer made a few negative comments, but, in the face of Ignacio's strong plea, he drew up an order to transfer the soldier to Somorrostro. And he went, leaving a package of food and drink for his mates, who remained behind to go on commenting on the shelling.

Ignacio was moved by a strange unease, an inner disquiet, an anxious longing to see something new and truly serious. He didn't feel at home with his comrades, who fitted into the narrow scheme of battalion life with all its arguments and petty rivalries and who were adapted to the monotonous life of guard duty. In his moments of discouragement and vacillation, before he made his decision to leave, he had told himself "I am who I am," and he had remembered Pachico's aphorism: things are as they are and they cannot be any other way. When he thought of Pachico he felt the inner emptiness of the war, and he tried to conjure up more lively emotions. He had brought with him into the country the spirit of the city streets.

When Pedro Antonio heard of Ignacio's decision, he grew livid with anger and wanted to go knock the idea out of his son's head. But realizing how stubborn the boy was, he changed his mind and began to write letters urging him to give up his reckless plan.

Inside the city things were going from bad to worse. During the suspension of the bombardment following the Feast of St. Joseph, the rumble of cannonfire could be heard in the direction of Somorrostro. People began to feel the pang of hunger, and mortality rates were five times normal. Children suffered from the lack of air and sunshine. The infants who were born in the warehouses seemed scarcely fit to live, as if born to trouble.

The spiritual atmosphere was growing dark, and the merrymaking gradually ceased. The siege was no longer a joking matter.

Doña Micaela's death left behind a wake of sorrow in the Arana family. Like profound harmony, the feeling of death shrouded all the small events of daily life, giving them unity and depth, and colored the infinite fabric of ordinary life. For a time the realization that we all must die became a living reality, but then gradually death again became an abstract and lifeless idea. To Rafaela it seemed at times that she could hear the echoes of her dead mother's lamentations, and that her ghost still wandered fearfully about the warehouse, as if she were uneasy over her family's well-being.

Don Juan was conscious of the break in his customs and habits, and although his daughter's presence filled the house, he felt every morning a silence in his soul, the absence of a continuous murmuring noise which he had never really noticed until it was gone. He missed his wife's sighs and soft complaints, and he began to sigh inside himself, seeing everything in a darker light than before. Don Epifanio tried to raise his spirits, as he used to do for his own late wife. Soon after his loss, Don Juan's turn to serve at the cemetery post came up, and there, as his years of married life ran through his memory, he wept within himself, bracing himself against his rifle. *He, too, would die . . .*

"Sentry, wake up!" a voice called out to alert him to his duty.

"I'm awake all right." That poor suffering woman, she had kept his house in order, had kept him from troubles, and had embellished his life with her tender and sweet and modest laments. She had been for him the fragrance of his home and hearth. He recalled the cold damp winter nights when he would find Micaela sitting by the fire. Now, in the silence of the night, he was listening to the distinct calling out of the sentries in the enemy camp.

"This is all irreparable!" Don Epifanio repeated. "What destruction! They're saying now that when the Carlists come in, they'll wipe out the very name Bilbao. *La Guerra* is right: the only enemy is the priest and the villager."

La Guerra fanned the flames of hatred against the villager, against the entire rural population around Bilbao. Calling attention to the villager's enmity against Bilbao, it demanded all manner of rights for the city and none for Vizcaya as a whole. It called for the secession of the city from the regional government, so that Bilbao would not have to pay obeisance to the Sanhedrin at Guernica. It called for an end, once and for all, to the long quarrel between those who walked in crowded streets and those who lived scattered on the mountain, the quarrel that filled Vizcaya's history, the struggle between the city and the countryside, between the farmer and the merchant.

"For once the Bilbaínos are saying clearly what they want," came the reply from the countryside.

During the week of cease-fire after the Feast of St. Joseph, people began to guard against the growing scarcity of the necessities of life. Rationing was introduced: a pound of bread for each person under arms, and half a pound for everyone else. Military requisitioning was imposed on all warehouses. Don Juan was able to save two sacks of flour, though some people paid twenty-five duros in fines for such hoarding. As one of the current songs of those days put it—

> On the twenty-fifth of March
> They put us on a ration;
> But what does bread matter
> If we have a lot of heart?

Frequent firing could be heard in the distance, and because of the truce the curious were able to go out and watch the smoke of the liberating army and then talk about it. Some spoke of the Black Mountain or the Artillery Mountain, some said they could see the liberating columns, and many said they could see nothing at all.

"There's smoke in Nocedal!"

"No, sir. It's in San Pedro Abanto!"

"I tell you all that the smoke is from beyond the estuary of Somorrostro."

"Beyond, is it? You're a bit Liberal, you are!"

"Listen, Zubieta, why didn't you bring out your curved spyglass?"

"But don't you see, there to your right? Of course, if you're going to keep your spyglass shut . . ."

"You've got cobwebs in your eyes . . ."

"And you see visions . . ."

One morning the lookers-on were assembled in the house of one of them, who had put up a sign which read *Model Madhouse. From Here to Leganés.*

"It means the defeat of Serrano!" some cried when they heard the church bells pealing on the 27th.

"The army advances victoriously!" exclaimed Don

239*

Epifanio, using the slogan then in vogue, a phrase first uttered by the Brigadier-General.

Ever since the death of her mother, Rafaela felt herself changed, another person. The calm with which she had cared for her mother was gone, and she inherited her mother's anxiety and unease for the safety of her father and brother. During the day she was anguished by the round of events. At night she kept asking herself, *Will they break in? Will we lack for food?* She felt herself a mother in spirit, the soul of the house; and yet her love for Enrique, faint and still not confessed to herself, was the real rhythm to which her heart beat. Don Epifanio, a frequent visitor, called her Little Mother, or Landlady.

"I'm going to move in here. . . . The fact of finding your clothes clean, with all the buttons sewn on, has no price. . . . There's something missing, you go and find it for me. . . . God give you a good husband! . . . You turn red? Why, if I was twenty-eight. . . . Let's see now, where do you stand with Enrique at this moment?"

"What things you say . . ." And she stared into the darkness of the warehouse.

On the 28th, the bombardment began anew. For four days the enemy mortars thundered over the city. On April 1st, Holy Tuesday, the Easter truce went into effect.

Wheat flour was scarce, so bread was made of forty percent bean-flour at five cuartos a pound. It was a bread laced with weevils, inedible because of its rough hardness.

"There's still bread! Forward march!" exclaimed Doña Mariquita.

While they still could do so, they fed themselves on the belief that man does not live by bread alone.

On Holy Wednesday the Aranas read out loud the proclamation by the commander in charge of the siege in which he counseled Bilbao to surrender. One of the generals of the liberating army had been buried, and another was dying. It was painful to see Spaniards killing each other without justification. A sensible population, one which was also flourishing, rich, and exclusively devoted to the prosperity of its industry and commerce, would put political passion aside and decide to save lives by surrendering. The King, out of compassion for the city, wished to speed the decisive hour by ordering the bombardment of San Juan de Somorrostro. Abnegation and heroism of the type shown by the inhabitants of Numantia, explicable only towards a foreigner, were among Spaniards senseless, inhuman, and cruel. The King was not impatient to subdue Bilbao, for its fate was sealed; but he saw with sorrow that a handful of obdurate men, who doubtless had charges pending against them, judging the Carlists to be vengeful, had deceived themselves and others, dragging them along to put up a self-centered resistance, under the mask of patriotic abnegation. The King, King of all the Spanish and not of one party alone, would bring prosperity to the nation, being Spanish by race and heart . . .

"Stop right there!" exclaimed Don Epifanio. "What kind of Spaniard is he really? He's French, French by race, Austrian by birth, and Italian by education. . . . The real one was the one who died at Oroquieta, and not this one who's a cobbler from Bayonne who only looks like the real one, the real pretender . . ."

The proclamation ended by saying that when the King marched into Bilbao by main strength, all the

efforts of the leaders of the besieged would not suffice
to keep back the excited masses.

"The sword of honor given him as a present by the
armchair patriots of Bayonne must be good for something . . ."

The King, in short, opened his arms to them, faithful, in his exhortations, to his own conscience as a
Christian, a Spaniard, and a soldier. The bloodshed
would fall upon the blind and obdurate. Would that
Heaven would illuminate the truth for them. The world
would judge all parties, and history would assign each
man his place.

"So be it. Amen," Doña Mariquita said. "And let
them get on with the assault once and for all!"

"Will they break in?" asked Rafaela, in a tone of
voice that caused her father to look at her and feel a
chill, for she seemed like his dead wife come back, as
if her sorrowful ghost stood before him.

Meanwhile Don Epifanio was exclaiming, "The Army
advances victoriously!"

The besieged turned a deaf ear to enemy admonitions.
La Guerra vociferated against the Carlists and against
the abuse heaped on Bilbao by the besiegers in *El
Cuartel Real*. There was a real hunger for news.

La Guerra maintained that the Carlist insurrection
was a product of Jesuit lodges and of the conspirators
of the Vatican, and that Bilbao defended the cause of
freedom of choice, of rationalism against dogmatic faith.

"Not quite . . . not quite . . . ," murmured Don Juan.

The days during which the Church celebrates the
Passion of Christ were spent in enforced fasting. The
churches were in ruins and deserted; no worshipers
attended or even gathered at the sites. The church of
San Juan was in disorder. Children romped about

inside, picking up the pieces of prismatic glass which had been the candelabra, in order to make colored light. They played hide-and-seek around the altar and climbed the pulpit, delighted to be able to play and run and shout in such a solemn place.

On those same days *La Guerra* amused itself by attacking the former director of the Holy Week procession, now a guerrilla chief. It called Don Carlos an assassin, adding that he was worthy of papal blessings, and on Holy Thursday it made a frontal attack on the Church itself, in an article called "Jesus."

"God will punish us for such blasphemy," said Rafaela.

"I've already told you—they'll never break into the city!"

On Holy Saturday, issues of *El Cuartel Real* arrived, with detailed descriptions of the fighting in Somorrostro.

People began to hide their discouragement. Horsemeat came on sale at twelve cuartos a pound. An hour later the price had risen to three reales. At the end of the day it reached one peseta and then three—for those who could pay. Those who could not ate cat, at thirty to forty reales each, and even rat, at one peseta. How Marcelino and his playmates stared at the street-sweeper when, early in the morning, he emerged from the warehouse with the rats which had been caught during the night hanging from his waistband, rats which had fed on Don Juan's hidden flour!

The bombardment was resumed. But, what was the shelling compared to hunger? . . . Shells? . . . Rafaela went with some friends one night to the Arenal to watch the effect they produced as they fell through the darkness. The shells had become part of ordinary life, they were a common phenomenon, but hunger! Hunger dissolves the social tissue, corrodes it!

"The government is making mock of us," Don Juan would repeat.

When the bells pealed a warning, the pedestrians would take refuge in the doorways, and the spirit of the people showed itself in the dialogues carried on there.

"Do you all know," an old woman was saying one morning, in the Arana doorway, "that they're digging a mine under us so they can come in at night?"

"Don't talk such nonsense, for God's sake, woman!"

"Nonsense? Surely the nonsense is in putting up such a stubborn resistance . . ."

"Be quiet!"

"Shut her up!"

"She's a Carlist! Go to the woods! To jail with her!"

"One has to see it to believe it. . . . Some people eat cat . . . ugh! how disgusting! . . . Others eat rat. . . . And as for the wine! Cannonball firewater, the worst kind, and logwood . . ."

"Well, listen here, the defenders of religion are putting our churches in fine shape. . . . The things one sees!"

"I should say . . . a miracle a day. . . . What about the bombshell that fell next to a cradle and didn't explode? The child's guardian-angel must have defused it . . ."

"What about the shell that killed the priest sleeping in the vestry and tore the head off a saint's image? Was that a miracle, too?"

"Last night they put a piece of white bread down alongside our black bread . . ."

"So?"

"We've got a lot to tell. . . . A chicken at seven duros;

milk at six reales for a quarter of a liter; a couple of
eggs at twelve reales. . . . Live and learn!"

"That's right . . . and them, the rich ones, hide away
white bread, while the poor . . . I know one of *them*
has the house full of hams."

"Be quiet, you witch!" Don Epifanio yelled at her
from the warehouse.

"As if I didn't know . . . the rich ones, they . . ."

"What rich ones, and what kind of nonsense are you
talking? The very rich are not in the city, and if they
are, they pay in gold. The poor have the cheap places
to eat in. The people who have to put up with everything are those of us who are in the middle . . ."

"Just as always, as always," murmured Don Juan,
"the middle class . . ."

"And then you spoiled young men who can't learn
to eat cat . . ."

"Even though they were pickled witches!"

"And now they're saying that the Law is going to
set what can be charged for everything! . . . About
time!"

"You can say that for a certainty . . . this is a
scandal. . . . There may be some who laugh. They
want the shelling to keep up, so they can put on boots,
and that way they won't surrender . . ."

"Out on the street with you! Get out of here fast!
And may a shell land on you!"

"Get out of here, you witch; to jail with her!"

"Carlist!" screeched Doña Mariquita, after the fleeing
woman. "*La Guerra* was right, death without mercy
to these schemers! Pluck off their feathers! Did anyone
ever see such cheek!"

"Poor woman!" murmured Rafaela.

The authorities did, in fact, introduce price control,
and all goods began to be sold under the counter at a

price higher than before, despite the consequent danger of fines.

"I said it before. This is sheer mathematics. . . . Supply and demand, and there's nothing more to it," muttered Don Juan, with the smile of one in the know.

Don Juan worried about the price of food, feeling himself bound to the habit for professional reasons. The price of articles sold retail had increased much more than those sold wholesale, and selling by middlemen and bargainers was on the increase. Poor families who kept chickens took great care of them, so as to sell the eggs at the highest prices. The city, reduced altogether to its own resources, all work paralyzed, spontaneously responded to an urge to divide up the riches, while the poor exploited the swollen needs of the rich by simply withholding supplies. Meanwhile, the usurers grew fat; their lairs were brimful of jewels which had for long been treasured and guarded as family heirlooms.

And thus, slowly, the city was being consumed, as if by a nondelirious fever.

"This is ignominious!" yelled Don Epifanio, losing patience. "Let them carry out an attack as in '36. Let them rush our trenches in man-to-man combat! . . . This means to lose without glory! . . ."

"Without glory to put up with hunger and living in storehouses?" asked Rafaela.

"The Army advances victoriously!" replied the émigré, pulling himself together.

On the 10th the bombardment was suspended; on the 11th the river waters came down on them like a cataract.

A windstorm blew over the city: chimneys were carried away, trees were uprooted. A bridge was rent by the force of the water. The superstitious were terrified. Simple souls, already suffering from the effects of the shelling, were convinced it was the end of the city, recalling the ancient prediction that it would perish by a flood. Don Miguel, who had listened calmly to the warning bells signaling shells on the way, hid under his bed, stopping his ears against the sound of thunder. Don Juan hurried to transfer his grain for fear of leakage. As the water invaded the already wrecked houses it finished the demolition left by the shells; the waters flooded the deserted houses, undermining them and assuring their ruin, forming deep muck in the debris. And the threat of typhus floated, invisible and threatening, over all, leading to hysteria. A pitiless heaven vented its fury on the fallen.

In an attempt to raise spirits somehow, a patrol of men playing guitars toured the streets, on a merciful errand of consolation.

The prime and utmost consideration, in the face of the flood, was given to saving the supply of powder: it was stored under one of the arches of a bridge that had been left intact and dry, close by the estuary.

The inhabitants of the besieged city imaginatively put the overpowering current to work, even as it was beginning to subside, by throwing into it bottles topped with small white flags, containing descriptions inside of their situation, like castaways on a desert island. The children, when they heard about it, were delighted with this device right out of *Robinson Crusoe*. Meanwhile, the authorities thought of launching balloons and setting up a system of semaphores.

The same day the flood began, news was received of the approach of the liberating army, of its latest battle, and of the advance of twenty thousand reserve troops under the command of the marqués del Duero.

"At least he's a serious man," remarked Don Juan, who had looked on General Serrano with suspicion ever since the Covenant of Amorebieta.

A military communiqué raised their spirits. It had been brought into the city by an ingenious customs guard who disguised as a villager, had crossed the rugged mountains by night under cover of the storm. He was treated like a hero. His news, all oral, was published. Songs were written to him, a collection was taken up to reward him, and his photograph was put on sale. Single-handedly he had brought the city hope, awakening in her a bit of hero worship.

There was intense hunger for communication with the outside world, for some word of what was happening among the folds of those hills and mountains which loomed up so serenely a short distance away. Some mariners set up a semaphore.

"Are they answering?" Rafaela asked her father when he arrived home after watching the experiment.

"Yes, the Carlists have answered by showing us a fine slice of ham on a pole, as well as some bread, a wineskin, and a cooking pot."

"But haven't we made mincemeat of those stupid jokesters with our cannon?" asked Doña Mariquita.

"Bah! It's their idea of a clever joke. . . . They have to show their tenderness towards us in some way . . ."

And that was their way of demonstrating it. Often they left written admonitions in the advance outposts, along with the silent device of displaying the black bread of the besieged alongside the white bread of the besiegers.

During this last cease-fire, which lasted twenty days, the city felt its poverty even more vividly. Don Juan, his flour remaining hidden after a second search for such goods, ingeniously managed to bake a loaf of white bread, which his children ate crumb by crumb, as if it were pastry.

As the truce was prolonged, people began to visit each other, to go from warehouse to warehouse, and even to stroll in the streets. They exchanged observations with one another, thus enlarging their understanding of the bad times they were going through together. Domestic unease, held within the bounds of each house and enveloped in the louder succession of public events, began to turn into a public depression made up of individual ills. Those who sorrowed felt their sorrow melt when they shared it with others, extending it and coloring the small world in which they were all confined. The women gossiped and composed variations on the theme of disaster, with all the delectation of the sick person who involves the entire world in his illness. Fear melted into sorrow and discouragement, anger and impatience into forced joy, care into optimism.

Rafaela went up to the floor where she normally lived, to her old home. It broke her heart to see it filled with trash and dust and to find a lovely wardrobe of hers smashed, a wardrobe she remembered fondly from her earliest childhood. She heard a mewing and found her cat reduced to bare bones, like the spirit of the abandoned home. As she looked at the ruin where order had once reigned, she remembered her mother. Leaning against the wall of the lonely house she cried in silence, while the cat, watching her every move, stared at her in a fixed gaze.

What was it all leading to? Why so much destruction? What was all this about Liberals, Carlists, Republicans, Monarchists, Radicals, Conservatives, and Progressives . . . the Liberty of Worship, Catholic Unity, Universal Suffrage . . . they were nothing but things for men to talk about! And they were claiming to defend religion! What did men understand by religion? Religion! The sweet reign of peace! The constant impulse to make one hearth and home of the entire world! When she went to Mass, when she withdrew to the cloister of St. James, there to pour out the most intimate impulses of her soul, what did she care about all those things over which the manly defenders of religion were fighting?

After she had dried her eyes and gone back to the warehouse, she ran into Don Miguel.

"Well, hello, my little niece! Now you're the mother of the house . . ."

She wondered if he could tell that she had been crying.

Don Miguel recounted a thousand comic details of the goings-on at the so-called Tribunal of Canned Goods, after the altercations concerning food, most of which was indeed canned.

"What battles rage! 'This woman here wouldn't hand over a can of tuna-fish in tomato sauce for less than twelve reales, when the municipal order stipulates that they are to cost six' . . . Tomorrow there is a performance at the theatre in homage to the beauty of women: you'll go, won't you, Rafaelilla?"

"I'm in mourning . . ."

"No such thing . . . now. There's no question of formality these days, certainly not of mourning."

Rafaela went, after all, to the theatre, which was filled. The city made it a meeting point, where the lively spirit of the gathering might affect them all by extension. The orchestra played and the chorus sang: the *jota*, the song of the auxiliaries, was performed, and all hearts resounded to the words:

> We are auxiliaries—without colors or slogan.
> We are defenders—of an invincible people.
> We are Liberals—and will shed our blood
> all our blood—for liberty!
> . . . .
> God who guards us—God who tends us
> Knows that his people—defends its glory.
> If its fate is sad—we die battling.
> Let it be known—we die for liberty.

And the word "Liberty!" was reiterated with haughty insistence, for it meant the same, apparently, as the glory of God.

Rafaela was deeply and sadly moved at another song, sung slowly and drawn out, in which the peaceful merchant was represented, now under arms, saluting his God, his Fatherland, and his mother.

> When we are all at our tasks
> Working in busy peace
> Recalling the sorrows of the siege
> Perhaps our mothers will weep.

No, her mother would not weep, not ever again.

They left the theatre recomforted, with new spirits.

Outside, the serenades went on: clumsy and vulgar songs were sung, wherein the jokes turned into insults, and the enemy was called assassin, incendiary, Pharisee, Carib, coward; songs in which the *escarapelas*, those with Phrygian caps and cockades, appeared before the Bilbao girls, the *niñas*, who smiled despite the Caribs hidden in the mountains. But the girls sang back:

> We have sworn to die
> Before we give in.
> If you take our forts,
> We'll fire our powder—to the sky!

Meanwhile, bean-bread gave way to maize-bread.

During the truce, the children at the Arana warehouse were sent to school, so as to keep them out of the way. The school had been improvised in a lower floor, and there the boys could exchange the latest rumors, thus enlivening their inner world.

"At my house, four shells landed . . ."

"In mine, six . . ."

"Twelve, in mine . . ."

"Shut up, dummy! Wouldn't you like that to be true!"

"No, that's the truth! As there is a God!"

"Hold on or I'll slap your face . . . just look at him, hasn't he told you a dozen shells fell on his house . . . What cheek! Just to give himself airs . . ."

"I've picked up more shell-fragments . . . !"

"Here's another one!"

"My grandmother says they're digging a mine under us, to get in. . . . They did the same the other time, too . . ."

"Fibber! You're worse than a fibber! Your grandmother must be an old Carlist . . ."

"An old Carlist? My grandmother? . . . Why I'll give you a punch. . . . Take that back, or dare to say it again. If you say it again, I'll bust your snout . . ."

"How are they going to get in? Why they're even scared to death of our cheval-de-frise . . . ! Isn't that plain to see?"

"No! Tell us!"

"Those at La Sendeja, at the Battery of Death. . . . They've got some spikes to them . . ."

"So? The last time they brought some Moors with them to jump the trenches . . ."

"This guy keeps pissing in our eye. . . . Is that what your grandmother says too?"

"Some Moors? Like those who jumped in the bull

ring, jumping over the bayonets? . . . Don't you remember? Like those . . . ? Ay, and they'll cover themselves with pitch-tar from the bogs to jump even safer and better . . ."

"Stop right there, stupid! You'll be believing that fellow there soon, and he can fib to his grandmother. . . . As soon as they catch sight of Vinagre's people, watch out!"

"Who, the Moors?"

"The Carlists, stupid!"

The children built up a fresh and poetic vision of the war, an entirely Homeric vision embroidered out of things they had witnessed, out of dreams, out of the scraps of things they had half-seen or overheard.

What a pleasure it was to hear those things told and to have to tell them! What fun it was to elaborate lies on a tissue of truths and make epics out of war. They listened with mouths half open: while their elders endured the war, they made poetry of it. Living for the day, their wills still virgin, uncaring for the morrow, and uninterested in the passions behind the fighting, blind to the consequences and the core of it all, they saw only pure form; it was a game pregnant with unheard-of emotions.

Meanwhile, the longed-for liberty took its time in arriving. On April the 25th, the chief of garrison summarized all the anguish of the city and its growing despair in a report addressed to the Minister of War: "Tomorrow marks the end of the corn. The population is without bread, without rice, and there is no ham or bacon to be bought. The troops are on half rations, and without wine. I'll find them some coffee. The situation grows ever more acute. I am attempting to keep up their morale, but it is low, and there is a deepening lack of confidence in our being able to save ourselves, or in anyone else's being willing to do it. I am taking active measures against this idea and will even put it down if it persists and spreads."

During the truce, as scarcity worked its silent damage, spirits fell faster than during the actual bombardment. Discontent was turned into rumor and the word "capitulation" was beginning to turn up quietly. It was whispered that battalions of Catalans were about to swoop on the town, and some people already dreamt of the giant mustaches of Savalls, and called any further resistance mere stupid obstinacy.

Don Epifanio no longer spoke of nearby smoke. On the 27th the cry went out: "There is no bread left!"

"Why don't they attack? The cowards!" shrieked Doña Mariquita.

And Don Epifanio answered her with a song:

> Come out of your trenches, come out,
> And come up to our battlements, come.
> Carlist cowards, come attack our forts.
> Out there, hidden in your trenches,
> You haven't the courage to fight.

But under the sound of the songs lay the silence of despair.

Some demanded a weeding-out: that all those suspected of Carlism, all the country people (whose number they exaggerated), be rooted out and expelled from the city. One effect would be, incidentally, to lessen the penury of those that remained: they would have slightly more. It was said that there was a working relation, an intelligence system, between the peasants inside the city and the besiegers outside; that they passed information at night by means of light signals. It all amounted to pure suspicion, an itching to put the finger on an imaginary traitor. Others were blamed for spreading word of the discouragement and alarm felt in the city, of planting the word "capitulation," so that, whispered from person to person, it would have its effect. This last crime was thought of as poisoning the city's faith, a worse crime than poisoning the water to cause an epidemic—and no less fantastic.

"Those peasants, those peasants," Doña Mariquita would repeat. "I can't get it out of my head that Arteta is in the auxiliaries. . . . Arteta! Why, I knew his parents, and his grandparents, his whole family . . . Carlists to a man, all Carlists, life-long Carlists . . ."

"And what has that to do with it?" Don Juan would ask.

"What? A Liberal from a Carlist family? It can't be—it's like having a Carlist from a Liberal family!"

"Can you possibly mean that being Carlist or Liberal is hereditary, and perpetually so?"

"I may not be able to explain myself, Don Juan, but I know whereof I speak. These things are taken in with the mother's milk, and what's sucked in flows out in the shroud. Thus it was in my time, and thus it will always be. . . . Anything else would be unnatural . . . one could not believe in anyone, if he can be one thing as well as another . . ."

On the morning of the 28th, when a number of foreigners were leaving the city, Juanito and Enrique happened to meet at an advanced Carlist post, where they ate white bread and spoke with Juan José.

"One of these days you'll have us inside the city."

"We'll receive you with gunfire."

"That's the kind of friends I like. Let's shake on it!"

They spoke with more warmth than ever, their communion of friendship stronger than ever. Juan José and Enrique talked together like old comrades, calling up ancient memories, but without alluding to the fist fight they had once fought to see which of them would be chief of their street. The fist fight was in their memories the dominant link between them, tingeing all other memories. More than anything else, it united them. That day was still present in their minds, the day when after beating each other to a white heat, they broke apart, covered with sweat and mud, and wiped their bloody noses.

That afternoon, Rafaela went out with a neighboring girlfriend, along with Enrique and Juanito, to take a walk around the outskirts. She scarcely heard Enrique's talk, for she feasted her eyes on the fields, on the orchards and gardens she had not been able to see for so long. When would all this be over, so they could go for long walks? Enrique was explaining the layout of the enemy positions to them when they saw people begin to run.

Turning pale, Juanito said, "Let's get out of here! Back home!"

Just then Rafaela's friend gave a cry, and stopped short.

"What is it?"

"I can't walk . . . they must have hit me. . . ." She began to turn pale as wax at the mere thought of having been wounded.

Rafaela looked at her brother and at Enrique, trying to get them to hurry. The two youths surrounded the girl, so that she might lean on them, but as she looked at the ground and saw blood, she fainted and fell into the arms of Enrique. Rafaela felt astonishment, terror, and, underneath it all, an unconscious stab of jealousy.

"Hurry, hurry! Into the first house. Right here, in this doorway!"

They carried her to the nearest place; people gathered; and Rafaela, scarcely knowing how, found herself beside her brother en route home.

"But . . . what of Concha?" she asked, suddenly stopping.

"Let her be. She's being attended to. We'd only be in the way."

What a brute! she thought to herself, and then: *Why did Enrique stay behind? Will he be more than "in the way"?*

The wounded girl had been hit by a peasant who had fired as if idly target-shooting, a volunteer in the enemy camp, a villager who wouldn't have hurt a fly normally but who was now playing at war.

When she found herself at home, behind the protection of its walls, Rafaela shuddered, thinking of the danger she had escaped. As soon as she heard what had happened, Doña Mariquita screamed, "Now, now we'll never surrender, savages! Pharisees!"

Rafaela, excited by the afternoon's happenings, felt her mother's fearful spirit come to life in her again, but soon she began to feel a vast irritation and hatred of men at war. She had an idea—an idea so deep that it wasn't entirely conscious—about the stupidity of war, about the stupidity and brutality of all those things men do. The things men do!—men who have not been guided by religion, by the spirit of the family which draws together and combines in itself both the masculine and the feminine. They had wounded Concha, poor Concha, without meaning, without her counting at all in the war. Those men played at war like children, and then they tried to convince women to believe that they were fighting for serious reasons!

The people, downcast in their wretchedness, straightened up under fire. The shooting only served to give them courage, taking their minds off their hunger. Another appeal was sent off to the Minister of War.

On the 29th at six in the afternoon, without prior warning, the church bells began to toll as the shells again rained down: the report of the enemy howitzer sowed confusion and sudden flight. Everyone hurried home, and many of those who had moved back to their dismembered houses during the long truce returned to the storerooms and warehouses. The firing was ferocious at the start, a shell a minute. Within three hours, more than a hundred and fifty had fallen. Dire anxiety again took hold: at Don Juan's no one went to bed until after midnight. And, at dawn of the 30th, they received word that Uncle Miguel, who had been put to bed three days before, was getting worse by the moment and was calling for Rafaela. She went to him as soon as she could, during a lull in the shelling.

The poor man was downcast, sad, his insides all wrong; he sighed at every turn and spoke only of his approaching death, so that his niece might tell him, "It's nothing. . . . You men! As soon as you have the least little pain, you all get scared . . ."

"Do you think that's it?"

He watched his niece in silence, as she came and went, bringing him broth and medicine. He followed her with his eyes and once, when she was out of the room, set about musing on what he should have said to her, what she might have responded, only to feel a new sense of shame in her presence when she returned. Meanwhile, the pealing of the bells in alarm and the enemy fire did not let up.

That night, which Rafaela had to spend in her uncle's house, was filled with true anguish. The bombardment was violent. She had seen her father crestfallen. She knew that there was no more food and that resistance was impossible. She recalled that other sad night, the night of San José, when death carried off her poor mother. *Poor*. The obsessive song of the *carabí* which had sat atop a casket began again to resound in her mind.

"Rafaelilla!"

"What is it?"

He didn't want anything: only that she draw closer; that she answer him; that he might just hear her voice.

The next morning her uncle was much relieved of his pain, and Rafaela returned to her house, leaving him asleep.

"But when are they finally going to make their attack?" demanded Doña Mariquita.

On May Day, a new ray of hope was born, when they saw the Carlists marching along the rim of hilltops, in apparent retreat, with their gear and equipment in wagons. From time to time, news and rumors swept through the city, brought from the fortifications. Enemy battalions moved across the heights, to the left and to the right of the city, over which the thunder of the cannonade continued. There was talk about the death of old Don Castor, who had said that the city's liberators would have to pass over his dead body.

While awaiting the liberation now at hand, the people faced the shelling defiantly, with increased courage. "They're firing from sheer rage!" exclaimed someone who had deluded himself into thinking that shells fired from such a motive were less dangerous.

At last! At four in the afternoon the Spanish flag was seen waving far away, above the camp from which the smoke had come. Meanwhile a Carlist battalion was encamping at Pagazarri. The townspeople followed the outcome of the long struggle anxiously, watching how the liberators dislodged the besiegers. At nightfall, from the Santa Agueda height where the famous *romería* was held, a friendly cannon saluted the liberated town. And while hearts swelled with the longing for freedom, the shelling continued. But despite the shells the women came out to watch in the distance the liberating army crown the eternal height in the calm dusky light. There was danger no longer. They had been saved. There were even people who exclaimed, "The poor Carlists!"

That night, the desire for a realization of their dreams, plus the tag ends of doubt and uncertainly, scarcely allowed anyone to sleep. At eleven, the enemy ceased its firing.

On the 2nd of May, at dawn, the Arana family heard loud cries.

"We've been saved!" yelled Don Epifanio, taking out a package of white bread and sausage. "We're saved! I've just bought some hake from a village woman."

Rafaela remembered her Uncle Miguel, while Marcelino exclaimed, "Bread, papa, look, bread!"

"And the army?"

"At the door. At eleven-thirty last night those savages fired their last shot, yelling from their advance posts at us: 'There's our last one!' "

Everyone spilled out on to the streets, which seemed to grow wider. They were like anthills in the sun: people came and went, greeting each other as if on return from a long journey. Village women came along with their market baskets, and white bread went from hand to hand. Juanito, along with his comrades of the Guards, had gone out to meet the Liberators and, when first they ran into a group of correspondents from the foreign press, they amused themselves by pulling their legs, recounting stories made up of stupendous lies.

It was the 2nd of May, a date already twice glorious in the history of Spain.

The entrance of the liberating forces into Bilbao on the 2nd of May of 1874, awoke the memory of the 2nd of May of 1808, and recalled the almost-forgotten battle of Callao on the 2nd of May of 1866; so that from then on a triad or even a triangle could be formed, of the three dates:

$$\frac{\text{May 2nd}}{1808 - 1866 - 1874}$$

Three! Three, like Liberty, Equality, and Fraternity. Three, like God, Fatherland, and King. Three! From the Trinity on down, a figure pregnant with mystery and full of symbolic life. Nothing, but . . . not for nothing! Was it now perhaps also providential that the formal liberation of the city was postponed, with no harm done, from the 1st, when it was actually freed, to the historic 2nd? The inscrutable mystery of numbers!

Don Eustaquio and Don Pascual ran into each other on the street. Beginning with near embraces, they ended by venting on each other the pent-up wrath they had so long nurtured. And then, having insulted each other, they parted, greatly relieved of a weight, and caring deeply for one another.

While most of those who had stayed in the Arana warehouse went to the Arenal, Juanito climbed with some of his companions to the top of the Archanda cordillera to look at the abandoned enemy forts and to contemplate the town in ruins, as they filled their lungs with the free mountain air. How much they had to tell! The past now past, who was not glad to have been an actor in that drama, a witness to it?

Pillars of smoke arose from the houses the enemy had burned in its retreat. Other houses were prey to marauders who made merry by sacking them, by swooping down on chicken yards, and by knocking down girls of the village whenever they had a chance. They were giving free rein to their instincts, intensified during their enforced confinement, to get even with the country people. Some of these fellows even paraded a stolen cow in triumph through the town's central streets.

On that day the Arana household ate white bread—in the usual room, now a wreck, beside a wall in shambles. The memory of Doña Micaela—whose invisible shade was said to wander in distress through her ruined home—outweighed their joy in liberation.

They had left the warehouse with a certain regret for the place which had served them as shelter and hearth through all the days of their anguished confinement, a place which from then on would be consecrated with the spiritual fragrance given it by the slow death of the poor mother of the family.

In the afternoon, the women and children went out to a park bench at the Arenal to watch the victorious troops march in, while Juan, Juanito, Enrique, and Don Epifanio fell in along the highroad, with the battalion of auxiliaries. The veterans assembled under the flag bestowed by the ex-queen Isabel on the National Militia in 1836.

The liberating army, battered and wretched-looking, entered the city across the Puente Viejo, the only bridge left standing, the old bridge of ancient memories for the town, the blazon of glory of their arms, witness of their own inner turbulence. The army was received by the City Council, and then they marched through the ruins. They passed by, their faces pale with fatigue, between the rows of faces white with misery and stamped with the sign of darkness; there was no wild enthusiasm shown at their passage, merely a few shouts of "Viva!" many demonstrations of solicitude, and a current of mutual compassion. An immense mourning hung in the air, above the happiness, along with the dreamlike lassitude of convalescence. One would think they had all just emerged from a painful nightmare. They felt, one and all, an ardent thirst for rest.

A soldier fainted near Rafaela, and they sat him down on a bench and brought him water. The women fanned him with their fans as if he were one of their sons.

The children were the ones who truly enjoyed the spectacle: the rumble of the drums beating time along the street, the artillery pieces going by with the gunners seated on the gun-carriages, the uniforms and their braided trim, the flags, the colors.

"Those are the Marines!"

"Look, look. . . . There's a colonel! . . ."

"No, dummy, he's a lieutenant-colonel . . ."

One soldier had his arm in a sling, another his head bandaged. All of them were covered with dust. They brought bread, meat, codfish, newspapers with news of the outside world, delayed letters.

The Arana household was assigned six officers and six common soldiers, walking with the lightest of treads and whispering very low. The officers told fanciful stories of their days at Somorrostro; and both the liberated and their liberators competed in recounting setbacks and misfortunes, like old friends, each one dwelling on his own sufferings competitively. They had so much to tell! Now they could take pleasure in the past, now that it was reduced to memories, now that their sufferings were purified of a painful presence and had entered into the past, the inexhaustible source of poetry. How much they would have to tell those who came after them! It was only now that the city people learned that the army had been stranded without ammunition, struggling between life and death.

Doña Mariquita gave vent to her delight and showed a grand disdain for the vanquished besiegers, comparing them to those others who had attempted to assault the city in the previous war.

At nightfall, Rafaela went to visit her uncle, who, in much better spirits, was able to make jokes about the recent bombardment.

That night they heard a disturbance break out in the officers' room. One of them, used to sleeping on the ground, had barely fallen asleep on the bed when he awoke from a nightmare in which he was falling through space. He was lost without contact with the earth; he felt suspended in space and finally had to throw a small mattress on the floor and sleep there. He had learned, during the hardships of the campaign, to love the contact of mother earth.

On the 3rd of May, the first Mass was celebrated, a military Mass in the open air, under the wide sky above them all.

It was something to see all that multitude, silently and almost mechanically following the habitual course of the liturgical office, while each one mused over his own problems, his past pain, the many tasks which the future would require. That silent multitude was the same one which, days before, with no misgivings

on their part, had read that in Bilbao they were defending "free will" against dogmatic faith.

After the column had marched in, friends and relatives of the besieged followed. Long-delayed letters
arrived, telegrams poured in. The relief of Bilbao awoke
all Spain. In La Coruña, the city of the militiamen of
'23, there was dancing in the streets. Santander, Bilbao's rival, sent a special commission. Barcelona sent
money for the poor. Salutes to the "new Numantia"
were dispatched, as well as to the "Pearl of the Seas,"
"The Gravestone of Absolutism"; and even verses were
composed to the city.

At the Aranas', one of Don Epifanio's relatives was
overwhelmed with questions. There was one consolation in what they learned: despite all their hardships
inside the city, it had been far worse for those who
had left. The Liberals outside had lived only by a
miracle, and the Carlists were more amused than ever.
What *tertulias*, what woeful gatherings had assembled
in the villages, baited by the Carlist émigrés from Bilbao! What taunts! What wretchedness!

"And what fanaticism, my lad, what fanaticism! What
sermons! The churches were more like clubs or taverns. . . . 'You Blacks!' here, there and everywhere. . . . Can you imagine that at Eastertime one
couldn't sell a fine lamb at any price, if it were black.
One day when Matrolochu and I went to church, the
people who filled it gave us a wide berth, wide, wide
. . . so as not to touch a Black. You know that priest
from here, I forget his name. . . . He told them that
the statue of Mercury on the fountain in the boule-
vard was a pagan idol, the god of commerce and of
robbery . . ."

"And the god of the people of Bilbao, isn't that so?"

"He didn't have to go much further. In short, after that sermon, into the river with Mercury!"

"And what do they say about us?"

"Bells ringing at all times, and taunts on all sides for any reason whatsoever. . . . The worst were the émigré Bilbao people . . ."

"There's no worse enemy than one cut from the same wood. And did they assume they would break in?"

"Break in? They couldn't have been more certain. Imagine: there was no question of credit for Liberals, and some Carlists celebrated the death of their creditors . . ."

Liberation actually brought a rise in the mortality rate in the city. And further conflicts. Don Juan was impatient because the army did not go out to pulverize the Carlists, while Don Epifanio assured him, in private, that they were busy laying plans to proclaim Alfonsito, son of the dethroned Queen, as King of Spain.

"About time," said the ex-supporter of King Amadeo I. And, thoroughly vexed at the bombardment, he resolved to play no further part in these affairs. He would go on hearing Mass like a good Catholic, of course, but to pay for it? Give his money to the priests so that they might take advantage of it like that one who had gone to the village? Never!

A relapse carried Uncle Miguel to the gates of death. When they brought him the effigy of the Lord (as a matter of pure devotion they told him, for it was a time for general felicitation), he pretended to believe them, but his spirits were sunken and he was living within his lonely fantasies about the approaching final hour.

One morning when his niece brought him his medicine, his tongue grown loose from the weakness of his spirits, he clutched her by the hand, seeing her as in a dream, like a half-real apparition. He drew her head down toward him and kissed her on the brow, saying, "How I have loved you, little Rafaela! Will you remember your poor uncle, the odd old bachelor?"

"Come now! What's all the fuss about? Now's the time to pull yourself together. This is all nothing."

Rafaela felt short of breath. When she left the room she cried silent tears of pity and pain.

The sick man called out to ask if the clock had been wound. Then he began to think about the comedy of death and about what he would say and do if he had been accompanied at his deathbed by a woman who cried over his hand, if he had been surrounded by children he could bid farewell, comforting them with halting words, giving them his advice and his blessing, taking the supreme step with all the appropriate ritual. Drowsy, half-asleep, he heard his niece's footsteps. Then, when the exhortations began, the dying man, immobile and silent, in a cold sweat, began to go over his entire life with immense sadness. *He had never really lived.* He felt a vast sorrow because his fear of being happy had caused him to throw his life away. He longed to return to his past life. He felt left alone in the midst of an immense sea. All his confused thoughts were accompanied by an apparent serenity, as in a vision. In truth, he was unable to fight the languor which gradually overcame him. Finally he surrendered to his sleepiness and entered peacefully into his final moment.

When Rafaela saw those dry, unmoving eyes staring at her, she closed them, looked about her, and then kissed his forehead. Her cheeks burning, she broke into silent weeping. *Poor Uncle! Poor Uncle!*

Once again the sense of death had come to color all

her thought and feeling, tingeing everything with a deep and pure indifference.

Don Juan looked at his dead brother for a while and thought about their life together, about the games they had played as children. The image of death invaded the innermost recesses of his soul, and deep anguish overtook his entire being.

When the will was read, they learned that the niece had been named as sole heir and the maid left a sum for daily household expenses. Notebooks filled with detailed accounts of the bombardment were found in drawers, along with pieces of bean-bread, shell fragments, a portrait of Rafaela as a child, and a lock of hair labelled "My niece's." When Don Juan came upon a collection of obscene photographs and books in a wardrobe, he could not keep from tears and murmured, "How often I tried to cure him! Poor Miguel!"

IV

WHEN IGNACIO reached Somorrostro, where he was assigned to a battalion of the San Fuente reserves, he took with him some tumultuous longings mixed with growing disillusionment. He caught a passing glimpse of his commander in chief sitting on the balcony of a farmhouse, his cheeks burning and a bottle of cognac at his side as he watched in the distance the flashing Carlist mortars firing down on Bilbao. At the general's orders, an oak had been cut down to give him a clearer view.

The boys of the battalion had crowded into another farmhouse like sardines in a fish-basket. The landowner, who had had to give up his bed and sleep elsewhere, was a crafty old man, full of complaints. His wife, who kept covering the soldiers up with their blankets, like a mother, nevertheless stole from them whenever it pleased her. The old man could not understand the thoughtlessness of the young soldiers. Once they broke a window and then hung up a blanket instead to keep out the cold air. They burned a staircase, so that they had to climb in through the balcony. Anything to do damage, for its own sake! The officers' horses trampled his planted fields, and the officers wouldn't let him climb the hillsides, threatening to shoot him as a spy if he did. But when the wine would arrive and the soldiers from Navarre would cry out, "Here comes the spirit of genius," the old man would smile and glance at the floor, thinking about his secret wine-cellar in the basement. And then he would glance at the quartermaster, with whom he had made certain arrangements and deals.

The soldiers did not look kindly on this old peasant, who patiently put up with their taunts and their disdain and meanwhile swindled them whenever it pleased him. Since he wasn't allowed to work in peace, he had no other recourse but to squeeze a little profit for himself out of the war. When confronted with the violence of the men who made war, he, a peaceful man, resorted to cunning. Since there was to be war, it was only right that there should be something in it for everyone.

Ignacio spent his days hoping for a great battle, as war filled his imagination. Meanwhile he played games or hunted for snails to pass the time. The lovely valley of Somorrostro stretched before him like the circle of a vast amphitheatre, divided into unequal parts by an estuary. Beyond the estuary, beginning with the mountain of El Janeo, which dominated the valley, were the mountains where the enemy was encamped, mountains receding into distance until they were lost to view. On this side of the estuary, guarding its entrance and dominating the valley no less than El Janeo, stood El Montaño with its terraced slopes and its sharp peak; then the slopes of Murrieta, in the form of a half-moon, the rough hill of San Pedro de Abanto, and across from San Pedro, on the other side of the gorge where the highway ran, the hill of Santa Juliana. From there, the spurs of the sierra of Galdames climbed like a staircase. The valley itself rose in a smooth slope to join the network of hills linking it to the surrounding heights where clouds usually rested.

The lines of the Carlists extended in a semi-circle across these mountain slopes, climbing up to the abrupt eminence of Galdames. They had laid waste to the

watershed of Santa Juliana, and their trenches sliced
the ground all the way to the heights of Triano. They
had cut the mining railroad which runs along the slopes
of the mountains. There were pits and trenches everywhere, covered roadways without visible outposts or
fortifications; everything was dug underground, so as
not to offer the enemy cannon the least target. The
mines in the area were a help to the Carlists, for they
cut the terrain and made it even more irregular. The
Carlists controlled the highway, the valley's axis, with
their fire. Everyone, even the women, had worked as
furiously as ants to dig in. Who could dislodge them
now? Not even God could get through there!

And further on, in other folds in the terrain, before
Bilbao, additional lines made access doubly difficult.

Among his new comrades, Ignacio breathed like a new
man. Even if these men weren't all volunteers in the
strict sense, they were volunteers in the sense that they
did what they had to do willingly. One of them, a man
called Fermín, had taken to the hills with his cudgel
one day when the bread he was eating suddenly tasted
bitter after someone told him of "the horrors of revolutionary impiety now being unleashed." The men all
loved Ollo and loved Radica even more. Radica, a
stonemason from Tafalla and a hero of the people, had
led them to victory more than once with his cry of
"Long live God!" The two men were their natural
born leaders, men they had followed by choice. Ollo,
a veteran of the Seven Year War, represented the party's military tradition and was the organizer of its forces.
Radica bore inside himself the forceful impulses of the
people, the freshness of its enthusiasm.

The men still remembered the bloody days of the
24th and 25th of the month before. After a long march,

they had reached Navarre to cut off Moriones, who
was on his way to liberate Bilbao. Ollo had made a
long speech haranguing them. Bilbao was being shelled.
The King was thinking of them. They returned to
their positions singing. Then the Republican game-
cock, having crossed the estuary of Somorrostro, attacked them frontally, across the most difficult terrain,
as was his manner. His soldiers enveloped El Montaño
and were about to take its pointed top, swarming up
its rocky sides, almost drunk from the rain of stones
and rifle-fire coming down on them. Suddenly they
rolled up their sleeves and fixed bayonets. But then
the troops from Alava poured in on the San Pedro
side. The Republican cock had to retreat and ask for
reinforcements, while another general took command.
And they didn't take Bilbao—then and there! They
didn't take advantage of the situation to deliver the
coup de grâce to the besieged garrison in the city.
Instead, that stupid bombardment began, that slow,
heavy shelling.

"They came at us in columns, in threes," one of
Ignacio's comrades was saying, "and as they came out
on to open terrain, they came toward us, those poor
men. We fired at them from fifty paces, and the orders
had been to fire at a specific target. Anyone who didn't
follow orders or who fired without taking careful aim
was ordered twenty feet forward! Out of the trenches!
A hundred bullets, a hundred hits on target. Up there,
on that barren crest under the towering heights, we
found the next day a poor enemy soldier trembling so
from cold fear that he could hardly breathe. I told him,
'You can give thanks that you're not a carabinero.'

"Yes, I said that. It's easy enough to get into something, but what about getting out again? And they

were shooting at us from behind, once we had swept them from that slope."

"What good are Lamíndano and Montejurra?" wondered Ignacio, hearing tales about them on that height above the peaceful valley.

Everything raised Ignacio's spirit to the maximum. The bands of irregulars had come together. Out of fragments, an army had grown. The military spirit had taken hold of those now-battle-hardened volunteers, who no longer ran as before, from peak to peak. Now they were entrenched and awaited the attack. The sea air, tempered by the mountains, filled their chests. Their morale grew and their spirits swelled in readiness for the supreme moment. Meanwhile, the ordinary life of the battalion flowed on in its own simple tempo, with its arguments and its personal grudges and its envy and its fights—in short, with all the pettiness of peace. The men muttered about the poor treatment they got, despite the fact that they had all the meat and wine they wanted.

Ignacio could not get used to the unrestrained frankness of the men from Navarre, which was legendary. It struck him as showy and hypocritical, and he thought that anyone who keeps his mind in his mouth does not have it in the right place.

One simply had to hear them talking about their leaders. Leaders? Except for two or three, they were all rogues, interested only in drinking and tomcatting. Because one of the boys had some words with a peasant girl after she wouldn't give him some water to drink, one of the officers, a one-eyed man ugly enough to scare his own mother, sent him to be locked up in a bell-tower, where he was killed by an enemy bullet during an exchange of shots.

"Well, that may be one type of officer . . ."

"One? Well, there's another and another and still another . . . almost all of them. I tell you that no one has come here from Castile to make us rich." The soldier who was speaking then looked at another soldier, a man named Sánchez, a Castilian in their midst. A serious man, he was said to have joined up because he was wanted by the law and because he didn't want to be among men from his own region.

This serious man fascinated Ignacio. He was deeply and truly serious, in every fiber of his being, and he commanded respect. He was tall, sallow, and dry as the trunk of a grapevine. His air and bearing were such that he could easily be taken to be the scion of the ancient race of conquerors. The grim expanses of Castile, leafless and unwatered by streams, bone-dry and burning hot, seemed to have left on him the signs of their grave austerity. He spoke little, but when he did speak the words flowed out precisely and in order, each word solidly linked to the others. He thought clearly and plainly, against a violent chiaroscuro background, within the limited range of his thought. Ordinarily, it was not possible to be sure that he was thinking, for he lived lost in the spectacle of the things that were present.

"I've been told you killed a man," Ignacio said to him one day.

"No. Bad weeds never die. Unfortunately he got well."

"But . . ."

"You young kids don't understand these things. A thieving doctor and a pharmacist—may God strike them dead!—cheated me of his death. My harvests all failed and I was left without half a piece of eight. I took off for the city, and looked up that infamous . . . Those thieves are the ones who understand laws—

since it was themselves who invented them! . . . Times
were bad, no money, and he added fraud to my disasters. He got me to sign a paper which was retro . . .
retroactive. In short, he got me tangled up, the wretch,
so that he ended up with my house at a third what it
was worth . . . A little house like a sun! . . . Just think,
we were all in a continual state of fast, even my wife,
poor thing, so that when the time was up I was able
to get together some money, getting it from others, to
save my little house, and started out in time. As soon
as I reached the place I looked him up, but they told
me he was out of town, and I told that vixen of a wife
of his: 'Look here, I've brought the money. Esteban
Sánchez keeps his word. Here's the amount . . . You're
a witness.' It was useless, no good. When I went back
the bandit told me that the deadline had passed . . .
And everyone told me I was an idiot for not having
gone to court and depositing the money in front of
witnesses . . . Deliberate conniving! As if men of honor
who have to sweat to earn a gnawed piece of bread
had time to study the laws these thieves make up out
of their heads, every day some new ones and each one
more confusing . . . Naturally, they live off such things,
mixing everything up . . . And the filthy Government!
A gang of highwaymen! . . . I begged him, in the name
of his dead mother, I threw myself at his feet in tears
. . . yes, in tears, crying before that bandit . . . Nothing
doing! He looked at the floor, and he tells me, he says:
'I can't eat tears. . . . It's all an act anyway, a farce!
You're a bad lot! If I paid you any heed, you'd skin
me.' He suggested I stay on in my own house, my own
house, and pay rent! And the filthy pig even tried to
give me a handout. When I left I said to him, I said:
'You will remember Esteban Sánchez.' A few days
after he stole my house from me with the help of the

whore of a notary, my wife died on me, from sheer
grief, the poor little thing, so as not to witness such
goings-on, and then my son died, too, from disgust, I
think, so as not to go on living in such a world full of
thieves. And now you'll see what happened. When
they told me that the bastard was on his way to take
over my house, to take over the title, which he had
already stolen, I waited for him on the road and let
him have it, a direct hit. I told you already—he didn't
die. I was denounced, and had to run for it, away from
the world of the rich, from the pig's justice of the rich
and the lawyers, and made my way here, to kill Liberals. I couldn't stop. . . . The ones who treated me
worse, who were most against me, were the very ones
he had already left without a shirt to their backs, the
filthy dog. Whoremongers! Pimps! Cuckolds! . . .
Bandits! Thieves! They've invented a thousand ways
just to steal our wheat from us, our bread. . . . The
Law, the Law! They always bring out these damned
laws. The laws must be abolished, Señor Ignacio, and
one must go after the person who doesn't do right with
a stick! I'm going to fight, to wage war . . ."

Alone, without family, an outlaw wanted by the law,
that stern and serious man fitted into the wide frame
of the war like no one else. Listening to his confidences,
his confessions, Ignacio felt the fire of enthusiasm rekindled in his own breast, the fire which had warmed
him in the mountain when he read up there, along
with Juan José, the proclamations in which the poor,
the good people, were stirred up against "the gang of
cynical and infamous speculators, shameless merchants, local tyrants, bribed police, all of whom, like
toads, had become swollen in the contaminated swamp
of expropriated Church property." The day was at
hand when so much filth would be liquidated forever.

The King reviewed his troops once they were established in their positions, his body's bulk itself serving as a flag of flesh, as if stating: *Here am I, for whom you fight: Courage!*

On the 24th, the shelling resumed. The shells passed over the dugouts and raised huge clouds of dust as they hit the ground and exploded. Far off there would be some white smoke, followed by a dull explosion, and then a strong humming sound would make Ignacio lower his head. Dust and smoke would rise close by, along with a deafening report, and then the rumble of air that was rent by the projectiles. Ignacio's heart turned hot, then cold. But most of the shells landed at a good distance away, and were audible only as they were fired. That rhythmic thunder, whose low and awful notes widened out until they finally died into silence, might have been, in the world of living men, the inarticulate voice of the terrifying god of war, a hard marble divinity, blind and deaf. It was hardly the noise of human struggle, of confused cries, of the excitement of body against body. And there was nothing to do there in that place but to stand firm and receive the projectiles with resignation, with passive courage.

The night of the 24th, Ignacio slept in anticipation of the great day. At dawn they were ordered to Santa Juliana. The battalions milled about, coming and going from side to side, as they occupied new positions, in the easy movement of a cool dawn, just as one goes, refreshed by sleep, to one's daily labor.

At dawn of the 25th of March, the Liberal cannons opened up. From El Janeo and from the sea, a continuous cannonade resounded in the distance, as the Nationalist troops, under cover of the fire, invaded the valley and deployed in a circle around the front.

The center of the forces crossed the lower estuary

under a hail of bullets. The left wing was attempting to envelop the sharply pointed Montaño where it had run into a stone wall in February; the right threatened to capture the positions of the Carlist left, up on the heights.

At nine-thirty the firing became one continuous roar, and the entire scene lay under a cloud of smoke.

Ignacio loaded his rifle with regularity, as did all the others around him. It was a job, a necessary job, to which they all paid heed, absorbed in the moment's action, without thought of danger. They worked like workers in a factory, with no thought of the goal of their work, no idea whatever of its social value. Fermín was furious because he was not allowed to smoke a cigarette, not so much as a single one.

They had scarcely been at their job for an hour when they received orders to move again. Where? "Over there!" their chief answered, pointing to a peak on their left. They began to clamber up higher, crossing roads; sometimes the battlefield was blocked from view, though they could hear the incessant drawn-out thundering. At times they caught sight of the smoke, like a low cloud, over the pleasant valley, at the foot of the silent eternal mountains. They penetrated mining terrain, desolate and dismal, where only a few tubercular plants grew among the light-brown ore; everywhere were platforms and dumping pits, gradations and enormous steppingstones leading straight up. The whole ground seemed eaten away by a filthy leprosy, all possible space for vegetation eaten away, the earth displaying its very entrails, punctured by intermittent holes. And up and up they went, without ever stopping.

The night before, one of the passes in the sierra, the Portillo de Cortes, was assigned to a battalion of men from Guipúzcoa, a force reorganized with recruits following the internal insurrection of the priest Santa Cruz. They had scarcely reached their guard post in the dugout assigned them when a shell landed in their very midst, killing nine of them. The survivors spent the night, a night of desolate brooding, in the company of the dead men. The silent calm had crystallized their fear and, early the next day, when they heard the homicidal whine of the shells overhead, they abandoned their post to the enemy, which occupied the abandoned parapet. Meanwhile, in the nearby batteries, formations of men from Castile, Aragon, and Alava fought on bravely, cursing the recruits who had been shattered by fear during their awful night.

As soon as Ignacio's battalion reached its goal, they were emplaced on some crags in front of the surrendered parapet. They were on a height, in a shaded crease in the sierra, dominating the field of battle. Ignacio was overcome by a sense of being isolated, abandoned by his own side. Shivering, thirsty, and in need of relieving himself, he felt totally enervated. The task of firing at point-blank range took his mind off himself to some extent.

"Let's go after them!" yelled a joyous voice which brought some cheer, steadying his sight and bearing.

"We're going to have some action," Fermín said to him.

They began to move forward. They heard a bugle call and a voice yelling out "Let's go!" They hastened their pace, and the lively move calmed Ignacio's anxiety.

"Hold on!" yelled their chief now. "Who gave you orders to move on, you barbarians?" He was running after them, carried along by the mass, like a satellite by its planet.

Who ordered the bugle call? The circumstances, the very nature of the situation, of the moment. *Something* had ordered them on.

"Go get them!" the men yelled from the neighboring parapets, urging them on.

"After them!" their officer now called out, giving way to the anonymous order, to the moment's inspiration.

Ignacio, with his bayonet fixed, like all the others, clearly saw that the enemy was firing at them from their parapet to stop the drive, and then that the firing was coming from a line further back. Shortly after, entering the parapet, they found it abandoned. One of his comrades was brandishing his bayonet over a poor soldier who, crouching next to the trench, was gazing at him stupidly.

"Leave him be, you barbarian!" yelled an officer.

"Can't I even wet my bayonet?"

Ignacio was not sure how he and some others came to find themselves in the abandoned parapet, with shells bursting in the air around them. They quickly left it and took cover in a circular depression, shaped like a dishpan. A comrade was hit and fell, and they let him lie. The mass of men was halted, but then they began to break down into smaller units in order to cross a flat stretch open to the enemy's fire.

Ignacio thought he was running a fever. Watching a companion crossing the stretch of open terrain, he kept thinking, *Now, now, now. . . .* His fellow soldier got a bullet in the head, the part of his body most exposed to fire. He bounced and jerked like a rubber doll until he finally hit the ground, perhaps never to rise again.

Meanwhile the shell fragments kept rending the air.

Every time a comrade fell, the rest of the men waiting would squeeze off a bullet.

When the order was given, Ignacio began the crossing, avoiding a man lying in his way. Next to him, a comrade cried out and gave a sudden leap. He fell in a grotesque somersault, like a bundle, and Ignacio wanted to laugh.

"We're born again!" Fermín called to him when he had cleared the open space. Ignacio was choking, trying not to laugh at the grotesque somersault of his fallen comrade. Fermín's joyous call gave him a chance to break into laughter in reply. But when he laughed, he wet his pants, an act which somehow eased his anxiety.

Once he regained his calm, his laughter having relieved him, he saw the enemy coming at them again, their bayonets fixed. Concentrating on one of the attackers, he took careful aim, said to himself, "Let's see if I'm lucky," and squeezed the trigger. When he withdrew with the rest of the men, he cast a last glance at the poor enemy boy, on his knees, seeming to drink from a puddle of blood.

At last, exhausted, they found themselves in a strong defensive position, outside the line of fire. Night was falling, and they hadn't eaten a bite since morning.

"Boys, there's only this for all of you!" said their chief, handing over a loaf of bread, from which Ignacio took a bite, immediately handing it on to the first man in the line. This fellow took his bite, passing the bread on to the third, who, with the remark: "Just like taking Communion," sent the bread on its course, which now made the rounds along with the phrase, amid laughter, from mouth to mouth. When it came to the last man, a morsel was still left over.

After a time, a basket of food was brought to their leader. A couple of lads stepped forward to serve it.

He looked at the basket a moment, and, aware that no one had eaten, he gave it a kick and sent it rolling.

"Bravo!"

"That's a man!"

Voices could be heard crying out "Into the valley! Cowards! Chicken! Get them out! Go home! Back to your knitting! You don't wear the pants!" What was happening was that the wretched boys from Guipúzcoa, those who had abandoned the parapet, were marching past, crestfallen before their comrades-in-arms from Castile and Navarre.

"They get the ripe ones, and we the hard ones," a man from Castile was saying.

"They're the ones who in the end get the best piece," answered another. "With their damned Basque talk, which even God doesn't understand, and with their shrugging of shoulders and saying 'Me don't understand. I'm from Vizcaya, yet': they always end up getting their own way."

The fray had been bitter. At the end of the day, they knew nothing about the rest of the line.

That night a glacial wind blew. Ignacio, wrapped up in his blanket, felt the penetrating cold numbing his exhausted body. Some of his companions held on to each other to lend each other more heat, mutual heat; many of them were blackened with gunpowder and with dust kneaded with sweat. Under cover of some rocks, not far from the dead, they silently waited for the night to turn into daylight—when they might perhaps die.

Unable to sleep a wink, Ignacio made an effort to go over the day, and all that was left was the confused memory of a nightmare in which clear and vivid scenes were outlined: among them the recollection of the poor enemy boy, on his knees on the ground, drinking his own blood.

And that laugh? Why had he been overcome by that stupid laugh? Filled with regret, he felt like crying as he recalled in the silence of the night that tragic somersault. And the unfortunate Julián would never again play the guitar for them; he, too, had made that tragic somersault, that truly supreme mortal leap.

For a moment Ignacio felt torn from the earth and held suspended in the air. *Die? What does that mean?* he thought to himself, unable to think of himself as dead. And, if he were to die, what of his poor parents? . . . He offered a Paternoster for the boy who had died on his knees . . .

What must his father think of his crazy move in leaving behind the battalion he had lived with for so many months and going to Somorrostro? It had been a piece of madness! . . . But how could he go back on it? Nothing could be done about it now. What's done is done!

On those solemn and motionless evenings when time seemed to halt and flee into eternity, the spirit of death moved through Ignacio, in a mist of dark forebodings. He would hear people around him snoring and breathing heavily in the night. Further off, some soldiers would play cards by the light of a fire.

One night, a man next to him started screaming, until Ignacio shook him awake. "What's the matter with you?" Ignacio asked.

"I was dreaming . . . dreaming of a dead man I saw when I was a child," answered the man, opening his eyes wide and breathing hard. "A dead man I saw one night alongside a road . . ."

"I just can't sleep in the country at night," another

spoke up. He was crouched down, leaning on his rifle. "I just can't help it!"

They all shuddered when they heard a shout. "The sentry is half-frozen, stiff with cold!"

"Who's out there? Let's find out. Some one is missing from the line! . . ."

"Bah! It must be Soriano, out there going through some dead man's pockets . . ."

"What a dog's life . . ."

"I don't know. . . . It's better than before," said Sánchez. "At least out here we don't have to work . . ."

"That's worse yet."

"There's nothing worse than working."

"Well, work at least . . ."

"Yes, I know. It's very honorable."

"They say it's a virtue . . ."

"Yes. When someone else does it. All that talk about work is something told to us by the masters, so we'll bust supporting them. We're nothing but brutes. We're good for nothing. Here, everyone is busy not working, and if a person can get away with it, more power to him. . . . Work is the biggest of the dirty tricks. . . . Let the others bust with work! Just wear themselves out; sweat like a pig; fall apart in some obscure corner, covered with as many lice as their ancestors . . . and leave their children an honorable name, as good as any man's, a few teeth in their mouths and empty-handed, so they can fall apart with more work. . . . Let the nuncio go to work! It's all a swindle. Only brutes work. . . . Why have most of us volunteers come out here?"

"To play! To play cards!" yelled one of the men seated around the fire.

Presently they were all swapping stories, most of

them obscene. They soon went on to talk about the campaign.

The daylight began to filter in and, as it did, they heard the fresh sounds of dawn. The sky was clearing, and they began to think now only of the coming battle, of their task, their obligation.

Before the sun was fully up, the noise of war began. The enemy could be seen advancing all along the line; a cloud of smoke, from which issued a continuous rattling sound, covered the valley. An impassive and serene sky reigned over the whole smoke-filled scene. It was a radiant spring day that covered the green of the mountains, where insects and plants continued their slow silent struggle for life.

They were ordered up above Pucheta, where, from within dugouts, they opened fire on the Liberals. The Liberals made three bayonet attacks in an attempt to take the Carlist position, and three times they were driven back. When they attacked, they did so with all the blindness of a bull, rushing forward with their heads lowered, looking at the ground.

The unfortunate Liberal conscripts went down like golden sheaves of wheat on the plains falling before the sickle. They bit the dust, riddled with bullets; some spit out their souls; others died with a sigh; still others died with a curse on their lips. They charged with their teeth clenched and their eyes fixed, ready to sink their iron in hot flesh, and, when they didn't succeed, since their enemy was not disposed to hand-to-hand combat, they fell like bundles. One man, a woodcutter back home, felt unnatural running along brandishing a rifle with a bayonet at its end, as if it were a lance he was carrying, and was overcome with a longing to use it as an ax.

Torn from their homes—places full of life—and from

their parents and relatives, from their own world, carted off to this place to die, they were sons of their own fathers, after all, and perhaps had scarcely ever heard of the humble villages from which their fellow soldiers came. When these unfortunates died, their memories died with them, along with their vision of their quiet fields and the sky there, their loves, their hopes, their world, the entire world dissolved; when they died, worlds died with them, entire worlds, and they died without even having known one another.

More than ten thousand rifles and thirty cannons a minute were firing at the Carlists, and not even that firepower was sufficient to enable the Liberals to extend their line around the Carlist left, which they were striving to envelop.

Ignacio was stunned by the noise, his mind filled with a tumult of blurred impressions. He spent that night, along with his fellows, in digging more trenches, to gain even greater cover from the enemy's artillery. They all called for picks and shovels, and all the men from the different regions—from Navarre, Castile, the Basque provinces, and Aragon—tried to outdo each other. Anyone might have said that they were busy digging their own graves.

At midnight Ignacio and the others began marching once again, and before dawn they were at Murrieta. The last two days had made a deep impression on his mind. For the first time he wondered: *What is this war about?*

The feast day of Our Lady of Sorrows, the Generalísima of the Carlist army, dawned splendidly. The two preceding days had hardened every spirit, and when the first firing broke out early that morning everyone felt the kind of sultry oppressiveness that comes before two highly-charged storm systems are about to collide. During those early and solemn hours there was a delivery of mail to the troops. Some men learned the latest news about their children; others read about their wives' sorrows; still others placed in their breast pockets their mothers' final farewells. It was very silent, as each man thought about his own affairs, the things that made up his own private and personal world.

Ignacio and his comrades crouched in a forward parapet before Murrieta. Some of the men passed the time by cleaning their rifles. Others calmly awaited the task at hand. At noon, the Liberal artillery concentrated its fire on the San Pedro hermitage, which it reduced to a sieve, and on Murrieta. Beyond the Musques bridge, the Liberals sent a strong column toward El Montaño to distract the Carlist right wing. Meanwhile, in the center, they advanced towards San Pedro, to open a wedge in the Carlist lines.

From time to time a cloud of smoke hung over the crest of El Montaño, but whenever it went away, the Carlist chiefs could be seen, on foot, laying about them with their swords. Some one thousand men burrowed into the ground like worms, seeking whatever cover the rocky peak could offer. Their hearts beat against the ground as the shells swept over them from El Janeo, and yet they managed to fire back, to repel the enemy's advance.

At one o'clock, under a luminous sky, the Liberal columns suddenly and forcefully attacked the Carlist center. The thundering of the cannons drowned out the crackle of the rifle fire.

As soon as Ignacio made out the distinctive uniforms of the National forces and heard a command to fire, he fired. Through the smoke and haze he could see men falling and others taking their places, while their officers waved handkerchiefs like shepherds herding hesitant sheep into a slaughterhouse. They set out in formation from the Carreras hermitage, and after a few steps they had lost every tenth man. Out of the fear of each individual person, each isolated tremor, there grew a collective and communal fear. The mass of men would halt for a moment, then suddenly retreat in a run, abandoning equipment and leaving the wounded behind. Then they would regroup and surge forward again in a new wave. These men went to their deaths with savage resignation, not knowing where they were bound, nor why, nor for what reason they were setting out to kill someone they didn't know—or to be killed by someone they didn't know. Like wretched sheep, totally resigned, all vision of the future closed off, they died. They died absorbed in the immediacy of the act, caught unawares by the death that was everywhere present.

Firing extended along a front of about seven miles. The Nationals continued to advance under cover of their artillery fire, like a sea moving forward in the ebb and flow of its waves.

In front of the houses of Murrieta, at a crossroads formed by paths leading off the highway to the foothills of El Montaño, death reaped its harvest hurriedly. The National forces took refuge where they could, behind hedges or fences protecting the curved slopes. There they breathed in the invigorating smell of the earth, while they listened to the constant shriek of shells above their heads. Their officers, now carrying long sticks, urged them forward, occasionally striking out at those who hung back. In some places, the living used the bodies of the dead to protect themselves. On the San Pedro side, the tide of men crashed against the hillside repeatedly, leaving behind in its ebb and

flow, like so much flotsam and jetsam, the bloody bodies of fallen comrades. There were moments of panic,
but the general fear caused everyone, cowards together
with the brave, to flee forward. Some slipped and fell.
The gazes of the living, on their way towards death,
fell on the unmoving eyes of those who had already
entered into its mystery. Some of the wounded ceased
their cries when they were wounded a second time.
Others complained of being trampled, and many of
thirst. They all let themselves be pushed forward, moving as if in some lucid fever.

Ignacio kept firing regularly. He was calm and aware
of everything around him. It was as if time had gone
to sleep within his soul, through which passed the
disconnected but clear and precise impressions of the
moment. He watched one of his comrades climb out
of a trench and then others after him. He followed
them just as the enemy entered the trench, bayonetting
the wounded and those who were slow in leaving.

It was the great mass of soldiers which made the
decisions, even though no individual soldiers saw clearly
the reasons for them. The officers did no more than
order that the things that were already happening be
carried to their completion. By giving orders, the officers preserved the illusion that they were in command, but the actual decisions of battle were produced
spontaneously within the body of the men they led.

The Carlists climbed up to the houses of Murietta,
where they thought they might find further points of
defense for themselves.

"They won't get us out of here unless they shell
these houses to splinters . . ."

The enemy troops advanced by blows. New waves
of attackers pushed the others forward, forcing back
some who were lingering behind. Watching the enemy

uniforms appear from behind hedgerows along the paths, coming into the open, Ignacio thought: *Now!* There was firing from his own side, and he watched some of the attackers drop their rifles and fall like broken dolls. One of his comrades lay on the ground beside him, breathing very hard, as if trying to store up air.

The house Ignacio was firing from suddenly filled with noise and dust, and one wall began to come apart.

"They'll blow us to bits with their damned artillery! Let's move up higher in the town."

"First we have to set fire to this house!"

At these words, a peasant suddenly appeared out of nowhere, offering them money, begging them not to set his house on fire.

"It's no good. This house is of no further use to you."

Ignacio and some others gathered a thick bundle of hay from the haystack above the house and set it alight. As they began their escape to the houses higher up, they saw the brilliant red flames reflected in the dead face of the soldier who just a few moments ago had been breathing so hard to store up air. When they left, the enemy came in. The two sides mingled in confusion, as if dazed, at the foot of the house. They were practically touching each other, in total surprise over their proximity and with little idea what to do. A Liberal officer brandished his stick at one of the last of them to leave.

Many of the Carlists were recuperating in the houses higher up in Murrieta. The cannons of the Nationals ceased, since their soldiers had taken the houses lower down. Ignacio and his companions led themselves along a deep and protected roadway to take over a parapet on the heights of Las Guijas.

Ignacio took a moment to catch his breath. They were in a beautiful landscape filled with gorse and heather, overlooking the open area in front of Murrieta. Their fire controlled the entire road from Las Carreras to Murrieta and also that crossroads where death had reaped its quick harvest. Like a vast panorama, almost the entire field of battle lay before their eyes: San Pedro, amidst its underbrush, and the hermitage of Santa Juliana, which seemed to contemplate the slaughter like a gigantic owl with two enormous and terrified eyes formed by the holes the shells had made in its towers. At their backs, behind the position they occupied, lay the ravine where the soldiers from Navarre had carried out their famous charge in February. Above it all rose El Montaño; between it and El Janeo a bit of the calm sea was visible, the small cove next to the beach at Pobena, where the waves came in gently, lapping at the sand. In the depths of that sea, now tranquil and serene, in its quiet abysses, another struggle was taking place—a slow and silent battle among the creatures who dwelled there, the struggle for existence. On every side, the horizon was closed off by mountains piling on top of one another, like a staircase toward the sky. Their peaks seemed to raise themselves higher in order the better to watch the battle. In the background, far in the distance, lay Begoña and the outskirts of Bilbao. A cloud in the shape of a semicircular crown veiled the valley.

The enemy cannon were fixed in a vineyard at their feet. More fearsome were those that fired at them from the side of El Janeo, where groups of peasants gathered to watch the spectacle of war with the help of spyglasses, binoculars, and even opera glasses.

The men of the battalion were crouched behind a tongue-shaped parapet, on their knees in the ditches.

The day had turned cloudy and the battle continued with intermittent pauses, as if saving up breath.

"They couldn't have picked a worse place to climb. One has to come up here to see it and believe. . . . This is a trap," said one man.

When he heard the word "trap," Ignacio glanced mechanically in the direction of Bilbao, his birthplace, his little corner of the world. He thought about the poor eel fishermen who on winter nights cast their nets again and again under the tremulous glare of the lights they use to attract their prey. For a moment he was distracted by that vision of peace, that memory of peaceful fishermen deceiving eels in order to eat them later.

They heard a great outcry coming up from the enemy camp, and a little later they saw a new wave of men advancing towards San Pedro. The general in command, once he had taken a little nap in his straw chair to allow his meal to settle, had in a sudden martial outburst ordered his horse brought to him, after his adjutant had been wounded, so that he might show himself to his troops. Aroused by his gesture and filled with enthusiasm, his soldiers cheered him like crowds at bullfights do when the matador takes off his hat and positions himself for the supreme moment of going in for the kill.

Unexpectedly, Ignacio's ammunition gave out. Finding himself made useless, he was overcome by violent anxiety. He didn't know what to do with his rifle nor what to do with himself. Unarmed, it seemed to him that he was somehow more exposed to enemy bullets. He watched one of the men nearby, thinking to himself that the fellow was too much out in the open. *If they were to put him out of action, I'll* . . . After a short while, the man fell, as if overcome by fatigue, and dropped his rifle. In fact, he had been wounded. Ignacio went over to him quickly, seized his ammunition, and began to fire again, leaving it to others to carry off the wounded man.

As the afternoon declined, the struggle grew more intense. It was as if everyone was in a hurry to finish the task at hand before night descended. The enemy seemed almost annoyed by the resistance, a matter of pure tenacity and stubbornness. Things could not remain as they were. And underneath that overexcited and instinctual stubbornness, fatigue was growing, enormous fatigue. They had to bring things to a conclusion before their strength failed them, so that they might be able to lie down somewhere and fill their lungs deeply in the open air.

I'm going to be left alone, thought Ignacio, as a feeling of solitude invaded his soul. *Alone, alone among so many people, abandoned by everyone like someone shipwrecked, with no one to stretch out a friendly hand. People were killing each other without wanting to, killing out of the fear of death. Some terrible hidden power was mowing them down in harvest, inundating them in a fleeting present in order that some men might annihilate others.*

He received new ammunition and he kept firing, like some people keep walking even though they're overcome by fatigue, because their legs continue to carry them forward.

The Liberals, the poor Liberals, what did they know of these things? They were smashing themselves to pieces against the rocks of San Pedro. Of the companies which were sent out, their ranks full of men, only a few made their way back past the bodies of men cut down in the flower of their youth. Death was reaping its harvest, distributing the blows of its scythe by sheer chance.

At the end of the afternoon, Ignacio stuck his head

up out of the trench, out of mere curiosity, and felt a
stab of pain just under the Sacred Heart embroidered
by his mother. He felt there with his hand, then his
sight grew dim and he fell. He felt himself weaken
with every second, his mind going, his vision of things
present turning to water. Then he sank into a deep
sleep. His sense of the present moment left him, all
sensation departed, his memory collapsed. He was left
alone with his soul and out of it surged forth a thick-
ened and dense vision in which he saw his entire childhood in a split second. His body lay on the ground,
and his soul hung on the verge of eternity. And there
he relived his days. In a single instant, spanning years
and years, the panorama of his life appeared to him.
He saw his mother when she sat him on her knees and
washed the dirt off his face after he had been in a fist-
fight. He relived his school days. He saw Rafaela when
she was eight, dressed in a short skirt and wearing
braids. He relived the nights when he listened to his
father telling stories about the Seven Year War. He
saw other nights when he knelt down by his bed in
his night clothes and prayed with his mother. In his
vision he now moved his lips in prayer. His dying life
was now reflected in his eyes. From there on, he got
lost, letting his mother the earth suck back his body's
blood, all that was left of it. The expression on his face
showed a serene calm, as if he had conquered life and
now was at rest, in the peace of the earth, through
which no moment passes. Close by, the roar of combat
resounded, while the waves of time broke against eternity.

The 28th dawned dismal and cloudy. The Carlists at
El Montaño were still under artillery fire, some of them
already making the Act of Contrition aloud. A fog put

the firing to an end, the clouds opened up, and mud puddles began to form next to the dead.

The Nationalist battalions who made up the reserve went into battle already battered and worn out. The force from Estella had lost two-thirds of its effectiveness. Of its twenty-one officers, only five were left. The battlefield was littered with greatcoats, knapsacks, cartridges, uneaten bread, the refuse of one side mixed with that of the other on that common ground which gathers up the past and encloses the future. Bodies lay strewn about, some with eyes wide open staring at the sky, others with drowsy eyes, still others with eyes blackened in stony terror. Some appeared to be sleeping; some grasped their weapons in a convulsive grip; some lay sprawled out full length; some lay face down in a heap; some were still on their knees. One man's stilled breast cradled another's cold head. Some soldiers had been surprised while absorbed in carrying out their military tasks, following orders; some had been caught in the midst of a moment of drowsy surrender to hopelessness; some when overcome by terror and anguish; some during the languor of their last dream, their last melting dream.

During the sad night of the 28th, the living slept next to the dead, while crows gathered on the heights. The men from Navarre muttered their protests at having been dragged from their land to this slaughterhouse—all because of that damned Bilbao. The leaders were disillusioned. That night at a meeting of generals presided over by the old warrior Elío, the hero of Oriamendi during the Seven Year War, eighteen of those present, including the King, favored lifting the siege of Bilbao to save both blood and time. They were opposed by Berriz and the old Andéchaga, the soul of the Basques and a knight-errant. Elío, following the authority of two men instead of eighteen, decided to continue the siege. Protests were to no avail. The apathetic old man remembered nothing but the stubborn battle of resistance waged before his own eyes in these same mountains in 1836. In his senile mind the present time was pictured without color or perspective. The brutal power of the last three days of battle in the valley were only a misty vision for him, a dull echo recalling reminiscences of the Seven Year War. The recent battles impinged on his dreaming senses only to reawaken the vivid memories flowering out of the youthful days of his consciousness. These latest battles affected Elío's weakened spirit only by bringing back the illusions of his years of glory and stirring up the lees of his most cherished memories. The other ancient general, Andéchaga, the man of the goad and the shield, the man of the dagger made of iron and of wood from the Basque forests, also fastened on his own war memories. Their spirit of tradition bound the Traditionalist youths to take up the challenge of '36 and revenge themselves. The old ones were the experienced ones, natural guides for inexperienced youth. They were, besides, the flower of Carlist loyalty.

Both sides gathered on neutral ground to bury their dead. They dumped them in deep trenches as if they were burying locusts. Buried without their mothers' last kiss, men of both sides were laid in the earth together in the holy brotherhood of death, to rest forever in peace beneath the battlefield watered with their blood. Along with the earth thrown in upon them fell the last prayers, the last laments, and then—an immense forgetfulness. With heads bared under an impassive sky, the living answered the prayers said for the dead by the chaplains, who prayed beside the bodies of the dead that God's kingdom come; that His will be done on earth as it is in heaven, done in the world of reality as it is done in the world of the ideal; that they be given their daily bread; that their trespasses be forgiven as they forgave those who trespassed against them; that they might be delivered from evil. And as they all asked for these things mechanically, only with their mouths and with no thought of what they were saying, merely conscious that they were carrying out a pious and ritual act, they gazed on the bland dead, the inert dead bodies, gazing on them without solemn seriousness in the face of the eternal mystery of death. What were those men there watching the dead but men asleep? What went on within them? What did they feel at that moment? In most of them the spectacle produced not so much as a single concrete thought or expression of an idea: they were merely wrapped up in deep feelings of seriousness.

Looking at the body of Ignacio, Sánchez could only remark, "He did well to die. To get rid of all that bother . . . to free himself from all care."

The farms had been laid waste and trampled, the wheat fields were ruined, the houses were deserted and in shambles.

In the presence of the dead, men from one side and from the other had begun to mingle with one another. They began with insults, but they ended by drinking from the same glasses and singing together.

On the 29th, the news of the deaths of Ollo and of Radica hit the men from Navarre like a lightning bolt. Both leaders had been the victims of a shell while they were observing the enemy camp. The men had lost their heroes. Ollo, who in '33 had exchanged his seminarian's soutane for a Royalist uniform, left his King an inheritance of thirteen thousand men facing the enemy, of the twenty-seven thousand who only fifteen months before had crossed into Spain. And they had lost Radica, their Lord Bayard, the stonemason from Tafalla who had led them so many times to victory. Despair, unease, and discouragement seized the men of Navarre, but they also wanted to go after the cannon that had killed their leaders and take it by bayonet charge. They spoke angrily about the mad effort to take Bilbao, an effort Ollo had opposed, just as Zumalacárregui was said to have opposed it during the Seven Year War. Each man recounted the terrible event in his way. It was said that Dorregaray and Mendiri had escaped in time after they were warned by a spy. Much was made of the fact that a single shell had taken the lives of their incorruptible leaders. Some said that as the dying Ollo was taken away, Dorregaray had stood up straight and announced in tragic tones that blood so vilely spilled must be avenged. Among so many dead, these two men stood for and symbolized them all. These two leaders who had let their men into death had died without glory or honor. And soon the fatal word was heard everywhere: "Treason!"

Finally, their anger died down and the parleys between both sides went on anew. Soldiers on both sides joined in, and soon they were drinking, singing, and gambling together. What did they want money for? Fermín offered up what he had won from one of the enemy soldiers to the Virgin of his home town, if she would bring him safe and sound through the war—and if his money held out.

A group of officers from both sides talked about the events of the war.

"Who would have said, when we first started out, that we would ever have come to this! We thought it would be a simple matter, just a walk into Madrid in the twinkling of an eye . . ."

"And we thought that you were just a pack of alley cats who would run away as soon as you saw the National uniform, and that as soon as we sent in a well-organized column you'd be routed and the uprising put down as if by magic . . ."

"And just see what we've come to! Who would have believed it? And the sad thing is there's no way to turn back now. A settlement seems impossible, and besides, it would be a shame after we've shed so much blood for the Cause . . ."

"Isn't it more a question of not shedding the blood still left in our veins?"

"What a pity that there's not some other campaign going on now like the one in Morocco in which you and I could fight on the same side," a Carlist colonel told a Liberal colonel. "Facing a common enemy, we would all be united . . ."

"Damn it all! Still, it's a pleasure to fight against brave men. . . . On both sides, after all, we're all Spaniards . . ."

As they parted, there was new warmth in their handshakes, for now that they had fought against one another—much better than fighting against heathens—they felt deeply for their common Fatherland and they understood the sweetness of human brotherhood. In fighting each other, they had learned to feel compassion for each other. Beneath their struggle there was a great sympathy. They felt mutual solidarity, out of which came brotherly compassion. Brothers feel more like brothers after strife between them.

But it was brutal and what's more, stupid, absolutely stupid, all of it. They were killing each other for the sake of other people, and they were forging their own

chains. They didn't even know why they were killing
each other. They made up two enemy armies. That
was that. The enemy was the enemy, nothing more:
the man on the other side, the other. War was their
obligation, their job.

Several men from both camps were eating, drinking,
playing cards, and singing when they were approached
by a peasant.

"What are you here for? Isn't it enough for you to
clean up our lodgings?"

"He's a usurer, a skinflint, a Jew. . . . He's come
around to see if anything turns up for himself . . ."

"Beat it, peasant. Get away from here! Get busy!"

He had to go away with his head hung low, for all
of them were united in the rejection of the man of
peace.

They played hard, competing with each other to
show off their lack of care for what tomorrow might
bring. In a chorus, they all sang—

> While our liquor holds out
> Fellows, have at the bottles.
> It's a joy to be alive
> And forget about tomorrow
> For maybe tomorrow
> We'll be called on to die.

Then one of them picked up a guitar and made it cry
out slowly, as he sang a long and drawn-out song, slow
and as monotonous as the furrows on the plowed plains.
Then came the sound of an impetuous wild dance—
the *jota*.

Meanwhile, using a priest as an intermediary, the
high commands of the two armies discussed the terms
of an agreement. Recognition of all military ranks,
offered one side. The others answered, either Carlos

VII as absolute monarch or nothing. We need a national plebiscite, came the reply. The right of tradition and never mind these modern notions about "popular sovereignty," came the counter-reply. With more determination than ever, the Carlists kept their flag flying, the flag which read "God, Fatherland, and King." Many in the National Army were for unfurling the flag of Alfonsito, for they needed a King, the only national symbol to be used in war, and a King who would be, above all, the First Soldier of the Nation, the Supreme Chief of the Army, a leader imposed on the country by discipline and not a president, a mere civilian. The Republic sent out commissions to keep up the Army's spirits and to sow their ideas in those fallow fields. There was no lack of ideas. Some even wanted to make Serrano—then President of the Republic, the handsome general of the dethroned Queen, the man who had cooked up the last covenant—into an emperor.

Every day, the hour when firing and shelling would begin was announced beforehand, and later the artillery fired only blank shells, merely to do their duty. These were days of laxness. There was even one case in which a Carlist corporal in an advanced post guided a lost relief party of the enemy back to its battalion. At some points in the Carlist line it became necessary to prohibit the boys from visiting the enemy positions.

As the beginning of April, furious windstorms flattened the shelters made of branches and sod, and the clouds let loose a downpour of rain. The tempest lashed the mountains, and landslides into the valley did great damage to the banks of the overflowing rivers. Mud covered the cannon, ran under the campaign tents of the Liberals, who shivered as they lay on the rocks, and filled the trenches of the Carlists with water up to the knees. The soaked Carlists could neither cook their food nor dry their clothes. The sky's fury brought the two sides together at some points, forcing them to seek shelter in a neutral house, uniting them in facing a common enemy. When the storm died down, the valley was the richer for it, the blood having been washed away. The camps were in wreckage.

Holy Thursday dawned in splendor. Using earth from the heights, cloths from the tiny churches in the area, and some boards, the pious Lizárraga made an improvised altar on a high spot on the Carlist left. From time to time, bugles announced the phases of the liturgical office. When the Host was elevated, cannons thundered, the Royal March was played, weapons were presented, and heads bowed. In memory of the ideal Redeemer, who died for mankind and to bring, along with war, eternal peace, the Host was lifted up, in the face of the enemy, for soldiers still drenched from the waters of the storm.

That night the windstorm started again. Torrential rain destroyed what was left of the shelters, leaving the men in the open. The sea could be heard roaring against the mountains. At dawn on the 12th, the encampment looked like the remnants of a shipwreck. The water from the sky, dripping drop by drop upon the dead, assured their more rapid decomposition. Swarms of spring flies arrived. Crows cawed on the mountain-crests. Pestilent vapors, which always follow on battles, swept down the valley.

When the echoes of the events at Somorrostro reverberated throughout Spain, a huge clamor of hatred and pity swept across the land. The nation sent off fresh batches of its sons to save Bilbao. Many voices demanded that the Basque country be razed, drowned

in blood and fire to put an end to that turbulent race
once and for all. Others thundered out against the
clergy. Many blamed the government for its inepti-
tude. As usual, numberless people went on simply
enjoying themselves. A great many pictured to themselves the Carlist positions at Somorrostro as being
placed on abrupt precipices, inaccessible peaks, incred-
ibly narrow passes, and craggy hideaways, so that in
their minds that lovely valley was turned into a network of insurmountable defenses, all due to some mad
dislocation of the earth. In short, Somorrostro became
fodder for the press, a topic of conversation and discussion in the café, something for everyone to talk
about—and cause for pain and weeping in many a
home.

The venerable ladies of Madrid gathered to make
bandages, meanwhile whispering rumors about each
other. And under the pretext of organizing pious as-
sociations to help the wounded, they carried on a conspiracy in behalf of Alfonsito. In the course of all this
ferment, a third body of the army was formed. When
General Concha took command, under orders to sur-
round the Carlists, he told his officers that they had
the entire enemy gathered together and thus could beat
them in a single battle, something the regiments in
Flanders had once also ardently wished.

Old Elío, ever-faithful vassal of his King, prepared
to fulfill his mandate to stop the Liberal advance, his
hopes pinned on the resurrection of his ancient memories, namely, that they would come at him by the
route used in '36. It was the known way, the natural
way, the way that experience marked as obligatory.
As a mere precaution, he sent reinforcements on the
27th to old General Andéchaga, thus diverting them
from guarding the pass engraved in his memory. But

on the 28th Concha sent his columns to take the height
of Muñecas, and there, on the highway a bullet ended
the life of old Andéchaga, the seventy-year-old knight
errant, the iron soul and spirit of the siege of Bilbao,
leaving his men like orphans. Poor old Elío was left
alone among the newer generals. Meanwhile, the Liberals invaded the valley of Sopuerta, opening up the
line. Facts were betraying the memories of the old man
of Oriamendi. The operation was getting off the track
laid down in his memory. Perhaps the enemy was
trying to confuse him. He ordered Sopuerta abandoned
and handed himself over to fate, while Lizárraga directed the retreat of the troops.

During the night of the 28th, the Liberals advanced
along rough paths, lashed by an obstinate rain, to link
up with the line established by their own men from
Somorrostro. On the 29th they continued their advance through the rain, and the Carlists retreated to
a new line of their own.

The Carlist commander in chief waited. He waited
to see where all that would end. He waited with full
confidence in himself, his loyalty to the Cause, the
truth of his memory, and the resources of the terrain.
The skein must be allowed to unwind a bit more, so
that he might seize some loose string to pull it apart.
It was needful that the enemy should show his hand.

There came the moment when old Elío saw that
Concha was taking the ancient route, the one of yes-
teryear, the one he had fastened in his memory, the
one that experience indicated: the highway to Valmesa.
Among his memories, old Elío trod with a steady step.
He went to Güeñes, only to find that once again he
had lost the thread of the operations engraved in his
senile mind. The Liberals were attempting the impossible, something they hadn't thought of in '36: they

were going up the mountain, to scale the sierra of Galdames. Had anyone ever heard such madness! The troops the old man was leading according to chance, weary of leaving one pass to cover another, began to mutter against the old general, that withered and worn-out antique, that old dog with nothing left in him but his loyalty. Some of the Carlist leaders wanted to act on their own, without paying him any more heed. Reluctant to leave themselves to fate, they burned with the desire to do something, make some move, to draw up a decisive plan of operations and carry it out. A plan? A decisive plan? But to commit oneself to a single plan means rejecting every other possible plan. Impatient youth! Impatient and inexperienced youth, who believe that getting up early makes the dawn come quicker! A plan? Can any plan be greater than those mountains, put there by God to defend men of loyalty?

The 30th arrived. The old man, shaking off his drowsiness, received and read reports, immersed in quiet resignation, and waited for events to happen. The Liberals moved forward, stone by stone and tree by tree, and seized the spurs of the sierra of Galdames, driving a wedge between the two wings of the Carlist forces. The Carlist chiefs met to urge Elío to re-take the sierra. But the old man, still deeply entrenched in his old experience and as loyal to his memories as he was to the Cause, answered that the enemy had been mad to scale the sierra. It was only a feint, a strategy to sow confusion. He needed all his forces to wait for the enemy on the road they took in '36, the road that experience indicated, the road they would have to take sooner or later. But he finally gave in a bit before their insistence and assigned a force of a hundred men from Castile to the paths in the sierra, so that they could not say that he was as stubborn as a mule.

But the poor old man of Oriamendi was in fact unhinged. The world, this world, was getting out of
kilter. The enemy was confusing him by climbing the
sierra, something that would not have occurred to them
in the good old days. On the bridge at Güeñes, which
was already mined and ready to be blown up, he received confidants, read reports, and kept on the look-
out, while a wild rush of new impressions played hob
with his memory. What these modern generals wouldn't
try!

By nightfall, the firing was taking place in a formal
pattern. The Liberals, some of them on all fours with
their weapons between their teeth, climbed the heights
on all sides. Their wounded fell, bouncing from rock
to rock. They fought in the shadow of the peak, above
the moonlit valley.

It was then that the enemy plan became obvious:
the Liberals meant to break the Carlist line and sur-
round the men of Somorrostro, stranding them on the
field of their heroism, between the mountains and the
sea. The old general ordered the Güeñes bridge blown
up and he went to Sodupe. Dorregaray, whom he
ordered to withdraw from Somorrostro, had already
begun to do so by his own decision, not waiting for
the order from that old man, whose mind lagged so
far behind the actual course of events.

On the peaks of Erézala and of La Cruz the battle
raged under the moon's intermittent light. The men
from Castile whom the general had grudgingly trans-
ferred there resisted the Liberal advance for some five
hours, perhaps thereby saving the men of Somorrostro
from complete surprise.

Under a midnight moon shining on the summits,
the Third Liberal Corps crowned the desolate extent
of the sierra, and the soldiers burst out onto the desert-

like mesa, the haunt of hawks, to rest among the gorse
and heather and fern. The Carlist line was broken, and
from those heights could be seen the fold in the network of mountains where Bilbao was hidden as it anxiously waited for liberation.

The old man of Oriamendi, the last one to leave
Sodupe, marched away in loyal resignation, without
knowing where it would take him. The two corps
linked up at Castrejana, where the old general remembered the three months of resistence they had put up
there during the Seven Year War. The King had ordered him to stop the enemy advance, and stopped it
must be. When he asked a young man what he thought
of their position and was told that it seemed very weak,
he answered that it was too much to say such a thing,
for in his memories the place was a stronghold. But
the artillery of '74 was not the artillery of '36. The
enemy did not need to take their position. It was sufficient simply to deploy batteries on the mountain and
pin the enemy down between the forces on the heights
and those outside Bilbao. So cannons appeared on the
heights.

The old dog of the proscribed royal family, the cour-
tier of outlaws, loyal to the wishes of his Lord, left
Mendiri and went off with Dorregaray to see the King
at Zornoza and make him understand the necessity of
changing his mind. At dawn on the first of May, Mendiri received the order to retreat, written in the King's
hand. At two in the afternoon the last Carlist battalion
crossed the pontoon bridge. Bilbao was free.

Thus it was that the Carlist army again suffered the
defeat of '36, led by the old *caudillo* of Oriamendi, the
living symbol of loyalty and faith, of tradition and experience. His own memories were defeated, but he
resisted with an old man's faith. Concha was acclaimed

by his troops on the height of Santa Agueda, and he
fired off a twenty-one gun salute to Bilbao.

The Carlist forces trooped away over the hills which
dominate both sides of the estuary of the Nervión River
upon which Bilbao lies, leaving their mortars to con-
tain the city. Some younger soldiers threw away their
rifles or broke them against trees. Among their curses
could be heard the cry of wounded will: "They've sold
us out! Treason!" They looked back with greedy desperation at the battered city which was slipping from
their hands, just as it had slipped from their fathers'
hands in '36.

And many dreamed of revenge.

On the night of May 3rd, the Marqués who had
been the immediate director of the siege had to be
bled, so great was his rage! The men from Navarre
remembered Olla and Radica, sacrificed to the Basque
cause, and the Royalist outlaws repeated the words
attributed to Andéchaga, the old knight-errant: "If
they enter the city, it will be over my dead body."

The battalions gathered in Zornoza like a camp of
gypsies. The men sprawled on the ground, battered
in body and soul. Some of their officers thought about
the bitter fruit of exile, while others dreamed of having
new cannon. Meanwhile, the King paraded his human
presence along the highway, arguing, apparently, with
his generals.

"Cannons! Cannons!" they all began to shout. The
officers offered their pay to help buy them. They all
wanted to believe that machines, not men, had conquered them.

To console his people, the King decreed on May
3rd that Vizcaya was entitled to be called "Excellent,"

in addition to the title "Most Illustrious," which it already possessed: icing on the cake!

When Ignacio's parents received notice of his death, his mother cried out, "My son!" and fainted. With a terrible serenity, his father murmured, "May it all be for the glory of God," and then lay down. Days later he was still repeating these words. The wound in Josefa Ignacia's soul soon healed, as the pain spread through her whole being and numbed her. She said her devotions more intently, but, as always, without thinking about the words or savoring them. She prayed mechanically, not even lingering over the words "Thy will be done." And thus her prayers, pure to the letter, were the incarnation of her feelings and her anguish, the subtle music in which she slowly expressed her emotion. She pictured her son to herself as being alive, as she had always seen him, but being in some remote region now. She did not picture him lying on the ground, with white unmoving lips, his eyes dry, blood on his chest. She felt sorrow that she had not been able to collect his body, so as to give him burial in a holy place, and she wished that she had the heart she had embroidered for him, the heart he was wearing on his breast when he was killed.

"My poor son! Buried in a heap of others . . ."

"Be quiet, woman, and calm yourself. God has willed that it be so, and may everything be for His greater glory! No need for crowns of flowers and placards. What he needs are Masses. . . . Our duty is to feed the living and pray for the dead."

When she went to Mass, the mother hid her tearful eyes behind her ancient, worn, and grimy prayer book printed in large type, the only book she knew how to read any longer. A sob shook her when she reached the passage she had read out day after day over many years to ask God for that son. The open book invited her to ask for the special grace she hoped to obtain, and she asked, "Let us see him soon."

Among the cards and letters of condolence, there was one from Uncle Pascual: one of his homilies. He counseled that they submit to the Divine Will. What else could they do? He wrote that Ignacio had died with glory. They should not weep over a death that would grant him eternal life. They should not forget that whosoever would be a disciple of Christ must take up his Cross and follow Him, forsaking father and mother, wife and sons and brothers. God, they should know, has accepted those lilies offered up at Somorrostro as expiation for terrible impiety. Ignacio was the lamb of war who washed away with his blood the stains of Liberalism and placated God's anger, putting a halt to the whiplash of anarchy by the weapon in his hand . . .

"Yes, yes, all that's true, but my poor son! Dead and buried in such a way . . ."

"But that's dust now, woman of God!"

"Dust? My son, dust? My poor little boy!"

The letter from Uncle Pascual softened Pedro Antonio's soul, but when he felt that he was about to burst into tears and let loose his tender feelings, he was kept from it by a painful lump of dryness which filled his entire being.

Alone with himself, he became alarmed at the strange calm with which he had taken that blow of fate, at the stupor which kept him from seeing the full extent of his loss. *I've lost my son, my only son*, he said to himself, trying to realize the meaning of that trial, which had seemed so natural to him. He did not manage to convert the cold cry of "I've lost my son" into the mysterious words "My son has died." His son, of course, had left, as had so many others. He had not, also of course, returned, but he might return some day. Between that memory and this hope, both equally alive, there intervened as a present reality only the possibility of a word of news, mere news, something said.

Neither father nor mother were entirely convinced that their son had died. There might be some mistake. And every day they waited for him at dawning, never really aware of their hope. And every day they despaired of ever seeing him again.

In the Arana house the family was at the table, talking about what they had been through and about the memory of poor Doña Micaela.

"What an outburst of joy she would have felt on the 2nd of May!"

"Ah!" exclaimed Juanito. "Ignacio, the son of the chocolate-shop owner, is dead . . . killed at Somorrostro."

"Poor boy!" exclaimed Rafaela, feeling her heart leap in her chest. "His parents must be suffering terribly at having allowed him to go there . . ."

"Who knows what they expected!" said Don Juan. "They've gone away somewhere, leaving the shop and everything. At the very least, they hoped that Chapa would make them confectioners to His Majesty. In short, they brought it on themselves."

"The truth is," Rafaela said, "that I think it's savage for men to kill each other over ideas, over a difference of opinion . . ."

"You don't understand these things," her brother interrupted. "It's not a matter of opinions at all. It's jealousy, isn't that it?"

What a brute, she thought, turning red as she felt his slap at her soul.

"My daughter, you don't understand the world," said her father, as he put a morsel of food in his mouth. "It's sad, but they deserved what they got. If only they would learn from it . . ."

"Don't talk like that. Some men, just to prove that they're men . . . ," she began, thinking of her brother's brutal words.

"They're capable of finding joy in having a martyr for a son. . . . I'm not like them, and I don't wish them any harm, but they deserved what they got . . ."

"If they've done anything wrong, they should be forgiven, Papa."

"Forgive them?" He helped himself to some rice and milk. "All right, let it pass! But forget it all? Never!"

They spoke then of other matters, but as the conversation ended Don Juan exclaimed, "Poor folk! It's a shame, a real shame. What a state to be in! Poor parents! . . . It's an irreparable loss, irreparable, irreparable . . ."

He was thinking of his dead wife.

Rafaela spent the entire day in deep dejection. From the darkest corners of her memory, from the well of oblivion itself, gushed out recollections of the bashful looks Ignacio, poor, unfortunate Ignacio, used to give her when they met on the street. Now she would never see him again, solid and somewhat ungainly, walking firmly on the earth.

When the siege of Bilbao began to make itself felt, towards the end of 1873, Don Joaquín took his nephew Pachico with him to settle in a small town on the Bay of Biscay, far enough from the theater of war that neither its immediate effects nor its noise could reach them.

The uncle lived more absorbed than ever in his prayers and devotions, and he was less and less interested in political strife, which only led to arguments among other people, who didn't even know what they were arguing about. Every day he grew more aloof from "those people," whose number grew before his eyes.

What did these disputes about the government of the temporal world mean to him? God had given these things over to the disputes of men, but Don Joaquín, interpreting God's will in his own way and translating men into "those people," kept his distance from the world and its vain disputes, from which he expected no lasting good would ever come. He prayed for the conversion of nonbelievers and sinners, incorporating this request into the orderly system of his prayers. He prayed for them, and inasmuch as there must be all kinds of things in this world since the ways of God are infinite, he felt compassion for those who had to serve the inscrutable designs of Divine Providence in some other way. *A strange madness, this madness of people who take it on themselves to impose on others their own solutions to the problems of the temporal world, who kill each other over differences of opinion, whether great or small*! Thus he thought, as he meditated on the theme that at the Last Judgment he would have to give an account of his own doings and not those of others.

He withdrew from friends and acquaintances so that God and His holy angels might draw closer to him, believing that it was better to hide himself away and tend to his own soul than to try imprudently to work miracles. What were war and its hazards to him? His holy peace was best preserved by staying at home and not listening to news. News! If he were to see all things in front of him, what would this be but a vain vision? He watched over himself, admonished himself, and took no chances with himself, no matter what happened to others. He tried to rise above earthly things on wings of simplicity and purity, devoting his being to eternal things and taking earthly things only for immediate use. It grieved him only that his efforts to achieve simplicity got more complicated with every passing day.

The most important thing was not to allow himself to be disturbed in the tranquil round of his devotions and his pious habits, whose endlessly rich variety unfolded in complete tranquillity within a profound and all-inclusive unity. Devotional calendar in hand, he varied the ordered course of his pious exercises according to the time of the year and the different devotions assigned the months and the days. Novenas followed novenas, prayers of particular intention followed other prayers of particular intention. Adding and subtracting the days to be given to each exercise gave him complete contentment. And then there were the meditations, the pious readings, especially in *The Imitation of Christ*, his most constant spiritual nourishment. No element of the extraordinary intruded, nothing outside the narrow round common to all humble souls, merely the current devotions, for he remembered that those who made their nests in heaven had been humbled and left with nothing so that in their humility and poverty they might learn not to fly with their own wings but to await beneath the wings of the Lord.

The life he lived helped keep his mind off his persistent, but not acute, physical ailments, distracting him from continuous worry over the chronic illness which was slowly consuming his life. He welcomed this Cross the Lord had been pleased to give him, without his meriting it. His attention fixed on this Cross, he had been able to make it the nucleus of the external world in which he thought himself forced to live and to whose needs he was yoked. His infirmity forced him into some relation with the transitory events of the low world of the senses. In his devotions, he lived in his own inner world, a place of secret consolation, among the enduring senses of his soul. The two worlds were linked in him, the world of his illness and the world of his devotions, and the idea of death was always fixed in his mind, although he did not always see it present. But death, always at an invisible distance, approached him more closely, losing itself in eternity.

A fortunate affliction indeed, which by the Grace of God he was able to convert into a fountain of inner consolation. The pain impeded him but did not oppress him. O, to be able to abandon himself to the Lord, to receive without distinction the good and the bad, the sweet and the sour, the joyful and the sad, and to give thanks for everything! He did not deserve such a good; perhaps his illness was a consolation unmerited.

His chief mortification, comforting and distracting him at the same time, was the battle he waged inside himself against the evil enemy which surrounded him at all times and watched for him to be careless. It would occur to him that perhaps he had committed some misdeed. He remembered the idea that men cannot know whether or not they are in sin, that it is not we ourselves but sin within us which commits mortal sins. And then he began to quibble with himself. "May this not be some vain scruple by which the devil is trying to distract me? Or may it not be rather that the devil is trying to distract me with the suggestion that this is a vain scruple, so that I will ignore it? Or is it perhaps this *last* thought which is the temptation of the devil?" And thus he would go on. Once, when he decided to fast to mortify his flesh, it occurred to him that since he found gratification and intimate spiritual delight in fasting, he really should mortify himself by not fasting, so as to deprive himself of such gratification. And this tempting idea in turn gave rise to repentance, the state which corresponds with the inner life of a perfect man.

The truth was that his inner life was endless in its variety and never bored him. How could all that talk about war which so much concerned other people compare to the intimate battle inside a soul, his soul? Compared with the heavy battle in his soul, sustained by Grace against the Tempter of Men, what were all those other battles that filled the newspapers worth? But when this thought came to him, it occurred to him that such ideas were the fruit of infernal pride, and calling to mind that he was no more than a clod of mud, a vile earthworm, he gave himself over to acts of contrition, acts which constituted one of the obligatory elements of his own most diverting representation of the life of his soul.

As regards his nephew, he no longer was worried by the boy's ideas, for despite everything Pachico continued to be the same Pachico, with the same character, the same habits, the same humor. No, it was impossible that he might have changed so radically as to become someone else. Had he, perhaps, left off seeing him a single day? Had anything happened in the boy's life, one of those tremendous turning-points which might cause God to withdraw His grace from the unfortunate one, bringing about a complete change in that person's existence? *Mere idiosyncrasies*, he thought. *Each one believes in his own way*. When this thought crossed his mind on one occasion, he managed to entertain a disrespectful judgment, which only gave him cause for repentance and a new experience in his inner life. What happened was that just after he had told himself that *Each one believes in his own way*, the words in his mind continued, as if in play, to add: *Just as everyone has his own way of killing fleas*. He then told himself that he was getting light in the head and becoming featherbrained. *There's so much left to correct in myself*, he thought, determining to dedicate himself for a while to more acts of contrition.

Ah, the blindness of those persistently blind people who ignore the inexhaustible interest of the life of the soul and who occupy themselves only with attaining their own health! Those people outside, the worldly, might think Joaquín bored and boring, a man poor in spirit, a fool, but what did they know about the inner consolations and the ceaseless novelty of that life? Better, far better, that they take him for a simpleton, even for an imbecile, for thus he would be humbled, to be exalted one day. But . . . was it not perhaps an act of pride to want to be humbled so that he might be exalted? To do something with a view to being exalted? How could he become one of the least, with his sights thus fixed on becoming one of the first? Ah, holy simplicity! Unattainable holy simplicity, unattainable to those who seek it deliberately!

Uncle and nephew lived in an impenetrable closeness one to the other, each one totally unlike what the other imagined him to be, and yet joined together by an infinite network of habits, by the subtle fabric of living together a long time. The uncle could not say his long rosary peacefully at night unless he knew his nephew was in his room reading his books, and the

nephew could not read in easy comfort during those
same hours unless he could hear, somewhere below
the threshold of his conscious mind, the muffled whisper of Don Joaquín saying his pious exercises, in the
thought that the rosary would be able to make him
simple of heart.

After the noon meal Pachico would take himself off to
kill time in a low café, fitted out to look like a club,
where all the town's idle congregated to play cards, to
drink coffee, and to talk about the news of the war as
carried at second hand by the newspapers.

Each of the café regulars was a character unto himself, his own man, an irreplaceable individual, even if
he were no more than a son of the neighborhood.
Pachico was amused to see them take part in the in-
terminable card games and in the arguments the games
brought on. As they took part in the changing battles
of cards and in the endless arguments, they became
more and more themselves. In this play, they fed their
spirits. Their arguments were sometimes violent,
wearing them down to a frazzle, after which they would
only begin again, shuffling their cards and continuing
their confrontations.

They argued about the war news in the same terms,
shuffling the names of generals and places, or dis-
cussing the movements of the warring columns. Their
military talk differed in no way from the talk provoked
by the diverse combinations of cards in the different
games. They went on and on about such small facts
as the distance between Somorrostro and Bilbao—three
leagues or four or five?—and whether the Carlists would
be able to hold out for two more months, or three, or
five?

Pachico was attracted by these loud arguments, very

loud indeed, between these men of flesh and blood, who let their spirits show through in these bellowing matches, while the reports the newspapers carried, which he knew about only from the lively discussion in the café, irritated him. It was really something to hear when a famous captain who had retired would exclaim, as he took out of his pocket the unvarying gold doubloon which he always carried with a certain sense of respect, "Nothing to it at all, just so much talk and nothing else. . . . I'll bet ten duros that the Carlists won't last a month. . . . As if I didn't know that terrain inch by inch."

Alongside those discussions, everything in the press was mere notetaking, newsmongering, a tiresome heap of disconnected items—pure history, at most.

Of the entire war, what would remain? Pachico wondered. A few dry reports, a few lines at best in future history books, some passing mention of one of numberless civil wars whose meaning the actors in the drama would carry to their graves. The war was no more than another link in the life of the Spanish people, a link whose only function, perhaps, was to maintain the continuity of their history.

Whenever he tired of the café, Pachico would wander about the outskirts of the town, at random and with no fixed goal, sometimes along faint pathways, sometimes striking out across the countryside in search of new places, little corners he hadn't seen before. The landscape's variety interested him, even some tree new to him, or a shady grove or a farmhouse he hadn't known before. These discoveries fascinated him as much as new combinations of cards fascinated the cardplayers caught up in their game, or as much as the methodical round of his devotions and the varied struggle of his soul with the devil fascinated his uncle. Everything was always new and everything was always old, in the everlasting change and the eternal unchangeableness of all things!

In his wanderings he liked to stop for a while at a promontory overlooking the sea. There he filled his eyes with the sight of the immense deep waters and the sky which embraced them. The sea and sky—each one giving life to the other in solemn communion! The waves followed on one another in their noise, while cloud followed cloud in silence. When he lowered his gaze toward the vast and turbulent surface of the sea, he felt a dark intuition about life, the intuition that life is simply what it is, with no meaning beyond itself. Then he felt a strange sense that the fugitive moment of the present had come to a stop, that it had become immobile. From that promontory, the vast waves moving endlessly before him suggested the breathing of Nature, as it slept its deep and dreamless sleep. But at other times, moments when he watched the wind stirring up the waves and sweeping away the clouds, he thought about the Spirit of God moving upon the waters and imagined that at any second the august spirit of the Omnipotent and Ancient of Days would appear before him, exactly as He was pictured on altars—resting on clouds, His full, wide-pleated garments floating out behind Him as He makes new worlds surge into being out of the submissive waters.

Returning to himself after such visions, he remembered his period of intellectual crisis, the battle of ideas which had raged in his mind. None of his ideas was connected to his own world, to the world in which he was born. His ideas had been clad in the uniforms of their concrete expression, and they stayed under military discipline—columns of dialectical arguments guided by reason and obedient to the formal tactics of logic. His mind brimmed with these ideas and their marches and counter-marches and skirmishes and surprise attacks. And he had never noticed that they never met each other head-on, but that instead some would simply disappear when new ones appeared and grew clearer and more defined. In this battle, old ideas abandoned the field to newer ones, although sometimes the old army of ideas, seemingly vanquished, would assemble again and return to the fray in a sudden and impetuous assault.

But underneath these mental skirmishes, there throbbed for him a heartbeat, the vast and dark heartbeat of the world of peaceful, humble things, the humble and peaceful things of ordinary daily life which constantly nourished his mind. Compared to the tranquil quiet of this mental world made up of the images of simple things his intellectual skirmishes were mere playthings, entertainments, the source of the different kinds of pleasures found in surprise. But what did those supposed crises of intimate anguish come to, after all, when they died down, as if by magic, when, to take one instance, he sat down to eat? He had been playing out a comedy of doubt, pure illusion, a matter of being too suggestible!

At last he achieved inner peace. The contending armies of ideas melted away, and now his ideas lived together like brothers in his consciousness. Now that his mind was quieted, his ideas worked together in harmony. In his present serenity, Pachico thought with his whole being, not merely with his intellect. And he felt the deep life of true faith, of faith in faith itself. He got to the true and solemn seriousness of life, which is concerned not for reason but for truth. Only when he was reading books or engaging in the discussions he now rarely indulged in would the old battles awaken for him and his ideas seem to need to choose up sides and form enemy armies. But now even this combat seemed mere play-acting. Gradually, he came to realize that this combat had never been a part of him, that it was all a show staged in his mind by forces outside himself. He came to understand that he had never really felt the anguish of doubt.

In some moments of unexpected surprise, a surprise which welled up from the dark mystery of his own being, he prayed the prayers of his childhood. Like sweet perfume, they refreshed his soul, evoking the misty world which lies in the deep and dark places of the unconscious, where the noise of rushing ideas, their superficial waves, can never reach.

When Pachico learned in a letter about Ignacio's death, his heart skipped a beat. *Unfortunate boy*! He went home and locked himself in his room where no one could see his tears. He realized then how much he had cared for his friend. He wept harder, to find in weeping some hidden relief, and he lost himself in vague and wandering thoughts.

A life lost? Lost . . . for whom? Lost to him, the victim, poor Ignacio. . . . But such lives are the spiritual atmosphere of a whole nation of people, lives we take in with every breath, lives which sustain and spiritualize us all.

When he went out again, his eyes were dry and he was at peace. When he met people, he felt fresh, returned to himself, and wrapped in his usual strength. He had satisfied his tender feelings for his friend by giving in to his tears. He spent the rest of the day thinking about his friend's death.

That night he started to put down on paper the day's reflections, as was his habit. But when he expressed his thoughts in external form, a knot of anguish came to his throat and his eyes filled with tears. Out of his boiling feelings came only a few bare ideas which turned cold on the paper. Thus, his remembrance of Ignacio turned out to be like a stone epitaph, a dry and hard and intellectual reflection about death which was a mere fragment of philosophy. He thought to himself: *To think that some people, with their calm hearts and their cold souls, can make others weep by massaging them with trite and weary rhetorical commonplaces! Is it really necessary to exempt people from having to think in order to make them feel something? Nevertheless, what a depth of feeling lies in profound sorrow!*

The next day he went to the edge of the sea, where the waves broke at their foaming crests, in their eternal chant about the simplicity of life, and there his thoughts of the night before fell into the deep and fertile waters of oblivion.

Waves broke at his feet, dashing noisily against the rocks in a roar of spray, and disappearing into the sand of the beach. *A dead wave . . . but was it dead?* Another followed, also to die, while the sea itself remained the same. *Beneath the waves, which were the work of the wind on only the surface of the vast sea . . . beneath the waves, perhaps in a rebellious contrary direction, there was only the incessant eternal movement of the deepest waters, a round dance without beginning or end.*

V

PEDRO ANTONIO AND HIS WIFE were living in his native village with his brother, the priest Don Emeterio, who did his best to take their minds off their loss. Don Emeterio took his brother with him to the *tertulia* at the local inn to help him forget his sorrow by listening to the talk about the larger events of the war. Josefa Ignacia stayed home with her sister-in-law, a ship's officer's widow, who talked only of the dead boy and the last time she had seen him, at a dance, in his uniform. Ignacio's mother was drawn to this simple woman, who joined her in her constant complaints about the loss of her son, like the echo of her own incessant monologue. She looked forward each day to hearing the same appreciative bits of praise about Ignacio, just as a sick person looks forward each day to the same healing balm to ease the pain. Little by little, her grief spread out into all the things of daily life, even the most insignificant. The mere act of mending stockings or allowing her gaze to rest on household utensils helped her grief turn into something fixed, an idea not without its sweetness which tinged her every thought.

Meanwhile, Pedro Antonio abandoned himself to the comfortable habits of daily life, though deep inside him a growing sorrow could not break through and find expression. He thought of his poor son all the time, in wandering thoughts so slow that they seemed almost to be unmoving, in a vague vision that permeated his whole mind. Just as a single immense, dark cloud can dim the earth by its shadow, his son's memory filled his soul. His grief lay buried beneath this memory.

Ignacio's father enjoyed wandering among his childhood haunts, where he had spent slow, long hours, in the shade of chestnut and walnut trees, taking care of the cow. He went to listen to the everlasting murmur of the river, a song calling up his earliest memories. Along the way he would stop to chat with old friends he met at their farms in the country at their toil with the hard earth. He was pleased by their sympathy for him in those conversations whose essence amounted to "It is God's will . . ."

The peasants tended regularly to all their chores, and their fields resounded only with the usual voices of every day. At noon, watching the smoke from the farmhouse chimneys curl above their tiled roofs and lose itself in the air, Pedro Antonio could almost forget about the war, but it came back to him when he heard the talk at the *tertulia* every afternoon, when he heard the farmers complain about the constant levies exacted of them to supply rations for the Carlist Army, and when some battalion on the march passed through the area. His constant obsession over the death of his son dominated his consciousness without the slightest connection to the war in which he died.

"Go and find something to do. . . . Lord, what a man!" his wife would often say to him. His terrible calm alarmed her, she suspected that he had something wrong with him inside, and she feared that he might be struck down by some mental trouble which would leave him paralyzed—or, who knows, perhaps something even worse.

Pedro Antonio often went to a small corner of the

orchard of the house they lived in to sit under a chestnut tree beside a brook. There he found a certain amount of peace, watching the water flow by, listening to its meaningless babble, watching it cover the rocks with spray. He sometimes dropped a leaf into the current and watched it be carried away until lost to sight. He never tired of admiring the water-striders, who walked the waters in the quiet pools, just as other insects walked the dry land.

On mild nights he would spend some time on the balcony. Its daytime irregularities erased, the landscape appeared to him as a mass of shadows from which, in the dark, the far-off light of some farmhouse would speak to him of a home lost in the mountain. Having grown deaf to the everlasting noise of the brook through constantly hearing it, it came to him as a song of silence, a deep, unheard melody whose flow he allowed to carry away all his vague imaginings.

The hours of his slow days were marked off one from another by the mellow ringing of the church bells, whose sounds grew thinner as they melted away into the calm countryside. First came the bells of dawn, clear in their fresh serenity, springing out of the air to rid him of the last lazy grogginess of a night's sleep. The Angelus followed at noon, its tones full and solemn, a voice of rest which seemed to fall out of the whole sky. Later, when the outlines of the mountains were purified in the marble sky and when light was dissolved in shadow, the bells for afternoon prayer came, hidden and intimate, as if they rose from the weary earth. The last bells, the bells of evening, the bells for the souls of the dead, called on families now gathered by their hearths to pray for the souls of their dead, for the buried members of the everlasting family. The voice of the bells was always the same, but it seemed to take on different tones at different hours of the day.

On his solitary walks, Pedro Antonio stopped by habit at one particular farmhouse, where he could see over the entire valley. There he passed time with the old owner of the place, a decrepit man no longer useful as a worker, who sat in the lee of the house on a rickety chair in the sun, shucking corn, peeling potatoes— doing any little useful task to make himself less of a burden. His family had abandoned him as being in the way, and he was happy to see Pedro Antonio and to talk with him about his dead son. "I'll always remember the last time he came here to this village . . . what a handsome fellow! And as for you, I've known you since you were like him, a mere boy. . . . As for me, I'm now over eighty." The old man then repeated in Basque what he had said about his age, addressing Pedro Antonio in the formal mode of *berori* rather than in the Basque familiar, *zu*.

"And why, then, did you address me in the form of *berori*," Pedro Antonio asked.

"Oh, you're rich, and a gentleman . . ."

The chocolate-shop owner was pleased to hear the old man talk, even though he always ended, after looking all around him with a piercing look, by telling of his troubles in a low voice and by complaining about the conduct of his children who had left him there totally forgotten, with only the occasional company of a small granddaughter. "Children! They're all out for themselves . . . but that's the way of the world. . . . The poor things are fed up with work themselves, maintaining their own. . . . Children!" he would exclaim, thinking at the same time how he had treated his own parents in their old age. And he would conclude, in Basque, "I ask only that God may grant me a week-long death." That was the period of time he thought necessary to prepare his soul and to avoid being a burden to his children in his illness.

"Children!" he would mutter as he took leave of a dazed Pedro Antonio. And he would end his cloudy and formless meditations by repeating, "A week-long death."

The Carlists were so discouraged by their hasty retreat from Somorrostro that Don Carlos announced to them his coming entry into Bilbao and a triumphal march under his flag from Vera to Cádiz: he would swiftly take over any place where revolution and impiety were prepared to do battle with him. And he had not lost his taste for dancing, one of the official duties of every good monarch. He promised the *junta de merindades* victory or death. He harangued the young men from his pulpit in order to sow in their minds the miraculous formula: *No importa!* "It doesn't matter!" And he threw himself into an attempt to cover up the failure of the attempted government loan and the furious ill-will between the old and the new commanders, when Cabrera turned his back on the Pretender.

"Poor Ignacio," Juan José said. "He went and died before our triumph, just as we were preparing. . . . What a hurry he was in! A little more patience and we would have entered Bilbao together." He was more hopeful than ever, for it seemed to him that the vigorous effort at Somorrostro had exhausted the enemy's spirits and that they, the Carlists, were fresher and more ready for battle. The one who takes it during a fight and who saves himself for the end must finally be the winner. Two or three good blows delivered when the opponent is weary of fighting and . . . ready for the next round!

The two armies faced each other near Estella, the holy sanctuary of Carlism, where the liberator of Bilbao had come to smother the place. Dorregaray, who had succeeded old Elío as commander in chief of the Carlists, spoke out against the stupid fury of the Liberal soldiers, and the Liberal general spoke of the rabid outcries by which the Carlists had announced their powerlessness. Thus they insulted each other beforehand to build up their rage, like schoolboys spitting words at each other's ears before they come to blows. They finally confronted each other on the 25th of June. On the 26th, a storm broke which was especially hard on the Liberals, whose hunger drove them to devour potatoes from the ground and who in a panic set fire to some villages to warm themselves and to dry themselves out. On the 27th the Liberal artillery forced the Carlists back up to the heights. Then, ready for hand-to-hand combat, their weapons poised, separated by torrential downpours, they had to wait for the sky to clear. Next, in a decisive moment, the Liberal general Concha was killed, just as he appeared to buck up his soldiers who were advancing on the guerrillas. Here was revenge for the Carlists!—their way of getting back at the Liberals for Somorrostro, for the loss of Ollo, of the dashing Radica, of the spirited old Andéchaga. They vented their feelings by slaughtering the wounded the enemy had left behind in its retreat from those fields laid waste by man and by the heavens. As a trophy the Carlists hung on a balcony the bloody sheet where Concha's corpse had lain. On the 30th the inhabitants of the ruined town of Abárzuza begged at the feet of their King for all the prisoners to be killed: amidst the curses of the ruined peasants against those men, who were outsiders, one tenth of them, some twenty-two men in all, were duly shot in front of the

ruins left by the Liberal fires. A few days later, the
Pretender's wife, newly arrived in Spain, reviewed the
Carlist troops on the slopes of Montejurra, the moun-
tain which had witnessed their victory.

A strong breath of hope gave new life to the Carlists.
The most prestigious military man on the enemy side
had been killed before the enemy had hardly had time
to enjoy the glory of the liberation of Bilbao. Barely
two months had passed since their retreat from Somorrostro, and the Carlists had reassembled with victory in mind. The Liberals would see, now the Liberals would see, what armies sustained by Faith are
made of! Is there a greater proof of vitality than for a
shattered army to reassemble? As for the Liberals—
merely marching together always, like large rivers do,
is something that is proper to plains. They, the Carlists, were the army of mountain volunteers, the torrent
which flows down from the roughest terrain, gradually
wearing down all the rocks, even the largest.

Juan José could already see himself in Bilbao. He
burned with impatience because they did not set out
immediately on a march to claim what was theirs.

Pedro Antonio heard the news of the victory, embellished with a thousand details and comments. He
chanced to be in Guernica on July 8th, the day some
smuggled cannons came into the city. To greet them,
half the town turned out, everyone exulting over the
victory at Estella. In their eyes, Bilbao was as good as
captured already, Don Carlos sat on the throne, the
ancient Basque privileges were once again confirmed.
The Liberals had sunk in defeat, and the new cannons
had established peace. The cannons were paraded in
triumph, crowned with branches, through crowds which
gazed at them with adoring glances. Young boys hailed
them from trees they had climbed for a better view.

Some people hugged the cannons. One old woman wanted to kiss their bronze, glistening in the sun, as if to kiss a holy relic. One would have thought that an epidemic had just ended, that it was the day of Corpus Christi, and that the Monstrance was being carried in procession.

Feeling the gaze of those black-mouthed cannons, Pedro Antonio's slow and persistent thoughts gave a sudden start and his pain stirred up to take his soul by force. But the bonds could not be broken, and he fell back into the slow and drowsy current of sorrow, into the almost unmoving current of his hazy vision of his son.

In the village, the coffee-hour was given over to discussion of the news and to outlining plans based on what had been printed in the newspapers.

"They're just beating about the bush," exclaimed the surgeon. "Some brave initiative this is, taking Bilbao and defending Estella. It would be better to stop playing hide-and-seek in the mountains and to march directly on Madrid. Let the Liberals occupy the provinces if that's what they want. Strike at the head . . . at their head . . ."

"That was the craziness we had in the last war," said Pedro Antonio, "and you know what came of those famous expeditions."

"Don't go by that! It's not the same now. . . . Some could move from here, others from Catalonia, still others from the center . . . and goodbye, Madrid!"

"All right," exclaimed Don Emeterio, "let's suppose we're already in Madrid, what do we do then?"

"You want to know what we do then?"

"Yes, what do we do?"

"Why . . . that's not even a question!"

"Well, that's the question I'm asking . . . The main thing, and don't change the subject, is to take complete control *here*. . . . What comes after, we don't need to concern ourselves with that yet. This is the place, right here, under the protection of our mountains . . ."

What things must be running through the minds of Don Eustaquio, Gambelu, and even Don Braulio. If only they were here to say them! thought Don Pedro. The conversation diverted him and made him think of other conversations, those quiet and intimate ones in the coziness of his chocolate shop.

On the occasion of the entrance into Cuenca of the *Infantes* Don Alfonso and Doña Blanca, the brother and sister of Don Carlos, Don Emeterio feigned to be highly indignant over the horrors reported in the Liberal daily newspapers. But he read the papers again, nevertheless, in order to feed his imagination on those cruel details, saying to himself once again that there's nothing in the world worse than sentimentalism, one of the century's evils, which sympathizes with criminals and animals but lets impious schoolteachers poison the innocent souls of children in the name of liberty.

The entrance into Cuenca was indeed grand! After the city resisted for two days, the troops attached to the *Infantes* broke into the city, and while Don Alfonso and Doña Blanca went to Communion to give thanks to God, their soldiers—remnants of the Pope's Zouaves, cantonal troops from Alcoy, fugitives from the Paris Commune, and former convicts—carried out their own kind of divine justice, during two hours of "recreation." The Bishop was unable to stop the fury of these mercenary adventurers. They robbed, sacked, killed any hospital patients who were slow in obeying their orders, and destroyed historical archives. They reduced museum showcases given over to natural history and physics to splinters, ravaged print-shops and schools, breaking everything until they finally fell down for lack of breath. Doña Blanca paraded the Carlist flag through the terrified city to the sound of music, while her brother explained that the lads needed to let off steam.

"Every single Liberal city should be razed and covered over with salt!" exclaimed Don Emeterio. "Anything else will lead us nowhere, and all this will never come to an end."

"It will come to an end when God wishes," Pedro Antonio answered.

"When God wishes, when God wishes . . . ! That's the way it is, that's why everything's in turmoil. People keep saying 'when God wishes,' " Don Emeterio retorted, mocking the unconscious blasphemy of that phrase that suggests that everything is rightfully awry.

They all attributed bad faith to the Liberal press in its accounts of the taking of Cuenca, but then proceeded to use these same accounts as the basis of their discussion. They talked about the barbarism many people attribute to Spaniards, and then moved to discuss the distinction between gentle customs and luxurious customs, at the insistence of Don Emeterio, who had read in Jaime Balmes' *Protestantism Compared with Catholicism* that chapter in which the famous journalist excused the savagery of the running of the bulls, a "spectacle dear to our hearts which, while feeling the most gentle compassion for its fatality, still seem to be ill at ease if much time elapses without the relief found in scenes of pain, pictures sprinkled with blood."

To certain observations made by the surgeon, Don Emeterio exclaimed, "That's sentimental exaggeration, and nothing else! The people need something virile so they won't get flabby. It was people who cried

'Bread and bulls!' who knew how to face up to Napoleon. . . . you can't wage war with saintly old women, and war is a necessary evil."

On another day a manifesto was read aloud at the *tertulia*, the manifesto Don Carlos issued at Morentín, which was like music to accompany the bloody lyrics of Cuenca. The Pretender declared that he had saved Spain by defeating all the generals in the service of the Revolution, and went on to speak about the glorious sword of Philip V, the glorious example of Columbus raising the Spanish flag in the New World. He brought in God, the Throne, the Spanish Parliament, as well as the disastrous financial situation of Spain.

"With blows like the one delivered at Cuenca and manifestos like this one, Spain is as good as ours!" said the sly surgeon.

Ours? thought Pedro Antonio. *Spain ours? What does that mean? It will never be mine! Our Army! Our Program! Our Ideas! Our King! Our . . . Our . . . What was mine was my son, mine was the money I put into the Cause.*

They could not persuade him at the beginning of August to go to Guernica to see the King receiving his "Vivas!" Instead Pedro Antonio went to walk in the valley where he was born, to cradle his spirit by contemplating that serene landscape, the spiritual link between all the generations of his village; against the eternal background of its vision of calm the slow processes of the inner lives of the grandparents of grandparents had unfolded, just as would happen with the grandsons of grandsons.

"Go somewhere and try to distract yourself. . . . For the Lord's sake, Perú Antón, go on out somewhere!"

Josefa Ignacia's heart told her that her husband's calm was like that suffocating, still heat that burns up the fields and comes before the storm that flattens down the dry vegetation, once a living green.

Pedro Antonio was now showing a new symptom to alarm his wife: the frequency with which he talked about the savings he had given to the Cause.

"I told you so," she said, "I told you so many a time when you were about to hand over your money, to look sharp at what you were doing. . . . I told you. But of course we women don't know anything about these things . . ."

"It's not lost yet. . . . And besides, how could I turn them down? Can you tell me how I could have told them no?"

Pedro Antonio took secret delight in these scoldings by his lifelong companion and began to dwell on the subject of his savings whenever he got the chance— which increased his own worry. And she, sensing something of her husband's sickness, would say, "Don't pay any attention to that, it isn't worth your bother to get excited about it. . . . We won't lack for food . . . considering how few we are now . . . !" The couple fell silent as the persistent memory of their dead son came to stand between them.

"In any case," said Josefa Ignacia, "you've got nothing to lose by looking into your savings . . . go and see Don José María."

And finally, brooding on his savings, Pedro Antonio decided to go in Gambelu's company to Durango, where the Carlist State was being established.

Postage stamps had already been issued, the first step in any ordered system of communication. Carlist money had been put into ciruclation: *perros grandes*, as they called the copper coins which supplemented and served as fractions of the National silver pieces, bore the effigy of the King by God's Grace, crowned with laurel, like a Caesar. A telegraph system had been inaugurated, and the University of Oñate was about to start its courses. Decorations were handed about, as were the titles of count, marquis, and duke, with their corresponding territory. Little by little the complicated machinery of a state was being put in place, under armed protection. Movement is proved by going forward: from all that labor a definite program would arise.

"A beehive of drones!" Gambelu said to Pedro Antonio. "All this is no more than a Court, and we don't need a Court, but a Royal General Headquarters. The cafés, the sidewalks, the streets in this place are almost always full of people, all praying for victory and arguing about tactics. . . . And as for that Court of enthroned titles, they're all foreigners who maintain a horse at someone else's expense and take the best lads as orderlies . . .!"

"The same as in '39 . . ."

"Even worse. Now instead of Elío, Dorregaray—a Mason."

"A Mason . . .?"

"Yes, a Mason. There are a lot of them around here, and they answer to the central Lodge in Bilbao. And that Lodge answers to another, and so on until we reach the center, which they call the Invisible Valley. . . . No one can trust anyone . . ."

"The Invisible Valley," Pedro Antonio said softly to himself, so deeply startled that without meaning to he looked behind him, where he caught sight of Celestino.

When Celestino saw him, he composed his expression, came toward him, stretched out his hand, and said, "What it must be like . . . ! I was deeply moved, deeply . . . I loved Ignacio, poor Ignacio, with heart and soul. . . . What nobility! What sincerity! And, especially, what faith in the Cause!" After a prayer for the dead delivered in the same tone, Celestino spoke to Pedro Antonio and Gambelu about the splendid conditions in Durango. He went on without stopping to talk about the planned siege of Irún, which the King would watch over in person, and then he concluded by remarking that old and faithful Elío had returned to the grace of the Lord.

"Unless St. James the Moor-killer descends mounted on his white horse . . . or the Virgin," said Gambelu.

"The Virgin?" exclaimed Celestino. "The Virgin no longer appears to anyone but shepherds . . ."

The Invisible Valley! Pedro Antonio kept thinking about this strange phenomenon. As soon as he could get away from Celestino, he ran to look for Don José María, to deal with the question of his savings. But he could not find him, and so he returned to his village and his wife, pondering all the while about his savings, about the splendid conditions in Durango, and about the Invisible Valley. All these images floated vaguely in his mind, over the persistent background of his dim vision of his dead son.

Once he went to visit the home of a man with whom he could join in a duet of lamentations, for the man had also lost his savings. And, like himself, the man had also lost a son, and, like himself, he seemed now more keenly to remember the loss of his savings. He had given up his son's blood, and now they were sucking away the blood of his purse. A hard thing to give one's sons, their arms fresh for work, but in the end they can be replaced. One goes and another comes; the family continues. Moreover, a missing son means one fewer mouth to feed. But if the purse runs out, the trap has arrived. The house may disappear, and the family scatter to the wind. And if the family is broken up, who can replace it? Both men believed in the genius of the family, which men sacrifice themselves for.

"Console yourself that we will retrieve our loss a hundredfold in heaven," Pedro Antonio said.

"That's what the priests say. . . . My boys . . . one is serving the King, the other is dead. There's only myself and the women to work the soil. . . . If things go on like this, and I have to sell the farm, what will my son do?"

Pedro Antonio thought of the future, of his years of old age, and of the life which lay ahead for them. Sometimes he regretted that he could not mourn his son's loss more deeply, but then he would bring himself around at once by murmuring, "One must bear one's own cross with joy." And yet, it was strange that it weighed on him so little, so little. . . . Was that really his Cross?

Pedro Antonio returned to Durango just after the disaster at Irún, that shameful rout which amounted to "Every man for himself!" For that was the way the siege, watched over by the King in person, had ended. In its course, many unfortunate victims of an epidemic perished in the snow, after being forced to abandon the hospital. The disaster gave rise to new schisms and factions, and the King censured two commanders as cowards and traitors.

This time Pedro Antonio did indeed find Don José María, who gave him a sorrowful look and said, "God sends us tribulations to put our patience to the test. Those of us who are graced with the unmerited benefits of being able to rely on the ineffable consolations of faith . . ."

He went on in the same vein for some time. Pedro Antonio thanked him then suddenly exclaimed, "We're lost!"

"Of course! They insist on wasting time, instead of marching straight to Madrid . . . to Madrid!"

The war atmosphere had reduced for him the concrete program he had sought for with such zeal before the war to the single phrase: "To Madrid!" For him everything now depended on taking control of the ruling center: lay hands on the threads of government for twenty-four hours, and then everything would be done and the program would be on its way.

"And what about the interest on my loans?" asked Pedro Antonio.

"To Madrid! To Madrid!" exclaimed the armchair theorist, as if he were just ending out loud a mental monologue in which he had been absorbed.

"To Madrid? What for? To take over the Bank, perhaps?"

They talked a bit about money, and Pedro Antonio somewhat calmed down.

But his obsession over his money was turning into mania, beneath which the vision of his lost son throbbed persistently, trying to break out into open sorrow.

"Pedro Antonio is in a bad way," Josefa Ignacia told her brother-in-law. "He's about to go mad. He does nothing but tell me at every turn that we're ruined, and he scolds me because he says I spend too much. . . . And not a word about our poor Ignacio. My son! . . . Lord Jesus, how much misfortune!"

On winter evenings at the end of '74 Pedro Antonio would visit a relative's house, and there, in the large kitchen, by the hearth where supper was being prepared, while listening to talk of a thousand trivial matters, he would stare into the moving flames which crackled and climbed in search of freedom, the changing tongues of flame licking at the smoke-blackened wall. He would then recall the brazier, now dark and silent, in his shop, thinking of the way he poked the fire to turn it into a palpitating red glow just as the discussion grew more heated between Uncle Pascual and Don Eustaquio. It had been such a humble fire, curled up at his feet, submissive as a dog, consuming itself for its master like a burnt offering. Then those flames in that country kitchen would call up for him the image of Purgatory. Seeing his son there, he would murmur a Paternoster for his soul.

The Christmas season began. For Josefa Ignacia the days were doubly sad. Her husband accepted them with the resigned calm with which he had accepted everything else since the death of his son. There were neither the joys nor the memories of other years now. To try to cheer him up, his brother the priest would talk to him about the Carlist triumph at Urnieta on Conception Day and about the Liberal army's *pronunciamento* at Sagunta supporting Alfonsito, son of the Queen dethroned in the September Revolution. He spoke with some exasperation, like all enthusiasts, about there now being two kings ranged against each other on the field: one king who would draw to his side people who were for order and for money, and one king who must be a living ensign for the army.

The priest thundered out against the new King's manifesto, in which he had proclaimed that he would never stop being a good Spaniard and a good Catholic, like all his predecessors, and a good Liberal, as his century demanded. "Our Don Carlos gave his cousin a good reply: 'I am the Legitimacy!'"

"His cousin, is he?" asked Pedro Antonio. "In that case, everything stays in the family . . ."

"What madness! To proclaim himself King now, just when we are at our strongest. . . . And to call himself a Catholic Liberal! . . . A Catholic Liberal! It is against this kind of person, this very kind, that the Pope has launched his most energetic condemnations . . ."

"Will they finally come to recognize the Carlist debt?" asked Pedro Antonio.

His brother looked at him in alarm, and his wife, frightened by the priest's strange look, also became alarmed.

He's going to go mad if he continues like this, Don Emeterio thought. Then, raising his voice as if to drown in noise his brother's black mania and also to smother the slight fear he felt in his presence now that he had mentally consigned him to madness, he shouted, "*Now*, precisely *now*, when we are at our strongest, now that we are within grasp of victory. . . . Why, we've never shown more vigor or more strength."

"That's what we said last time. . . . And what seven long years they were!"

Pedro Antonio felt, somewhat dimly, that since his son was dead, the Cause for which he gave his life had died with him. In his mind, Somorrostro had been the high point of their strength, and everything that had followed had only been a regrouping of forces which up until then had grown and been hoarded like a treasure. He had a vague intuition, dark and undefined, that they were present at a moment when their resources and their energies could only decline. They were no longer at the moment of juvenile strength, before destiny is decided. It was no longer springtime, when the forces of growth still throb beneath the earth, but summer, the season of harvest. The moment of fullness of action had passed. The time of freedom, the time of the energy that springs up out of the concentration of force, had come to an end. Somorrostro had been the climax, and the retreat from Somorrostro had been the old defeat of Carlist memory. Already at Abárzuza Carlism wore its destiny engraved on its brow.

Pedro Antonio thus listened to everything with indifference, and his comments were doubting ones. Thus, he shrugged his shoulders when he heard that the two kings had faced each other on the field at Lácar, that the Carlist Mounted Guards had issued a challenge right out of history books to the Pavia Hussars, and that Alfonsito had been forced to quit the field. And when Gambelu told him on one of his visits to the village that Cabrera had recognized the Liberal King, he exclaimed, "It's clear enough now! We're sinking, and there's no help for it! ... And my savings are going too."

"I told you some time back that Cabrera is not our Cabrera," Gambelu answered. "He's a Mason and a Protestant, married to a Protestant woman. ... He doesn't believe in the Virgin. ... A Mason, a Mason ..."

The gigantic figure of Cabrera in Pedro Antonio's memories grew even larger, partly hidden for him in the smoky mists of the Invisible Valley, and attracted him with a strange splendor. And while the Carlists were insisting that the old *caudillo's* defection meant nothing to them and busying themselves making up insulting names to call him, as Carlos stripped him of all his honors, Pedro Antonio read to himself, almost syllable by syllable, the legendary hero's proclamation, feeling as he read it the deepest memories well up in him as if conjured up. He could hear the very voice of the old man once known as the "Tiger of Maestrazgo," who now—disillusioned, repentant, and invoking his son—forgave his enemies, just as in the Seven Year War he sowed terror invoking his mother, who had been lined up and shot. Pedro Antonio heard the voice of the hero who bore his wounds as living testimony to his merits, and whose dead titles and decorations had been stripped from him by the grandson of Carlos V, who had bestowed them upon him. He could hear that voice telling his former followers that he was leaving the King in order to go with God and the Fatherland and that they were vainly trying to fill a vacuum of ideas with mere words. It was a strange echo, indeed, that voice of the old guerrilla, loaded with wounds and glory, who now spoke, from out of the mysterious Invisible Valley, about ideas and peace, about the power of doctrine over blind faith, pleading for compassion for the Fatherland, begging that they reject once and for all the insult to their dignity on the part of those who claimed that the Spanish were ungovernable, and exhorting them that they, being *conquistadores* by tradition and by character, should carry out the greatest conquest possible to any people: the conquest of triumphing over their own weaknesses!

This isn't Cabrera, thought Pedro Antonio. *This is a missionary.* Then he recalled that other preacher who, in the open air, in the Bilbao cemetery, spoke of peace, evoking memories from the Seven Year War and of the night of Luchana, at the foot of the matron of stone who gave crowns to the defeated as well as to the victors. They also said that he was a Mason, that preacher. What did those Masons have, by which they could thus stir up the soul?

Pedro Antonio found himself prepared to believe the old caudillo. Under the spell of his proclamation, he felt reborn in him his spirit of the year 1840, when in one of the battalions led by Maroto he had heard his own voice joining his comrades in yelling, "Peace! We want peace!" And then, when he heard Gambelu exclaim, after news of some shootings at Estella, "There's still hope," he remembered Muñagorri, where Juan Bautista Aguirre rose up in revolt to the cry of "Peace and local statutes! Long live the Catholic religion! Long live Alfonso XII! Long live General Cabrera!"

Meanwhile, Durango was a beehive of activity: the decisive blow once and for all, and then, "To Madrid!"

Juan José lived in hope of victory from one day to the next. The pruning worked by the shootings at Estella would serve as a future warning to all traitors. And the very fact that the enemy now had a King on whom to pin their hopes and as a living symbol for their most zealous efforts would furnish the Carlists with the vigor needed to defeat them. He'd soon see, that little Catholic-Liberal King. Juan José would sing, between his teeth:

> In Lácar, my boy,
> You were in a fix;
> If Don Carlos had given you
> The boot with his foot
> You would have landed in Paris.

But Celestino had arrived at such a point of disillusionment that he confessed privately to himself his pessimism and his fears. Who was going to get those Basques to move out of their native terrain? In the ancient times they had not cared to go on the offensive beyond the Malato tree, unless they were given a stipend. Fighting close to their families and with their own countryside as support, they didn't much fancy going to Madrid, to provide Castile with a King. What for? They go there? The Carlists had already planted on their own, by way of experiment, the roots of a small, independent state, with their own postage stamps and their own coins. And they distrusted the unknown plains. It was enough for them, strongly entrenched behind the Ebro River, to nurture their incipient State— thanks, in large part, to the help of those old Castilian volunteers who had come north, some to make a living from the war, others to satisfy atavistic instincts, some to put on airs, and most all of them to suffer derision and scorn.

But what wasn't the worst of it, no. For Celestino, the worst thing was that there was nothing fixed about the program, so that most of the men did not know what they were defending. For he, in need of formulas in order to understand a movement which did not spring from the depths of his soul, was of the opinion that a formula engenders a movement. Listening to him talk one night Juan José interrupted to say, "Without all that, we've taken to the hills, and even with all that everything will fall apart, if that's the way God wants it. What we need is fewer self-important know-it-alls. . . . And as regards the Castilians, who invited them here?"

The Pretender understood that he had to lend himself to the supreme ritual. Many people were already murmuring that he was a Mason, or at least was influenced by Masons and Liberals, and the story was being endlessly repeated that his grandfather had resisted taking

the oath to respect the *fueros*. Not even the consecration of the Carlist army to the Sacred Heart of Jesus
stopped the gangrene from spreading. The time arrived when it was necessary to hold the general Councils of Vizcaya at Guernica. On the 30th a petition was
presented asking that the King be proclaimed Lord of
Vizcaya. When she heard the news, Josefa Ignacia
urged her husband, "Go and see that, for God's sake.
Take your mind off things, find some distraction. Go
and see it . . ."

Don Carlos was King by right and by deed, it was
said, and now he would be King by the will of the
people, being consecrated by the true democracy of
tradition and *fait accompli*. Those were Councils, those
were! "Of the 177 signatures on the message," Gambelu said, "only fourteen, just fourteen, had Castilian
surnames. As for the rest—what good Basque surnames! Gabicagojeascoa, Muruetagoyena, Urionaba-
rranechea, Mendataurigoitia, Iturriondobeitia. . . .
Lovely! Just let an outsider try to grab the land . . ."
Those were the real thing, those Councils! There was
no representative from Bilbao, so as to preserve peace.

As the 3rd of July drew near, the day designated
for the King's oath, Guernica began to fill with people.
Pedro Antonio gave in to his wife's urging and was
now going every day with Gambelu to the city of the
Oath. Amid the thronging crowds of people, awaiting
the ceremony and hearing inside him the noise of gut-
deep passions, Pedro Antonio began to feel rekindled
in his spirit the fire his son's death had extinguished.

On the 3rd, having stayed over to sleep in the city,
Pedro Antonio was awakened by the twenty-one-gun
salute, which reverberated through him. Gambelu arrived and the two of them, as impatient as children,
rushed into the streets. What a crush! The tumultuous

flow of the multitude stirred up the depths of Pedro Antonio's soul, where slept his old memories. He recalled the times he had visited the city on market day. The countryside, the calm air, the placid fertile plain nestled among evergreen woodlands, the woodlands of his childhood, the maritime freshness of the atmosphere—all of these things penetrated to the very center of his being.

Childhood memories welled up into his consciousness from the places deep inside him where they had been lovingly stored up, memories all mixed up with each other. "Here, in that shop, my father bought me some shoes. The woman who owned the shop was cross-eyed. . . . And there, right there, we were stopped with the cow, the day he brought her in to sell . . ." His recollections gave the entire scene around him new life, fresh and intense, and he took an interest in all the people crowding the town.

They were swept along by the crowd to the central plaza, reaching there just as the appointed retinue went to find the King. Pedro Antonio stood on tiptoes to see over the heads of people in front of him. The *Miqueletes* set out. The noise of the crowd, the sound of clarions and kettledrums, the parade of people behind the banner—it all shook Pedro Antonio's spirit. When he saw the image of the Virgin Most Pure on a waving banner of white satin hoisted high, he crossed himself. He recalled one day when he was a boy and his father had brought him to watch a procession on Holy Thursday: the memory seemed to awaken in him his old childhood longing to devour everything with his eyes before everything disappeared forever.

All the houses were bedecked with hangings. Some people hung out their bedsheets on their balconies, like tokens of their intimate and innermost lives. Fireworks burst over their heads, as if the tumult of the crowd had risen toward heaven and formed there a cry of jubilation. All the bells that were set ringing might be said to be a greeting from the countryside. From time to time the thunder of the artillery gave a profound note and a chord of unity to that festival in which everyone forgot that they were at war. For Pedro Antonio, the uproar eased the mute and silent grief which he had kept pent up since his son's death, as he felt himself being overcome by the life of the crowd. The ringing of the bronze bells, the bursting of fireworks over the noise of the multitude brought him back to memories of the Seven Year War, and his soul no longer sought peace.

The swarm carried them along until they found themselves in front of the house where the King was staying. When he appeared, a loud shout of "Viva!" drowned out even the sound of the bells. The King! The King who was about to take an oath before the people.

Gambelu and Pedro Antonio ran like little boys to Santa Clara, and they barely managed to stay together beside a tree to watch the ceremony. The retinue entered the space set off by railings. Don Carlos and his rather dim father took up positions on a dais under a damask canopy, sheltered by the great oak, while the representative authorities stood on the porch of the small temple shrine. The Mass of Consecration began. The multitude, spread out on the treeless field, seemed to be paying homage to the Oak of the Statutes. Between its branches, Pedro Antonio could see the enormous back of the giant Oíz, that somber mountain beneath whose gaze his child's soul had been formed. This child's soul beat in him now, in unison with the multitude listening to Mass in the silence of the open air,

all of them communing with one another and caught
up in the ceremony. Nearby there were some young
girls, their cheeks as red as apples, full of themselves
and of their youth, whispering and giggling. An old
woman, distracted from her prayers, grew indignant
at their irreverence. The Host was elevated. Everyone
who could, in that throng of people, knelt. Everyone
bowed his head. In the silence of the multitude assembled at the foot of the old oak symbolizing Basque
liberty, under a clear, bright sky, the Host was lifted
up for the adoration of the people, of whom scarcely
one had any understanding of it all. When Don Carlos
descended from his throne and knelt before the altar,
the crowd stood up. Pedro Antonio longed to let his
soul leap inside him and to let flow the tears he had
so long kept back. He resisted his longing out of shame
at crying in front of so many people, but his resistance
only excited him more.

Torn out of his withdrawal into himself by the crowd
surrounding him, he seemed to awaken from his leth-
argy. He realized that he was just one father in that
crowd who had lost his son, his only son, by whom
he would have perpetuated himself among them. When
he returned to himself, he found the pain which had
been germinating in his soul. The cold words "I have
lost a son" turned to the burning words "My son is
dead," a phrase like fire in his vitals. He was a man,
a man like all the others, wounded by an incurable
hurt in the midst of human society. He had been a
father among men, among those who surrounded him
now, many of them fathers still.

The priest took the Host and his voice resounded
in the living silence of the crowd, saying that it was a
spectacle worthy to be seen by angels, the sight of a
King prostrate before the immense Majesty who in-

habits the heavens; that the King had never before appeared so great; that it was a consolation and a wonder to see him there now and in such a posture, when nearly all the kings of the earth made pacts with the nefarious revolution . . .

"Take that, Alfonsito!" Gambelu mumbled.

. . . That it was admirable to see him join his people in a close religious tie by means of a solemn vow . . .

Pedro Antonio could take no more. He choked back his sobs while the priest, armed with his weapon of the word, seemed to take pleasure in having the King before him on his knees.

. . . That the people had spoken through the mouths of their cannons; that they had done so with the blood of their martyrs, generously shed on the field of battle . . .

At the words "blood of their martyrs," the wound in Pedro Antonio's soul opened and he began to bleed silent tears which brought him sweet acceptance of the death of his son. He cried in silence, and the memory of his son who died for the Carlist faith grew in him and he felt a sense of enormous peace. The hazy vision which had been in the depths of his consciousness grew larger and took on life. The more he tried to hold back his tears, the more they flowed, so that he finally allowed himself the intimate comfort of crying in public. He, too, had his sorrow and carried his Cross. . . . Let them understand!

The merry young girls with the apple-red cheeks took it all in and could not keep back their laughter at seeing that poor old man so carried away by the ceremony.

"Poor old fellow! How desolate he is!"

"Keep quiet, girl, don't make me laugh more," said

the other, as she held back her laughter and gazed at the King with her eyes wide.

Others, especially those who knew who he was, looked at Pedro Antonio with pity. One old woman seemed ready to cry for him herself. Through his tears, he could see those fresh young faces who had laughed at his weeping, and he tried to restrain himself by fixing his attention on what was going on in front of the altar. He heard the priest tell the King, "If you do thus, God will reward you, and if not, He will call you to account."

The pact between the King and the people had been sealed. The Mass continued, and the tears of the old man kept falling in silence.

"Some upbringing those girls must have had. Probably the daughters of some *Black*," Gambelu was saying, indignant at the behavior of the apple-cheeked young girls.

"Leave them be. They're young."

Gambelu gave the girls a furious look, and they laughed even harder.

As soon as the Mass was over, the air filled with enthusiastic shouts of "*Viva!*" The syndic came forward, silenced the crowd, and called out, "Noble Basques! Hear ye! Vizcaya, Vizcaya, Vizcaya, for the Lord Don Carlos, the Seventh of this name, Ruler of Vizcaya and King over all the regions of Spain, that he may live and reign over glorious triumphs for many happy years." He raised a damask standard, waving it in all directions amid delirious shouts of "Viva!" He repeated his invocation twice more, waving the pennant each time at the end. Pedro Antonio's tears were vanishing.

The King stood up. There was the noise of people hushing each other and finally complete silence. The

King thanked the people and said that he would always remember them in his heart and also their sons, who were generously shedding their blood on the battle-fields. A tender feeling welled up in Pedro Antonio's heart. The King went on to say that God, who never abandons those who fight in His cause, would soon grant them victory. The people thundered out more shouts of "Viva!" The old confectioner could no longer hold back his tears, and he was grateful to be able to cry amidst the noise. No one knew what was passing through the soul of that man, alone and isolated among so many people.

The chief magistrate of Guernica stepped forward and called out, "People of Vizcaya! Do you vow and swear homage to Don Carlos VII, the legitimate ruler of Vizcaya and King of all the regions of Spain?" Pedro Antonio's muffled "yes" was lost in the people's roar of "Yes!" which resounded through the branches of the old oak under the wide sky until it lost itself on the plain beyond. Then the deputies and the representatives of the people filed past the King for the ceremony of kissing his hand.

Pedro Antonio felt a great sense of rest and peace which he had not felt since the death of his son. It filled his spirit with the freedom of the air, the serenity of the sky, the expansive life of the crowd of people among whom he had expressed his grief. He was filled with thoughts of his village, memories of the Seven Year War, and the knowledge that his son had died without his having kissed him. He was free of a great weight, as if he had gotten rid of an oppressive disease which had kept him in a daze. Now he breathed freely again, and his mind was fresh. Once it was the people's turn, he drew near to kiss the King's hand. His eyes swollen, he kissed it with all his soul. It was just one more kiss for the King, among so many. But it was also that last kiss, saved so long a time, he had not been able to give his son.

Breathing free of that weight and feeling the curing calmness spread within him, he looked around for the red-cheeked girls so that they might see him in his serenity. He lingered for a brief time watching the rest of the ceremonial, in order to calm himself completely. When it was all over and the retinue of representatives remained on the dais as guards around the King's portrait, he went with Gambelu and the crowd to attend the Te Deum in the parish church. There he prayed as he had never prayed before. Peace had come to his soul little by little. He understood clearly the restful solitude left to him and his wife, and once again he believed that the world was a place of passage. His will to live was strengthened—to live for the joy of awaiting the hour when he would again be united with his son, when he *must* be reunited with him. Leaving the darkness of the church, he found everything outside restful and solemn as people went their separate ways.

When he got home, he looked at his wife, and then the two of them looked into each others' souls. They saw themselves alone in their old age after thirty-five years of marriage, bound together by an invisible shadow and a common hope, a son who was spiritually alive. The father burst into tears, exclaiming, "Poor Ignacio!" The mother said, "Thanks be to God!" and then cried with her husband.

The war was dwindling away, and in a convlusive rage the official Carlist paper called the Liberals cowards, criminals, slaves, Saracens, and eunuchs. Only a few days after the Oath to the Basque *fueros*, Don José

María counseled against stubbornness: they should abandon the King and save the *fueros* by making a pact with the enemy.

The proclamation naming the son of the dethroned Queen as King of Spain was having its effect. The people of order and money pinned their hopes on him. Many of those who had been helping the Carlists under the table began to abandon them. The episcopate began to preach charity, peace, and concord. The conflict of forces which provoked the war had found their diagonal: the counter-revolution was accomplished.

The moment of desperation was at hand for Carlism in arms. They had fallen back in Catalonia, after having lost the center when the Liberals took Cantalavieja. Within fifteen days some fifteen hundred men had been scattered, and others were routed at Treviño by the National cavalry. On the Carlist side, fury reached a paroxysm. Anyone thought to be a Liberal was hunted down ever more fiercely. Meanwhile, the towns were becoming convinced that the Government at Madrid did indeed have troops at its command. Even Gambelu spoke—though not in front of Pedro Antonio—of accepting the offer of a pact proposed by Quesada, when Lizárraga and the Bishop had to surrender at Seo de Urgel with more than a thousand men, for lack of water.

The uprising in the north having been contained, final desperation took over. The Madrid press was filled with insults against Don Carlos, who issued a new proposal: that in case of war with the United States over Cuba a truce should be declared between the opposing sides and his men shipped out as privateers. At the end of the year, the heavens launched heavy snowfalls and the government launched an avalanche of battalions against the Basque country. The thirty-five thousand Carlists who remained of the eighty thousand who had enlisted at the start now awaited the final push, under the command of a foreigner, a relative of the King. Don Carlos harangued them: the desired hour had struck. They were on the eve of great battles. They would not count the number of the enemy until after the victory. . . . Let them come! Awesome and terrible days waited ahead, but the French invasion had also begun with the occupation of Spain by Napoleonic troops. If bad days lay ahead, they would repeat the slogan of *No importa*! of the heroes of 1808: "It doesn't matter!" In Catalonia they would soon hear the traditional cry of "Take up arms!" that of old had rallied Christians against the Moors, and the immaculate banner would again crown the heights. They could expect hunger, cold, fatigue. But their King, even as he assured his followers of triumph, was himself looking for a decorous and seemly way of giving up. That last noisy expression of hope—"Now! Now that we've cleaned out the traitors!"—was born of despair.

Juan José felt his reservations reborn, but he wanted to deceive himself. It was impossible that the war should end as tuberculosis ends, in sheer weakness. Before succumbing they would do something resounding, something inspired and heroic. From the last effort of faith the miracle would come.

The year 1876 began with more heavy snow and with growing insubordination. In the Carlist ranks, growing thinner day by day as desertions increased, there was talk of amnesty, of surrender, of crossing into France.

When, towards the end of January, Juan José saw everyone in Durango looking for carriages and carts, emptying their houses, and beginning to disband upon hearing that the enemy was upon them, he exclaimed, "Everything is lost! They will win, yes, but their victory will cost them dearly! Let them win by their sweat!" And, who could tell? Perhaps at the sight of some supreme heroism to come, enthusiasm would revive in the weary, and the bonfire would kindle again.

And then came the last dying fit of anger. They defended themselves like a cornered cat, trying to kill while being killed. They defended themselves from the avalanche, falling back from peak to peak, from mountain to mountain, giving ground valley by valley, holding onto each handful of earth in the small State they had been building, with its own postage stamps, its own coins, its own university. At Elgueta they made the most of their weakness.

Juan José had to leave his disbanded battalion and join another, from Navarre. They went to Estella in the snow, only to have to abandon it in the middle of the month when that holy city of Carlism was lost. Each man was given two pesetas. They had no sure knowledge of the enemy's movements. When they left Estella, only thirty-four men were left of the eighty-two who had formed the company when Juan José joined it. They were beaten by the march of events. Now it was only a matter of falling back with dignity, without giving in, so that they might keep the right to fight again and rise up once more. The nation deserved to be left without the man who could have saved it. It deserved its fate because of its apathy, its stupid resignation, its culpable indifference. Spain was unworthy of a better fate. It was handing itself over to a mere boy infected with the anemia of Catholic Liberalism. It preferred peace without glory to glory without peace. It would become a mockery among nations.

Pedro Antonio had to see the entrance of the Na-

tional army, which was occupying the towns like a
river at flood. The boys who had run alongside the
Carlist troops now ran beside the Liberals. More than
one girl exchanged a Carlist sweetheart for one from
the new army.

The rout was general all over Vizcaya. Everywhere
the cry went up, "Long live peace!" The commander
of Ignacio's battalion shouted "Viva!" for the new King,
Alfonsito. At Tolosa, a Carlist battalion entered the
city to surrender, still armed and marching to military
music. The boys went home as if on a festive religious
pilgrimage.

What a different end, thought Pedro Antonio, *than
the solemn Covenant of Vergara which put an end to the
Seven Year War, to my war, than that embrace between
Espartero and Maroto in the middle of the fields and
between the two old armies, who cried out for sweet peace
after so much war and so hard a war!*

On the first day of Carnival the remnants of the Carlist
army, still loyal to their King, most of them Castilians
and courtiers of misfortune who had fought far from
their native region, made their way to Orbaiceta and
then to Valcarlos, their souls full of the sad memories
of hope and their throats full of the air of the country
they were going to leave.

"Poor Ignacio!" Celestino said to Juan José, who
was walking at his side.

"How terrible life is!"

In Valcarlos, while the King spoke to them for the
last time, many wept. Before their arrival at the border
on the Arnegui bridge, the money that was left in the
military coffers was distributed.

"This will buy masses for Ignacio," said Don José.

On the bridge, Don Carlos turned his plump body

around and exclaimed theatrically, "I shall return, I shall return." The Volunteers, some ten thousand men, wept and broke their swords and rifles. On the next day, the vanquished King, now on foreign soil, reviewed his remaining, unarmed battalions.

The people began to enjoy peace as convalescents do good health. Everything returned to its normal course. The emigrants came home, and the workaday world took on new life. Business took up where it had left off. Capital had not ceased to amass new capital, sometimes from the profits of war. Industry, weakened by the war, regained its strength. The muds of rancor were carried away. Open warfare was at an end, but the struggle of government kept on. The minority, which commanded the executive power, would continue to rule over the mass, keeping an armed peace over the order sprung from war.

The streets were joyous with the faces of a new generation of youth, a link between past and future, who kept society fresh and new. These young people gave meaning to the lives of their elders. In them lay the virginal wisdom and the sacred treasure of innocence which keeps the world from ruin. When they would come up to kiss Uncle Pascual's hand, the old man would think, *These are the just for whose sake God does not destroy us.*

One of war's fruits was new games for the children. The constant presence of troops had allowed them to learn something from the soldiers. They recovered spent cartridges to enliven their stone-throwing battles and make them more serious. With powder and brass balls of the type used to decorate old beds, they manufactured explosive bombs to throw by hand.

Juanito and his company from the battalion of auxiliaries took their leave of the war with big feasts, dancing, drums, balloons, skyrockets, and other fireworks.

The new King of Spain toured his country at peace. He visited the battlefield at Somorrostro, where he issued a proclamation threatening the Basques. On the 20th of March he entered Madrid with a part of his army of the north, and was received deliriously by the people who had dethroned his mother. Then part of his troops went to Ciudad Real to make war on the swarms of locusts who were devastating the fields of La Mancha.

The village enjoyed its peace with sighs of relief. The young men returned to working their ancestral fields. The continual Carlist levies and confiscations to provide rations for their soldiers and—an even more painful matter for the farmers—for the many Castilians who had been forced to emigrate to the Basque country and live off the land because they had relatives who served in the insurrection, these were now things of the past. The village now enjoyed its sweet peace, but when would the damage of war be repaired? And who would pay them for the debts amassed by the Carlists?

In this family and in that, a son had died. Someone or other had done his family a favor by dying. But what of the family that had totally disappeared? These were remarks made to Pedro Antonio by a landlord with whom he exchanged stories. The disappearance of an entire family, its members scattered in misery God knows where—that was tragedy, irreparable tragedy. In such a family, happy were those who died!

Uncle Pascual came to see his cousins, with the plan of bringing them back to Bilbao with him. Both wanted to go, but each hid the desire from the other, each hoping that the other would be first to confess the willingness to make the sacrifice.

"We must be resigned!" said Pedro Antonio.

"Well enough, for you. But not for our Communion!" exclaimed Pascual, whom peace had made more bellicose.

"What else can we do?"

"What else? If our Communion resigns itself, it dies. Now we can understand what the Liberals mean when they tell us to enter the road to legality. We're beaten, yes, but not conquered. Now it's our time to pray, we from here on earth, your son from heaven, but without forgetting our works—faith and works. Without this war, without our blood of propitiation, who knows how far the Revolution might have gone . . . ?"

"And without our money . . ."

"Do you see? You see? They've beaten us because we haven't purified ourselves yet. We should never forget the beautiful pastoral letter of our Bishop Caixal, which we should learn by heart. You remember what he says in it, that in the Seven Year War it wasn't Espartero's battalions but God's wrath that hurled the Carlist Volunteers back to the frontier. The same thing has happened again. . . . It's clear enough! They sought power, not the victory of God, King, and Fatherland. Ah, if only they had asked for the kingdom of God and His justice. . . . But no, they were ambitious, traitors, blasphemers . . . !"

"Anyone might think, then, that the Liberals who beat us were a band of saints . . ."

"No, no. We weren't beaten by the Liberals, but by God, by the God who makes it rain on the fields of the wicked and the good alike . . . There, in his inscrutable plans. . . . For this life is merely a passage . . ."

360*

"And, for the bird of passage, a shot in passing, is that it?"

"Don't joke about holy things. . . . As our Caixal says, 'It's true that the Liberals are worse than we are, but God uses the wicked to chastise the good . . .'!"

"In that case . . ."

"In that case, we praise the Lord and let them have it. . . . Above all, the moral triumph is ours."

"Bah! the same as ever. When everything material is theirs, they can laugh at all the rest . . ."

"They'll laugh? He who laughs last . . ."

"Yes, yes, have faith in the Virgin and don't run . . ."

"You're still only clay. Leave off. They'll have their *dies irae* . . ."

"Their what? A lot of good that will do us!"

"You think not? Listen, even here below, though beaten, we're the victors . . . ! You'll see how they'll take us into consideration. After all, who brought in Alfonsito, if not we Carlists?"

"Whoever doesn't find consolation doesn't want it. . . . What we need is peace."

"Peace, peace! . . . Peace can be apostasy, a devilish pact with Hell. . . . No, not peace, but continuous war with the enemies of God. . . . The cry of Julius II: Out with the barbarians! One must know how to understand the question of the religion of peace . . . Our Lord Jesus Christ came not to bring peace to the world, but a sword and fire. He said so Himself. He came to sow dissension and war and to divide every house against itself. . . . Peace, peace! Yes, peace with God and peace with oneself, but war, continuous war against the wicked . . ."

"You're right, you're right," answered Pedro Antonio, to pacify him.

When Pedro Antonio finally yielded to his cousin's insistence, Josefa Ignacia said, "If you want to . . . good!"

With what was left of the ex-confectioner's savings and the priest's, the three of them lived comfortably, united by the invisible shadow of Ignacio.

"Remember when we left?" Pedro Antonio asked his wife as they came in sight of the Begoña Tower, now ruined by the war.

She started to cry, but at the same time she was glad to be back and to set about their new life immediately. What she found strangest and most bothersome was to have her former parish church, where she had gone daily to Mass, so far from her new neighborhood. The priest had to reprimand her because she insisted on going to her former church on the day of Annual Obligation instead of to the one in her new parish.

A few days after her arrival, the poor woman went to the church of Santiago furtively, like someone going into a strange house. She made her way into the loneliest and most hidden part of the apse, behind the high altar. There, among the somber little corner chapels, in the melting soft light which filters down from the little rotunda, stood the statue of the pale *Soledad* Virgin, her lustrous face given expression and life by the slowly changing reflections cast by candles. The Solitary Virgin gazed up at Heaven, on her lap her dead, naked son, his limp arms hanging down, abandoned to the will of his Heavenly Father. Josefa Ignacia wept, sobbing out the *Salve* which those who are exiled to this vale of tears lift up to Mary their Intercessor. When she was a bit more serene, she read mechanically and without understanding the words written on the border overhead: *mater pietatis, flaviobrigensis patrona, ora pro nobis.* The calm half-light in that withdrawn corner and the unchanging expression on the face of The Mother of Sorrows, the *mater dolorosa*, that face which seemed to be given serenity and purity by the pain fixed on it, took hold of Josefa Ignacia. She thought of her own son. She saw him leaving his room in early morning, still not quite awake from his slumber. She saw him sit down to breakfast, the picture of good health. And the way he broke his bread, yes, just like that, as she saw it now, and then dip it in his hot chocolate! And that was the way he gripped his glass, the way he rinsed his mouth! And there, that was the way he looked at her, at his mother, with that tranquil calm of his serene eyes! "Well, see you later," every morning, and he would go off to the office, while she tended shop and waited for him to come back for lunch. Then she suffered a momentary vision, the glassy and brilliantly lugubrious gaze of the devil wearing rouge and low shoes. She covered her face with her hands to weep, thinking of the sins of spiritual pride and carnal desire. *No, no, my son was good, and you, Mother, who are good, who are a mother, gave him time to die in a state of grace.*

Josefa Ignacia left the church consoled, as a slow rain of light and peace seemed to sift down through the rose windows of the Gothic nave of the basilica. Among the women she left behind her—some seated on the floor or on their heels, their heads down, looking at their prayer books, their faces covered with the shawls—perhaps one was silently asking the Mother of the eternal Son to give her a son.

During the first days of his return, Pedro Antonio itched to go by his own shop. He would get as far as the beginning of the street, gaze at the kaleidoscopic spectacle of its trade and the goods displayed outside, stop for a moment, and then turn back. One day, after drinking a little more than was his usual habit in order to get up his nerve, he entered the street, his street. His old neighbors came to the doors of their shops to greet him and offer their condolences. As he went about talking first to this one then to that, he recovered his spirits and felt like a new man. He was satisfied that in their eyes he seemed to be content with his Cross, which he bore in a fitting way for an old soldier.

He arrived in front of his old shop and found that it was being renovated, to put a new and deluxe confectionery shop in its place. They had already knocked down the partition which separated the working area from the shop proper. They had taken away the old counter on which he had once leaned to dream of a tranquil old age in the care of the son who would continue his business. Despite his recollections, the changes being made struck him as reasonable, the most natural thing in the world. *It won't look bad!* he thought.

Then he met Don Juan, who was watching him from the door to his shop. *That man still has his warehouse!* he said to himself.

"Hello there, Don Pedro Antonio . . . ! Back again, eh? What's new?"

"Ah well, the worst is over. . . . All well at your house?" answered Pedro Antonio, remembering the day Arana had come to his own shop to insult him.

"Yes, all well, thanks to God. . . . I heard of your loss . . ."

"And I heard of yours. . . . What must be, must be. . . . Patience!"

"What's past is past. . . . The way life is!"

"Yes, well . . ."

After a pause in which Pedro Antonio fell silent, the

other added, "Good, good . . . good. . . . So you're here again! . . . *Well!*"

"And your daughter?" asked the former confectioner, who was deeply hurt by something in the tone of the other man's "Well!"

"Rafaela? She married Enrique, our neighbor, one of the Zabaleta family. . . . Do you know him?"

"May they live happily for many years . . . !"

They took leave of each other. Pedro Antonio was about to cry: that meaningless conversation had stirred his soul. As Don Juan watched him go away, he took some pleasure in the thought that he himself still had his children and his warehouse. Later he felt sorry for his former neighbor.

Pedro Antonio went from there to a corner of his old parish church, where he wept inwardly for himself, his shop, and his lost illusions.

The church was his distraction and his refuge in that tranquil life in which he had to think neither about business nor about the morrow. Every evening when the bells sounded for prayer he went to say the rosary with others, many of whom were unknown to him. Gathered together, many of them drowsy, they repeated their Hail Marys mechanically, without pausing to pay attention to what they were saying, all of them mentally absorbed in thoughts of their own affairs and domestic cares: a child's illness, rent for the landlord, the bad fit of the latest pair of boots, a journey ahead, the latest thing they had heard or seen, whatever they knew about the person next to them. Once they began their pious devotions, their minds began to wander, free of care, unhindered by the prayer, which was like the wavelets raised by the breeze in a backwater over the slow-moving current. From that common prayer, interwoven with the humble concerns of each participant, from that vague spiritual music to which each gave his own words, there flowed the brotherhood of simple and humble people. The most pleasing thing was the litany: the *ora pro nobis* and the transition from it to the *miserere nobis*. Sometimes people would repeat a prayer more times than the litany called for; one had to pay a little attention! Then, the prayers over, they would all suddenly become clear-headed and move out into the fresh air of the street. Sometimes someone, perhaps a total stranger, would offer holy water to Pedro Antonio at the exit of the church. They would bow slightly to each other, and each would go his own way.

From time to time Pedro Antonio would see his old friends. But Don Braulio scarcely left his house, complaining that his hinges and his bellows no longer functioned properly for the long walks of former times. Don Eustaquio was unchanged, but frequented a new *tertulia* of friends. Gambelu was evasive and sad, full of apprehensions, as alone as a toadstool and more caustic every day that passed. He lived on the charity of some of his old friends, but his lot improved a bit when Don Braulio died suddenly. His will left Gambelu a small pension for life, but named a nephew he barely knew as general heir, thus settling any question of intestate succession that might arise, so that the will was at once most convenient and also most respectful of tradition.

One morning Pedro Antonio ran into Don José María. The old conspirator spoke to him with his usual seriousness, wearing the same theatrical beard, and repeating at every step, "What we need now is peace, peace!" He was engaged in negotiations to buy public securities, mostly having to do with the war debt. He dreamed about the bonds the well-bled nation would

have to issue. In this way he would make up double
for what he had invested in Carlist bonds.

In their life in common, Pedro Antonio and his wife,
those two old travel companions, grew farther apart
with every passing day. As their minds turned back
to their childhood memories, to the time before they
knew each other, each grew more isolated. They had
begun to live beyond the memory of their son, and
now they never tired of repeating, if given the chance,
hundreds of times if they could, the sayings and the
doings of their parents, or those of the uncle who had
first taught Pedro Antonio his trade.

They scarcely saw each other except at breakfast,
lunch, and dinner. He went off to his visits and devotions, she to hers. Uncle Pascual remained to unify
them, and it was he who initiated all conversation and,
from time to time, brought up the memory of their
son.

Before the war was entirely over, and taking advantage
of its effects, Don Juan had bought land, for becoming
a landowner was his golden dream. To own land was
for him like a title to nobility and the consecration of
his fortunes. He would be addressed with formality
and respect. He would be able to count on a certain
number of votes in elections. He would savor the plain-
ness with which the renter is treated in this country.
When, about the time of the Feast of Saint Thomas,
he would be brought the rent money and the presents,
he would be able to picture himself in his own mind
in a scene right out of Bastiat, as the heir of those first
men to clear forests of their tortured tangle, to drain
swamps, and to break new ground in a wasteland.
Finding himself owning little parcels of ground in his

country, he felt a new surge of patriotism. His conservative sentiments were confirmed, and his childlike faith and his respect for the religion of his forefathers were strengthened. He began to hear Mass daily. He joined a pious congregation. When his daughter bought a pontifical bull he turned a blind eye, being now ashamed of the oath he had sworn never to buy one because of the bombardment. But he also proved his Liberalism by taking part in the civic procession on the 2nd of May, wearing the cockaded hat he kept like a relic.

Rafaela got married, to take up her part in life and to give flesh to her youthful longing and her unconfessed and secret desire for motherhood. Unless one loves the solitary life, the family is the fullness of life in the world. She wanted a complete life, and she was also afraid of being left alone one day, with relatives but no family. She was filling a vacuum, and that was the whole of it. Until then she had lived only through the apprenticeship of life. She simply got married, without any bookish sentimentalisms. To love, to love! What presumptuous words, so dramatic and literary! Only in books do people say, "*I love you!*" Affection and tenderness, these are simple and natural. To want someone? What did it mean to want someone? To want, only to want, to want for the sake of wanting? All of that was meaningless. To want and love a man was simply a way of attending to him, of caring for his cares, of living with him, of getting used to his habits, of contentedly enduring his weaknesses and adversities, of bearing his peculiarities . . . the peculiarities of men! She offered Enrique deep and warm affection, woven out of the thousand small details of ordinary existence, consubstantial with life itself. It was an affection that soon became habitual and thus unconscious.

For his part, Juanito kept busy looking for an heiress. He was now pinned down altogether at his writing desk, and he laughed at the radicalism of his former political opinions.

The Carlist Communion had long been nourished to some extent by sheer and simple loyalty, loyalty for its own sake, and by stubborn commitment to an idea of tradition that was both undefined and indefinable. Now, in its ancient depths, it was coming apart, breaking up into two component elements. For one thing, Carlism embodied the longing for a political order that would be completely and exclusively Catholic. It represented a bookish school of Catholic rationalism that was born of discursive reason and smelled of printer's ink, a Jacobin school that much resembled the very Liberalism it detested. But Carlism also stood for exclusivistic regionalism, blind to any breadth of vision, blind to everything beyond the immediate horizon. These two elements now stood separate and distinct, as a natural response to real circumstances.

Uncle Pascual, already murmuring against Don Carlos, calling him sometimes a Caesarist and sometimes a Regalist, began to preach the social kingdom of Jesus Christ—a facile formula whose vagueness allowed him to cram into it all his stillborn verbal games and embryonic ideas. It became more and more difficult for him to get outside of himself to understand the concepts of others. At every turn, he expressed abomination for Liberalism, a label that he used to include everything which escaped his ossified and formulaic understanding.

His cousin Pedro Antonio listened to all his dissertations as people listen to it rain. What did all those dogmas and doctrines matter to him, who lived in a holy simplicity of spirit? They were the noises made by wise men, and he paid them homage, knowing that "Holy Mother Church has doctors to answer to all that." "You're right . . . you're right," he would say. But in the depths of his being an almost wordless voice told him: *The point is to be good, and that's the whole truth.* And thus, while his cousin reposed in the truth, Uncle Pascual sought for reason, more than ever convinced that ideas and dogmas rule the world, that laws produce the things men do, that the body follows its shadow, and that Liberalism caused all the ills of the century.

Don Eustaquio, for his part, gave himself over to the church more and more. He killed half the morning hearing masses. He wandered the streets and abominated all politics. Convinced that a man's first duty was to tend to his own eternal salvation, he had some favorite sayings. "Each man in his own house, and God in every man's house." "There's not a finger's difference between one man and another." "We'll never be angels, none of us." And "Less politics, and more religion."

Juan José, beside himself since all the *fueros*, the Basque statutes, had been abolished, sparkled with fury. He called for unity among all the Basque country, including Navarre, perhaps for a new war to regain the *fueros*. He vented his rage on all outsiders. He wanted to learn to speak Basque, if he could learn it by scientific infusion, by mere enthusiasm, without a lot of slow labor.

In the atmosphere in which he lived, the old slogan—*Dios y Fueros*, "God and the Basque Rights," a slogan which had always underlain the later "God,

Fatherland, and King"—began to take on new force. The generalized ethnic currents running throughout Europe were felt locally. Underlying all the political nationalities which are symbolized by flags and glorified in military victories, there surged an impulse toward breaking them up into races and peoples of more ancient and prehistoric foundation, as symbolized by and embodied in their different languages and embodied in their private communion of daily customs peculiar to each. The pressures imposed by nations on these movements only made them run more deeply. It was an unconscious longing for a spiritual Fatherland, one not tied to the earth at all, an attraction felt by all people for the silent life underlying the passing tumult of history, and it pushed them towards their more natural redistribution, in accord with original differences and resemblances, a redistribution which would permit future free groupings of them all in the great human family. This impulse also represented the ancient struggle of races, the fountainhead of civilization. These ethnic currents, welling beneath history, are those which will be impelled into a confluence forming the peaceful humanity of the future, as they are joined to the development of the great historical nationalities which have been born of wars and which have sustained them. Within the great historic organisms is enclosed the living flesh of this variety of races, struggling to differentiate themselves in accord with the varied distribution of the originating elements. In each nation, mortgaged to the holders of the public debt, there still breathes the spirit of the ancient wandering tribes, which at one time were established on terrain held in common. Peoples, which form nations, impel the latter toward integration, dissolving itself into the people.

Yet the march toward this end is made with eyes closed, in an egoistic impulse of blind exclusiveness. Juan José and his aspiring comrades-in-ideas intoned the solemn hymn to the tree of Guernica, the living symbol of the authentic personality of the Basque people. They sang in Basque, scarcely understanding the words, the stanza—

Eman ta zabalzazu	Yield and propagate
munduan frutua	Your fruit through the world,
adoratzen zaitugu	While we venerate you
arbola santua.	Holy Tree!

In the invocation that the tree may yield and propagate its fruit through the whole world, those who sing the words do not suspect the intuitive genius of the wandering bard who traveled strange lands to bring them the enchantment of the song to liberty, set to music which everyone understood, though it was given body in an old language unknown to them.

Josefa Ignacia recalled her dead son more and more often. She could not picture him dead, for she had always seen him alive and well, as alive and well as she last saw him. Her own health was deteriorating, from some deep illness, as she said, but she would not allow a doctor to visit her, despite all of Uncle Pascual's exhortations. But he finally got his way by telling her that resistance such as hers bordered on sin, inasmuch as we all have obligations to the body. The doctor quickly made a gesture of hopelessness: it was too late, and she was old, it was too complicated . . .

It was in vain to keep from her the seriousness of her condition. She knew well enough, and gave it no importance. She felt the final sleep coming and had nothing to hold her to life. Efforts were made, nevertheless, to get her to go outside for air and sunshine and to find some distraction. All in vain. Her sight wandered, she looked at nothing, stared here or there indifferently, and simply smiled at whatever her husband said. She was failing, failing. She took to her bed, and they could see clearly that she was near the end.

She asked her husband to read out of the old missal from which she had prayed during the first years of marriage, asking God in a low voice day after day in tenacious humility for the son who would be torn from her by war in the flower of his youth.

But Pedro Antonio could not read the Basque, his own native tongue. She told him to take care of himself, to go for a walk, to pray for her and for their son, as they would pray for him, and to take his time about returning. "Now, I'd be of no use to you any more, merely a nuisance. . . . I can't do anything. . . . Even though you arrive late, it doesn't matter, for there will be plenty of time to be together later. . . . Take care, Pedro, take care . . ."

When they brought the Viaticum, Pedro Antonio was left to pray, on his knees before the Eucharist, beside the bed, glancing from time to time at the flames from the large tapers which danced about the darkness of the enclosed room during the slow, drawn-out *ora pro nobis* of the litany. The sick woman let the prayers lull her halfway to sleep, as a child is rocked to sleep by a lullaby. When she opened her mouth to receive the Host, her eyes met those of her life's companion and she felt pity for him, who was to be left alone. Her gaze rested on him, her gentle eyes sparkling with a smiling serenity, eyes which reflected, too, the long habit of living together with him.

When the ceremony was over, Pedro Antonio closed

373

the window halfway, approached his wife, covered her carefully, and kissed her on the forehead, something he had not done in a long time. Telling her "Now sleep, and get your rest," he went out.

Next came the prayers for the dying, which she scarcely heard, though they terrified Pedro Antonio. By dawn, she was dead, following her brief final struggle. Her husband stood for a while looking at her, at her eyes which looked back at him peacefuly from death. He closed them, covered her body, and cried silently afterwards, though he was feeling something like what he had felt at the King's Oath, a desire to live on in the sweet hope of soon being able to rejoin his dead son and wife. He piously took out Josefa Ignacia's worn prayer book.

He missed the presence of his Pepiñasi, then and for some time, longer than expected. Where was she? What had become of her? Sometimes he wondered why she hadn't appeared yet when it was time to eat. Were they going to have to go on waiting for her? Something was missing, something had broken the web of his humble life. And whenever, because of her absence, the image of death appeared to his mind, his heart softened.

Ever since being widowed, Pedro Antonio, alone in the world, lives peacefully and without counting the days. He is happy to wake up each morning to a life without surprises or griefs. His past sheds a tender diffuse light through his soul. He feels a deep peace which causes his memories to flower with hope of eternal life. Since his temporal life has been blameless, the evening of his old age is like a dawn.

His favorite walk is the ascent to Begoña along the road. At his feet he contemplates Bilbao, now so dif-

ferent from the city which received him in '26. He
watches the brilliant reflections of the estuary's twist-
ing silver band as it runs through green fields sown
with houses. In the warm twilight, as the empty silver
sky turns red towards the west, his soul feels fresh and
peaceful while he watches the silhouette of El Montaño
outlined in the reddening sky and the heights of Galdames, at times veiled by factory smoke, enclosing the
shining panorama. Down there below, at the foot of
those mountains, where the sky starts, his son sleeps.

He sleeps there forever, dead . . . and dead for what?
For the Cause! For the Cause? *The Cause for which
my son died*, he thinks. He thinks wordlessly that this
death has idealized and invested with grandeur the
Cause for which he himself had fought in his green
years of military glory. If the Cause were deprived of
the blood that was shed in its name, then what would
keep it alive? The puppet show put on by Don José
María? The babbled homilies of Uncle Pascual? The
fine, plump body of the King? It is martyrdom that
makes faith, not faith martyrdom.

Then he goes into the church at Begoña to pray to
the Virgin. When he comes out, he looks at the site
of the house in which Don Tomás Zumalacárregui was
mortally wounded, and then he sits for a while in the
fresh air under the plane trees. He contemplates the
heights from which Bilbao was bombarded and, in the
distance, the mountain of Banderas, at whose feet he
fought amid bullets and a snowstorm on the sad night
of Luchana. As he descends Las Calzadas he says a
Paternoster in front of the cemetery where his Pepiñasi
lies, and he enters the village serenely, along the way
he first entered it.

Sometimes in his wanderings he comes across a cow,
or a villager reading, or he notices the silvery reflec-

tions playing over the green fields of maize, like white-caps. Recalling his childhood, he hears the faraway echo of the cows mooing along the mountainside, and then the crackling of chestnuts on winter nights by the hearthside. He wonders at such times whether it would not have been better never to have left his native village, to have stayed and sweated over his mother earth and, innocent of all history, to have watched the sun come up anew each day.

His memories of the late war have begun to fuse in his mind with those of his own war, the Seven Year War, those two periods becoming entwined with one another in his mental perspective. The years are piling up for him, and the last bitter ones are beginning to fade. His ancient dreams of glory float high in his memory, like clean, serene, and distant mountain peaks in a misty landscape. But even these dreams end by becoming part of the incorporeal cloud of a lost ideal world, from which arises a silent, intimate epic song of his own.

The memory of his son tints everything with calm, giving nourishment to his resignation. Without the worries and alarms Ignacio sometimes gave him when he was alive, he enjoys his son now, in the secret recesses of his soul, when he is by himself, there where he has him in pure and serene memory. He remembers with grateful pleasure the moments when he would approach the child's cradle to make certain that he was still alive and breathing. Pedro Antonio's inward peace is reflected in his external world, the world of lines, colors, and sounds; and from its external reflection new currents of sweet calm flow back to him as from a living fountain. It is a reflection reflected, as if mirrors mirrored each other to give each other life. He is living in the depth of life's true reality, free of all transcendent intent and above time. Like a bare sky, his serene conciousness reflects the slow invasion of the gentle dream of final rest, the great calm of eternal things and of the infinity that sleeps within its closeness. He lives in the true peace of life, letting himself be rocked in indifference to daily events and cares, grown easier now as he grows more detached from those things which pass. In eternity: he lives the day in eternity. He hopes that this profound life will last beyond death, so that he may enjoy, on a day without night, perpetual light, infinite clarity, sure rest, steady peace—imperturbable, permanent peace, inside and out. Such hope is the reality which makes his life peaceful in the midst of his cares, and eternal within its short and perishable course. He is already free, truly free, not with the illusory freedom sought in action, but with the true freedom of being everything. Out of pure simplicity he had made himself free.

Often on his walks he meets a young man who greets him with respect. One day he took the opportunity to talk to the young man. It is Pachico. As he spoke about Ignacio, he called him "a beautiful soul." The father went off deeply moved.

Pachico has taken profit from the war, seeing in the struggle the public conscience at its greatest tension. He is recovering, although slowly and with setbacks, from the terror of death, turning it into uneasy restlessness about the uncertainties of the future. He feels discouraged by the shortness of life compared to the infinity of the ideal. He thinks that one day more means one day less. Sometimes he thinks that nothing should be done at all, since everything will be left incomplete. But he quickly shakes off the demonic temptation of "All or Nothing."

He continues his interest in walks in the mountains, and now that he has grown more robust he can climb with less fatigue. On clear and calm days he sets out as early as he can, fleeing the monotonous bustle of the street. The farther he gets from the noise of the city, the quicker his step. He stops at the foot of the colossus to rest a moment in order to recover his strength, stretching out under a tree in the shaded woods. There the humble ferns, the diminished descendants of a past race of giants, vanquished by beeches and chestnuts, hardly dare to lift their leaves above the ground. Around them small grasses carpet the earth, forming a soft seedbed for the beech trees above them, which repay them by giving humidity. Parasitic mosses cling to the trees' thick trunks and suck their sap, trying to recover by cunning what they had lost to force. Pachico contemplates the quiet peaceful forms taken by that silent warfare, seeing in the peace of the woods the alliance between the great and the small, the victor and the vanquished, the humility of the victor and the meanness of the parasite. The war itself is enclosed in peace.

He gets up and begins to scale the mountain. As he climbs, the panorama unfolds before his eyes like something alive while his breathing grows ever deeper. The air exhilarates him and, as he breathes it in, his senses also take in more vividly the surrounding countryside. He feels free to the very depths of his being, in the freedom of becoming one with everything around him, becoming possessed by it. Finally, he reaches the top, the kingdom of silence, and beholds the great congregation of the giants of Vizcaya, who raise their heads one behind the other, in a waving line where the sky begins.

The outlined battlements of the sharp white peaks left bare by centuries of water falling on them rise above the soft curves of the low green hills like lean ancients looking down sternly on exuberant youth. Within those green folds a scattered multitude lives seriously and disinterestedly, without looking for the quintessence of life: social coral reefs which form the base for human culture. In the distance, the unmoving peaks are intertwined with the moving clouds, which rest on them for an instant in their race across the sky.

He stretches out again on the top and loses himself in the immense peace of the august scene, the result and form of combats and alliances renewed repeatedly between the ultimate irreducible elements. Far off, the horizon line of the high seas is drawn like a hue of the sky, a contour over the tops of the mountains.

The mountains and the sea! The cradle of liberty and its proper ground! The seat of tradition and the seat of progress! From the height, where it is quiet and silent, he contemplates in the distance the restless and turbulent sea beside the quiet and silent mountains. Before man was made, the elements fought a turbulent war. Air, fire, water, and earth warred to divide among themselves the dominion of the world. That war continues, slow, tenacious, and muted. Drop by drop and second by second, the sea undermines the rocks. It sends armies of little animals against them which it spawns in order to eat away the rocks; and from the spoils of one and the other it pounds out its bed. Meanwhile, overhead the torrents from the clouds, blood of the sea's blood, wear down the haughty mountains, filling the valleys with the rich alluvial earth. Water, this levelling and egalitarian element which crosses all the earth, like the trader who traverses it, lives because it carries with it the heat of the Equator and the cold of the Poles, and undermines the overbearing ancient mountains which are chained to the place where they were born.

From where he gazed, Pachico could not see the waves rise nor hear the song of the sea. He saw it in its marmoreal quietude and it struck him as being as fixed and firm in its place as the mountains anchored by their rocky roots. He looked again at the mountains which defend and shelter various peoples, dividing them into races and nations, and which distribute the very waters that wear them away, and make the valleys lovely and fertile. In his mind, Pachico went on to roam over the history of the struggles and invasions of races and peoples and to think of the final brotherhood of all men, somewhere in the future. He thought of his Vizcaya, where some men live by the spade and water the mountainous land with their sweat, where others take their daily sustenance from the sea, and others get theirs by plowing through the sea to distant lands. He thinks of the blood spilled there in wars where the spirit of the merchant clashed with the spirit of the farmer, the ambitious man of the sea with the greedy man of the mountain. It is a clash that engenders life, like the clash in the ocean between the ice of the poles and the heat of the tropics. He sees history as the everlasting struggle of peoples, a struggle without truce or cease, whose end, an end that is possibly unattainable, is the true unity of all mankind. His thoughts of warfare lead him to think of the infinite idea of peace. Sea and earth, struggling under the blessing of heaven, celebrate their fertile union that brings life into being, a union initiated by the sea and sustained by the earth.

As he lay stretched out on the summit, resting on its gigantic altar under the fathomless infinite blue, time, the source of all cares, seems to stop for him. On

such serene days, when the sun goes down, all beings
seem purified to their very essence. In the distance the
blue and violet mountains sustain the vault of heaven
in pure outline, as clear and close as the heather bushes
within hand's reach. Differences of distance are reduced to differences of tonal intensity and quality, differences of perspective to differences of hue. The whole
scene becomes one immense plane, and the fusion of
spatial ends and perspectives leads him in that total
silence to a state of mind in which all temporal ends
and perspectives fuse together. He forgets the fatal
course of the hours, and, during an eternal and unmoving moment which never passes, as he contemplates the immensity of the panorama he feels the world
to its depths, its continuity, its unity, the resignation
of all its parts, and he hears unfolding the silent song
of the soul of all things in harmonic space and melodic
time.

The mountains then become for him part of the sky
on which they are embossed, and the aromatic, fresh
air seems to come from everywhere at once: from the
green earth, the purple mountains, and the marble sky,
bringing the freshness of their hues and the sublety of
their lines. The fathomless sky seems to denude itself
from space—totally by intention—and embrace the earth
with its fused infinity. A bird crossing the sky, a bum-
blebee buzzing, a butterfly fluttering, a gust of wind
stirring the trees and drawing forth a murmuring sound,
all seem like the breathing of Nature, signs of its profoundly hidden life.

A natural revelation of marvelous proportion allows
him to penetrate to the truth, to the immensely simple
truth: that the pure forms of things are, for the pure
in spirit, their innermost essence; that everything displays what it hides in an open light; that the world

gives itself wholly and unreservedly to anyone who offers himself to it wholly and unreservedly. "Blessed are the pure in heart, for they shall see God!" Yes, blessed are children and simple people, for they see all the world.

But, presently, his ideas are put to sleep by the quietude and silent symphony of his surroundings, and they cease to speak in him. His cares are all blotted out. His feeling of bodily contact with the earth disappears and he loses the sense of his body's weight. Absorbed by his surroundings and by the air, outside of himself, he feels overcoming him a deep resignation, a resignation which is the mother of human omnipotence, since only those who want everything to happen that does happen will manage to get all that they desire. In him a communion wakes up between the world around him and the world inside him: the two worlds fuse. Free from the consciousness of time and space, he contemplates them in their fusion. There in that silence beyond silence and in the aroma of the diffuse light, all desire extinguished and in tune with the song of the soul of the world, he enjoys true peace, as if in the life of death. How much there is that he will never express! . . . Rose-hued clouds in a golden sky which will never be painted! . . . There is an immensity of peace. The sea chants peace, the earth mutely speaks peace, the sky rains down peace. In a surpassing harmony of dissonance, peace wells up out of the struggle for life. There is peace within war and underlying it; peace sustains war and crowns it. What time is to eternity, war is to peace: its fleeting form. In peace, death and life seem to join as one.

When Pachico comes down from the heights and again walks past the fields, he greets a peasant working the reluctant earth. He thinks how much of this is the work of man which gradually supernaturalizes nature by humanizing it. Up there in the mountain the eternal sadness in the depth of his soul has fused with the temporal joy of being alive, and out of this fusion has come a fruitful seriousness.

Once back in the city streets, watching people come and go as they busy themselves with their work, he is assaulted by the temptation to doubt that all these worldly occupations have any eternal meaning. But when he meets someone he knows, he recalls the recent war, and then the warm spiritual calm he found on the mountain gives him courage for the unending struggle against the inextinguishable human ignorance which is the mother of war. Feeling that brutality and egoism are close at hand, he then gains faith to go on warring in peace, to make war on the warfare of the world, meanwhile resting in the peace within himself. War on war, but always war!

Up there on those heights time was vanquished for Pachico, and thus it is that he finds a taste for things of eternity and gains the determination to throw himself into the unrestrainable torrent of progress, in which fleeting things roll over permanent ones. Up there on the height, peaceful contemplation gave him an eternal sense of resignation which will never allow him to resign himself in temporal matters nor to be contented here below with endlessly seeking a larger salary. He has come back down from the height determined to arouse in other men the discontent which is the prime mover of all progress and all good.

Only in the refuge of true and profound peace is war understood and justified. It is here that sacred vows are made to go to war for truth, which is the only eternal consolation. It is here that war proposes to be transformed into holy work. Not outside war, but within it, in its very heart, peace must be sought: peace in war itself.

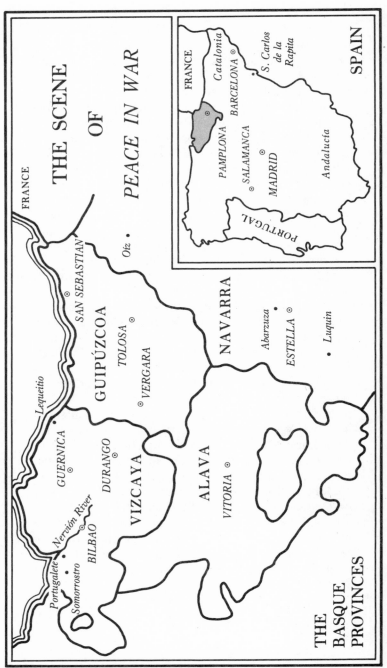

THE SCENE
OF
PEACE IN WAR

SPAIN

FRANCE

Catalonia

BARCELONA ⊙

S. Carlos de la Rapita

PAMPLONA

SALAMANCA ⊙

MADRID ⊙

Andalucia

PORTUGAL

FRANCE

Ofz. •

SAN SEBASTIAN ⊙

GUIPÚZCOA

Lequeitio

TOLOSA ⊙

⊙ VERGARA

NAVARRA

Abarzuza •

ESTELLA ⊙

• Luquin

GUERNICA ⊙

DURANGO ⊙

VIZCAYA

ALAVA

VITORIA ⊙

Nervión River

Portugalete •

BILBAO •

Somorrostro •

THE
BASQUE
PROVINCES

Map by Lisa T. Davis

Notes

Notes

Paz en la guerra was first published in 1897 at Madrid (Librería Fernando Fe). To the second edition, published in 1923 (Madrid: Renacimiento), the author added a prologue, reprinted here along with the "Author's Warnings" (Advertencias) that accompanied the first edition. A third edition was published in 1931 (Madrid: Companía Ibero-Americana de Publicaciones). The novel was reprinted in 1957 in Volume I of the series *Las mejores novelas contemporáneas* (Madrid: Editorial Planeta), and also appeared as no. 179 of the Colección Austral (Buenos Aires: Espasa Calpe, n.d.). It was published at Madrid in 1959 in Volume II (pp. 69-415) of the *Obras Completas*, published 1958-1964 under the editorship of Manuel García Blanco by Vergara, S.A., Barcelona (under concession from Afrodisio Aguado, S.A., Madrid, publishers of an earlier *Obras Completas*, 1951-1958, abandoned after six volumes were published); and again in 1967 in Volume II (pp. 87-301) of a third *Obras Completas* published by Escelicer, S.A., Madrid (© 1967 by Herederos de Miguel de Unamuno). Both the Vergara/Aguado and the Escelicer editions were consulted in preparing the present translation, the first into English. A German translation (*Frieden im Krieg*, tr. Otto Buek) was published in 1929, a Slovak translation (*Mir ve válce*, tr. Karel Eger) in 1932, an Italian translation (*Pace nella guerra*, tr. Gilberto Beccari) in 1952, and a Polish translation (*Pokój wśrod wojny*) in 1975.

In the citations below, *OC* indicates the Vergara/Aguado edition of the *Obras Completas*.

Throughout the text of *Paz en la guerra*, Unamuno makes prodigal use of points of suspension (. . .), which have been preserved in the translation. They indicate pauses and not omissions.

INTRODUCTION

ix. *Carlist Wars*: There are good summary accounts of the two Carlist Wars in Raymond Carr's *Spain* (Oxford, 1966) and in Gerald Brenan's *The Spanish Labyrinth* (2nd edn., Cambridge, 1960), and there are some wonderfully rich and gossipy essays on the major figures in the 11th edn. of the *Encyclopaedia Britannica*, which I have drawn upon.

xv. *En torno al casticismo: OC*, III, 185.

xvi. *"La enseñanza de la gramática"*: *OC*, VII, 635.
conference in Madrid in 1906: "Conferencia en el Teatro de la Zarzuela, de Madrid, el 25 de febrero de 1906," *OC*, VII, 679-80.

xvii. *conference in Barcelona in 1906*: "Conferencia en el Teatro Novedades, de Barcelona, el 15 de octubre de 1906," *OC*, VII, 742.

xxii. *"Dostoyeusqui sobre la lengua"*: *OC*, VIII, 1135.
Tragic Sense: in the present edition, vol. 4, p. 338.
xxiii. *"Sobre el cultivo de la demótica"*: *OC*, VII, 958.
xxvii. *"La ideocracia"*: *OC*, III, 435.

"Ultima lección académica": *OC*, IX, 1076-88 passim.

xxviii. *Untitled poetic fragment: Cancionero*, no. 394, 11-12 Sept. 1928 (*OC*, XV, 249):

> ¿Pretendes desentrañar
> las cosas? Pues desentraña
> las palabras, que el nombrar
> es del existir la entraña.

Hemos costruído el sueño
del mundo, la creación,
con dichos; sea tu empeño
rehacer la costrucción.

Si aciertas a Dios a darle
su nombre propio, le harás
Dios de veras, y al crearle
tú mismo te crearás.

xxxix. *a second poem: Cancionero*, no. 19, 12 Mar.
1928 (*OC*, XV, 192-93):

Padre, con este tuteo
de intimidad entrañable
en Ti me endioso, me creo,
se hace mañana mi tarde.

En Ti, Padre, *yo me* veo,
Tú te ves en mí, mi Padre;
tuteo se hace *yomeo*
y somos uno de sangre.

Tú me creas, *yo te* creo,
y en este diálogo que arde,
tumeo se hace *yoteo*
y las palabras gigantes.

Hablando se entienden hombres
y el nombre a la cosa le hace;
forjada a incendios de soles
fría palabra . . . diamante.

xxxiii. *The Tree*: (Boston, 1980), unpaginated. Quoted
by permission of the publisher, Little, Brown and Co.

AUTHOR'S WARNINGS ON THE FIRST EDITION

3. After the first paragraph, Unamuno listed several
ordinary typographical errors and pointed out that he
mistakenly referred to a journal called *El Pensamiento
Español* (Spanish Thought), which, during the years
covered by this novel, was actually called *El Pensamiento de la Nación* (The Nation's Thought).

AUTHOR'S PROLOGUE TO THE SECOND EDITION

6. *studies of landscape and skyscape*: Landscapes, Travels in Portugal and Spain, Spanish Walks and Vistas.

my novels: The translated titles are as follows (those published are in italics): Love and Education, *Mist* (present edition, vol. 6) *Abel Sánchez* (ibid.), *Tia Tula* (ibid., vol. 7), *Three Exemplary Novels*.

1898—to which generation I am said to belong: When Spain lost the Cuban War to the United States in 1898, a generation of Spanish writers—the so-called "Generation of '98," which included Unamuno, Antonio Machado, Juan Ramón Jiménez, Ramón del Valle-Inclán, and others—explored the themes of Spanish decline and the possibility of a regeneration that would bring their nation closer to the mainstream of European thought.

Walt Whitman: The quotation is a paraphrase of "Camerado, this is no book, / Who touches this touches a man" ("So Long!" 1860, epilogue to *Leaves of Grass*). For Unamuno's knowledge of Whitman, see *The Tragic Sense of Life*, vol. 4 of the present edition, p. 139 and n.

I

7. *Bilbao*: capital of the province of Vizcaya and the chief city of the Basque region, as well as one of the principal seaports and commercial centers of Spain. It lies on the Nervión River, which flows into the Bay of Biscay about 8 mi. to the north. In the 1870s, at the time of the second Carlist War, Bilbao was situated mainly on the right (east) bank of the river, in a narrow valley shut in by mountains; its population was about 18,000. Subsequently the "new town" developed on

the west bank and the river channel and harbor were improved; the present population is more than 400,000. The "old town," in which Unamuno grew up and which is the scene of much of *Peace in War*, was (and is) characterized by churches and other buildings dating from the 14th century and narrow streets leading from a riverside park and promenade called the Arenal. (Cf. *Encyclopaedia Britannica*, 11th edn., and Baedeker, *Spain*, 1901.)

The Seven Streets compose an ancient neighborhood which lies southwest of the Arenal and where Unamuno was born in 1864 and grew to manhood. (Margaret T. Rudd, *The Lone Heretic: A Biography* . . . , Austin, 1963, pp. 15-17.)

born with the Constitution, in 1812: In September 1810 the Cortes of Cadiz began meeting to draw up a Constitution. The result, which took effect on March 19, 1812, was a Liberal document, restricting the powers of the monarchy and the clergy.

the Hundred Thousand Sons of St. Louis: a powerful army led into Spain on April 7, 1823 by the Duke of Angoulême to restore full power to Ferdinand VII, as a result of a mandate granted to France by the Congress of Verona. This invasion began what Spanish Liberals called "the ominous decade of 1823-1833," a period of return to absolute monarchy.

8. *Apostolicals*: extreme monarchists who suspected Ferdinand VII of being swayed by covert Liberal advice, favored his brother Don Carlos, and wished to bring back the Inquisition.

the regency of Urgel: established by Absolutists in 1822 in Urgel, the diocese of the provinces of Lérida and Gerona, and the republic of Andorra.

the ominous *three-year period between 1820 and 1823*: There is a play on words here. Father Pascual finds the period from 1820, when a mutiny at Cádiz led by Colonel Rafael Riego and other Liberal officers limited the power of Ferdinand and left Spain in anarchy, until the French invasion of 1823, to be more "ominous" than the decade of absolute monarchy that followed.

Ferdinand VII died and the Carlist insurrection broke out: When Ferdinand VII died in 1833, leaving his throne to his three-year-old daughter Isabella under the regency of her mother, his brother Carlos invoked the Salic law to challenge his niece's right to the throne. The first Carlist War lasted from 1833 to 1840. The Carlists, whose strength lay in the northern provinces of Spain, were ultra-conservatives in both politics and religion.

Zabala: Juan de Zabala y de la Puente (1804-1879) came to Spain from Peru, when Peru declared its independence, and entered on a military career.

Frenchified sympathizers of Napoleon: The *afrancesados* were those who imitated French manners and attire and admired French "enlightened" thought. With the Napoleonic invasion of Spain, they collaborated with the French regime, either out of self-interest or in the hope that Spain could be liberalized.

the Imperial Eagles: the French army of occupation.

9. *seven glorious years*: the duration of the first Carlist War, 1833-1840.

Zumalacárregui: Tomás Zumalacárregui y de Imaz (1788-1835), the outstanding military genius of the first Carlist War, was diverted into military service from his original intention to be a priest. At twenty-four, he was captain of the Guipúzcoa regiment. At the death of Ferdinand VII he declared himself for the Carlist cause and was made a general of the growing Carlist forces in Navarre. Zumalacárregui was a master of guerrilla tactics and used terrorism to dominate the region where his forces fought. The year 1835 was fatal for him. Against his wishes, he followed the orders of Don Carlos to besiege Bilbao. During these operations, he was wounded in the leg. The military doctors thought the wound was not serious, but after great suffering he died of septicemia.

the Night of Luchana: The battle of Luchana, which took place on December 24, 1836, in bitter icy cold, with fierce combat between the forces of Espartero and his Carlist opponents, was won by Espartero, whose forces liberated Bilbao on the following day.

Maroto: Rafael Maroto (1783-1847), a Carlist general who fell into disfavor with Don Carlos after he unsuccessfully proposed ending the Carlist War by arranging a marriage between Isabella II and the Pretender's eldest son. Thereupon he abandoned Don Carlos, entered into negotiations with Espartero, signed the Pact of Vergara, and was commissioned an officer in the Spanish army.

Espartero: Baldomero Espartero (1792-1879) rose from humble origins to become Count Luchana and twice a duke for his military and political leadership from 1823 onward. Fighting on behalf of Isabella II, he was bold and resourceful in attacking the Carlist forces led by Zumalacárregui and Cabrera, becoming commander in chief of the northern army in 1836, when he forced the Carlists to abandon their siege of Bilbao. In 1839, after negotiating with Maroto and other Carlist leaders, he concluded the Pact of Vergara, securing the surrender of 20,000 Carlist soldiers in exchange for recognizing the ranks and privileges of their officers, thus putting an effective end to the war, although some guerrilla action continued for a time on the part of Cabrera and his men. A Liberal, Espartero went on to become regent for Isabella II after forcing out her mother, María Cristina. Falling into disfavor in 1843, when a pronunciamento proclaimed Isabella queen, Espartero fled to England for six years and then returned to Spain to work for Liberal policies while at the same time trying to keep them within bounds of moderation. After 1856 he retired from an active political role.

14. *the trouble stirred up later in Catalonia by the Montemolinists*: The Count of Montemolín, Carlos Luis de Borbón (1818-1861), was the eldest son of the Pretender Carlos V, who abdicated his claim to the Spanish throne in his favor in 1844, so that Carlist sympathizers regarded Montemolín as Carlos VI. Some Spanish intellectuals, such as Jaime Balmes, proposed him as a likely candidate for a marriage to Isabella II. In 1845, when it became apparent that no such marriage would take place, Montemolín organized a Carlist conspiracy in Catalonia; after the conspiracy failed in 1849, he fled to France, remaining there for ten silent years. In August 1860, Montemolín and some 3,000 troops under the command of General Jaime Ortega landed at San Carlos de la Rápita, near the mouth of the Ebro, but the military operation failed and Montemolín, returning to France, died shortly after crossing the border. Since his wife died seven hours later and his brother thirteen days thereafter, there are some who believe the three were poisoned.

Balmes: James Luciano Balmes (1810-1848), Catalonian religious apologist and political writer, the founding editor of a conservative Catholic weekly, *El Pensamiento de la Nación*, and author of *El protestantismo comparado con el catolicismo en sus relaciones con la civilisación euoropea*, a 3-volume work which went through many editions and was translated into English twice (London, 1849; Baltimore, 1918). His *Filosofía fundamental* (4 vols., 1846) was one of the few philosophical books in Unamuno's father's library. In *Recuerdos de niñez y de mocedad* (1908) Unamuno wrote, "What effect it had on me when . . . I read Balmes and Donoso, the only writers of philosophy that I found in my father's library! Through Balmes I found out that there was a Kant, a Descartes, a Hegel. I scarcely understood a word of his *Filosofía fundamental*—the most worthless of all his worthless books—but I nevertheless undertook to read it with great zeal. . . . I sometimes went to sleep with the book."

Montemolín's . . . Bourges Manifesto: In a Manifesto intended to be conciliatory toward Spanish Liberals, Montemolín spoke of "justice without violence," and indicated that he was not unwilling to consider a marriage with Isabella II: "There is no sacrifice in keeping with my dignity and my conscience that I would not be disposed to in order to put an end to civil strife and to hasten the reconciliation of the royal family."

Cabrera: Ramón Cabrera y Griñó (1806-1877), Carlist general. Cabrera's family hoped that he would become a priest, but he showed a much greater inclination and talent for warfare. An early defender of the Carlist cause, Cabrera became an unusually ruthless and ferocious fighter after his mother, María Griñó, was executed. After the end of the first Carlist War, he moved to England, although he returned to Spain in 1847 to lead new uprisings and skirmishes on behalf of Montemolín. In 1849 he left Spain permanently and married an Englishwoman with whom he had four children. Although Spanish Carlists continued to look up to him and to hope that he might return to lead them, he grew more Liberal in his political sentiments in later life; eventually he abandoned the Carlist cause by recognizing Alfonso XII as the legitimate ruler of

Spain, an act which gained him the title of count of Morella but lost him the titles and honors originally given him by Carlos V.

15. *Italian revolution unleashed against the Pope, the feats of Garibaldi*: Giuseppe Garibaldi (1807-1882), daring hero of nineteenth-century Italian nationalism, joined Victor Emmanuel II, the Italian king, in taking over the Papal States in 1860. Ten years later the King took Rome and called for a plebiscite on behalf of his rule, with his capital to be at Rome. The plebiscite passed, and Pope Pius IX announced that he was a prisoner in the Vatican, the only territory remaining within his temporal power.

Sor Patrocinio: Sister María de los Dolores y Patrocinio (1811-1891), a Franciscan nun, born María Rafaela Quiroga, who claimed to have received the stigmata and who exercised a great influence on Isabella II in both religious and political matters.

Consulate of the Sea ordinances: elements of a code of maritime law that was compiled as early as the 14th century and is the basis of modern maritime law.

19. *the assault of the priest Merino against the Queen*: Martín Merino Gómez (1789-1852) entered the Franciscan order at a very young age, but abandoned his habit in 1808 to participate in various military adventures. Deeply influenced by Liberal ideas, he left Spain for France in 1819-20 to avoid persecution. On July 7, 1822 he took part in demonstrations against the absolutist regime and was one of the victims of the repression which followed. In 1843 he won a lottery prize of 25,000 pesetas and began to augment his capital by lending money at usurious rates, thus making many enemies. On February 2, 1852 he surprised Isabella at a service of thanksgiving for the birth of her daughter and stabbed her in her right side. Making

no attempt to flee, he explained that his motive was to strike a blow against the ignorance of those who believed it was right to support the tyranny of kings. After a swift trial, he was executed in Madrid on February 7, 1852.

22. *Say*: Jean Baptiste Say (1767-1832), French economist of a Protestant family, deeply influenced by Adam Smith's *Wealth of Nations*. He edited the periodical *La Décade philosophique, littéraire, et politique* between 1794 and 1800, and was largely responsible for spreading the views of Adam Smith in Europe. His most important work, *Traité d'économie politique*, went through six editions and was widely translated.

Bastiat: Frédéric Bastiat (1801-1850), French political economist, best known for his book *Les Harmonies économiques*, where belief in a pre-established harmony at work in economic forces led him to be regarded as an optimist whose views were sharply opposed to the more pessimistic thinkers of the English liberal school of Malthus and Ricardo.

25. *African war*: In 1859-60, Spain undertook operations in Morocco, ostensibly to defend her garrison towns from the raids of tribesmen. The war provoked strong patriotic fervor on the part of the Spanish people. See Raymond Carr, *Spain*, pp. 260-61.

26. *Prim*: Juan Prim y Prats (1814-1870), marqués de los Castillejos, Spanish general; led successful campaigns in Morocco, 1859-60; organized the revolution of 1868; offered the Spanish throne to Amadeo; assassinated by unknown parties the day the new King landed in Spain.

Narváez: Ramón María de Narváez (1800-1868), Spanish general and politician who contributed to the fall of Isabella II.

Aparisi: Antonio Aparisi y Guijarro (1815-1872), a Spanish Catholic publicist and pro-Carlist orator.

30. *Magenta, Solferino, Savoy, Lombardy*: the sites of French victories over Austria in 1859.

31. *the Riego Hymn*: Rafael de Riego y Núñez (1785-1823), a Freemason, a Liberal, and colonel in the Spanish army, led a group of fellow soldiers in January, 1820 to proclaim the constitution of 1812, thus becoming a hero of Spanish Liberalism. The "Riego Hymn," composed by an officer named Miranda to a text by Evaristo San Miguel, was later set to another tune, in which form it became extremely popular as a tribute to Riego and a symbol of liberty and Freemasonry; for moderates and conservatives, both Riego and the song honoring him were symbols of revolutionary anarchy. Other political songs of this period include "El Trágala," "Canción contra el Trágala," and "Himno de Espartero." Riego was executed in 1823.

a nun with the stigmata: Sor Patrocinio.

32. *the poetic sediment of the centuries*: Cf. the 1896 essay "Sobre el cultivo de la demótica," where Unamuno writes: "One must seek the deep life of a people, its intimate life, more in legends than in factual chronicles. . . . History is a selection and condensation of events; it is to past reality what a topographic map is to the reality of terrain. The people make a landscape of the map, organize the inorganic stuff of history into legends and myths, supplant dead schematic representation with living symbols. . . . Without poetic meaning real historic meaning is not possible." *OC*, VII, 481-82.

32-33. *Judith . . . Cabrera*: the "legendary figures" that occupy Ignacio's imagination are taken from several sources—the Old Testament, Moorish tales, chivalric romance, and, in the case of Cabrera, 19th-century Spanish history. Fierabras of Alexandria in medieval romances was a Saracen giant, the son of a Babylonian king, who with his sister Floripes becomes a Christian after being defeated in a duel by Oliveros of Castile, a close friend of Roland; both were paladins of Charlemagne. Floris and Blanchefleur were lovers in an anonymous French poem from the 13th century, he Moorish and she Christian, who overcame many obstacles in order to fulfil their love for one another. Genevieve of Brabant, in an ancient Teutonic folk tale, is accused falsely of infidelity to her husband Siegfried, escapes with her baby son into the forest, and is miraculously fed by a hind for six years, until her husband finally realizes her innocence. José María the highwayman was a 19th-century Spanish folk hero, something in the mode of Robin Hood. Ogier (the Dane) was another of Charlemagne's paladins, who fought against the Saracens in Spain. Ferragús was a Saracen knight who lost his helmet and attempted to take Roland's. For Cabrera, see above, note to p. 14.

34. *General Nogueras*: Agustín Nogueras (1800-1848), fought successfully in the Seven Year War (1832-1840) against the Carlist uprising in the region of Maestrazgo. To retaliate for Cabrera's atrocities against civilians, he ordered María Griñó, Cabrera's mother, executed in February 1836.

41. *"Give me wine . . ."*:

> Dadme vino: en él se ahoguen
> mis recuerdos; aturdida
> sin sentir huya la vida;
> paz me traiga el ataud . . .

from "A Garifa, en una orgia," vv. 13-16, by José de Espronceda (1808-1842), Romantic and revolutionary poet, called "the Spanish Byron."

"*In a sea . . .*"

> Que en un mar de lava hirviente
> mi cabeza siento arder . . .

ibid., vv. 3-4.

49-50. "*The noise that cuts . . .*" (and following verses):

> Ese vago rumor que rasga el viento
> es el son funeral de una campana . . .

> ¡Au. . . , au. . . , aupá!, que el campanero
> las oraciones, ¡ay!, va a tocar.
> ¡Ay, ené!, yo me muero.
> Maitía, maitía, ven acá . . .

> Aunque la oración suene
> yo no me voy de aquí,
> la del pañuelo rojo
> loco me ha vuelto a mi . . .

from "En la tumba de Larra," by José Zorrilla y Moral (1817-1893), poet and dramatist.

52. *revolutionary proclamations . . . Prim, Baldrich, Topete*: Juan Prim (see note for p. 26); Gabriel Baldrich y Palau (1814-1885), a Spanish general who fought against the Carlists in the first Carlist War, supported Prim's revolutionary aims that led to the overthrow of Isabella II; Juan Bautista Topete y Carballo (1821), a naval leader who was badly wounded in 1866 in the battle of Callao (Peru) and who on returning to Spain from the Pacific also supported Prim.

54. *a Spanish '93*: Reign of Terror in the French Revolution, 1793.

55. *the mutinous Serrano*: The more probable reference here is not to Francisco Serrano y Domínguez (1810-1885), the important military and political leader who signed the manifesto of the September Revolution along with Prim and Topete, but to Francisco Serrano Bedoya (1813-1882), a member of the Union Liberal

party, who was deported to the Canary Islands on suspicion of plotting the September Revolution.

the revolt of San Fernando: On January 1, 1820, Rafael del Riego, with an army which had been assembled to put down revolt in Spain's American colonies, proclaimed the Constitution of 1812 and then, together with a Colonel Quiroga, entered San Fernando, a town in the province of Cádiz, to form a junta.

Lequeitio: small port in Vizcaya from which Queen Isabella II embarked for exile in France.

56. *Novaliches*: Manuel Pavía y Lacy (1814-1896), marqués de Novaliches.

58. *the* fueros . . . Señorío . . . ordinarios de hermandad: the word *fuero* designates, in general, the private rights of a person or a territory, and derives from the Latin word *forum*, in the sense of a place where justice is administered. According to long tradition, it was only the person of the Spanish king, who had to swear an oath to uphold their local rights and traditions or *fueros*, which bound the Basque countries to the rest of Spain. The *Señorío de Vizcaya*, or western Vizcaya, was governed by a magistrate or *corregidor*, based in Bilbao and representing the Spanish crown. Although Spanish monarchs were supposed to swear their oath to uphold the *fueros* beneath the tree of Guernica, the last one to do so was the Pretender Carlos VII. One of the underlying causes of the Carlist Wars was the intention of the Spanish liberal regime to take away the independence afforded the Basque countries by their local laws and traditional rights. The *ordinarios de hermandad* were the members of the governing assembly.

61. *Kant*: Immanuel Kant (1724-1804), whose *Critique of Pure Reason* is the fountainhead of modern

epistemology for its reconciliation of rationalism and empiricsm.

Krause: Karl Friedrich Krause (1781-1832), a minor German philosopher much influenced by Romanticism and by the systems of Hegel and Schelling; through the work of Sanz del Río he came to have enormous influence in Spanish universities in the 1850s and 1860s. "Krausism" gave the political liberalism and anticlericalism which had been building up in Spain from the beginning of the 19th century a philosophical base. Raymond Carr in *Spain* calls it "a curious blend of subjective mysticism and vague modernism" (p. 303). In the 1870s Krausism came under attack both from conservative Catholics and from the growing number of Spanish positivists influenced by Spencer and Comte.

62. *Balmes*: See above, note to p. 14.

Donoso: Juan Donoso Cortés (1809-1853), marqués de Valdegamas, an author and diplomat. Originally liberal in his sympathies, he was so alarmed by the Paris uprisings of 1848 that he wrote *Ensayo sobre el catolicismo, el liberalismo, y el socialismo*, denouncing reason as the enemy of truth and liberalism as the enemy of social order. At his death in 1853 he was the Spanish ambassador to France. The first philosophers Unamuno read in his father's small library were Donoso and Balmes.

Aparisi: See above, note to p. 30.

De Maistre: Joseph de Maistre (1754-1821), conservative French diplomat and philosopher; in his *Du Pape* (*On the Pope*, 1819), he upheld the primacy of the Pontiff and examined schismatic groups.

63. *Lepanto, Oran, Otumba, Bailén*: important battles in Spanish history. The naval battle of Lepanto took place off the coast of Greece in 1571 and was a

decisive victory of European Christian armies over the Turks. The conquest of Oran, a coastal city in North Africa, in 1509 gave the Spanish a foothold on that continent. In Mexico in 1520 Cortés captured Montezuma in a battle at Otumba (Otompán), thus leading the Aztecs to believe that the Spanish were invincible gods to whom they must surrender. The battle of Bailén, on Spanish territory, forced Joseph Bonaparte and his French troops to evacuate Madrid in 1808 and retreat beyond the River Ebro.

65. *Mendizábal*: Juan Alvarez Mendizábal (1790-1853), a Liberal politician and an influential member of the Masonic lodge of Cádiz, who was associated with the constitutional program of Riego. Mendizábal went into exile in London during the period of absolutism initiated by Ferdinand VII in 1823, returning to Spain in the 1830s. In 1836, as a governmental minister, he initiated a program of reform calling for the dissolving of religious orders and the dedication of their assets to education of poor children and aid to the sick.

The Second of May: See below, note to p. 261.

66. *"Ay, ay, mutillac!"*: the Basque refrain of a Liberal song against the Carlists. It literally means "Watch out, Carlist" and follows a song, in Castilian, to the effect that the Queen is coming to Bilbao with her son, the future Alfonso XII.

69. *Krausism*: See above, note to p. 61.

rationalizing his faith: Pachico Zabalbide is clearly an autobiographical character modelled on Unamuno himself. Two of Unamuno's letters shed light on Pachico's effort to "rationlize his faith." The first, written on May 31, 1895 to "Clarín" (Leopoldo Alas), states: "For some time I have been planning to write a story which can be reduced to the following outline: A youth arrives in Madrid bearing within him a profoundly religious education and fine religious sensibilities. . . . Then, from sheer desire to rationalize his faith, he loses it (which is what happened to me)." In the second, written in 1901 to Federico Urales, he wrote: "I have written a good deal of my own life into that of Pachico in *Peace in War*. What I say in a couple of pages of that book . . . is strictly true and gives the fairest picture of my spiritual state at that time. When I arrived in Madrid to study in 1880 at the age of sixteen, I was still in that same state of spirit and remained so throughout my first two years of school. I persisted in the attempt to rationalize my faith and, naturally, dogma fell apart in my mind. . . . And so one day, during Carnival (I remember it well), I suddenly stopped attending Mass. Next I set off on a dizzy chase through philosophy. I learned German from Hegel, that stupendous Hegel, one of the thinkers who have left the deepest imprint on me." Both of these letters are included in *The Private World*, vol. 2 of this present edition.

77. *Manterola*: Vicente Manterola y Pérez (1833-1891), a priest, politician, and writer who espoused the Carlist cause, debated its opponents with great eloquence, and traveled widely in Europe and Great Britain seeking funds for its support.

Suñer, who had declared war on God and tuberculosis: Francisco Suñer y Capdevila (1826-1898), renowned throughout Europe as an authority on tuberculosis, was known in Spain primarily for his republican and atheistic sentiments which he summarized in a tract called "Dios," published in Barcelona in 1869 and widely condemned by the Spanish clergy.

83. *Pelayo and his cross*: Pelayo was a Gothic warrior who fought against the Moors in 718 in the battle

of Covadonga; was subsequently named king by the Asturians; died in 737 and was buried in the Chapel of Santa María de Covadonga; the subject of many plays, poems, and historial romances. See also above, note to p. 32.

Philip II: (1527-1598), King of Spain, took strong measures in 1591 to put down factionalism in Aragon.

Charles I: (1500-1558), King of Spain 1516-1556; as Charles V, he was Holy Roman Emperor from 1519 to 1556; in 1521 he put down the revolt of *Comuneros* (those who wanted regional autonomy) in Castile. The *Comuneros* had wanted to restore Charles' mother, Juana la Loca, who had been insane since 1506, to the Spanish throne.

84. *battle of Sadowa*: usually called the battle of Königgrätz (Bohemia), a decisive battle in the Seven Weeks War in 1866 between Prussia and an alliance of Austria, Bavaria, and Hanover.

85. *Trágala*: "Trágala, tú, servilón" (Swallow it [the Constitution], you servile pig!), words from the refrain of a song with which Spanish Liberals reproached the supporters of absolutism during the nineteenth century.

86. *Syllabus errorum*: In 1864, ten years after Pope Pius IX proclaimed the dogma of the Immaculate Conception, he issued an encyclical, *Quanta cura*, condemning the depravity and corruption of modern thought. It was accompanied by a "Syllabus of Errors," some eighty propositions in all, which the faithful were exhorted to avoid. The Syllabus condemned pantheism, rationalism, naturalism, liberalism, communism, Freemasonry, divorce, secular control of education, civil marriage, and religious toleration. It upheld revelation, miracles, the teaching authority of the Church, and the superiority of Roman Catholicism over Protes-

tantism. In 1870 Pius IX convoked the first Vatican Council, which promulgated the dogma of papal infallibility, holding that when the Pope speaks *ex cathedra* on matters of faith and morals he is immune from the possibility of error.

105. *"Conspiracy of the Mantillas"*: the protest of the Spanish aristocracy against the Italian, Amadeo of Savoy. The ladies put on mantillas, a national garment, to protest against the foreigner.

Mendizábal: see above, note to p. 65.

106. *Cathelineau, the hero of La Vendée*: Jacques Cathelineau (1759-1793), one of the leaders of the conservative uprising against the French Revolution in La Vendée; inasmuch as he died in 1793, the expectation of his appearance demands something of a miracle.

Nocedal: Cándido Nocedal (1821-1895), first studied medicine, then law, and became a noted orator and political writer. Member of the Spanish Academy and an ideologue of Carlist conservatism.

II

110. *Rada*: Eustaquio Díaz de Rada (1815-1874), a Carlist commander who had fought in the first Carlist War and fled to France after the Pact of Vergara. He soon returned to Spain and resumed his military career in the Spanish army. In 1868 he was named commander-general in Burgos, but when his part in a conspiracy on behalf of the Carlist cause was discovered, he escaped to France and then began to raise troops for Carlos VII in Navarre. Died in the battle of San Pedro de Abanto.

116. *married a Protestant*: Cabrera married an Englishwoman, with whom he had four children.

117. *Savalls*: Francisco Savalls y Masot (1817-

1886), a Carlist general who specialized in guerrilla warfare; served in the Papal Zouaves between the two Carlist wars.

the priest Santa Cruz: Manuel Ignacio Santa Cruz Loidi (1842-1926) was a parish priest in Hernialde in 1870, when because of his Carlist sympathies he was persecuted by the Spanish government and forced to flee to France. Later that year he returned to Spain as a guerrilla chieftain. A figure legendary for his boldness and his fierce dedication to traditional values, he was nevertheless regarded with some disfavor by other Carlist leaders because of his independence. Late in the war, he gave up fighting and went to Rome, where he abandoned the name "Santa Cruz" in favor of "Loidi" and became a missionary to Jamaica. In 1922, at the age of 80, he joined the Jesuit order. Santa Cruz was depicted as a character in the novels of Valle-Inclán.

Ollo's deeds: Nicolás Ollo Vidarreta (1810-1874), Carlist leader from Navarre.

125. *Lagunero . . . Zurbano*: José Lagunero y Guijarro (1823-1879), Spanish general, exiled to the Canary Islands in 1862 because of his friendship for Juan Prim and his Liberal ideas; returned to work actively for the downfall of Isabella II; at the outbreak of the second Carlist War he was undersecretary of war. Martín Zurbano (1788-1845), Spanish field marshal during first Carlist War, executed in 1845 for fomenting a rebellion against Isabella II.

Sendeja: the calle de Sendeja, leading north along the Nervión River's edge from the Arenal, the central park of Bilbao (see below, note to p. 187).

Don't leave a guiri alive: *guiri* is an epithet originally denoting Basque anti-Carlist partisans of Queen María Cristina, Isabella II's mother and regent; later the term came to mean any Basque partisan of the Liberals.

132. *Amorebieta Pact*: made in March 1872 in the Vizcayan town of Amorebieta between representatives of the National Army and three Carlist deputies, granting concessions to any Carlist insurrectionaries who would lay down their arms.

Santa Cruz: see note to p. 117.

Lizárraga: Antonio Lizárraga y Esquiroz (1817-1877) entered the Carlist army as a volunteer at age seventeen in the first Carlist War, serving under Zumalacárregui. After the Pact of Vergara he entered the National army as a lieutenant. He returned to Carlist ranks at the outset of the second war as commanding general of Guipúzcoa. He was noted for his gentlemanly ways and his open piety.

137. *Miqueletes*: Basque volunteers fighting on either side.

139. *Cantonalism*: the movement demanding regional autonomy.

140. *"St. James and have at them!"*: "Santiago y a ellos!"

143. *Radica*: (?-1874), Carlist chieftain, killed at the battle of Somorrostro.

144. *Dorregaray*: Antonio Dorregaray y Dominquero (1823-1882), from Ceuta, was distinguished for his valor as a soldier in the Carlist force in 1836, when he was only thirteen years old; after the Pact of Vergara, became an officer in the Liberal army, but reaffirmed his Carlist allegiances after the Revolution of 1868, serving as a general of the Carlist army.

160. *Tree of Guernica*: an oak tree, beneath which the General Assembly of Vizcaya met every two years; here the Catholic rulers Ferdinand and Isabella swore in 1476 to respect the *fueros* or local laws and traditions of Vizcaya; the original tree died in 1811, but was replaced by a new tree grown from one of its acorns.

161. *Moltke's tactics*: Count Helmuth Carl Bernhard von Moltke (1800-1891), Prussian field marshal and strategist.

165. *Don Castor Andéchaga*: (1803-1871), fought in the first Carlist War, rising to rank of brigadier in the Carlist army; retired to private life after the Pact of Vergara; returned to the Carlist army in the second Carlist War; participated in the siege of Bilbao; died in the defense of the town of Talledo.

171. *Gómez*: Miguel Gómez (1796-?), Spanish Carlist general, in 1838 left the province of Alava with fewer than 3,000 men, crossed Asturias, Galicia, La Mancha, marched to Córdoba and Burgos in a daring six-month military expedition which met disapproval from other Carlist leaders.

177. *Elío*: Joaquin Elío y Ezpeleta (1806-1876), fought in the first Carlist War under Zumalacárregui, became a brigadier in 1836 and the commanding general of Navarre in 1839; emigrated with Don Carlos to France after the Pact of Vergara; in 1857 he took an active part in the conspiracy that led to the abortive uprising at San Carlos de la Rápita; a commanding general in the second Carlist War.

178. *Moriones*: Domingo Moriones y Murillo (1823-1881), Spanish general who fought in thirty-nine battles in María Cristina's army as a cadet in the Seven Year War and led an army against the Carlists in the second Carlist War. In 1875 Alfonso XII made him marqués de Oroquieta. The body referred to is, of course, not his.

III

187. *the Arenal*: a shady park and promenade on the Nervión River; it was the focus of life in the "old town."

189. *the "Battery of Death"*: In *The Lone Heretic*,

her biography of Unamuno, Rudd writes about the siege: "However, the children continued their games of war. In the midst of this suffering, even while the bombs rained death and destruction, they invented new games of playing at soldiers. One of the favorite sports was a sort of bowling game played *con tablones de la 'Batería de la Muerte.'* The purpose was, apparently, to knock down imaginary soldiers with make-believe 'death artillery' " (p. 33).

206. junta de merindades: township assembly in the Basque region.

226. Pitita: a mocking song that runs:

> Pitita, bonita.
> Con el pío, pío, pon.
> Pitita, bonita.
> ¡Viva la Constitución!
> ¡Pi, pi, pi, pi,
> Zorro, clo clo!

(R. Olivar Bertrand, *Así cayó Isabel II*, Barcelona, 1955, p. 62.)

228. *Floris and Blanchefleur*: See above, note to pp. 32-33.

239. *Leganés*: a village outside Madrid containing a madhouse.

241. *Numantia*: Celtiberian city of ancient Spain, near modern Soria; its inhabitants withstood a Roman siege for fifteen months (c. 130 B.C.).

Austrian by birth: Carlos VII was born in Leibach, Austria, in 1848.

248. *the Covenant of Amorebieta*: March 24, 1872, a pact concluded in the Vizcayan town of Amorebieta between the duke de la Torre and the Carlist deputies Urquizu, Urúe, and Arquinzoniz, offering concessions to Carlist soldiers if they laid down their arms. See above, note to p. 132.

252. *cheval-de-frise*: spikes or broken glass embedded in the top of a wall to keep out trespassers.

254. *Savalls*: See above, note to p. 117.

261. *the 2nd of May*: on May 2, 1808 (*el Dos de Mayo*) the Madrid populace rose against the Napoleonic troops. Goya painted two famous pictures (both in the Prado) of the events that followed, the first depicting the knifings of the Mamelukes by street fighters and the second the shooting on May 3 of the irregulars by French troops in Moncloa Park. On May 2, 1866 the battle of Callao took place on the coast of Peru, effectively putting an end to the war in the Pacific between Spain and both Chile and Peru. Both sides claimed victory.

265. *"new Numantia"*: See above, note to p. 241.

266. *plans to proclaim Alfonsito . . . King of Spain*: Raymond Carr (*Spain*, pp. 340-41), writes, "The greatest statesman of the Restoration, Cánovas del Castillo, has impressed on history his own conviction that the restoration of Alfonso was the work of organized civilian monarchism. In defeat and exile, Cánovas insisted that a restoration could only be successful if imposed by a great movement of opinion in favour of Alfonso XII, at the time a cadet at Sandhurst who would reach his majority (sixteen years of age) in November 1873. Alfonso, unlike his mother, could rally wide conservative support, from the faithful Moderates to repentant September conspirators now ready to work their passage as monarchist politicians."

IV

269. *Somorrostro*: a valley and river in the mountainous region northwest of Bilbao; between the estuaries of the Nervión and Mercadillo rivers.

295. *Berriz*: Elisio de Berriz (1829-1891), Don Carlos' minister of war.

298. *Dorregaray*: See above, note to p. 144.

Mendiri: Torcuato Mendiri y Correa (1813-1881), a Carlist general from Navarre.

303. *General Concha*: Manuel Gutiérrez de la Concha (1809-1895), Spanish general; author of a book on military tactics; killed in the Battle of Monte Muro; the first marqués del Duero.

Flanders: an allusion to the Spanish occupation of the Low Countries in the 16th and 17th centuries.

314. *his efforts to achieve simplicity got more complicated*: It may be noted that although Pachico Zabalbide is usually taken to be Unamuno's alter-ego, and properly so, his uncle's complicated efforts to achieve "simplicity" directly reflect Unamuno's meditations during his religious crisis of 1897. See the selections from his *diario íntimo* in vol. 2 of this edition, *The Private World*.

323. *Beneath the waves*: the imagery in this passage is extremely reminiscent of Unamuno's argument about "infra-history" in *En torno al casticismo*.

V

328. junta de merindades: See above, note to p. 206.

345. *Malato tree*: According to Basque tradition, *el árbol Malato*, near Llodio about 15 miles south of Bilbao, marked the northern limit of the recruiting powers of Castile. The Basque *fueros* granted exemption from recruitment. After the tree died, its place was marked by a stone cross.

360. *Caixal*: José Caixal y Estradé (1803-1879), Spanish prelate.

372. "Eman ta zabalzazu": these words are from the hymn "Guernicaco Arbola" (Tree of Guernica), by the Basque poet Iparraguirre, who left home in the 18th century to wander around France and England and then migrated to Argentina.

Library of Congress Cataloging in Publication Data

Unamuno, Miguel de, 1864-1936.
Peace in war.

(Selected works of Miguel de Unamuno ; v. 1)
(Bollingen series ; 85)
Translation of: Paz en la guerra.
1. Spain—History—Carlist War, 1873-1876—Fiction.
I. Lacy, Allen.   II. Nozick, Martin, 1917-
III. Title.   IV. Series: Unamuno, Miguel de, 1864-1936.
Selections. English. 1968 ;
v. 1.   V. Series: Bollingen series ; 85.
PQ6639.N3A25   1968   vol. 1   863'.62   82-61390
ISBN 0-691-09926-X